EOIN COLFER

ARTEMIS FOWL

THE GRAPHIC NOVEL

Adapted by **Michael Moreci**

Art by **Stephen Gilpin**

Disney · HYPERION

Los Angeles   New York

CHAPTER ONE

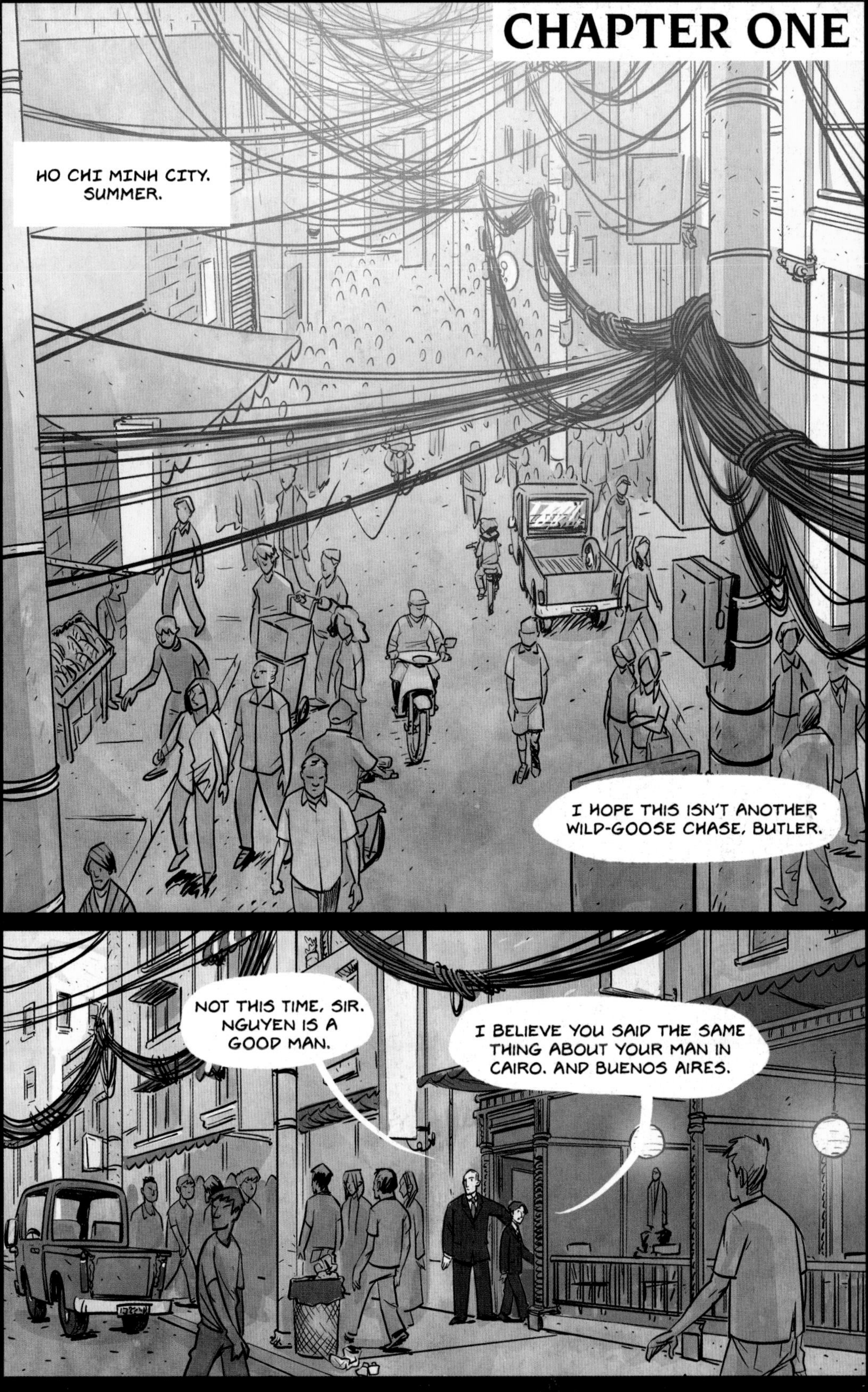
HO CHI MINH CITY. SUMMER.
I HOPE THIS ISN'T ANOTHER WILD-GOOSE CHASE, BUTLER.
NOT THIS TIME, SIR. NGUYEN IS A GOOD MAN.
I BELIEVE YOU SAID THE SAME THING ABOUT YOUR MAN IN CAIRO. AND BUENOS AIRES.

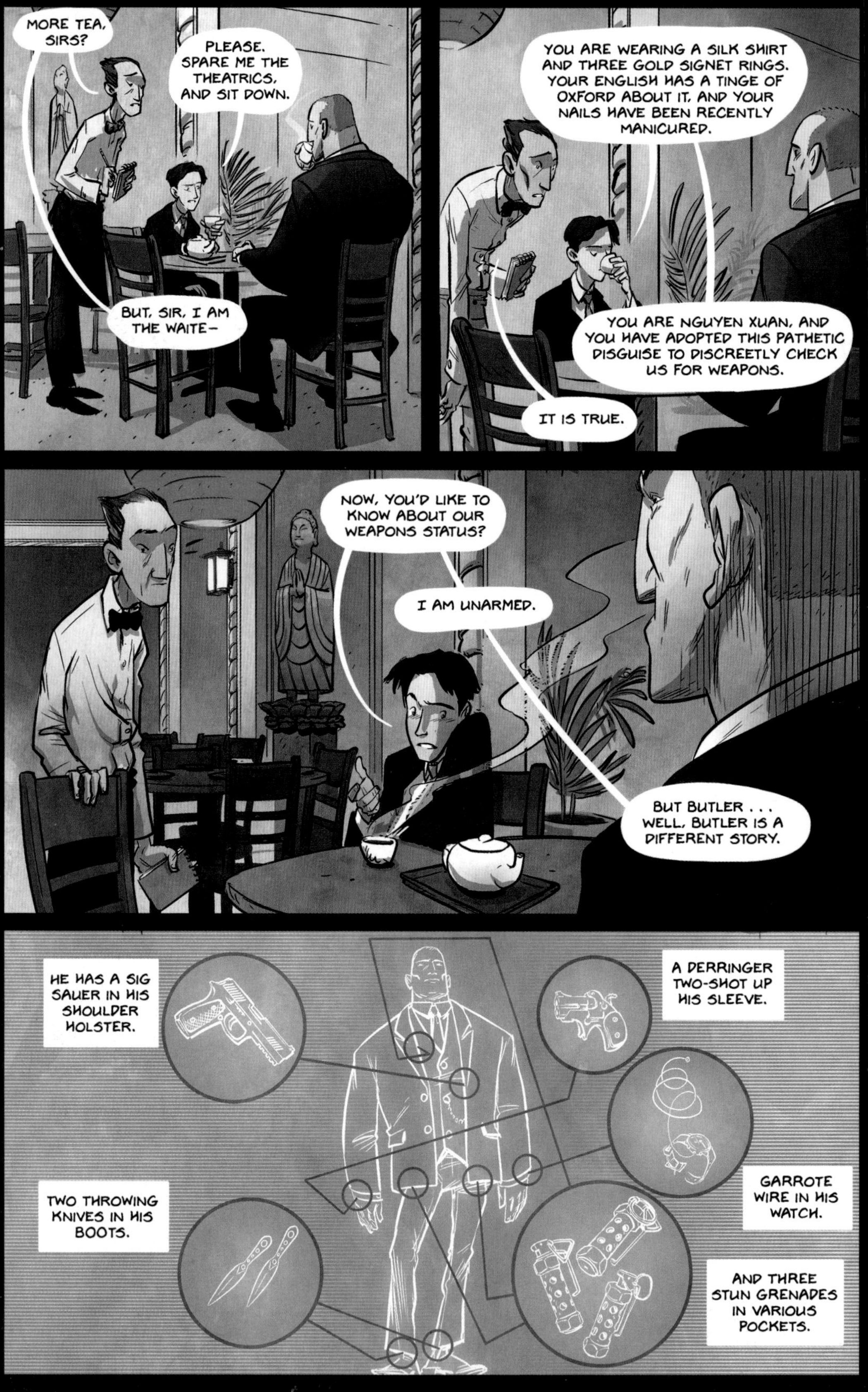
MORE TEA, SIRS?
PLEASE. SPARE ME THE THEATRICS, AND SIT DOWN.
BUT, SIR, I AM THE WAITE—
YOU ARE WEARING A SILK SHIRT AND THREE GOLD SIGNET RINGS. YOUR ENGLISH HAS A TINGE OF OXFORD ABOUT IT, AND YOUR NAILS HAVE BEEN RECENTLY MANICURED.
YOU ARE NGUYEN XUAN, AND YOU HAVE ADOPTED THIS PATHETIC DISGUISE TO DISCREETLY CHECK US FOR WEAPONS.
IT IS TRUE.
NOW, YOU'D LIKE TO KNOW ABOUT OUR WEAPONS STATUS?
I AM UNARMED.
BUT BUTLER . . . WELL, BUTLER IS A DIFFERENT STORY.
HE HAS A SIG SAUER IN HIS SHOULDER HOLSTER.
A DERRINGER TWO-SHOT UP HIS SLEEVE.
TWO THROWING KNIVES IN HIS BOOTS.
GARROTE WIRE IN HIS WATCH.
AND THREE STUN GRENADES IN VARIOUS POCKETS.

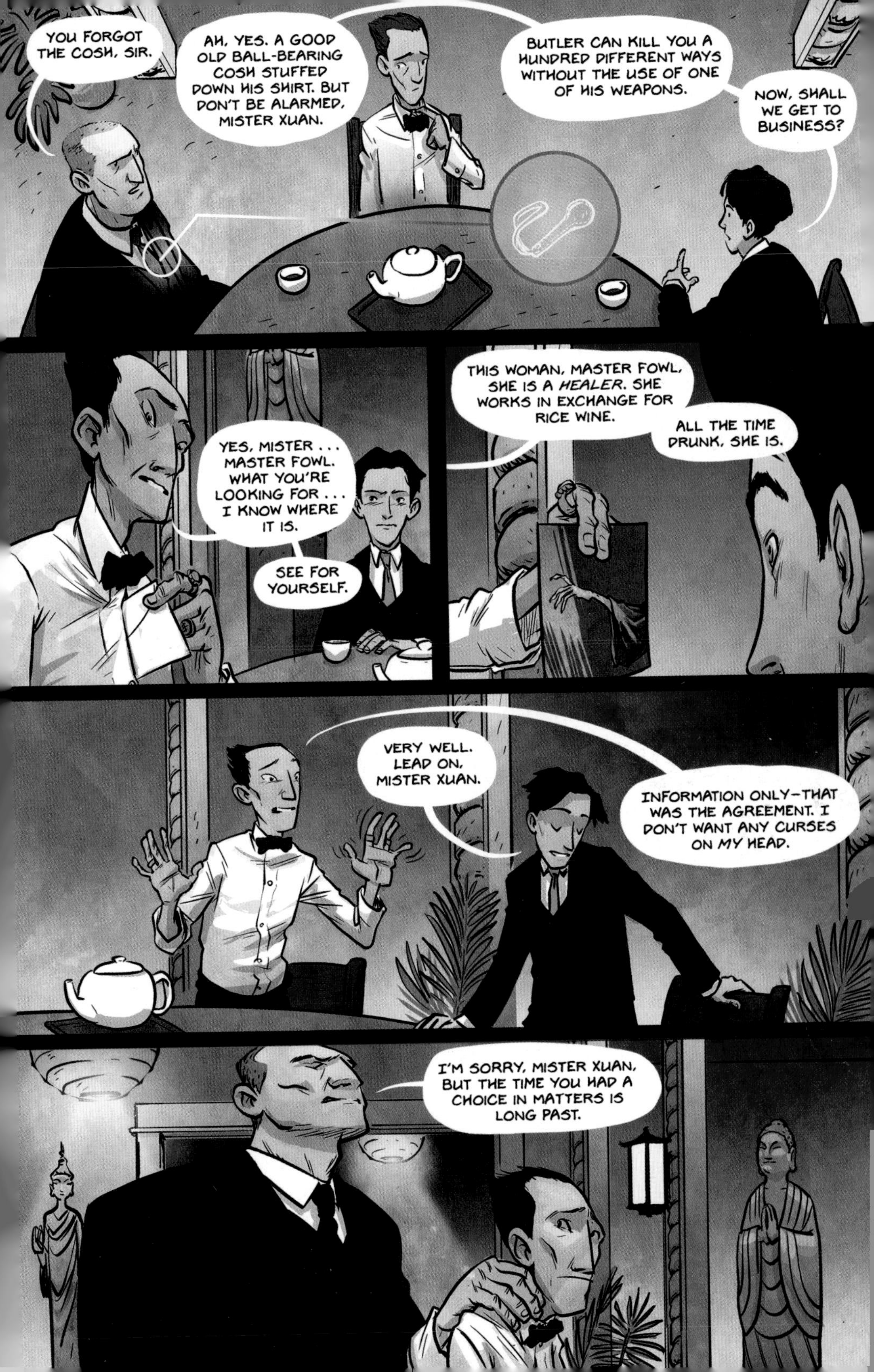
YOU FORGOT THE COSH, SIR.
AH, YES. A GOOD OLD BALL-BEARING COSH STUFFED DOWN HIS SHIRT. BUT DON'T BE ALARMED, MISTER XUAN.
BUTLER CAN KILL YOU A HUNDRED DIFFERENT WAYS WITHOUT THE USE OF ONE OF HIS WEAPONS.
NOW, SHALL WE GET TO BUSINESS?
YES, MISTER . . . MASTER FOWL. WHAT YOU'RE LOOKING FOR . . . I KNOW WHERE IT IS.
SEE FOR YOURSELF.
THIS WOMAN, MASTER FOWL, SHE IS A *HEALER*. SHE WORKS IN EXCHANGE FOR RICE WINE.
ALL THE TIME DRUNK, SHE IS.
VERY WELL. LEAD ON, MISTER XUAN.
INFORMATION ONLY—THAT WAS THE AGREEMENT. I DON'T WANT ANY CURSES ON *MY* HEAD.
I'M SORRY, MISTER XUAN, BUT THE TIME YOU HAD A CHOICE IN MATTERS IS LONG PAST.

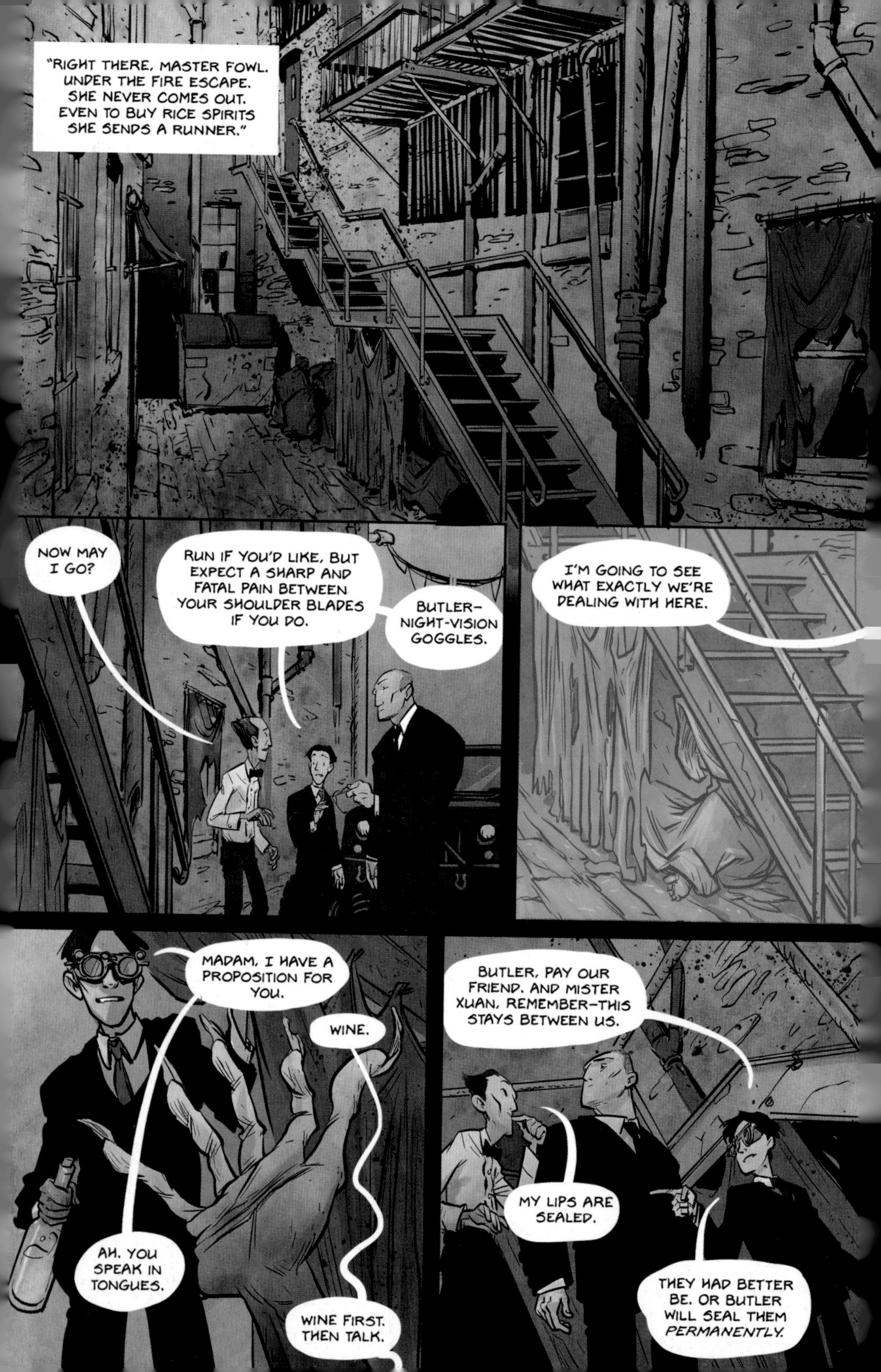
"RIGHT THERE, MASTER FOWL. UNDER THE FIRE ESCAPE. SHE NEVER COMES OUT. EVEN TO BUY RICE SPIRITS SHE SENDS A RUNNER."
NOW MAY I GO?
RUN IF YOU'D LIKE, BUT EXPECT A SHARP AND FATAL PAIN BETWEEN YOUR SHOULDER BLADES IF YOU DO.
BUTLER— NIGHT-VISION GOGGLES.
I'M GOING TO SEE WHAT EXACTLY WE'RE DEALING WITH HERE.
MADAM, I HAVE A PROPOSITION FOR YOU.
WINE.
AH. YOU SPEAK IN TONGUES.
WINE FIRST. THEN TALK.
BUTLER, PAY OUR FRIEND. AND MISTER XUAN, REMEMBER—THIS STAYS BETWEEN US.
MY LIPS ARE SEALED.
THEY HAD BETTER BE. OR BUTLER WILL SEAL THEM *PERMANENTLY.*

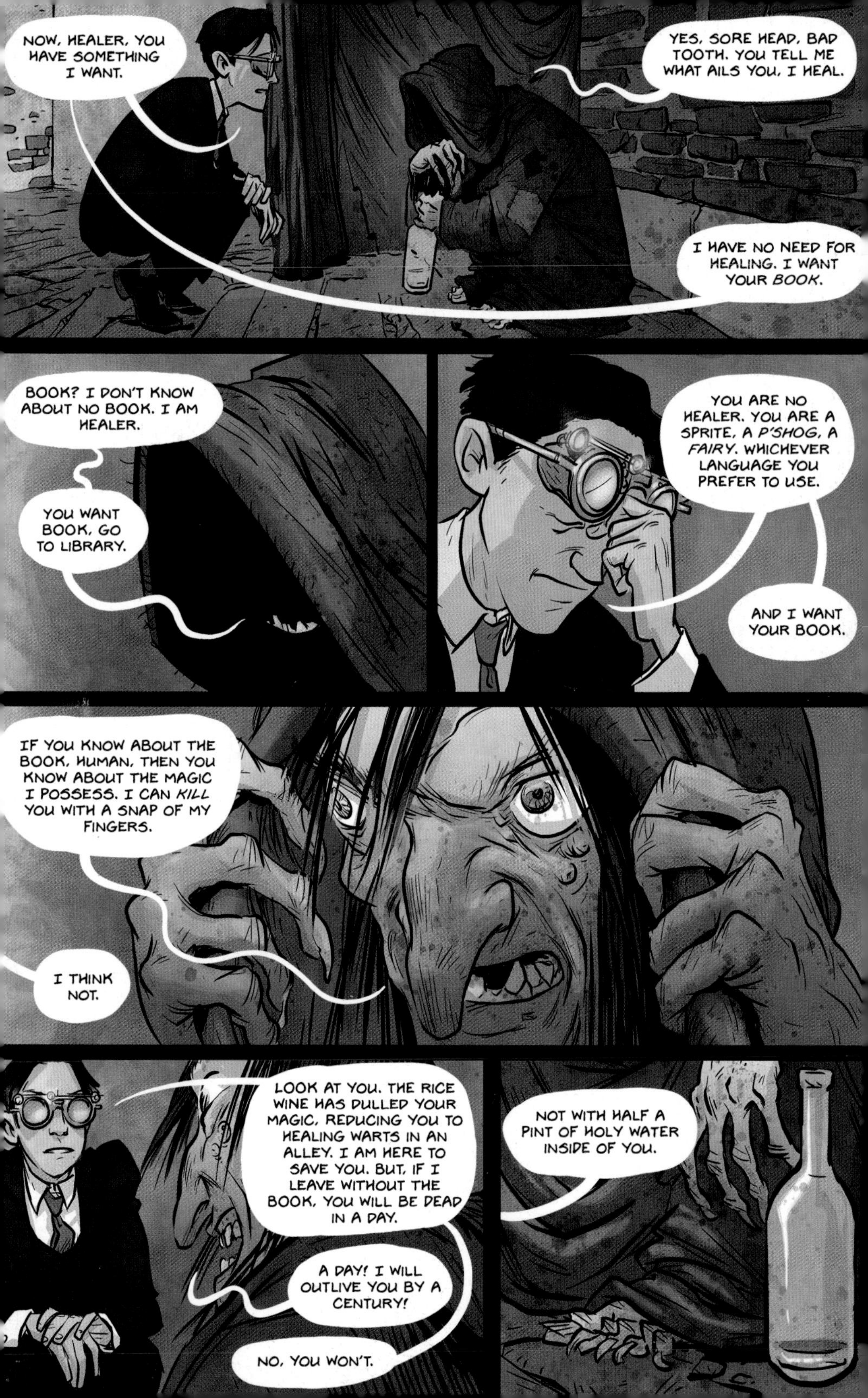
NOW, HEALER, YOU HAVE SOMETHING I WANT.
YES, SORE HEAD, BAD TOOTH. YOU TELL ME WHAT AILS YOU, I HEAL.
I HAVE NO NEED FOR HEALING. I WANT YOUR *BOOK*.
BOOK? I DON'T KNOW ABOUT NO BOOK. I AM HEALER.
YOU WANT BOOK, GO TO LIBRARY.
YOU ARE NO HEALER. YOU ARE A SPRITE, A *P'SHOG*, A *FAIRY*. WHICHEVER LANGUAGE YOU PREFER TO USE.
AND I WANT YOUR BOOK.
IF YOU KNOW ABOUT THE BOOK, HUMAN, THEN YOU KNOW ABOUT THE MAGIC I POSSESS. I CAN *KILL* YOU WITH A SNAP OF MY FINGERS.
I THINK NOT.
LOOK AT YOU. THE RICE WINE HAS DULLED YOUR MAGIC, REDUCING YOU TO HEALING WARTS IN AN ALLEY. I AM HERE TO SAVE YOU. BUT, IF I LEAVE WITHOUT THE BOOK, YOU WILL BE DEAD IN A DAY.
A DAY! I WILL OUTLIVE YOU BY A CENTURY!
NO, YOU WON'T.
NOT WITH HALF A PINT OF HOLY WATER INSIDE OF YOU.

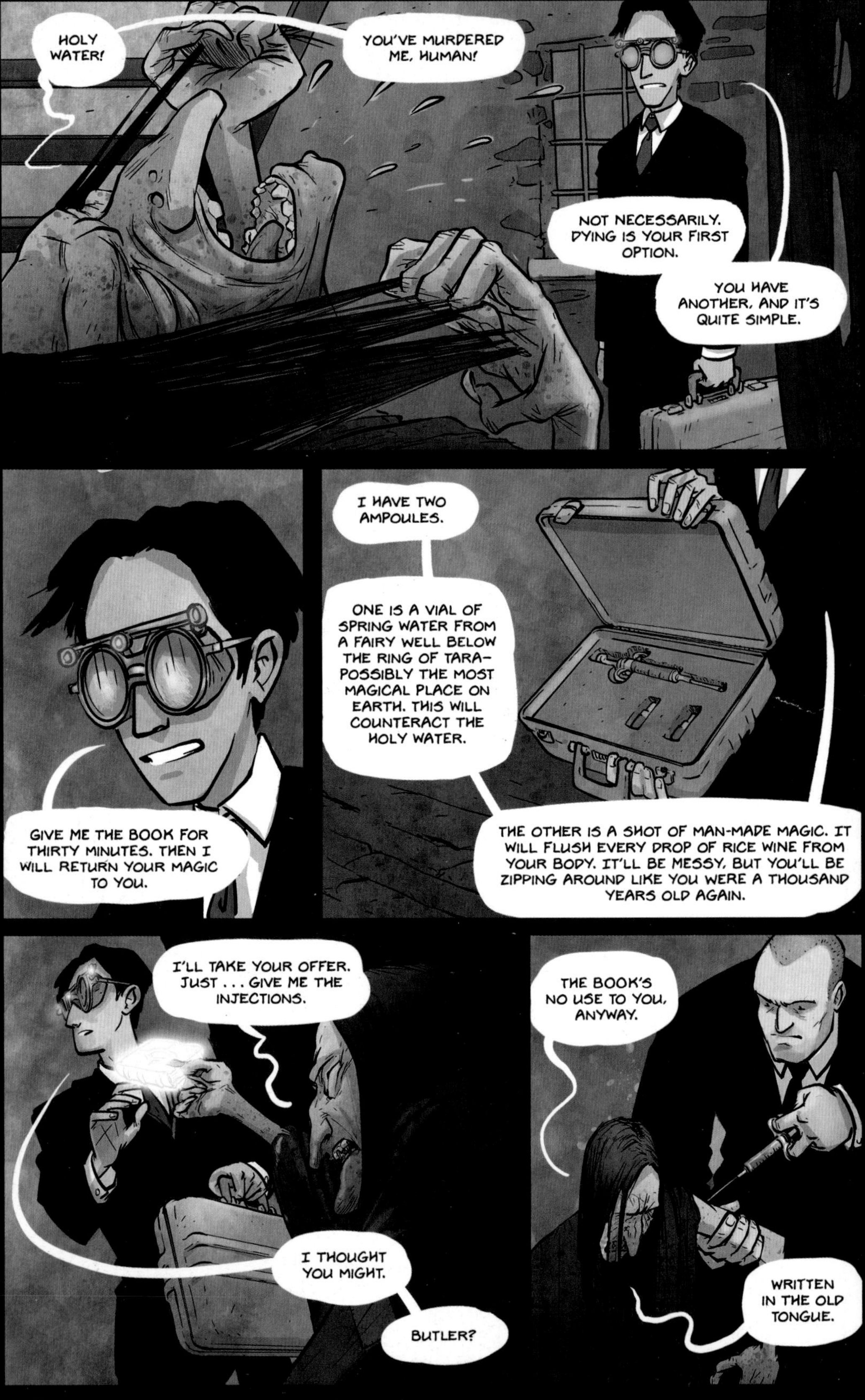
HOLY WATER!
YOU'VE MURDERED ME, HUMAN!
NOT NECESSARILY. DYING IS YOUR FIRST OPTION.
YOU HAVE ANOTHER, AND IT'S QUITE SIMPLE.
GIVE ME THE BOOK FOR THIRTY MINUTES. THEN I WILL RETURN YOUR MAGIC TO YOU.
I HAVE TWO AMPOULES.
ONE IS A VIAL OF SPRING WATER FROM A FAIRY WELL BELOW THE RING OF TARA—POSSIBLY THE MOST MAGICAL PLACE ON EARTH. THIS WILL COUNTERACT THE HOLY WATER.
THE OTHER IS A SHOT OF MAN-MADE MAGIC. IT WILL FLUSH EVERY DROP OF RICE WINE FROM YOUR BODY. IT'LL BE MESSY, BUT YOU'LL BE ZIPPING AROUND LIKE YOU WERE A THOUSAND YEARS OLD AGAIN.
I'LL TAKE YOUR OFFER. JUST . . . GIVE ME THE INJECTIONS.
I THOUGHT YOU MIGHT.
BUTLER?
THE BOOK'S NO USE TO YOU, ANYWAY.
WRITTEN IN THE OLD TONGUE.

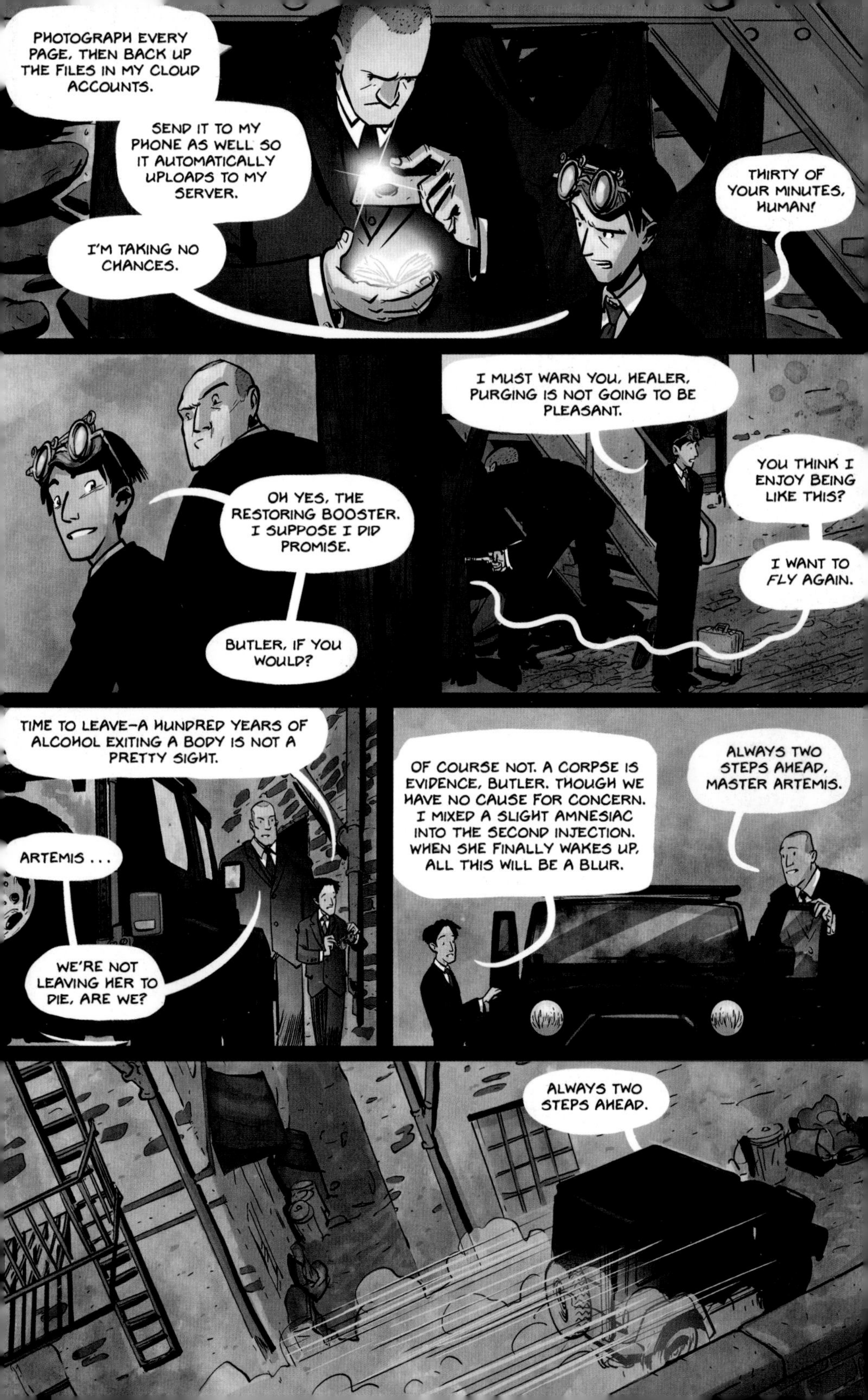
PHOTOGRAPH EVERY PAGE, THEN BACK UP THE FILES IN MY CLOUD ACCOUNTS.
SEND IT TO MY PHONE AS WELL SO IT AUTOMATICALLY UPLOADS TO MY SERVER.
I'M TAKING NO CHANCES.
THIRTY OF YOUR MINUTES, HUMAN!
OH YES, THE RESTORING BOOSTER. I SUPPOSE I DID PROMISE.
BUTLER, IF YOU WOULD?
I MUST WARN YOU, HEALER, PURGING IS NOT GOING TO BE PLEASANT.
YOU THINK I ENJOY BEING LIKE THIS?
I WANT TO *FLY* AGAIN.
TIME TO LEAVE—A HUNDRED YEARS OF ALCOHOL EXITING A BODY IS NOT A PRETTY SIGHT.
ARTEMIS . . .
WE'RE NOT LEAVING HER TO DIE, ARE WE?
OF COURSE NOT. A CORPSE IS EVIDENCE, BUTLER. THOUGH WE HAVE NO CAUSE FOR CONCERN. I MIXED A SLIGHT AMNESIAC INTO THE SECOND INJECTION. WHEN SHE FINALLY WAKES UP, ALL THIS WILL BE A BLUR.
ALWAYS TWO STEPS AHEAD, MASTER ARTEMIS.
ALWAYS TWO STEPS AHEAD.

CHAPTER TWO

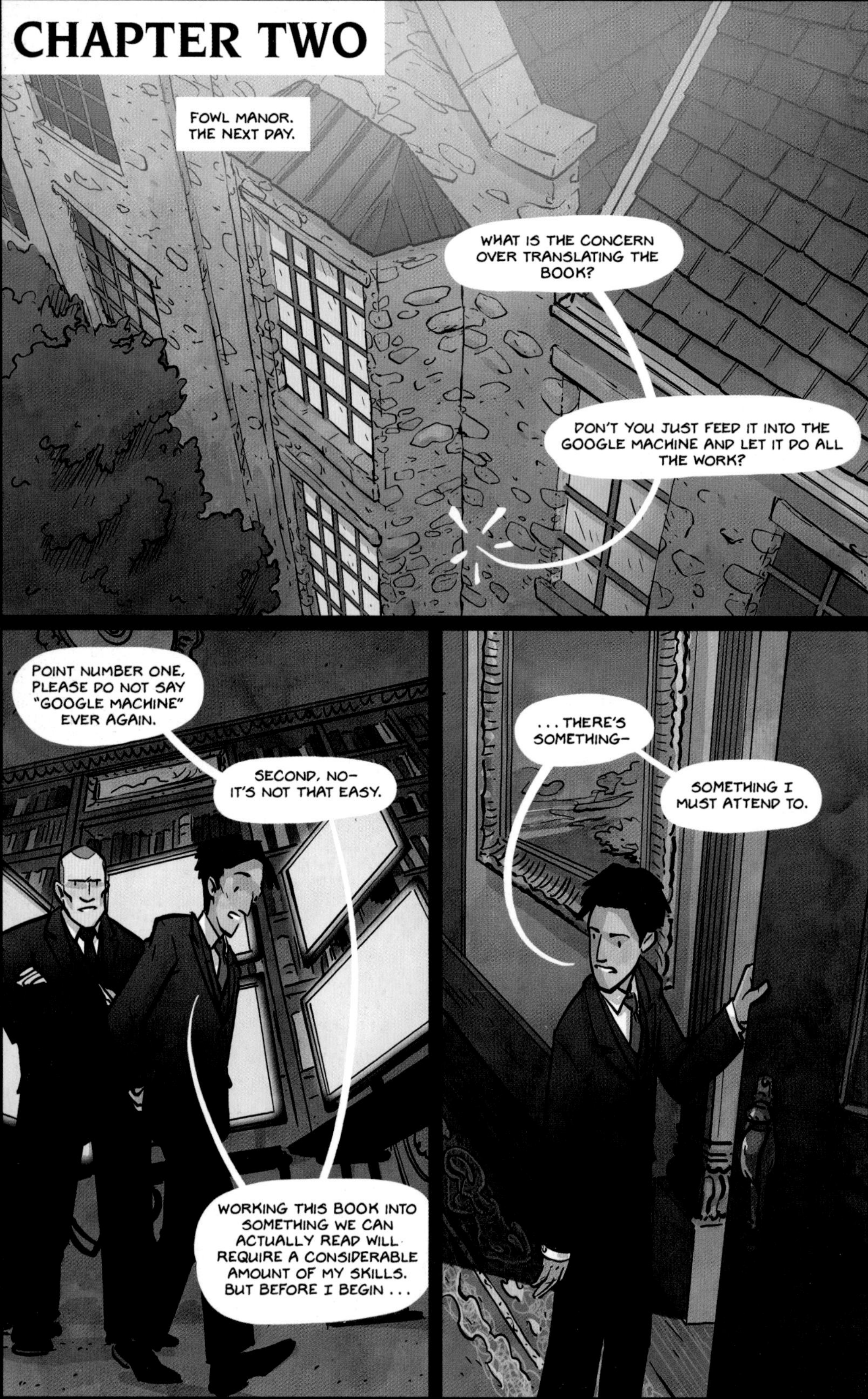
FOWL MANOR. THE NEXT DAY.
WHAT IS THE CONCERN OVER TRANSLATING THE BOOK?
DON'T YOU JUST FEED IT INTO THE GOOGLE MACHINE AND LET IT DO ALL THE WORK?
POINT NUMBER ONE, PLEASE DO NOT SAY "GOOGLE MACHINE" EVER AGAIN.
SECOND, NO– IT'S NOT THAT EASY.
WORKING THIS BOOK INTO SOMETHING WE CAN ACTUALLY READ WILL REQUIRE A CONSIDERABLE AMOUNT OF MY SKILLS. BUT BEFORE I BEGIN . . .
. . . THERE'S SOMETHING–
SOMETHING I MUST ATTEND TO.

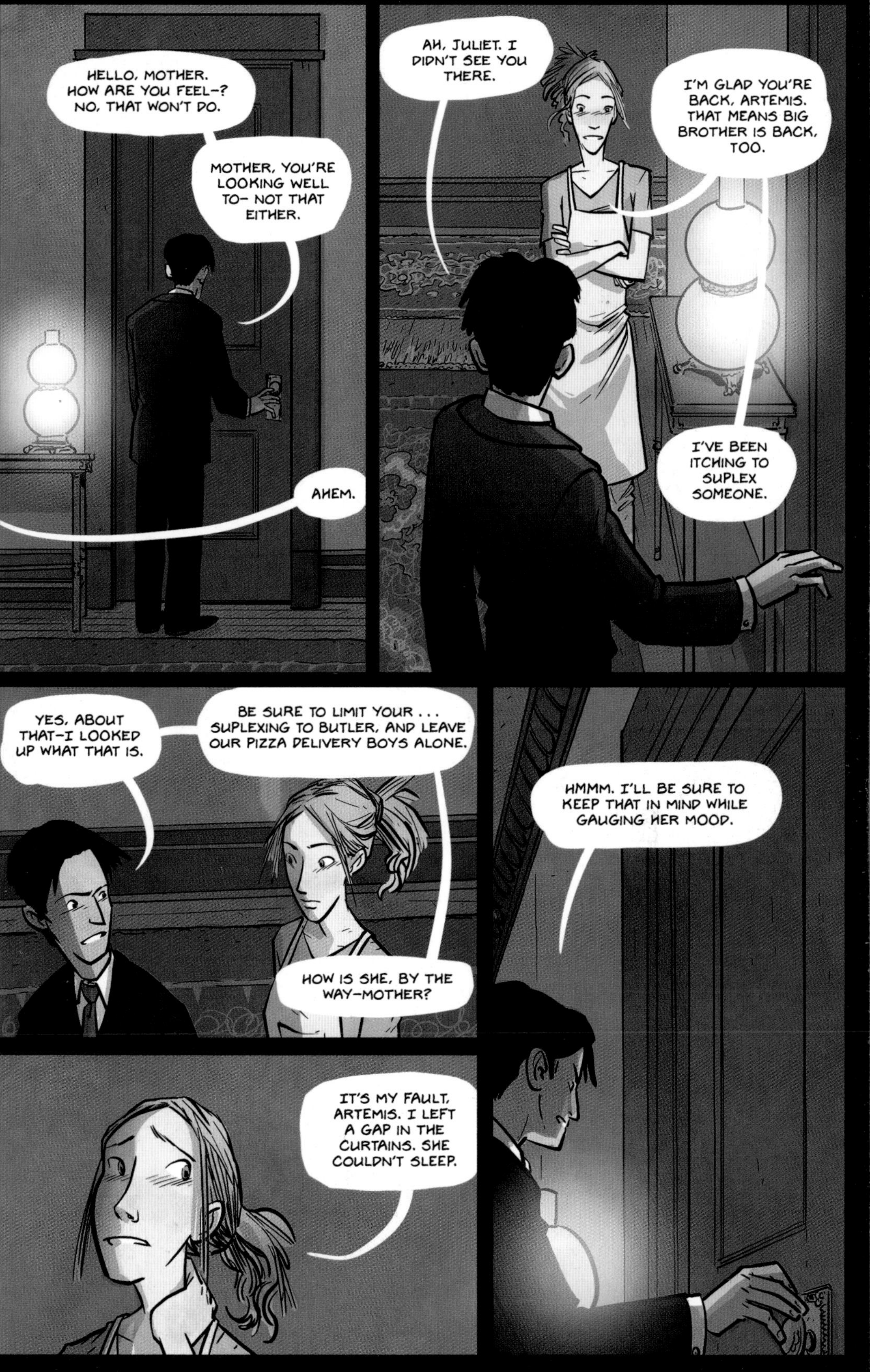
HELLO, MOTHER. HOW ARE YOU FEEL-? NO, THAT WON'T DO.
MOTHER, YOU'RE LOOKING WELL TO- NOT THAT EITHER.
AHEM.
AH, JULIET. I DIDN'T SEE YOU THERE.
I'M GLAD YOU'RE BACK, ARTEMIS. THAT MEANS BIG BROTHER IS BACK, TOO.
I'VE BEEN ITCHING TO SUPLEX SOMEONE.
YES, ABOUT THAT-I LOOKED UP WHAT THAT IS.
BE SURE TO LIMIT YOUR . . . SUPLEXING TO BUTLER, AND LEAVE OUR PIZZA DELIVERY BOYS ALONE.
HOW IS SHE, BY THE WAY-MOTHER?
IT'S MY FAULT, ARTEMIS. I LEFT A GAP IN THE CURTAINS. SHE COULDN'T SLEEP.
HMMM. I'LL BE SURE TO KEEP THAT IN MIND WHILE GAUGING HER MOOD.

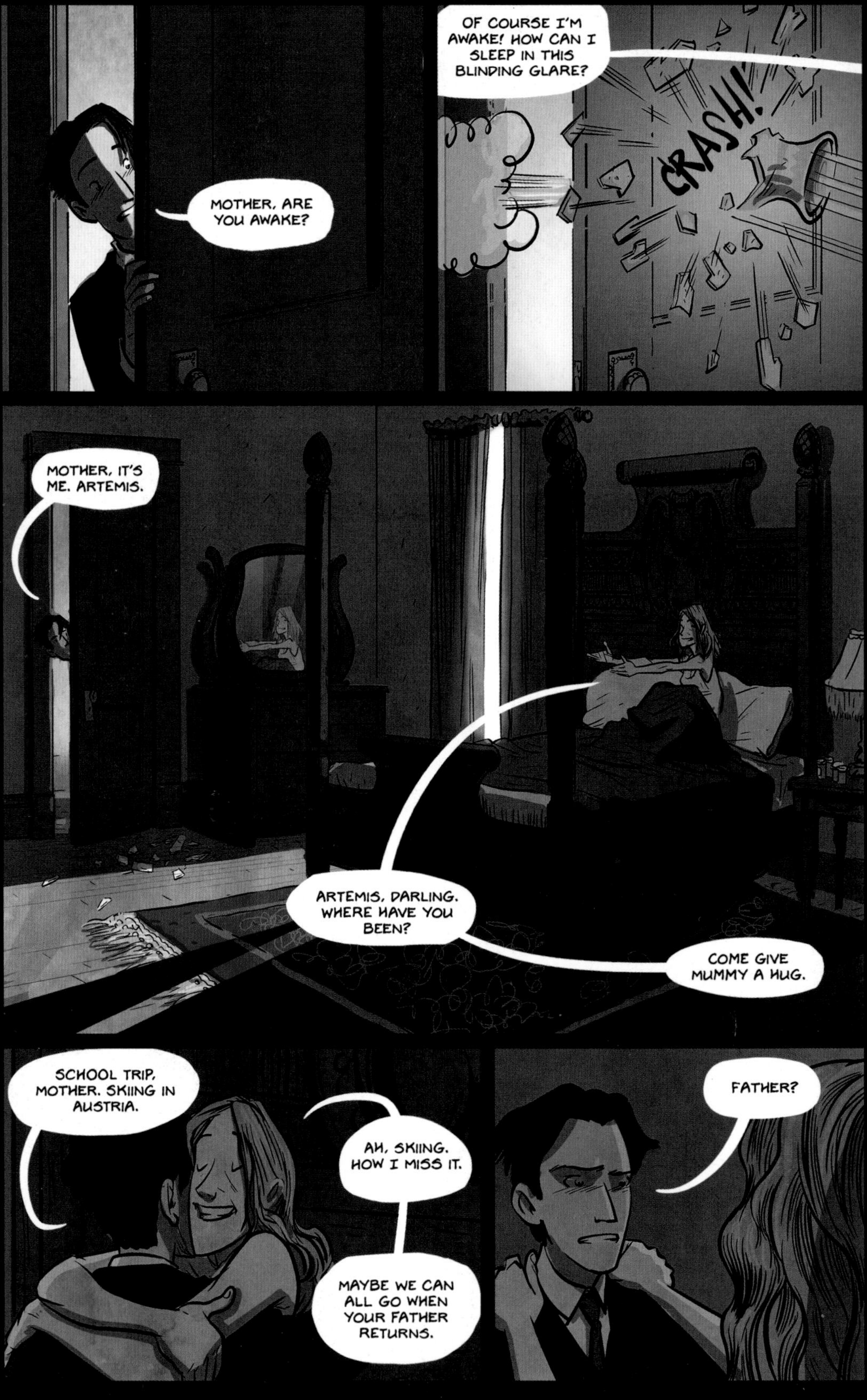
MOTHER, ARE YOU AWAKE?
OF COURSE I'M AWAKE! HOW CAN I SLEEP IN THIS BLINDING GLARE?
CRASH!
MOTHER, IT'S ME. ARTEMIS.
ARTEMIS, DARLING. WHERE HAVE YOU BEEN?
COME GIVE MUMMY A HUG.
SCHOOL TRIP, MOTHER. SKIING IN AUSTRIA.
AH, SKIING. HOW I MISS IT.
MAYBE WE CAN ALL GO WHEN YOUR FATHER RETURNS.
FATHER?

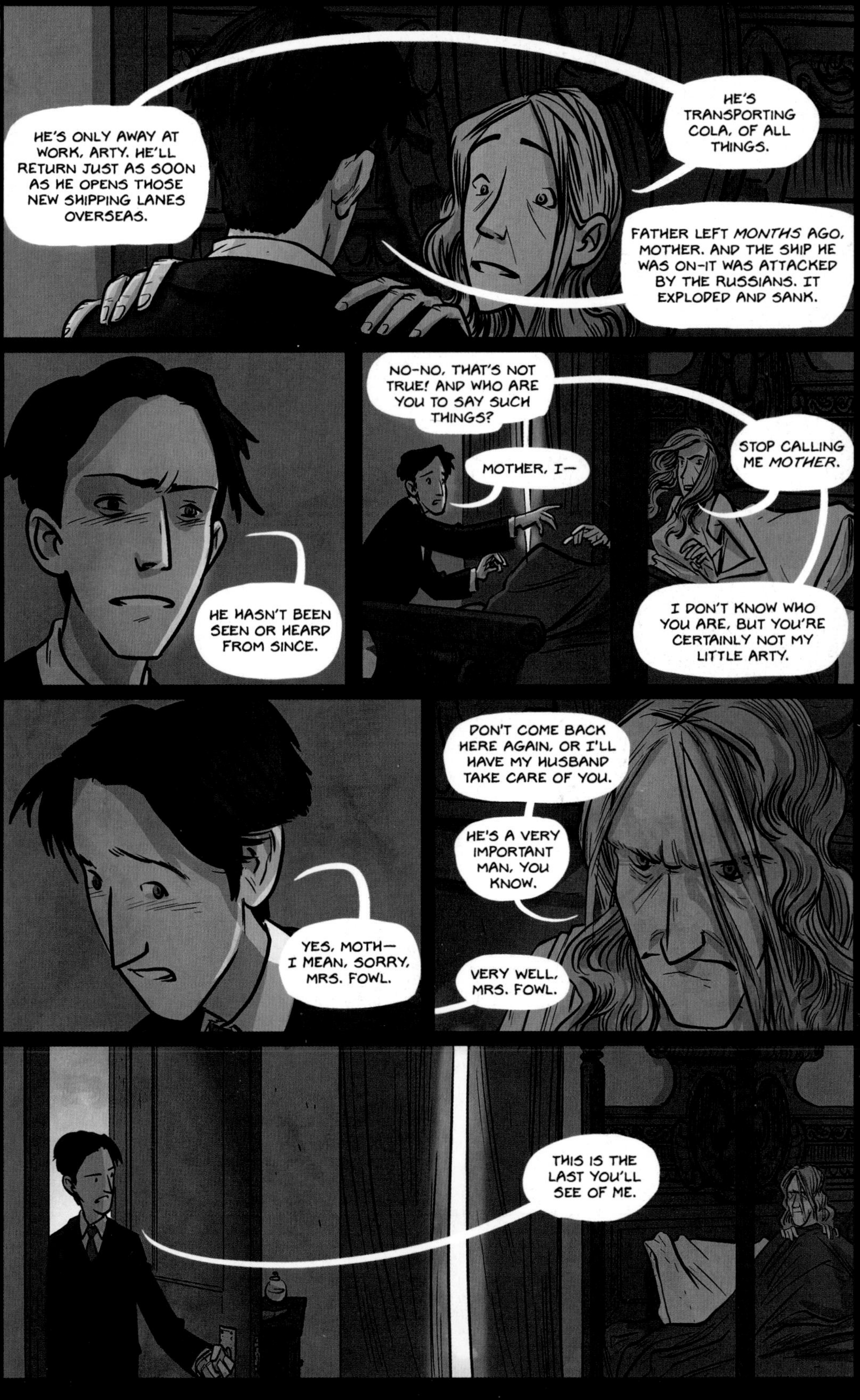
HE'S ONLY AWAY AT WORK, ARTY. HE'LL RETURN JUST AS SOON AS HE OPENS THOSE NEW SHIPPING LANES OVERSEAS.
HE'S TRANSPORTING COLA, OF ALL THINGS.
FATHER LEFT *MONTHS* AGO, MOTHER. AND THE SHIP HE WAS ON—IT WAS ATTACKED BY THE RUSSIANS. IT EXPLODED AND SANK.
HE HASN'T BEEN SEEN OR HEARD FROM SINCE.
NO-NO, THAT'S NOT TRUE! AND WHO ARE YOU TO SAY SUCH THINGS?
MOTHER, I—
STOP CALLING ME *MOTHER*.
I DON'T KNOW WHO YOU ARE, BUT YOU'RE CERTAINLY NOT MY LITTLE ARTY.
YES, MOTH— I MEAN, SORRY, MRS. FOWL.
DON'T COME BACK HERE AGAIN, OR I'LL HAVE MY HUSBAND TAKE CARE OF YOU.
HE'S A VERY IMPORTANT MAN, YOU KNOW.
VERY WELL, MRS. FOWL.
THIS IS THE LAST YOU'LL SEE OF ME.

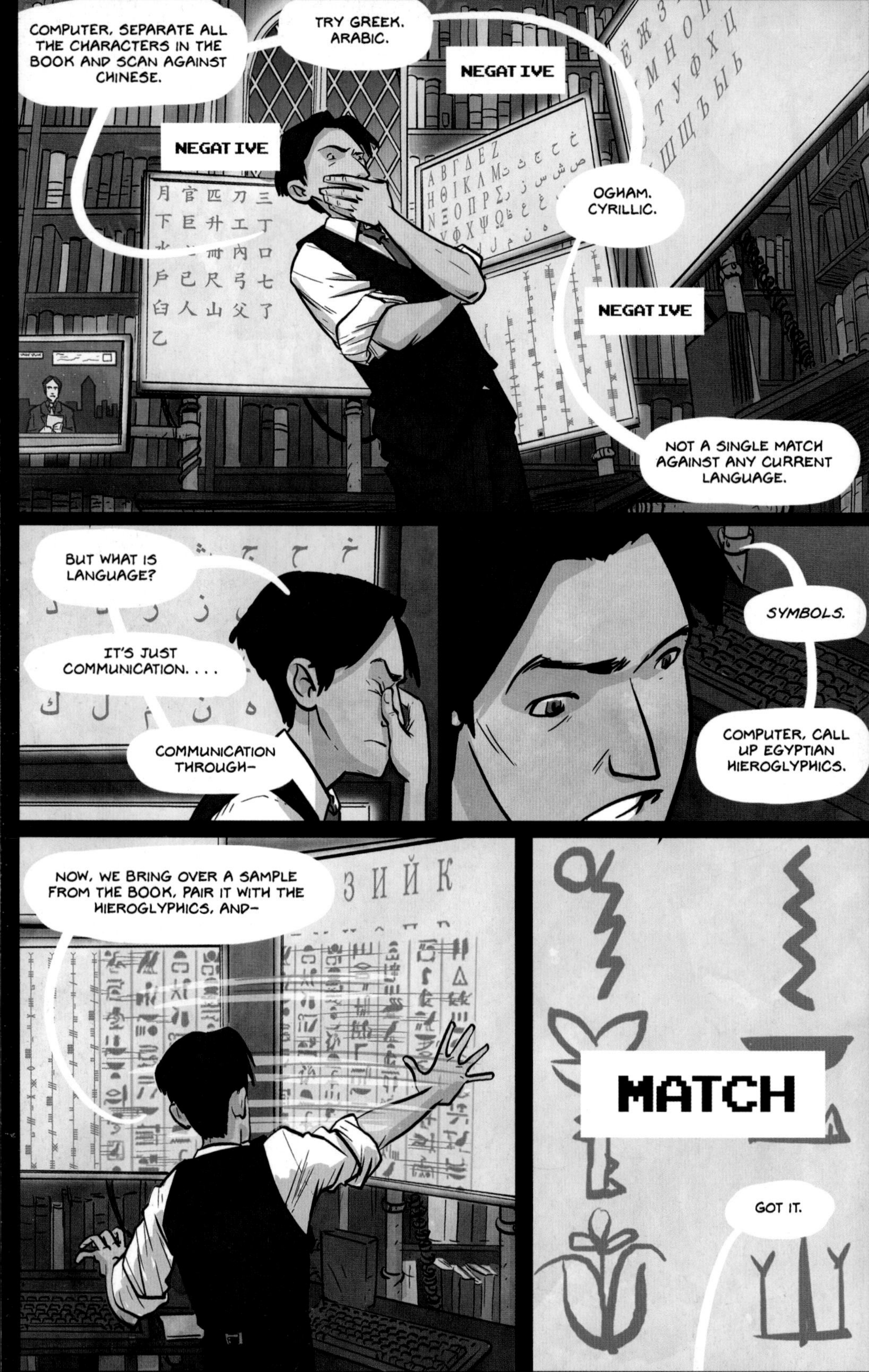

COMPUTER, SEPARATE ALL THE CHARACTERS IN THE BOOK AND SCAN AGAINST CHINESE.
NEGATIVE
TRY GREEK. ARABIC.
NEGATIVE
OGHAM. CYRILLIC.
NEGATIVE
NOT A SINGLE MATCH AGAINST ANY CURRENT LANGUAGE.
BUT WHAT IS LANGUAGE?
IT'S JUST COMMUNICATION. . . .
COMMUNICATION THROUGH—
SYMBOLS.
COMPUTER, CALL UP EGYPTIAN HIEROGLYPHICS.
NOW, WE BRING OVER A SAMPLE FROM THE BOOK, PAIR IT WITH THE HIEROGLYPHICS, AND—
MATCH
GOT IT.

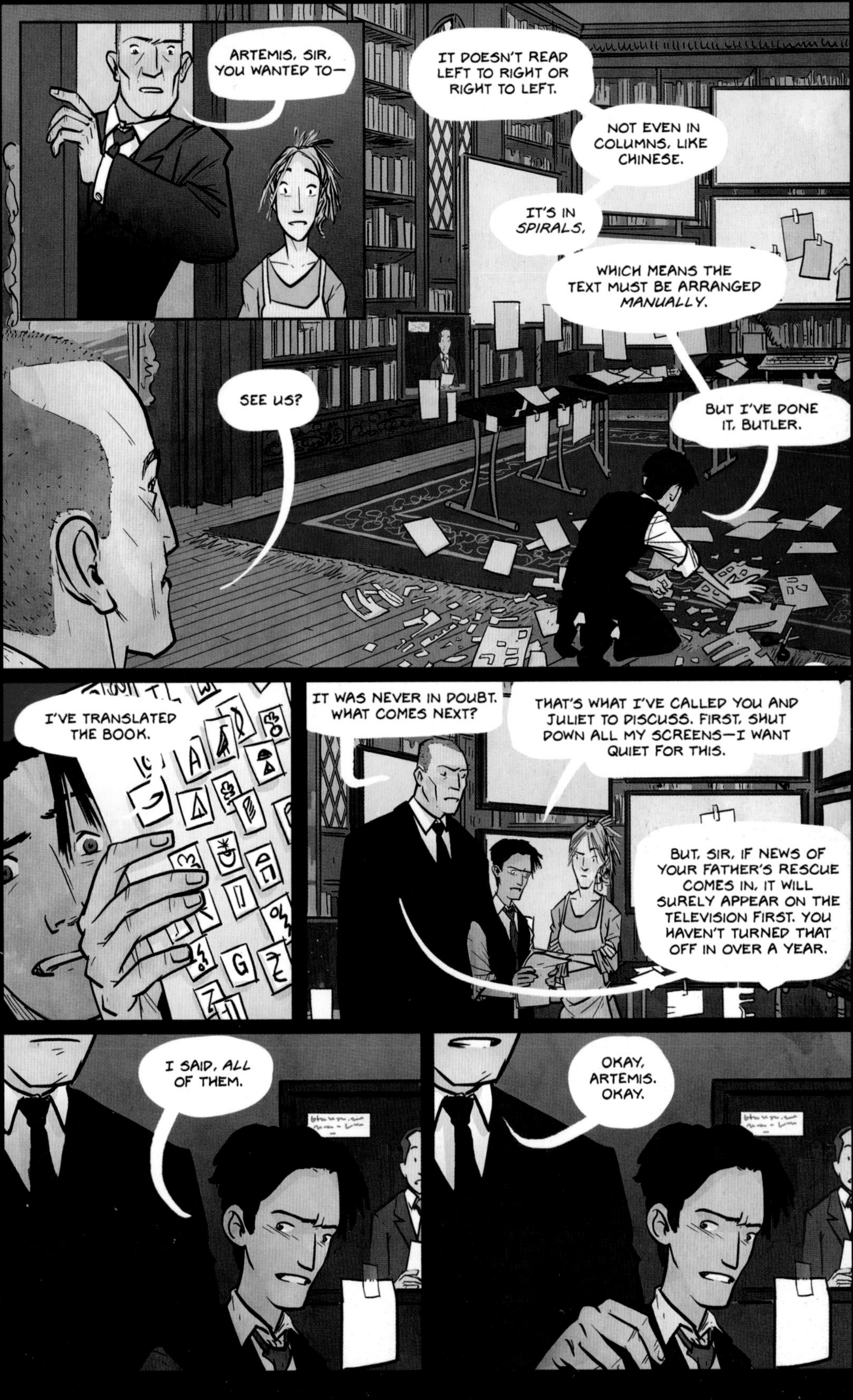
ARTEMIS, SIR, YOU WANTED TO—
IT DOESN'T READ LEFT TO RIGHT OR RIGHT TO LEFT.
NOT EVEN IN COLUMNS, LIKE CHINESE.
IT'S IN *SPIRALS*.
WHICH MEANS THE TEXT MUST BE ARRANGED *MANUALLY*.
SEE US?
BUT I'VE DONE IT, BUTLER.
I'VE TRANSLATED THE BOOK.
IT WAS NEVER IN DOUBT. WHAT COMES NEXT?
THAT'S WHAT I'VE CALLED YOU AND JULIET TO DISCUSS. FIRST, SHUT DOWN ALL MY SCREENS—I WANT QUIET FOR THIS.
BUT, SIR, IF NEWS OF YOUR FATHER'S RESCUE COMES IN, IT WILL SURELY APPEAR ON THE TELEVISION FIRST. YOU HAVEN'T TURNED THAT OFF IN OVER A YEAR.
I SAID, ALL OF THEM.
OKAY, ARTEMIS. OKAY.

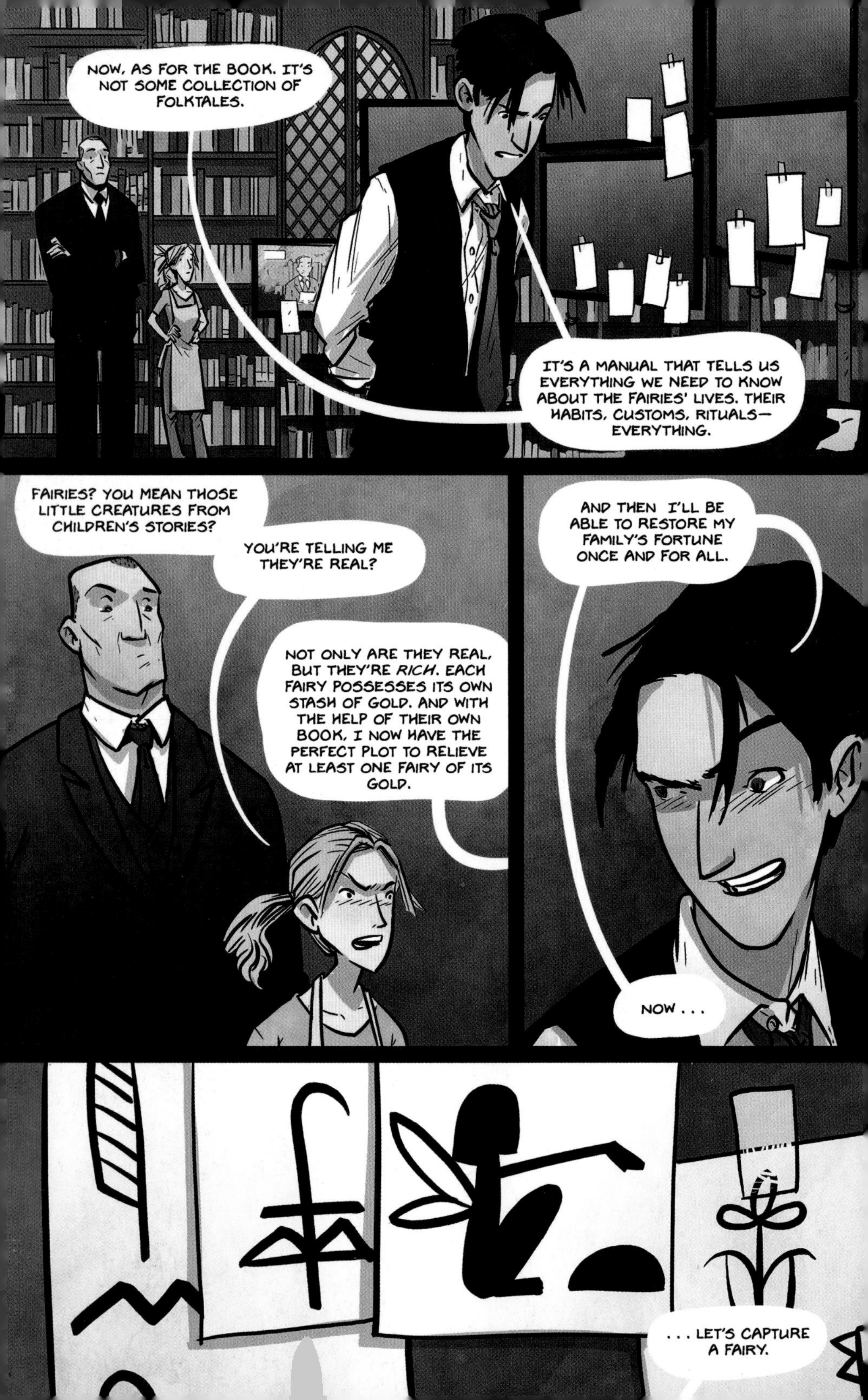
NOW, AS FOR THE BOOK. IT'S NOT SOME COLLECTION OF FOLKTALES.
IT'S A MANUAL THAT TELLS US EVERYTHING WE NEED TO KNOW ABOUT THE FAIRIES' LIVES. THEIR HABITS, CUSTOMS, RITUALS—EVERYTHING.
FAIRIES? YOU MEAN THOSE LITTLE CREATURES FROM CHILDREN'S STORIES?
YOU'RE TELLING ME THEY'RE REAL?
NOT ONLY ARE THEY REAL, BUT THEY'RE *RICH*. EACH FAIRY POSSESSES ITS OWN STASH OF GOLD. AND WITH THE HELP OF THEIR OWN BOOK, I NOW HAVE THE PERFECT PLOT TO RELIEVE AT LEAST ONE FAIRY OF ITS GOLD.
AND THEN I'LL BE ABLE TO RESTORE MY FAMILY'S FORTUNE ONCE AND FOR ALL.
NOW . . .
. . . LET'S CAPTURE A FAIRY.

CHAPTER THREE

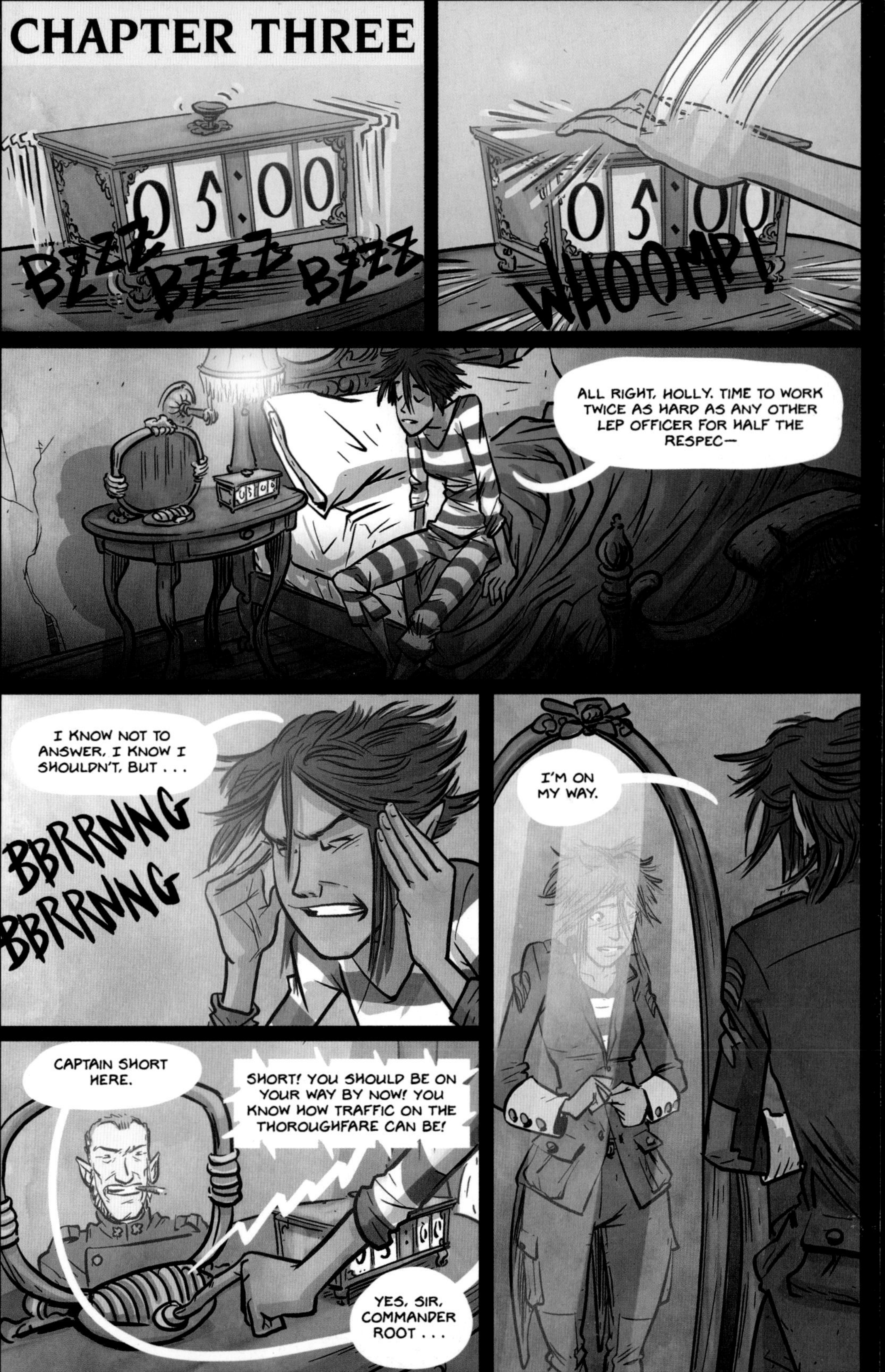
05:00
BZZZ BZZZ BZZZ
05:00
WHOOMP!
ALL RIGHT, HOLLY. TIME TO WORK TWICE AS HARD AS ANY OTHER LEP OFFICER FOR HALF THE RESPEC—
I KNOW NOT TO ANSWER. I KNOW I SHOULDN'T, BUT . . .
BBRRNNG BBRRNNG
CAPTAIN SHORT HERE.
SHORT! YOU SHOULD BE ON YOUR WAY BY NOW! YOU KNOW HOW TRAFFIC ON THE THOROUGHFARE CAN BE!
YES, SIR, COMMANDER ROOT . . .
I'M ON MY WAY.

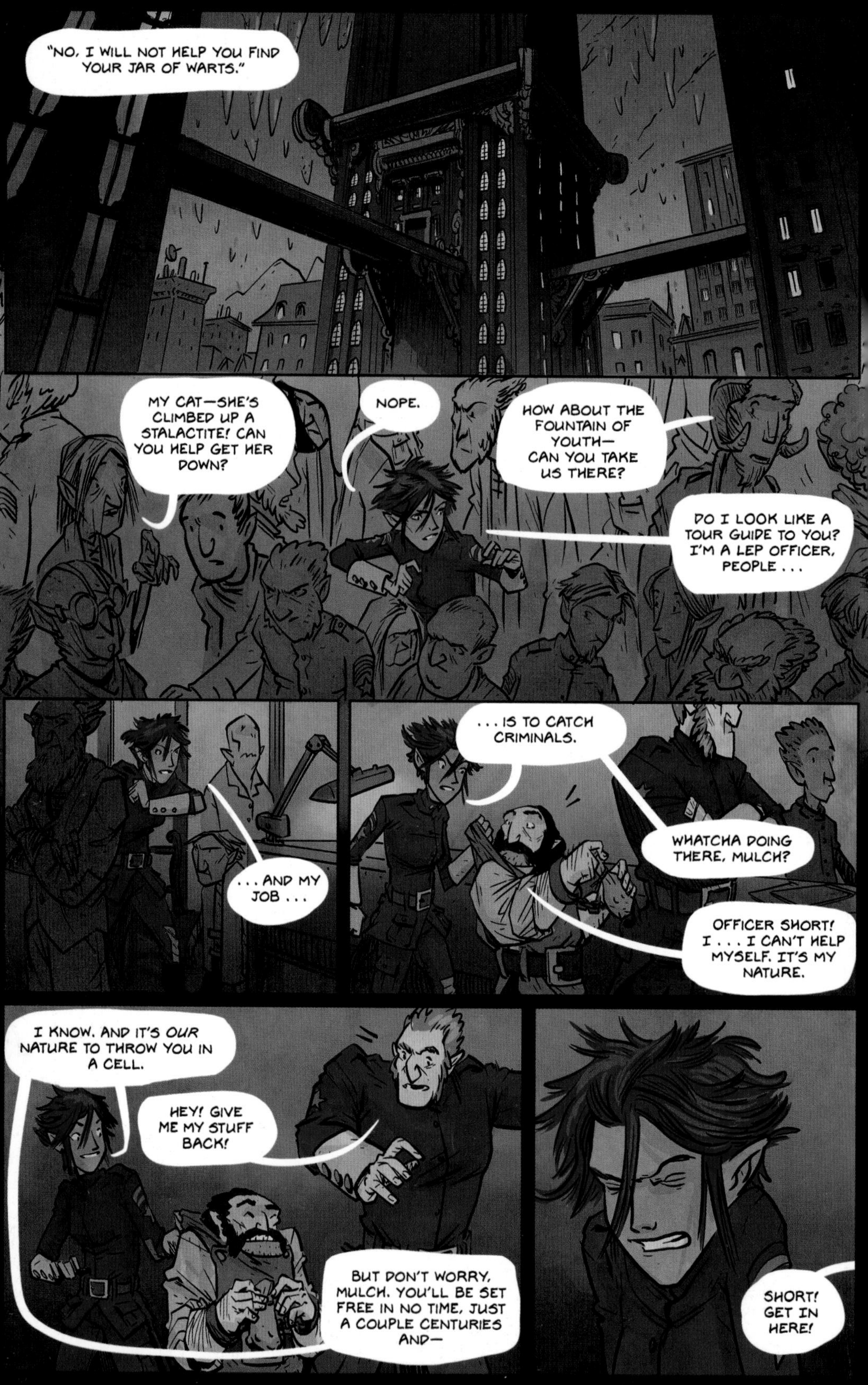
"NO, I WILL NOT HELP YOU FIND YOUR JAR OF WARTS."
MY CAT—SHE'S CLIMBED UP A STALACTITE! CAN YOU HELP GET HER DOWN?
NOPE.
HOW ABOUT THE FOUNTAIN OF YOUTH— CAN YOU TAKE US THERE?
DO I LOOK LIKE A TOUR GUIDE TO YOU? I'M A LEP OFFICER, PEOPLE . . .
. . . AND MY JOB . . .
. . . IS TO CATCH CRIMINALS.
WHATCHA DOING THERE, MULCH?
OFFICER SHORT! I . . . I CAN'T HELP MYSELF. IT'S MY NATURE.
I KNOW. AND IT'S *OUR* NATURE TO THROW YOU IN A CELL.
HEY! GIVE ME MY STUFF BACK!
BUT DON'T WORRY, MULCH. YOU'LL BE SET FREE IN NO TIME, JUST A COUPLE CENTURIES AND—
SHORT! GET IN HERE!

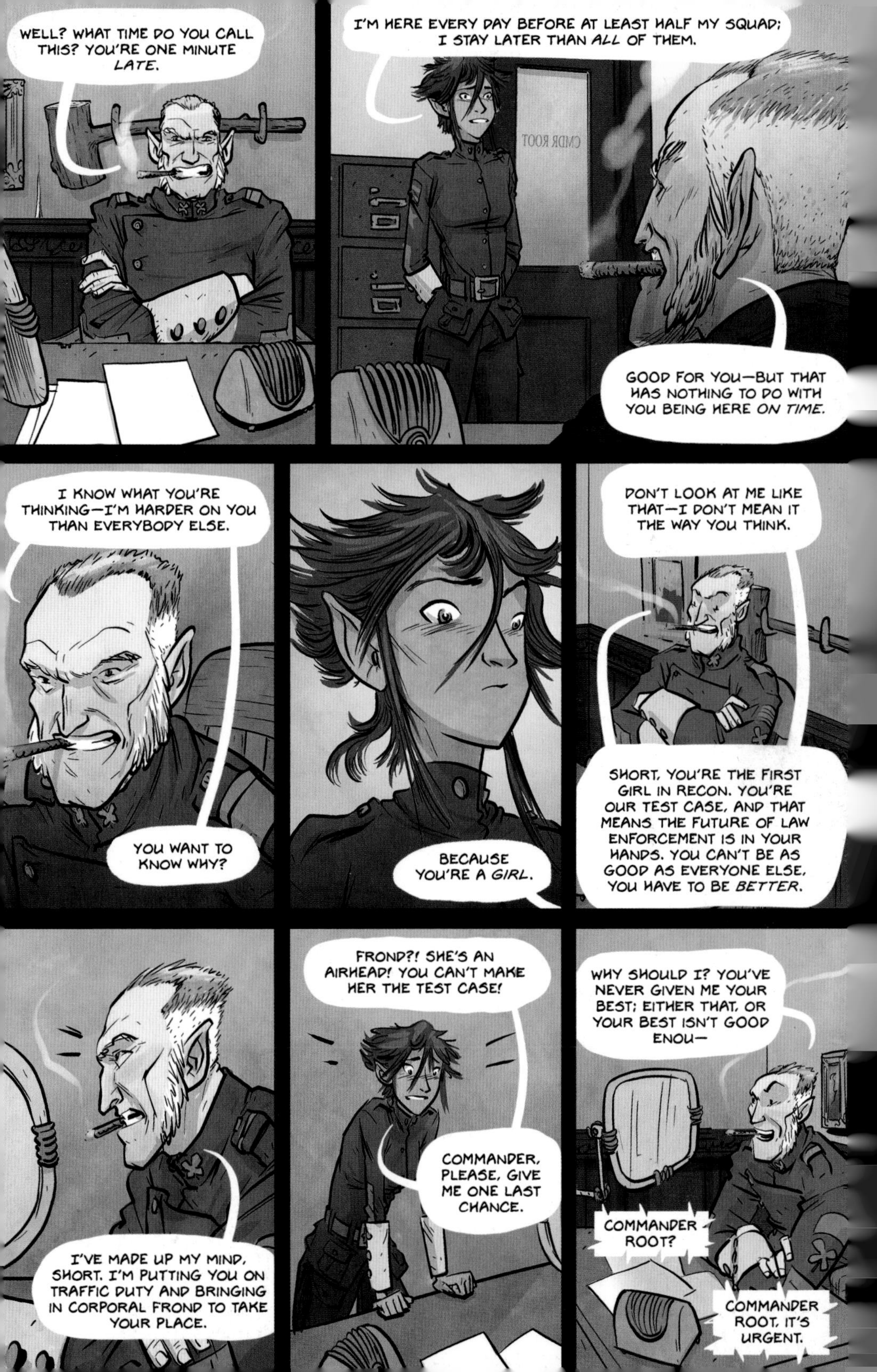
WELL? WHAT TIME DO YOU CALL THIS? YOU'RE ONE MINUTE LATE.
I'M HERE EVERY DAY BEFORE AT LEAST HALF MY SQUAD; I STAY LATER THAN ALL OF THEM.
CMDR ROOT
GOOD FOR YOU—BUT THAT HAS NOTHING TO DO WITH YOU BEING HERE ON TIME.
I KNOW WHAT YOU'RE THINKING—I'M HARDER ON YOU THAN EVERYBODY ELSE.
YOU WANT TO KNOW WHY?
BECAUSE YOU'RE A GIRL.
DON'T LOOK AT ME LIKE THAT—I DON'T MEAN IT THE WAY YOU THINK.
SHORT, YOU'RE THE FIRST GIRL IN RECON. YOU'RE OUR TEST CASE, AND THAT MEANS THE FUTURE OF LAW ENFORCEMENT IS IN YOUR HANDS. YOU CAN'T BE AS GOOD AS EVERYONE ELSE, YOU HAVE TO BE BETTER.
I'VE MADE UP MY MIND, SHORT. I'M PUTTING YOU ON TRAFFIC DUTY AND BRINGING IN CORPORAL FROND TO TAKE YOUR PLACE.
FROND?! SHE'S AN AIRHEAD! YOU CAN'T MAKE HER THE TEST CASE!
COMMANDER, PLEASE, GIVE ME ONE LAST CHANCE.
WHY SHOULD I? YOU'VE NEVER GIVEN ME YOUR BEST; EITHER THAT, OR YOUR BEST ISN'T GOOD ENOU—
COMMANDER ROOT?
COMMANDER ROOT, IT'S URGENT.

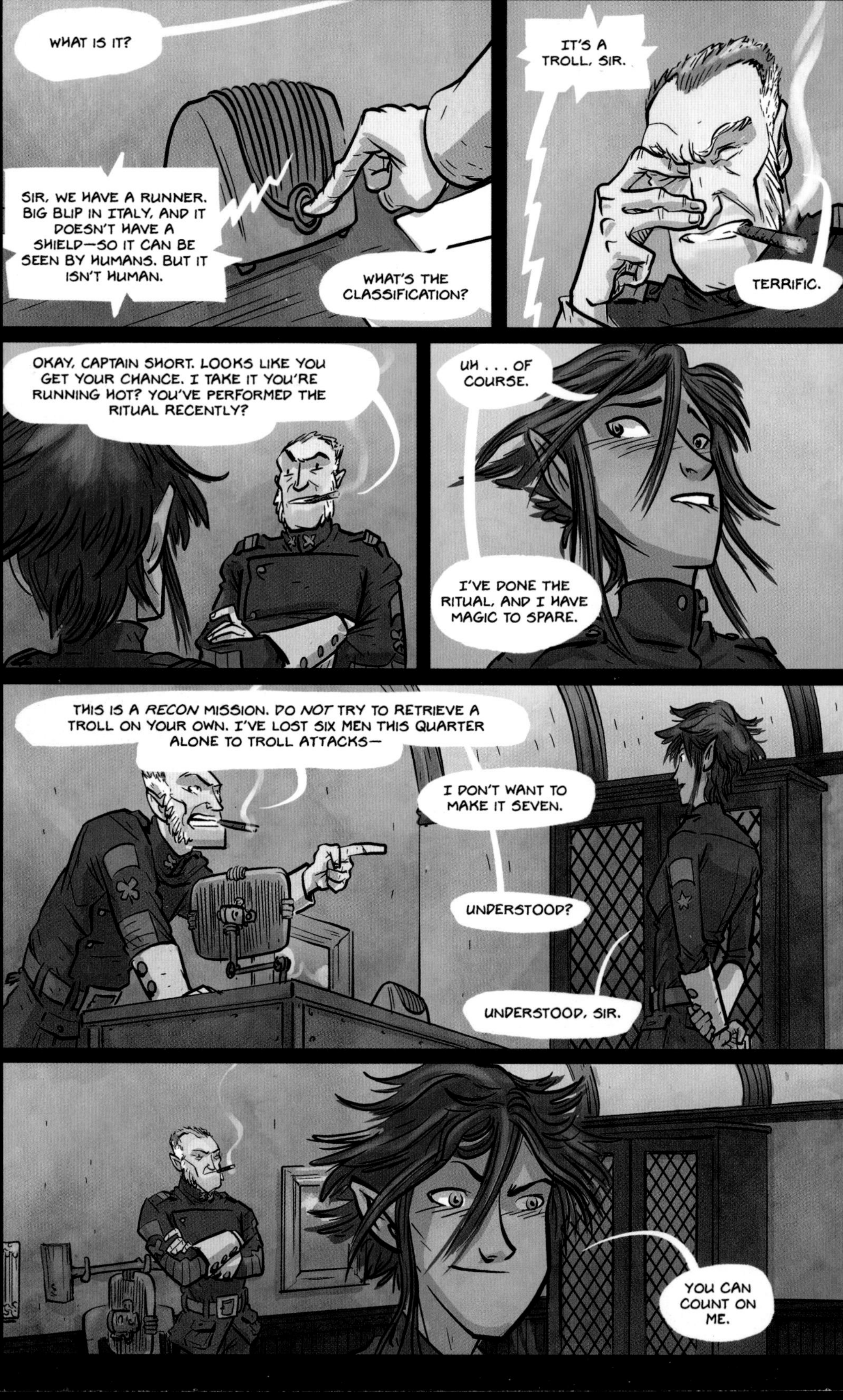
WHAT IS IT?
SIR, WE HAVE A RUNNER. BIG BLIP IN ITALY, AND IT DOESN'T HAVE A SHIELD—SO IT CAN BE SEEN BY HUMANS. BUT IT ISN'T HUMAN.
WHAT'S THE CLASSIFICATION?
IT'S A TROLL, SIR.
TERRIFIC.
OKAY, CAPTAIN SHORT. LOOKS LIKE YOU GET YOUR CHANCE. I TAKE IT YOU'RE RUNNING HOT? YOU'VE PERFORMED THE RITUAL RECENTLY?
UH . . . OF COURSE.
I'VE DONE THE RITUAL, AND I HAVE MAGIC TO SPARE.
THIS IS A *RECON* MISSION. DO *NOT* TRY TO RETRIEVE A TROLL ON YOUR OWN. I'VE LOST SIX MEN THIS QUARTER ALONE TO TROLL ATTACKS—
I DON'T WANT TO MAKE IT SEVEN.
UNDERSTOOD?
UNDERSTOOD, SIR.
YOU CAN COUNT ON ME.

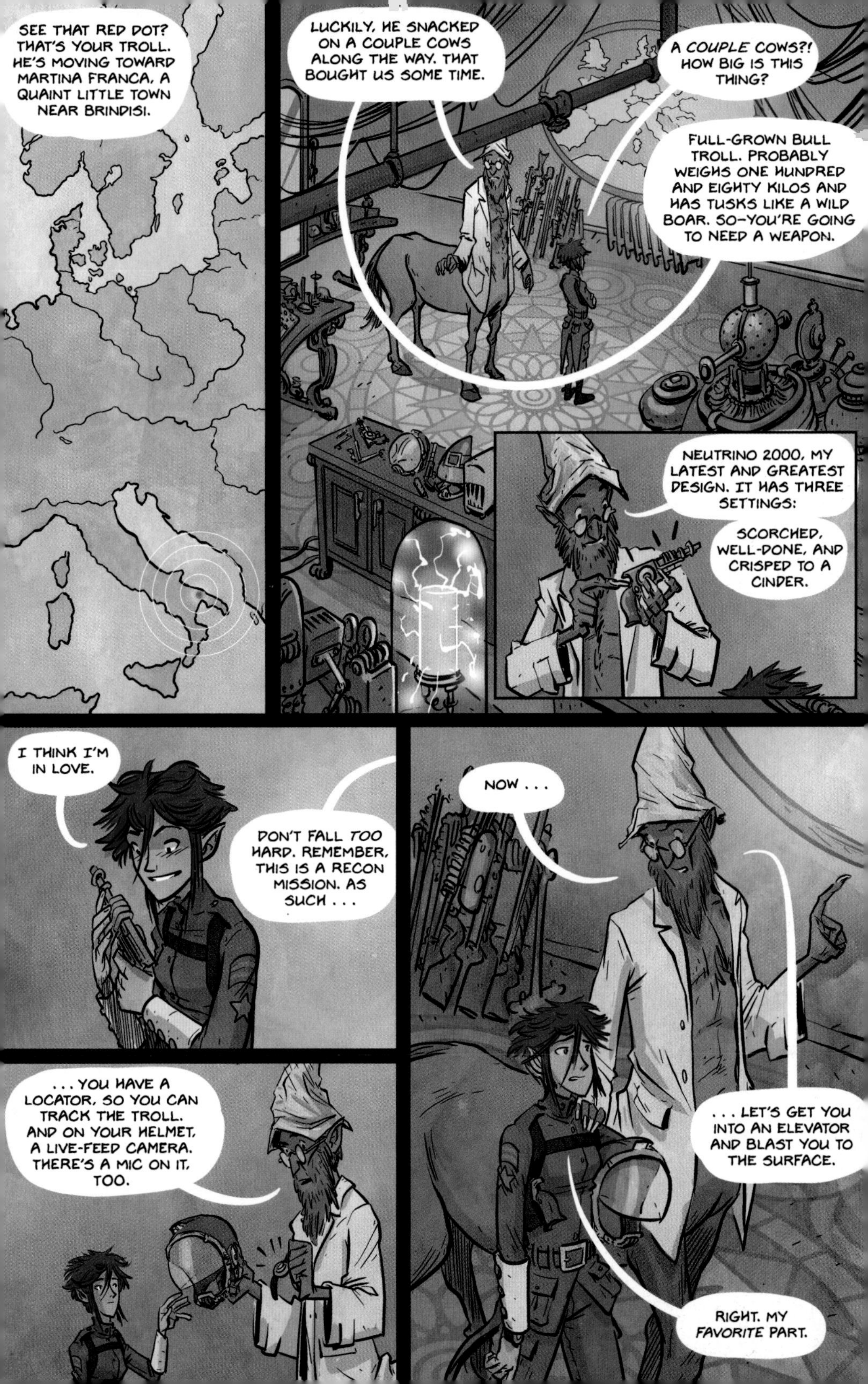
SEE THAT RED DOT? THAT'S YOUR TROLL. HE'S MOVING TOWARD MARTINA FRANCA, A QUAINT LITTLE TOWN NEAR BRINDISI.
LUCKILY, HE SNACKED ON A COUPLE COWS ALONG THE WAY. THAT BOUGHT US SOME TIME.
A *COUPLE* COWS?! HOW BIG IS THIS THING?
FULL-GROWN BULL TROLL. PROBABLY WEIGHS ONE HUNDRED AND EIGHTY KILOS AND HAS TUSKS LIKE A WILD BOAR. SO—YOU'RE GOING TO NEED A WEAPON.
NEUTRINO 2000, MY LATEST AND GREATEST DESIGN. IT HAS THREE SETTINGS:
SCORCHED, WELL-DONE, AND CRISPED TO A CINDER.
I THINK I'M IN LOVE.
DON'T FALL *TOO* HARD. REMEMBER, THIS IS A RECON MISSION. AS SUCH . . .
. . . YOU HAVE A LOCATOR, SO YOU CAN TRACK THE TROLL. AND ON YOUR HELMET, A LIVE-FEED CAMERA. THERE'S A MIC ON IT, TOO.
NOW . . .
. . . LET'S GET YOU INTO AN ELEVATOR AND BLAST YOU TO THE SURFACE.
RIGHT. MY *FAVORITE* PART.

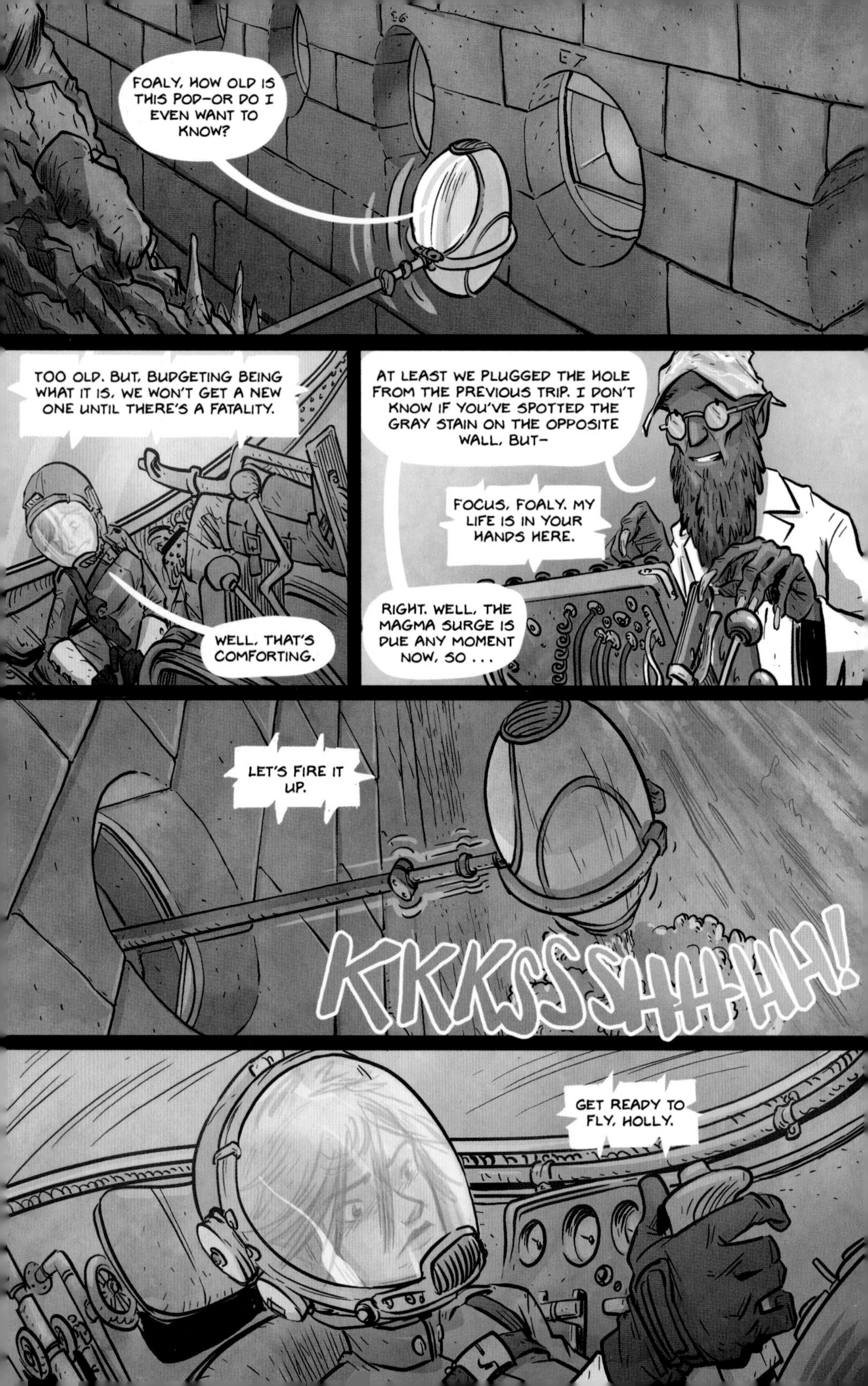
FOALY, HOW OLD IS THIS POD—OR DO I EVEN WANT TO KNOW?
TOO OLD. BUT, BUDGETING BEING WHAT IT IS, WE WON'T GET A NEW ONE UNTIL THERE'S A FATALITY.
WELL, THAT'S COMFORTING.
AT LEAST WE PLUGGED THE HOLE FROM THE PREVIOUS TRIP. I DON'T KNOW IF YOU'VE SPOTTED THE GRAY STAIN ON THE OPPOSITE WALL, BUT—
FOCUS, FOALY. MY LIFE IS IN YOUR HANDS HERE.
RIGHT. WELL, THE MAGMA SURGE IS DUE ANY MOMENT NOW, SO . . .
LET'S FIRE IT UP.
KKKSSSHHHHH!
GET READY TO FLY, HOLLY.

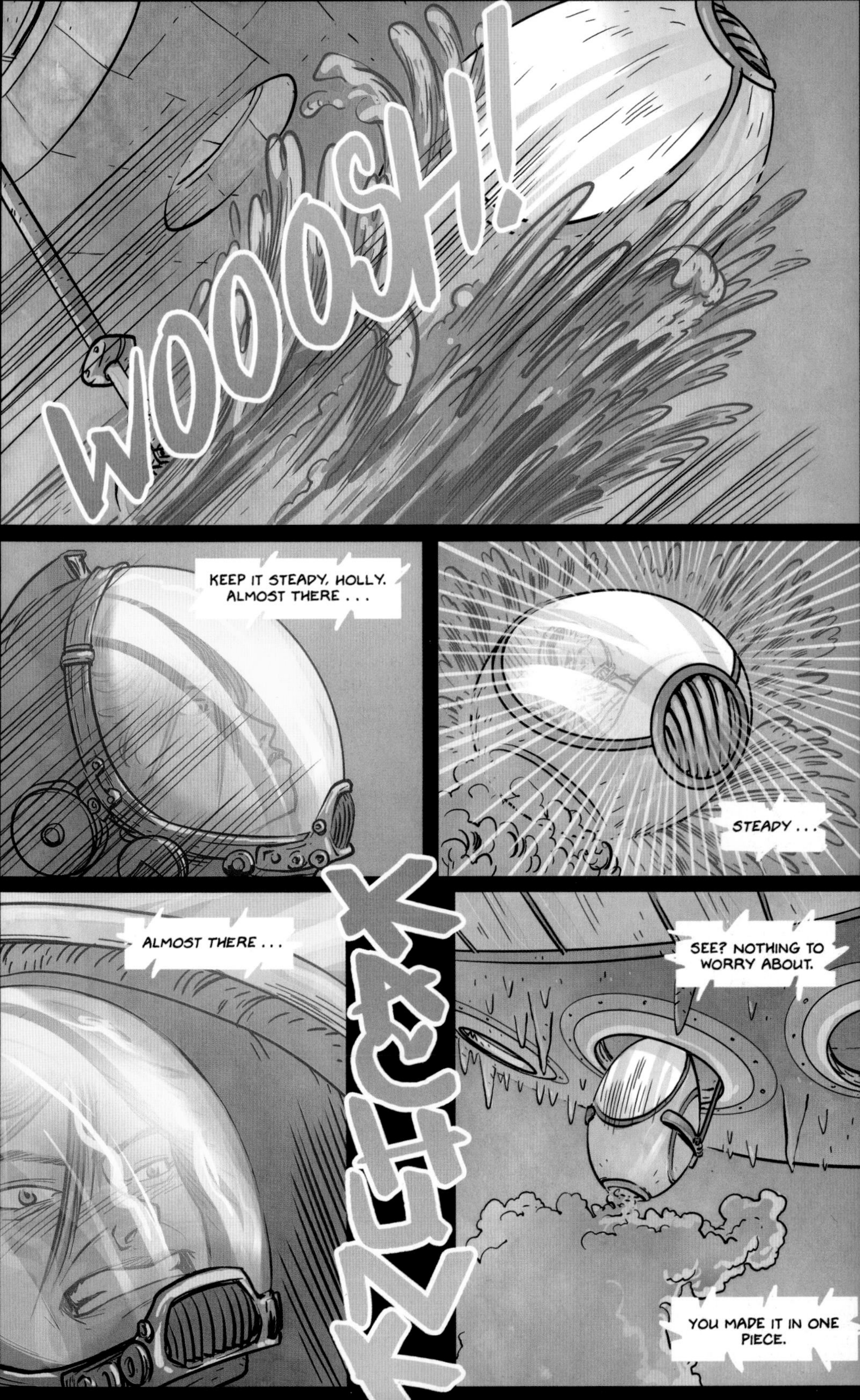
WOOOSH!
KEEP IT STEADY, HOLLY. ALMOST THERE . . .
STEADY . . .
ALMOST THERE . . .
KACHUNK
SEE? NOTHING TO WORRY ABOUT.
YOU MADE IT IN ONE PIECE.

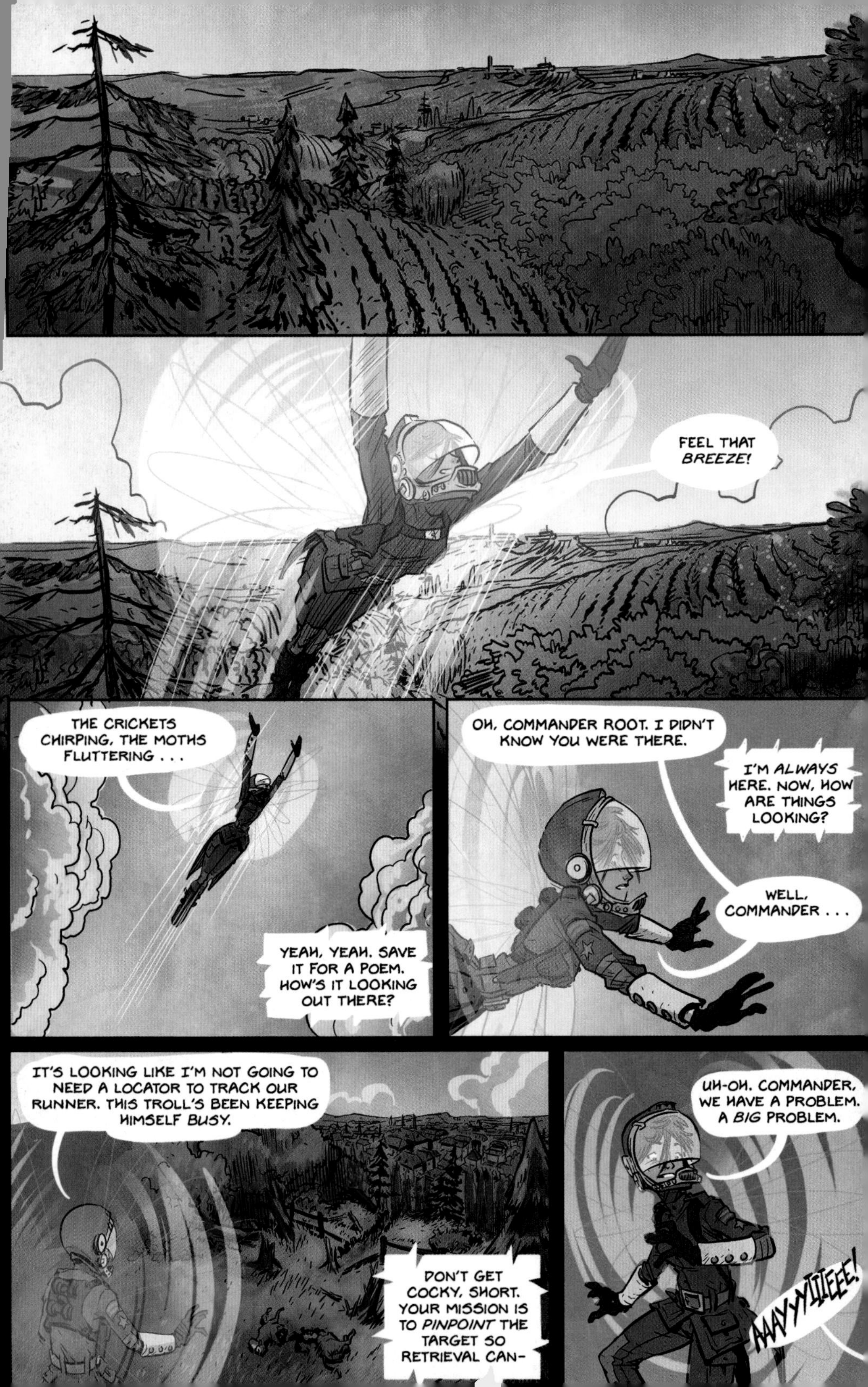
FEEL THAT *BREEZE!*
THE CRICKETS CHIRPING, THE MOTHS FLUTTERING . . .
YEAH, YEAH. SAVE IT FOR A POEM. HOW'S IT LOOKING OUT THERE?
OH, COMMANDER ROOT. I DIDN'T KNOW YOU WERE THERE.
I'M *ALWAYS* HERE. NOW, HOW ARE THINGS LOOKING?
WELL, COMMANDER . . .
IT'S LOOKING LIKE I'M NOT GOING TO NEED A LOCATOR TO TRACK OUR RUNNER. THIS TROLL'S BEEN KEEPING HIMSELF *BUSY.*
DON'T GET COCKY, SHORT. YOUR MISSION IS TO *PINPOINT* THE TARGET SO RETRIEVAL CAN-
UH-OH. COMMANDER, WE HAVE A PROBLEM. A *BIG* PROBLEM.
AAAYYYIIIEEE!

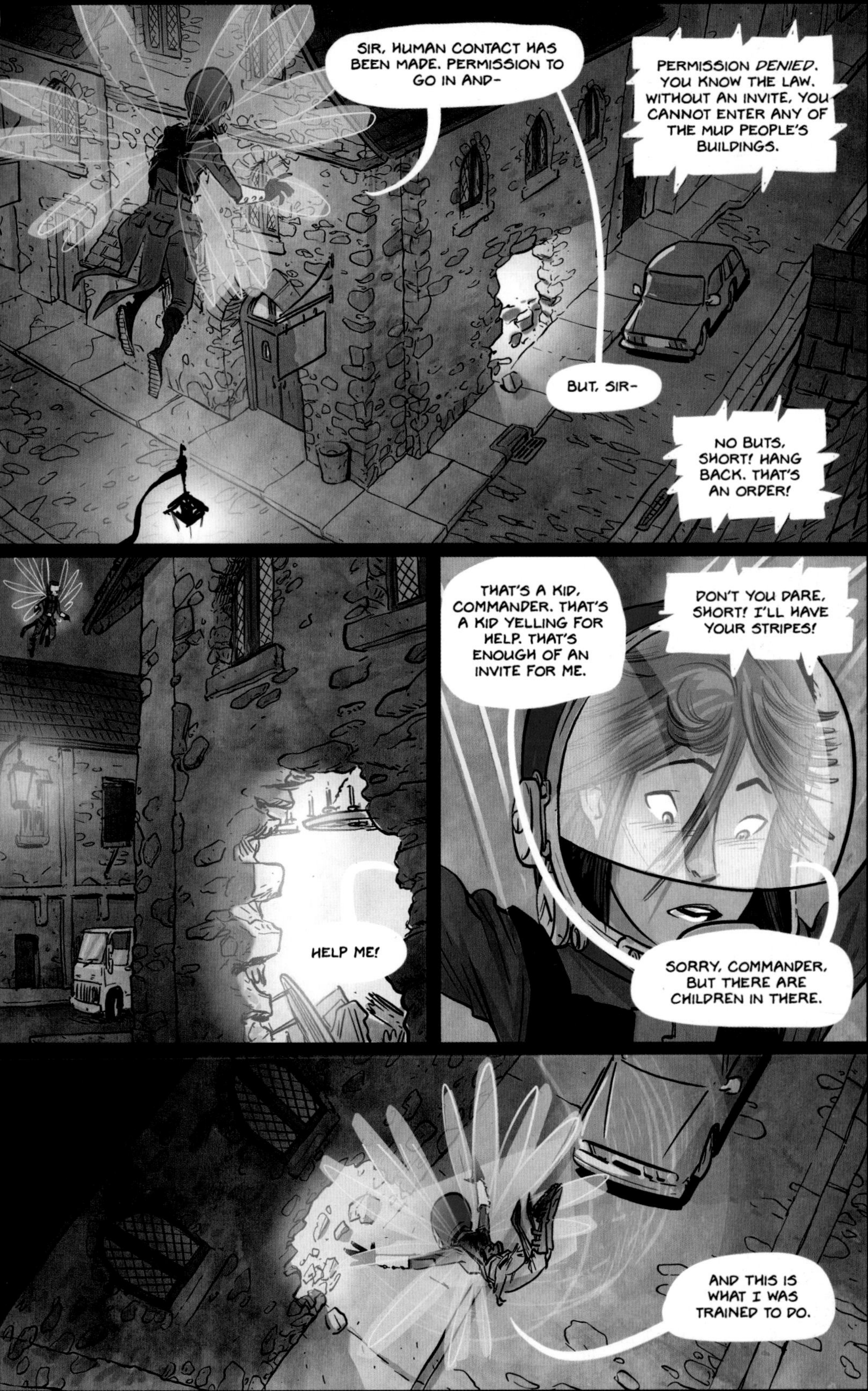
SIR, HUMAN CONTACT HAS BEEN MADE. PERMISSION TO GO IN AND-
PERMISSION *DENIED*. YOU KNOW THE LAW. WITHOUT AN INVITE, YOU CANNOT ENTER ANY OF THE MUD PEOPLE'S BUILDINGS.
BUT, SIR-
NO BUTS, SHORT! HANG BACK. THAT'S AN ORDER!
HELP ME!
THAT'S A KID, COMMANDER. THAT'S A KID YELLING FOR HELP. THAT'S ENOUGH OF AN INVITE FOR ME.
DON'T YOU DARE, SHORT! I'LL HAVE YOUR STRIPES!
SORRY, COMMANDER, BUT THERE ARE CHILDREN IN THERE.
AND THIS IS WHAT I WAS TRAINED TO DO.

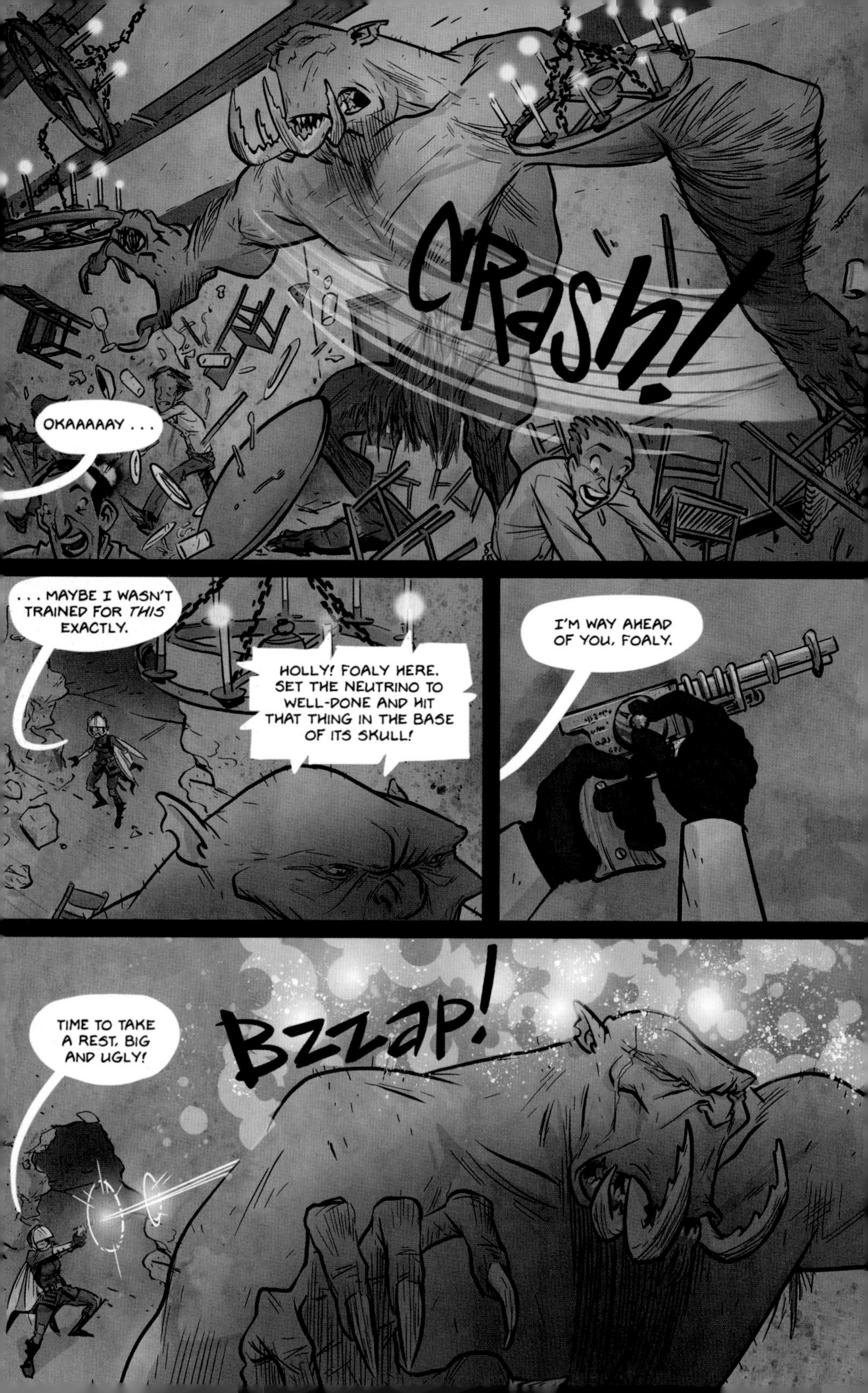
CRASH!
OKAAAAAY . . .
. . . MAYBE I WASN'T TRAINED FOR *THIS* EXACTLY.
HOLLY! FOALY HERE. SET THE NEUTRINO TO WELL-DONE AND HIT THAT THING IN THE BASE OF ITS SKULL!
I'M WAY AHEAD OF YOU, FOALY.
BZZAP!
TIME TO TAKE A REST, BIG AND UGLY!

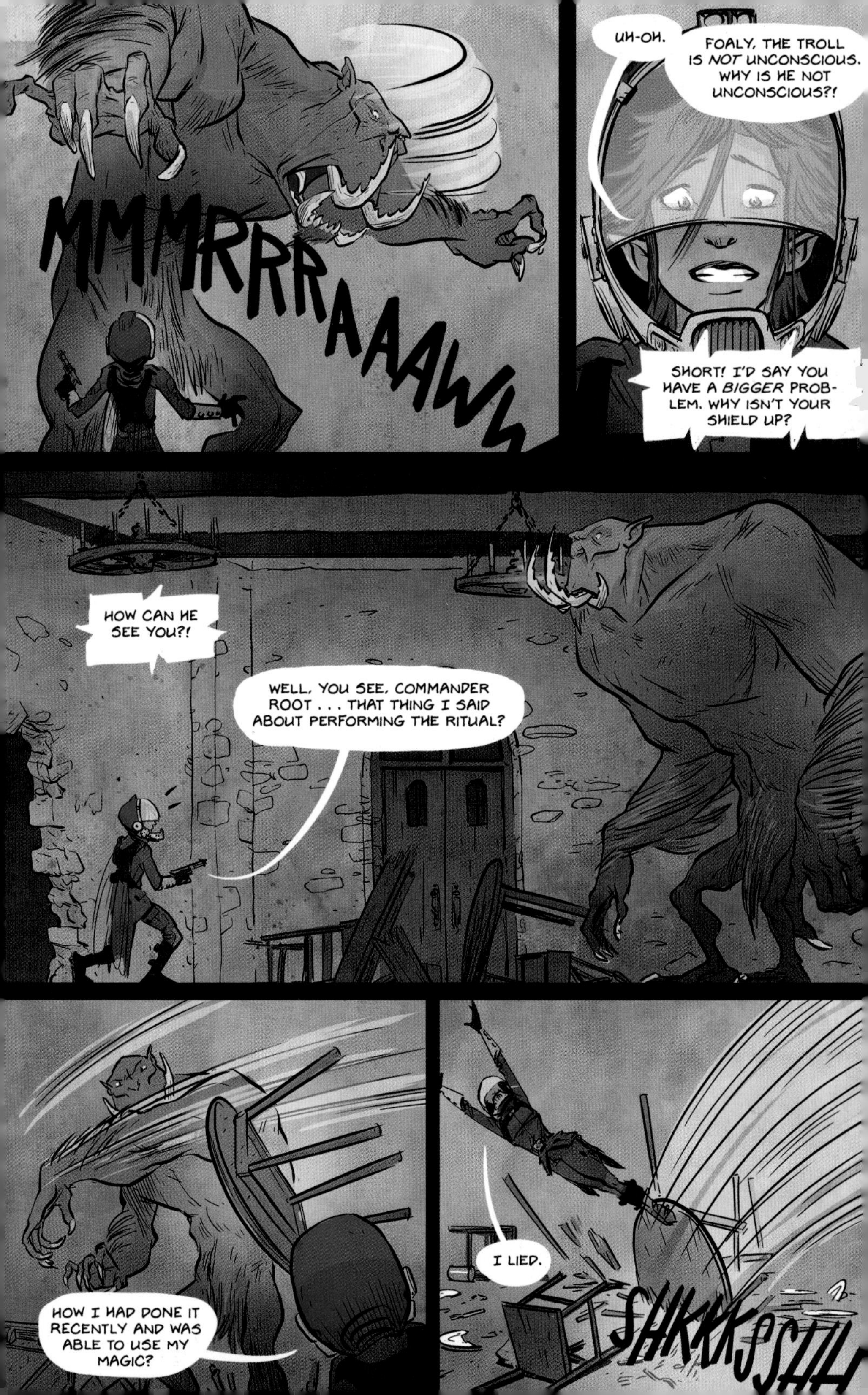
MMMRRRRAAAWW
UH-OH.
FOALY, THE TROLL IS *NOT* UNCONSCIOUS. WHY IS HE NOT UNCONSCIOUS?!
SHORT! I'D SAY YOU HAVE A *BIGGER* PROB-LEM. WHY ISN'T YOUR SHIELD UP?
HOW CAN HE SEE YOU?!
WELL, YOU SEE, COMMANDER ROOT . . . THAT THING I SAID ABOUT PERFORMING THE RITUAL?
HOW I HAD DONE IT RECENTLY AND WAS ABLE TO USE MY MAGIC?
I LIED.
SHKKKSHH

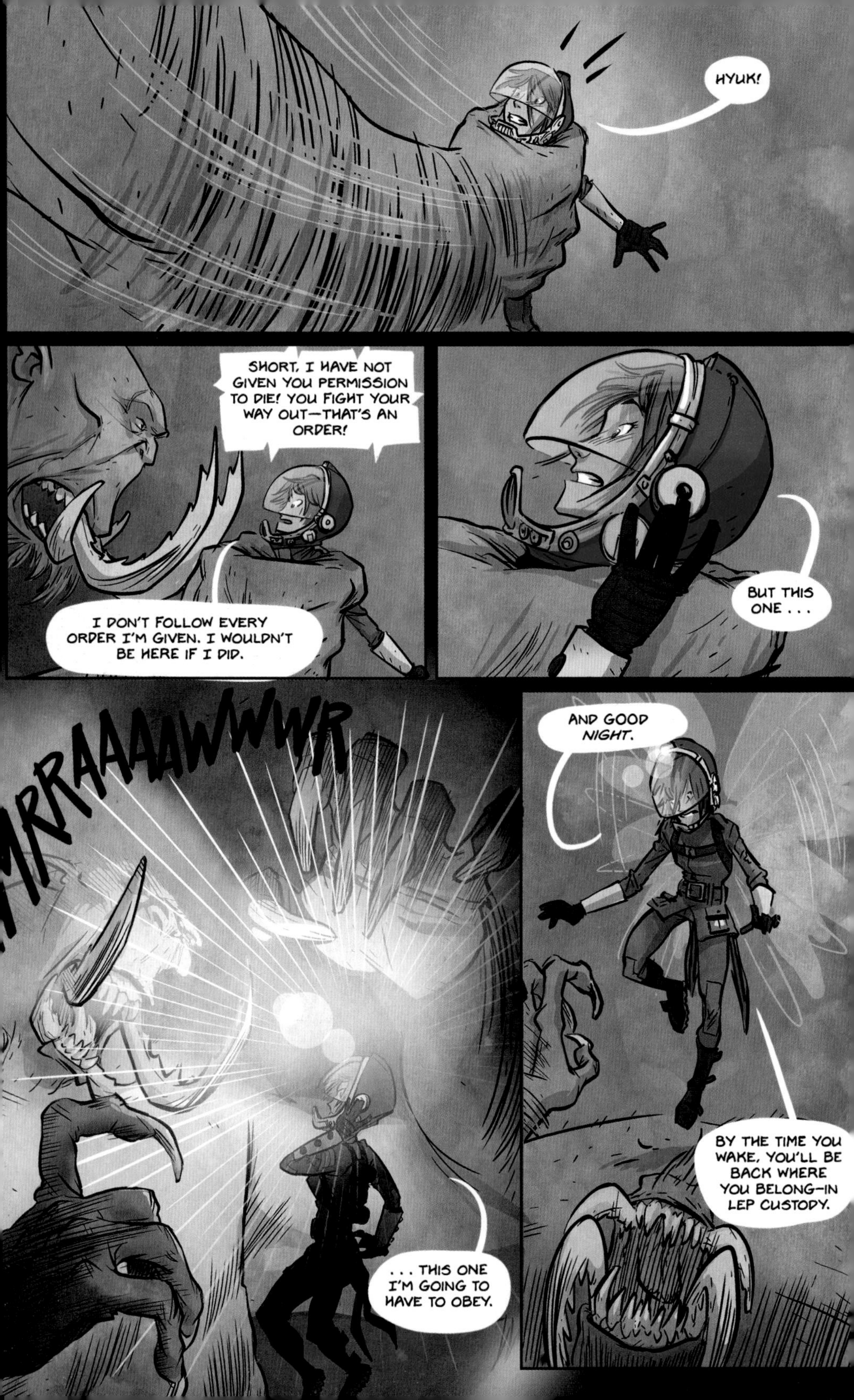
HYUK!
SHORT, I HAVE NOT GIVEN YOU PERMISSION TO DIE! YOU FIGHT YOUR WAY OUT—THAT'S AN ORDER!
I DON'T FOLLOW EVERY ORDER I'M GIVEN. I WOULDN'T BE HERE IF I DID.
BUT THIS ONE . . .
MRRAAAAWWWR
. . . THIS ONE I'M GOING TO HAVE TO OBEY.
AND GOOD NIGHT.
BY THE TIME YOU WAKE, YOU'LL BE BACK WHERE YOU BELONG—IN LEP CUSTODY.

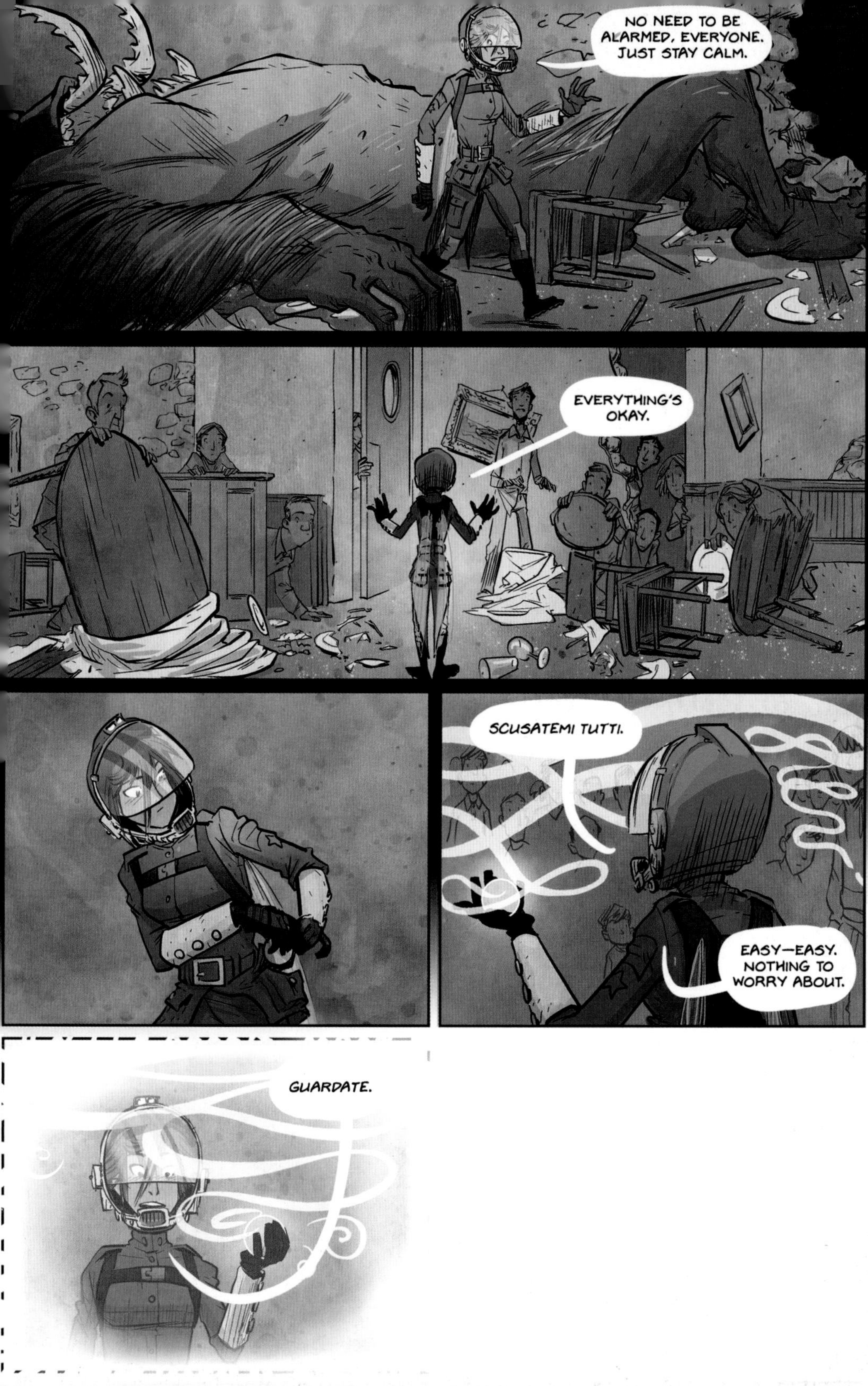
NO NEED TO BE ALARMED, EVERYONE. JUST STAY CALM.
EVERYTHING'S OKAY.
SCUSATEMI TUTTI.
EASY—EASY. NOTHING TO WORRY ABOUT.
GUARDATE.

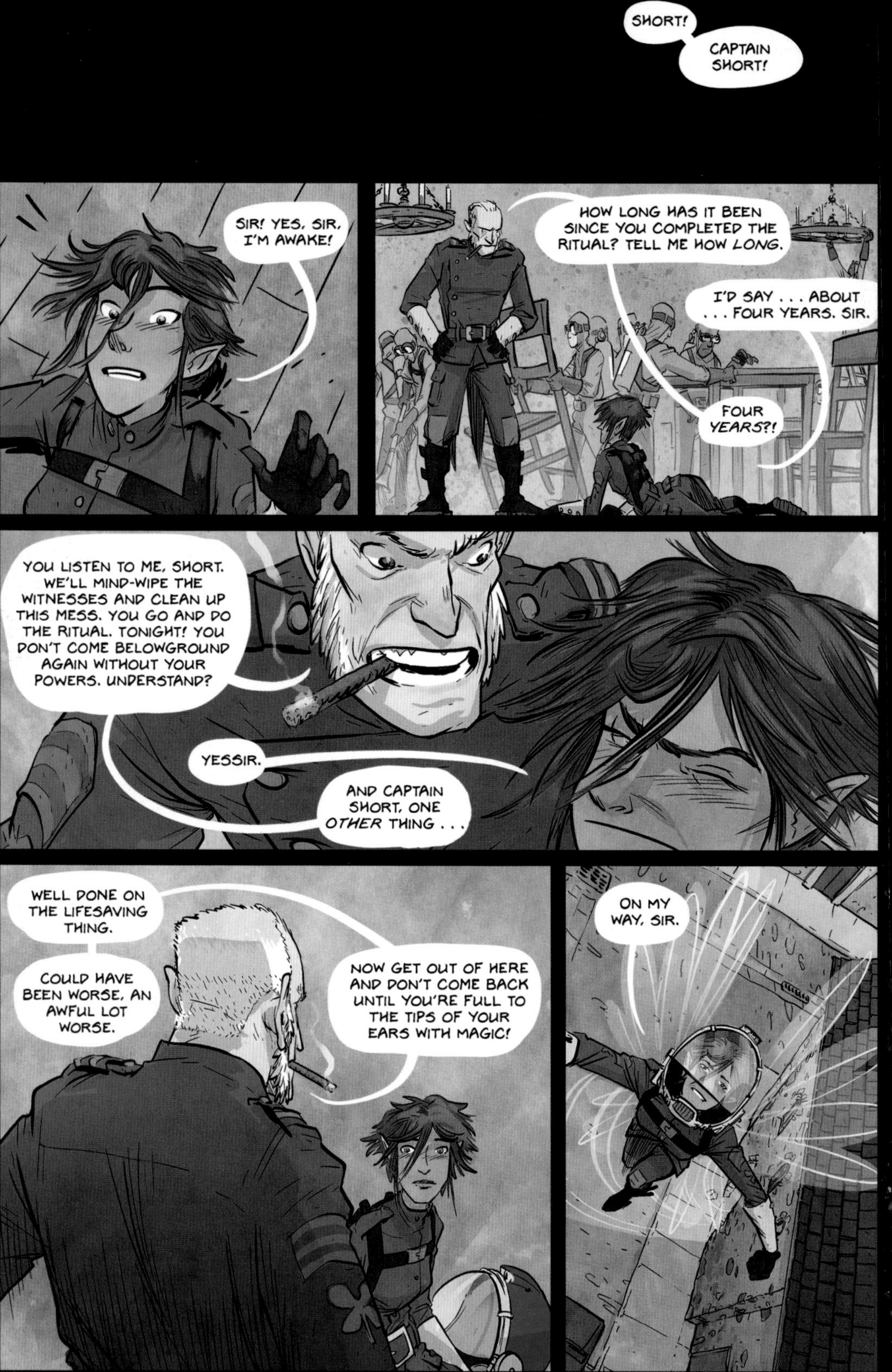
SHORT!
CAPTAIN SHORT!
SIR! YES, SIR, I'M AWAKE!
HOW LONG HAS IT BEEN SINCE YOU COMPLETED THE RITUAL? TELL ME HOW LONG.
I'D SAY . . . ABOUT . . . FOUR YEARS. SIR.
FOUR YEARS?!
YOU LISTEN TO ME, SHORT. WE'LL MIND-WIPE THE WITNESSES AND CLEAN UP THIS MESS. YOU GO AND DO THE RITUAL. TONIGHT! YOU DON'T COME BELOWGROUND AGAIN WITHOUT YOUR POWERS. UNDERSTAND?
YESSIR.
AND CAPTAIN SHORT, ONE OTHER THING . . .
WELL DONE ON THE LIFESAVING THING.
COULD HAVE BEEN WORSE, AN AWFUL LOT WORSE.
NOW GET OUT OF HERE AND DON'T COME BACK UNTIL YOU'RE FULL TO THE TIPS OF YOUR EARS WITH MAGIC!
ON MY WAY, SIR.

CHAPTER FOUR

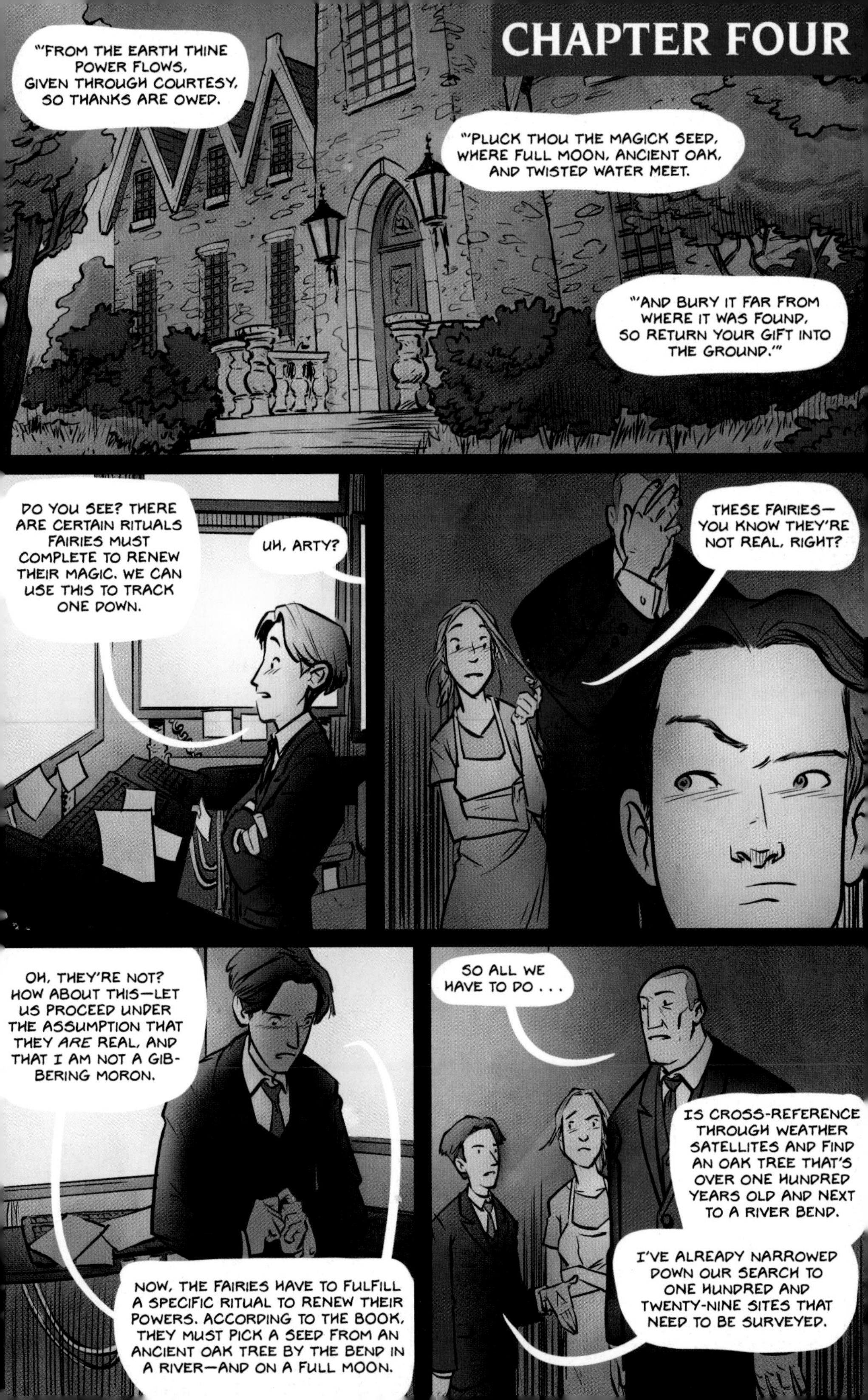
"'FROM THE EARTH THINE POWER FLOWS, GIVEN THROUGH COURTESY, SO THANKS ARE OWED.
"'PLUCK THOU THE MAGICK SEED, WHERE FULL MOON, ANCIENT OAK, AND TWISTED WATER MEET.
"'AND BURY IT FAR FROM WHERE IT WAS FOUND, SO RETURN YOUR GIFT INTO THE GROUND.'"
DO YOU SEE? THERE ARE CERTAIN RITUALS FAIRIES MUST COMPLETE TO RENEW THEIR MAGIC. WE CAN USE THIS TO TRACK ONE DOWN.
UH, ARTY?
THESE FAIRIES— YOU KNOW THEY'RE NOT REAL, RIGHT?
OH, THEY'RE NOT? HOW ABOUT THIS—LET US PROCEED UNDER THE ASSUMPTION THAT THEY *ARE* REAL, AND THAT I AM NOT A GIBBERING MORON.
NOW, THE FAIRIES HAVE TO FULFILL A SPECIFIC RITUAL TO RENEW THEIR POWERS. ACCORDING TO THE BOOK, THEY MUST PICK A SEED FROM AN ANCIENT OAK TREE BY THE BEND IN A RIVER—AND ON A FULL MOON.
SO ALL WE HAVE TO DO . . .
IS CROSS-REFERENCE THROUGH WEATHER SATELLITES AND FIND AN OAK TREE THAT'S OVER ONE HUNDRED YEARS OLD AND NEXT TO A RIVER BEND.
I'VE ALREADY NARROWED DOWN OUR SEARCH TO ONE HUNDRED AND TWENTY-NINE SITES THAT NEED TO BE SURVEYED.

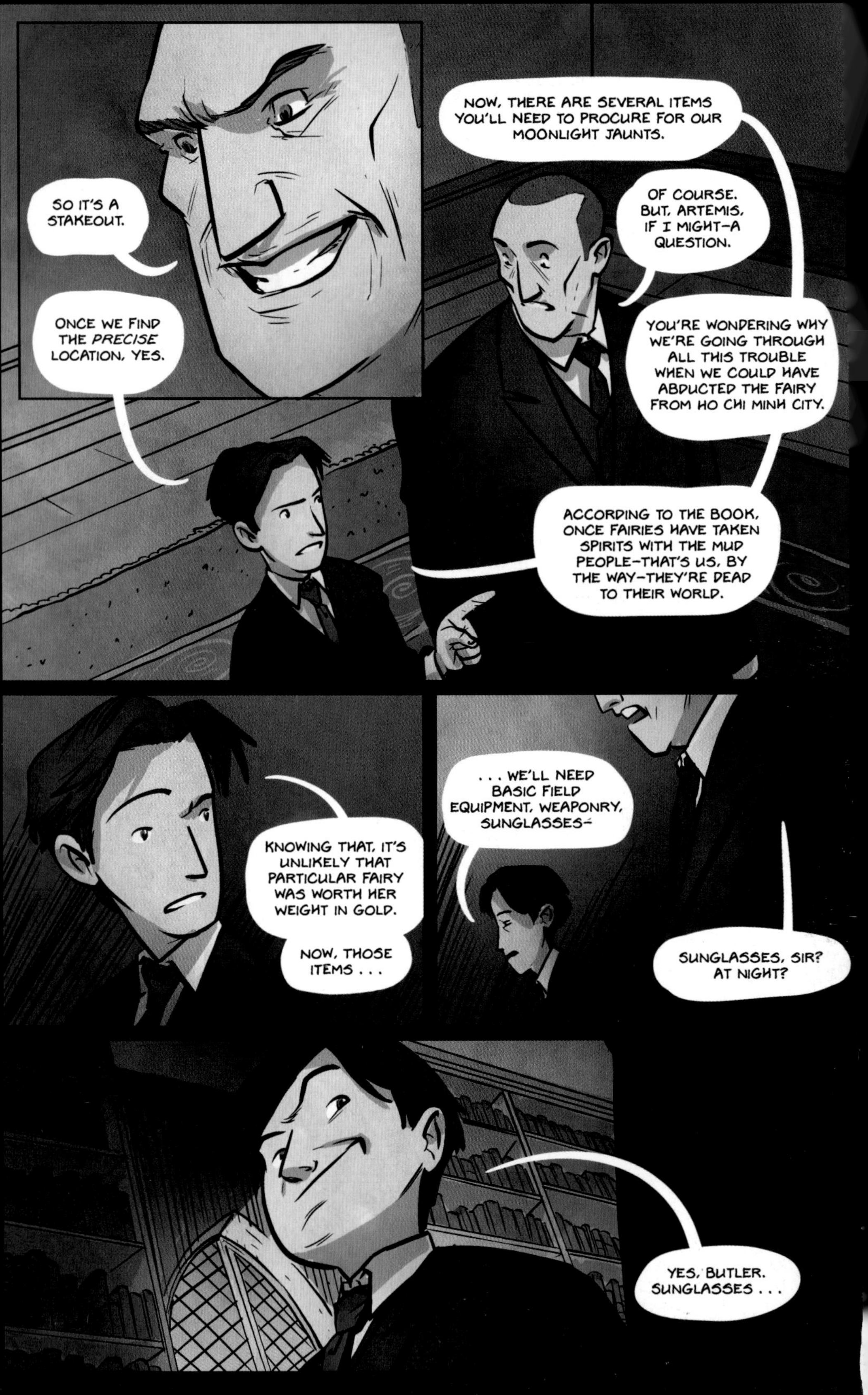
NOW, THERE ARE SEVERAL ITEMS YOU'LL NEED TO PROCURE FOR OUR MOONLIGHT JAUNTS.
SO IT'S A STAKEOUT.
ONCE WE FIND THE *PRECISE* LOCATION, YES.
OF COURSE. BUT, ARTEMIS, IF I MIGHT—A QUESTION.
YOU'RE WONDERING WHY WE'RE GOING THROUGH ALL THIS TROUBLE WHEN WE COULD HAVE ABDUCTED THE FAIRY FROM HO CHI MINH CITY.
ACCORDING TO THE BOOK, ONCE FAIRIES HAVE TAKEN SPIRITS WITH THE MUD PEOPLE—THAT'S US, BY THE WAY—THEY'RE DEAD TO THEIR WORLD.
KNOWING THAT, IT'S UNLIKELY THAT PARTICULAR FAIRY WAS WORTH HER WEIGHT IN GOLD.
NOW, THOSE ITEMS . . .
. . . WE'LL NEED BASIC FIELD EQUIPMENT, WEAPONRY, SUNGLASSES–
SUNGLASSES, SIR? AT NIGHT?
YES, BUTLER. SUNGLASSES . . .

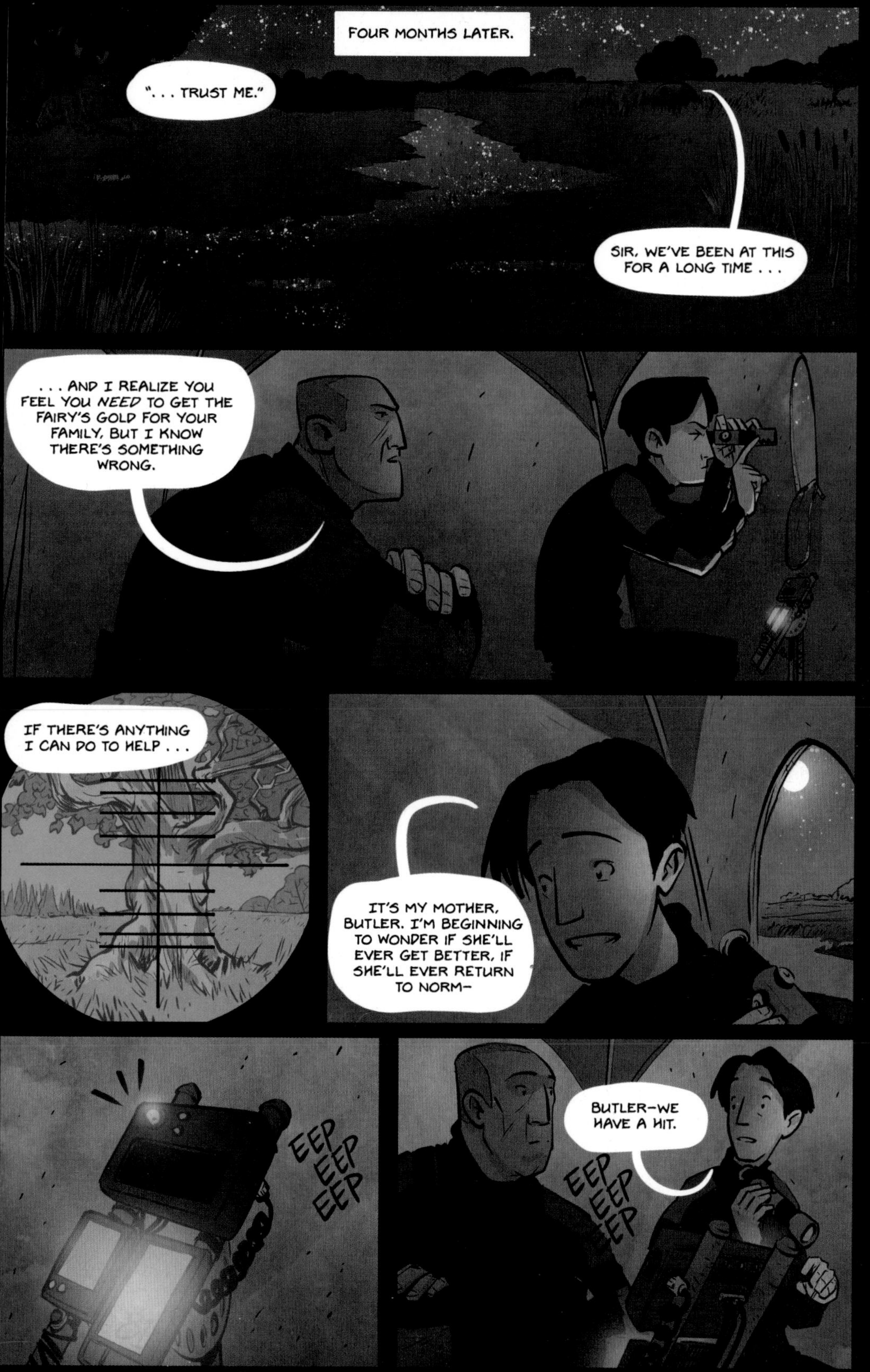
FOUR MONTHS LATER.
". . . TRUST ME."
SIR, WE'VE BEEN AT THIS FOR A LONG TIME . . .
. . . AND I REALIZE YOU FEEL YOU *NEED* TO GET THE FAIRY'S GOLD FOR YOUR FAMILY, BUT I KNOW THERE'S SOMETHING WRONG.
IF THERE'S ANYTHING I CAN DO TO HELP . . .
IT'S MY MOTHER, BUTLER. I'M BEGINNING TO WONDER IF SHE'LL EVER GET BETTER, IF SHE'LL EVER RETURN TO NORM–
EEP EEP EEP
BUTLER–WE HAVE A HIT.
EEP EEP EEP

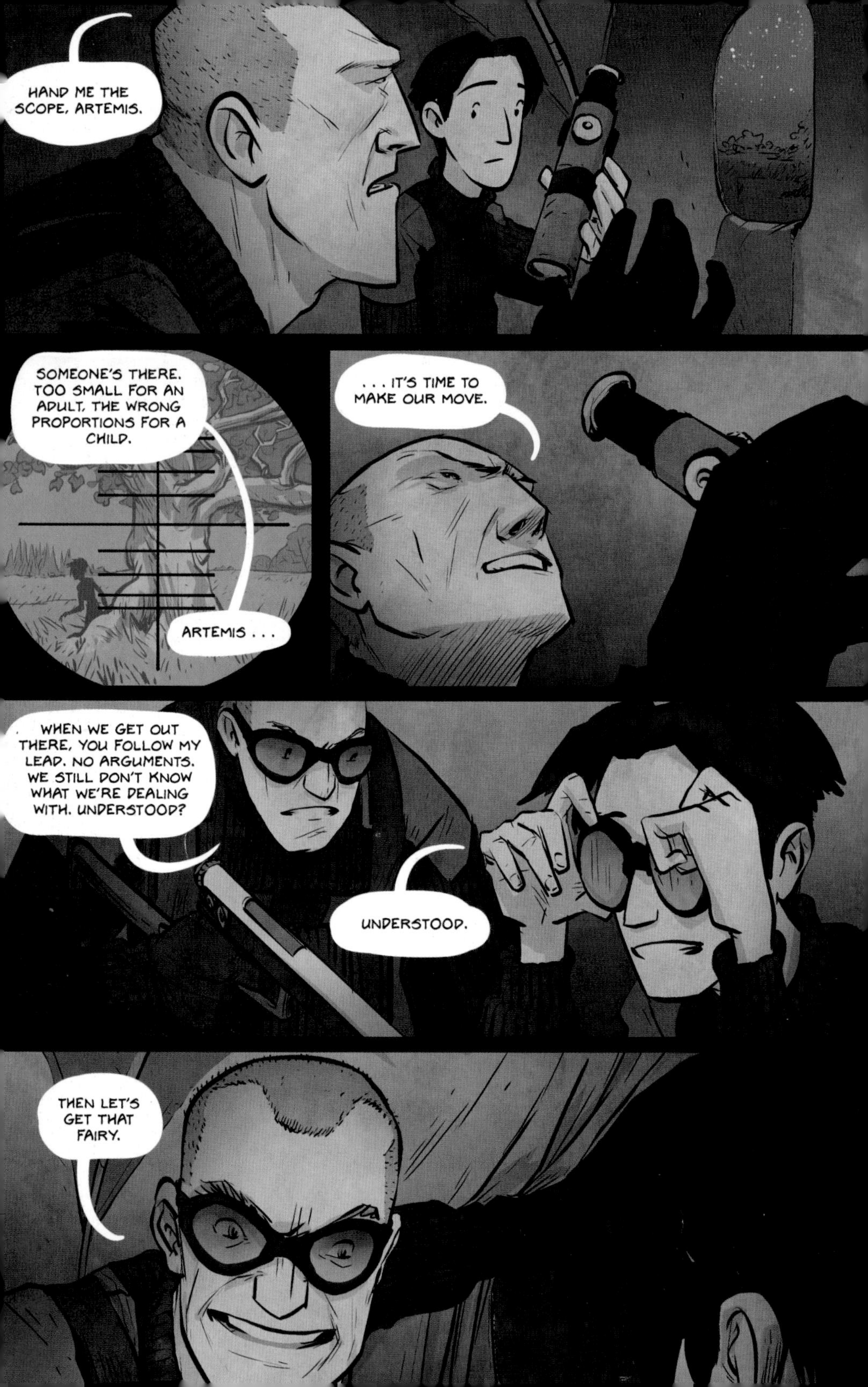
HAND ME THE SCOPE, ARTEMIS.
SOMEONE'S THERE. TOO SMALL FOR AN ADULT, THE WRONG PROPORTIONS FOR A CHILD.
ARTEMIS . . .
. . . IT'S TIME TO MAKE OUR MOVE.
WHEN WE GET OUT THERE, YOU FOLLOW MY LEAD. NO ARGUMENTS. WE STILL DON'T KNOW WHAT WE'RE DEALING WITH. UNDERSTOOD?
UNDERSTOOD.
THEN LET'S GET THAT FAIRY.

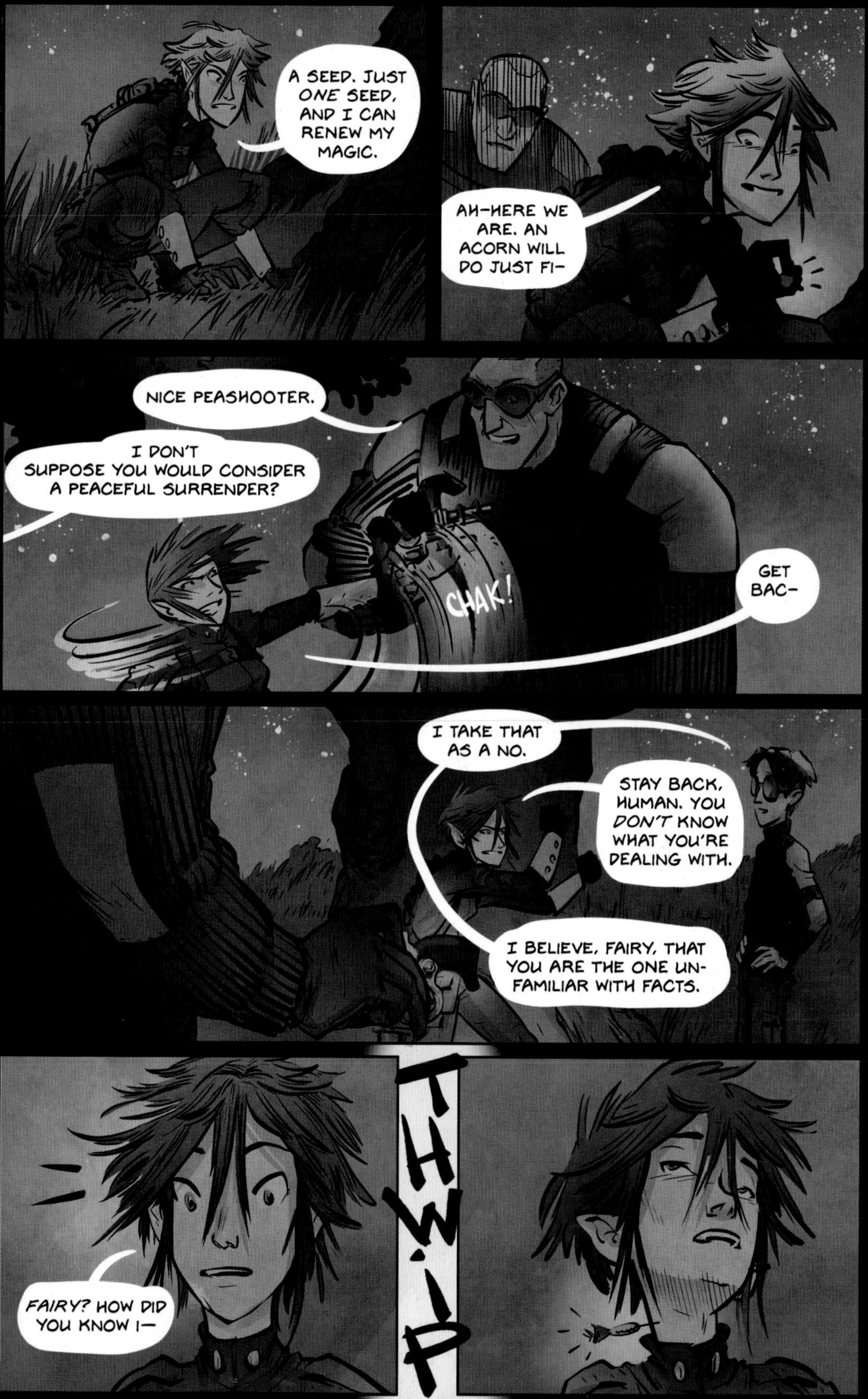
A SEED. JUST *ONE* SEED, AND I CAN RENEW MY MAGIC.
AH—HERE WE ARE. AN ACORN WILL DO JUST FI—
NICE PEASHOOTER.
I DON'T SUPPOSE YOU WOULD CONSIDER A PEACEFUL SURRENDER?
CHAK!
GET BAC—
I TAKE THAT AS A NO.
STAY BACK, HUMAN. YOU *DON'T* KNOW WHAT YOU'RE DEALING WITH.
I BELIEVE, FAIRY, THAT YOU ARE THE ONE UN-FAMILIAR WITH FACTS.
FAIRY? HOW DID YOU KNOW I—
THWIP

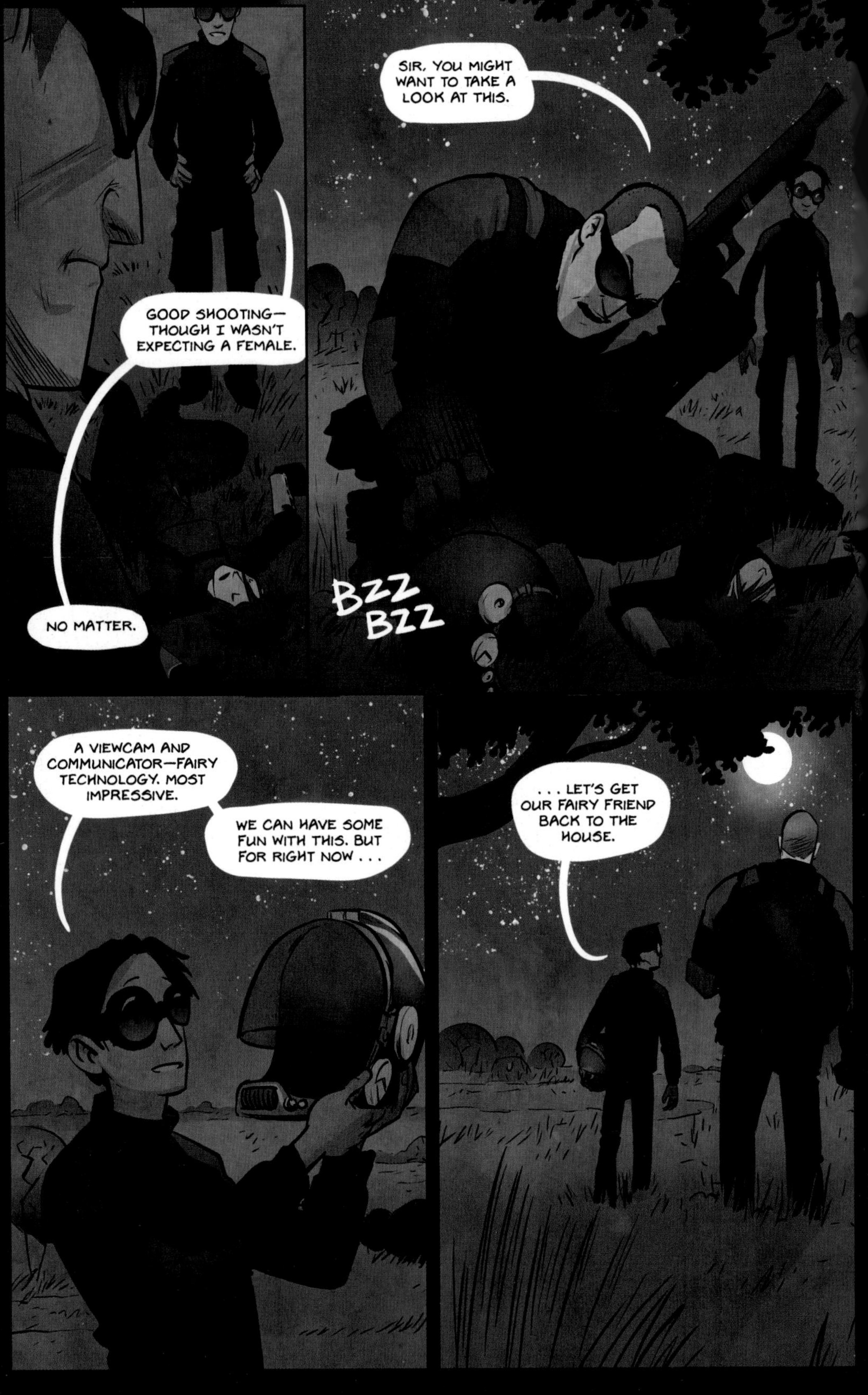
SIR, YOU MIGHT WANT TO TAKE A LOOK AT THIS.
GOOD SHOOTING—THOUGH I WASN'T EXPECTING A FEMALE.
NO MATTER.
BZZ BZZ
A VIEWCAM AND COMMUNICATOR—FAIRY TECHNOLOGY. MOST IMPRESSIVE.
WE CAN HAVE SOME FUN WITH THIS. BUT FOR RIGHT NOW . . .
. . . LET'S GET OUR FAIRY FRIEND BACK TO THE HOUSE.

CHAPTER FIVE

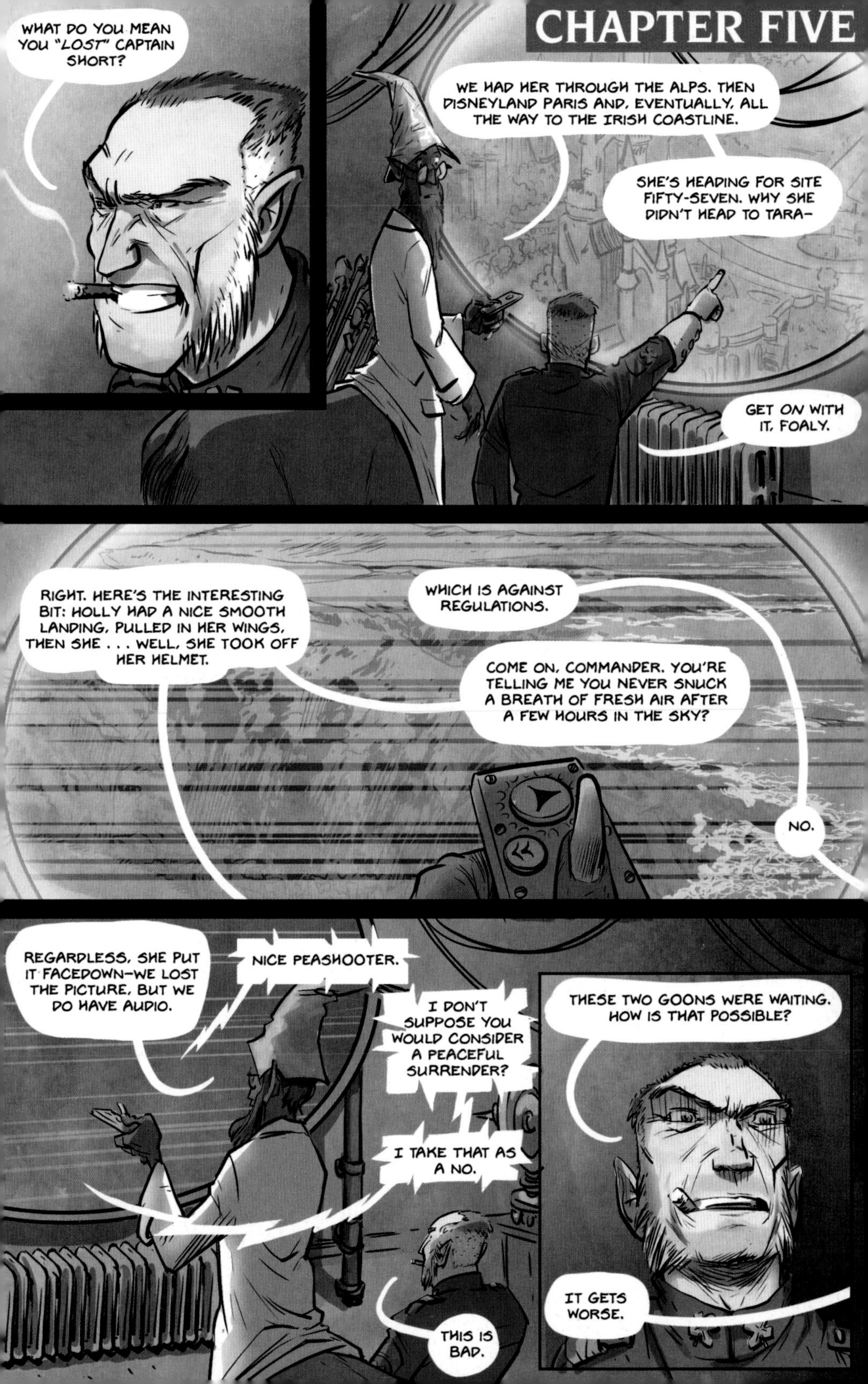
WHAT DO YOU MEAN YOU "LOST" CAPTAIN SHORT?
WE HAD HER THROUGH THE ALPS. THEN DISNEYLAND PARIS AND, EVENTUALLY, ALL THE WAY TO THE IRISH COASTLINE.
SHE'S HEADING FOR SITE FIFTY-SEVEN. WHY SHE DIDN'T HEAD TO TARA–
GET ON WITH IT, FOALY.
RIGHT. HERE'S THE INTERESTING BIT: HOLLY HAD A NICE SMOOTH LANDING, PULLED IN HER WINGS, THEN SHE . . . WELL, SHE TOOK OFF HER HELMET.
WHICH IS AGAINST REGULATIONS.
COME ON, COMMANDER. YOU'RE TELLING ME YOU NEVER SNUCK A BREATH OF FRESH AIR AFTER A FEW HOURS IN THE SKY?
NO.
REGARDLESS, SHE PUT IT FACEDOWN–WE LOST THE PICTURE, BUT WE DO HAVE AUDIO.
NICE PEASHOOTER.
I DON'T SUPPOSE YOU WOULD CONSIDER A PEACEFUL SURRENDER?
I TAKE THAT AS A NO.
THIS IS BAD.
THESE TWO GOONS WERE WAITING. HOW IS THAT POSSIBLE?
IT GETS WORSE.

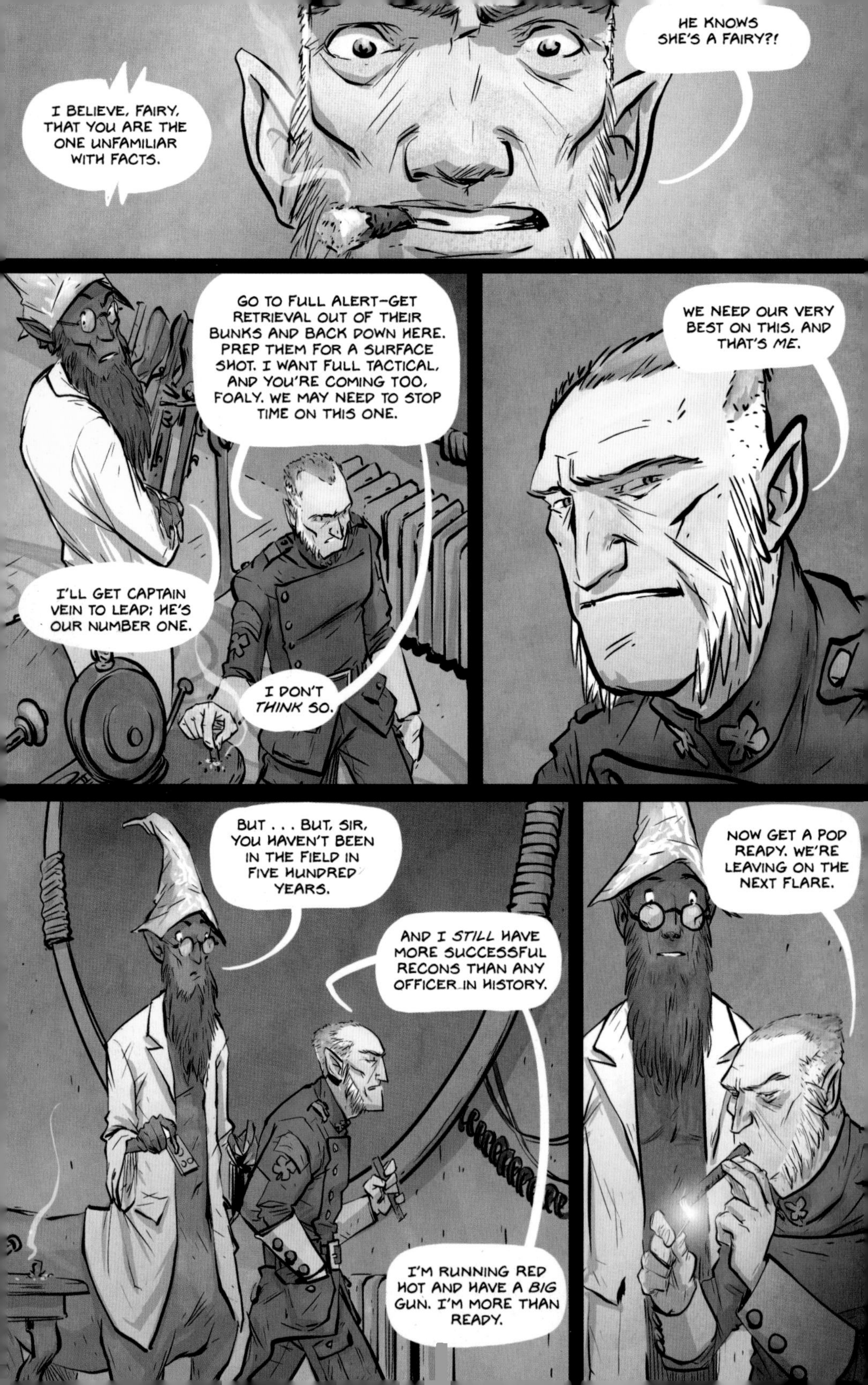
I BELIEVE, FAIRY, THAT YOU ARE THE ONE UNFAMILIAR WITH FACTS.
HE KNOWS SHE'S A FAIRY?!
GO TO FULL ALERT—GET RETRIEVAL OUT OF THEIR BUNKS AND BACK DOWN HERE. PREP THEM FOR A SURFACE SHOT. I WANT FULL TACTICAL, AND YOU'RE COMING TOO, FOALY. WE MAY NEED TO STOP TIME ON THIS ONE.
I'LL GET CAPTAIN VEIN TO LEAD; HE'S OUR NUMBER ONE.
I DON'T *THINK* SO.
WE NEED OUR VERY BEST ON THIS, AND THAT'S *ME*.
BUT . . . BUT, SIR, YOU HAVEN'T BEEN IN THE FIELD IN FIVE HUNDRED YEARS.
AND I *STILL* HAVE MORE SUCCESSFUL RECONS THAN ANY OFFICER IN HISTORY.
I'M RUNNING RED HOT AND HAVE A *BIG* GUN. I'M MORE THAN READY.
NOW GET A POD READY. WE'RE LEAVING ON THE NEXT FLARE.

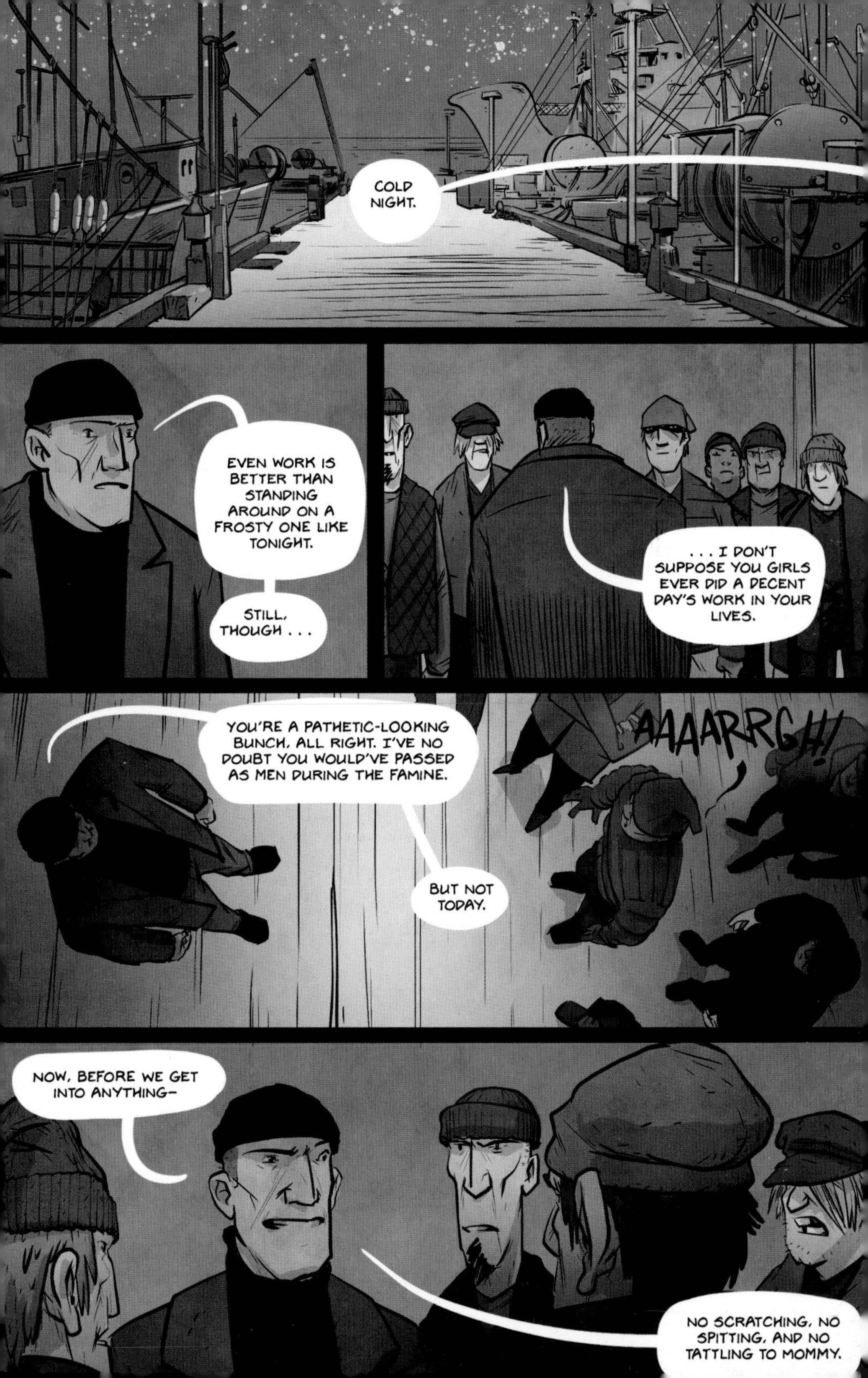
COLD NIGHT.
EVEN WORK IS BETTER THAN STANDING AROUND ON A FROSTY ONE LIKE TONIGHT.
STILL, THOUGH . . .
. . . I DON'T SUPPOSE YOU GIRLS EVER DID A DECENT DAY'S WORK IN YOUR LIVES.
YOU'RE A PATHETIC-LOOKING BUNCH, ALL RIGHT. I'VE NO DOUBT YOU WOULD'VE PASSED AS MEN DURING THE FAMINE.
BUT NOT TODAY.
AAAARRGH!
NOW, BEFORE WE GET INTO ANYTHING—
NO SCRATCHING, NO SPITTING, AND NO TATTLING TO MOMMY.

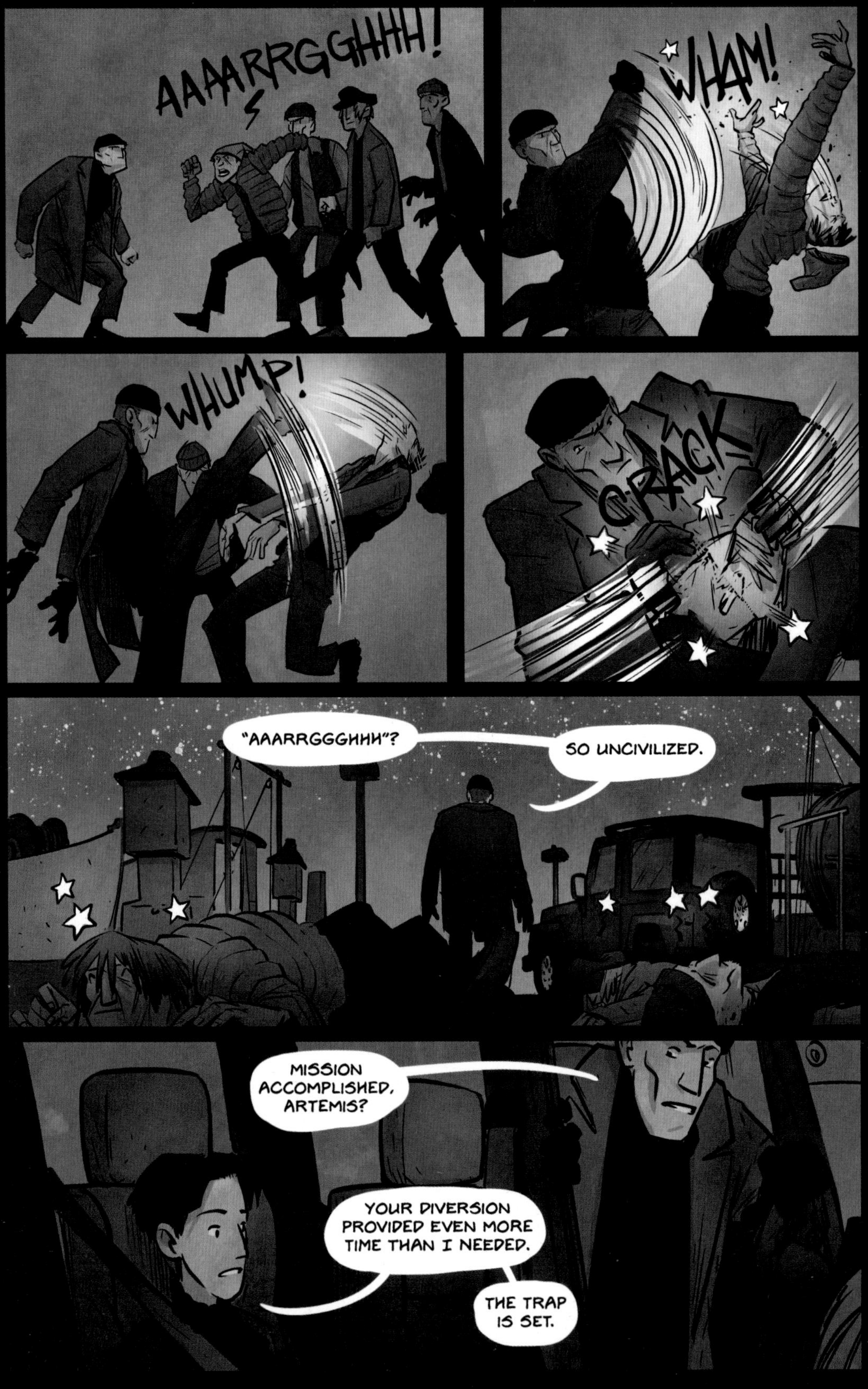
AAAARRGGHHH!
WHAM!
WHUMP!
CRACK
"AAARRGGGHHH"?
SO UNCIVILIZED.
MISSION ACCOMPLISHED, ARTEMIS?
YOUR DIVERSION PROVIDED EVEN MORE TIME THAN I NEEDED.
THE TRAP IS SET.

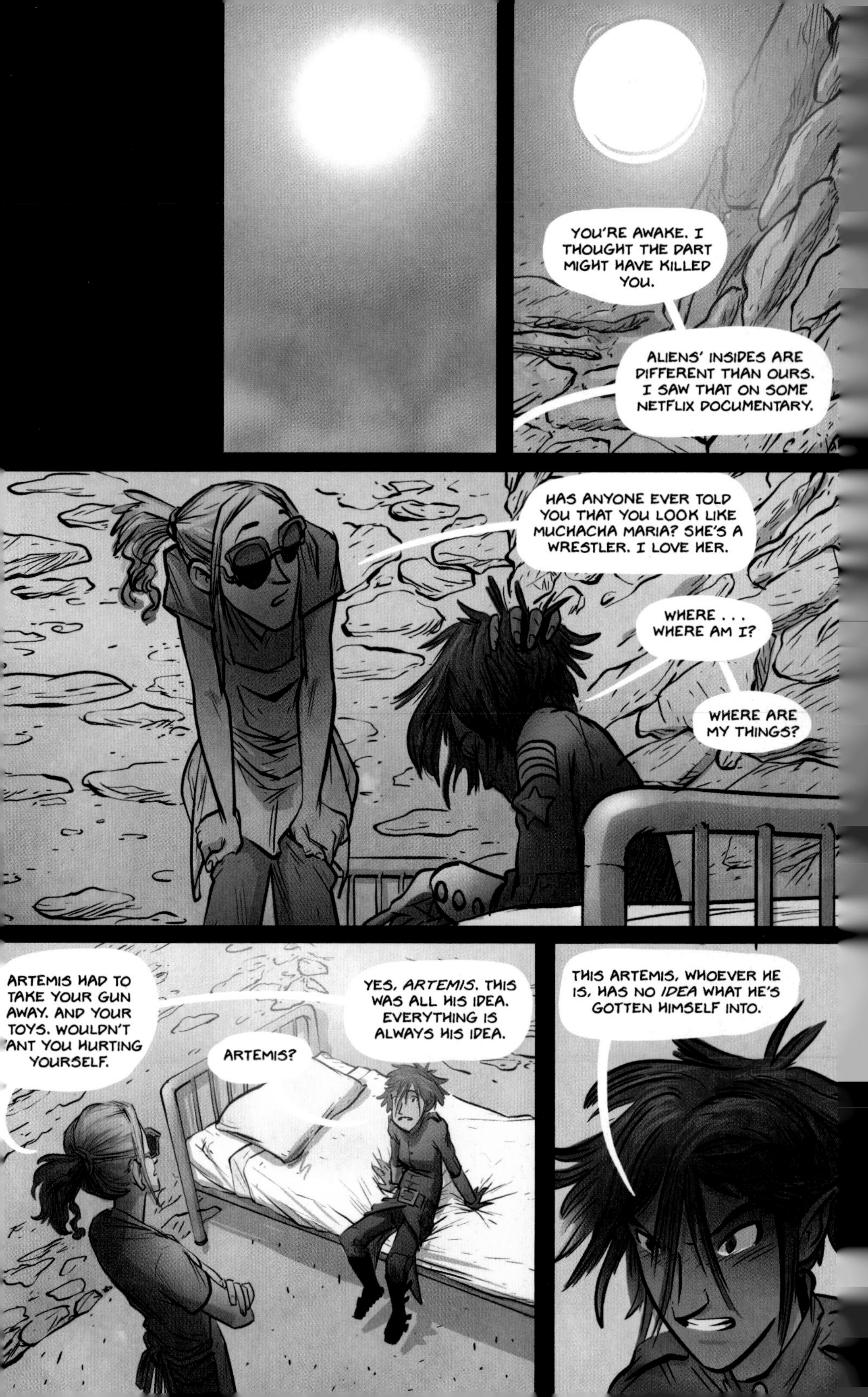

YOU'RE AWAKE. I THOUGHT THE DART MIGHT HAVE KILLED YOU.
ALIENS' INSIDES ARE DIFFERENT THAN OURS. I SAW THAT ON SOME NETFLIX DOCUMENTARY.
HAS ANYONE EVER TOLD YOU THAT YOU LOOK LIKE MUCHACHA MARIA? SHE'S A WRESTLER. I LOVE HER.
WHERE . . . WHERE AM I?
WHERE ARE MY THINGS?
ARTEMIS HAD TO TAKE YOUR GUN AWAY. AND YOUR TOYS. WOULDN'T WANT YOU HURTING YOURSELF.
ARTEMIS?
YES, *ARTEMIS*. THIS WAS ALL HIS IDEA. EVERYTHING IS ALWAYS HIS IDEA.
THIS ARTEMIS, WHOEVER HE IS, HAS NO *IDEA* WHAT HE'S GOTTEN HIMSELF INTO.

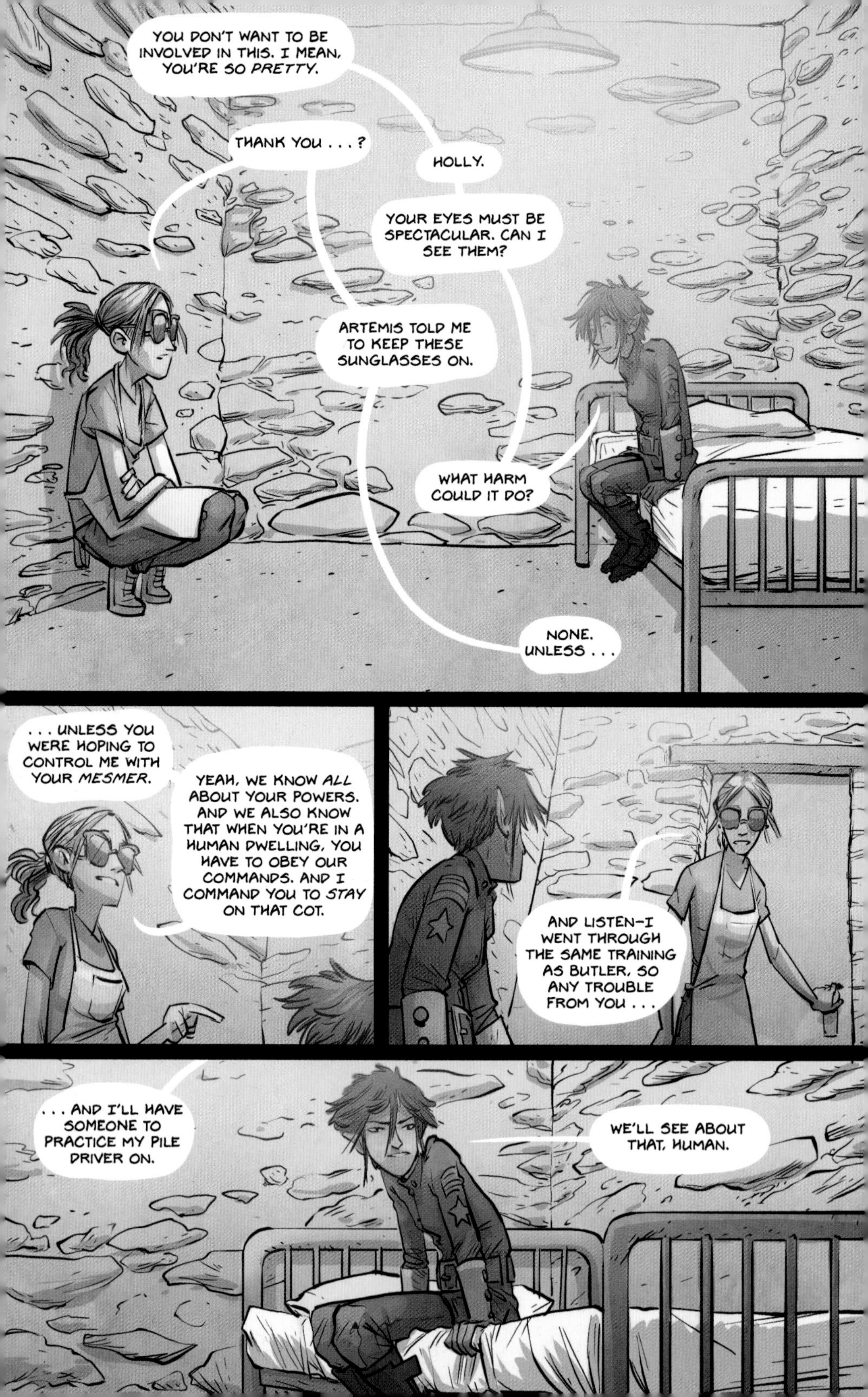
YOU DON'T WANT TO BE INVOLVED IN THIS. I MEAN, YOU'RE SO *PRETTY*.
THANK YOU . . . ?
HOLLY.
YOUR EYES MUST BE SPECTACULAR. CAN I SEE THEM?
ARTEMIS TOLD ME TO KEEP THESE SUNGLASSES ON.
WHAT HARM COULD IT DO?
NONE. UNLESS . . .
. . . UNLESS YOU WERE HOPING TO CONTROL ME WITH YOUR *MESMER*.
YEAH, WE KNOW *ALL* ABOUT YOUR POWERS. AND WE ALSO KNOW THAT WHEN YOU'RE IN A HUMAN DWELLING, YOU HAVE TO OBEY OUR COMMANDS. AND I COMMAND YOU TO *STAY* ON THAT COT.
AND LISTEN—I WENT THROUGH THE SAME TRAINING AS BUTLER, SO ANY TROUBLE FROM YOU . . .
. . . AND I'LL HAVE SOMEONE TO PRACTICE MY PILE DRIVER ON.
WE'LL SEE ABOUT THAT, HUMAN.

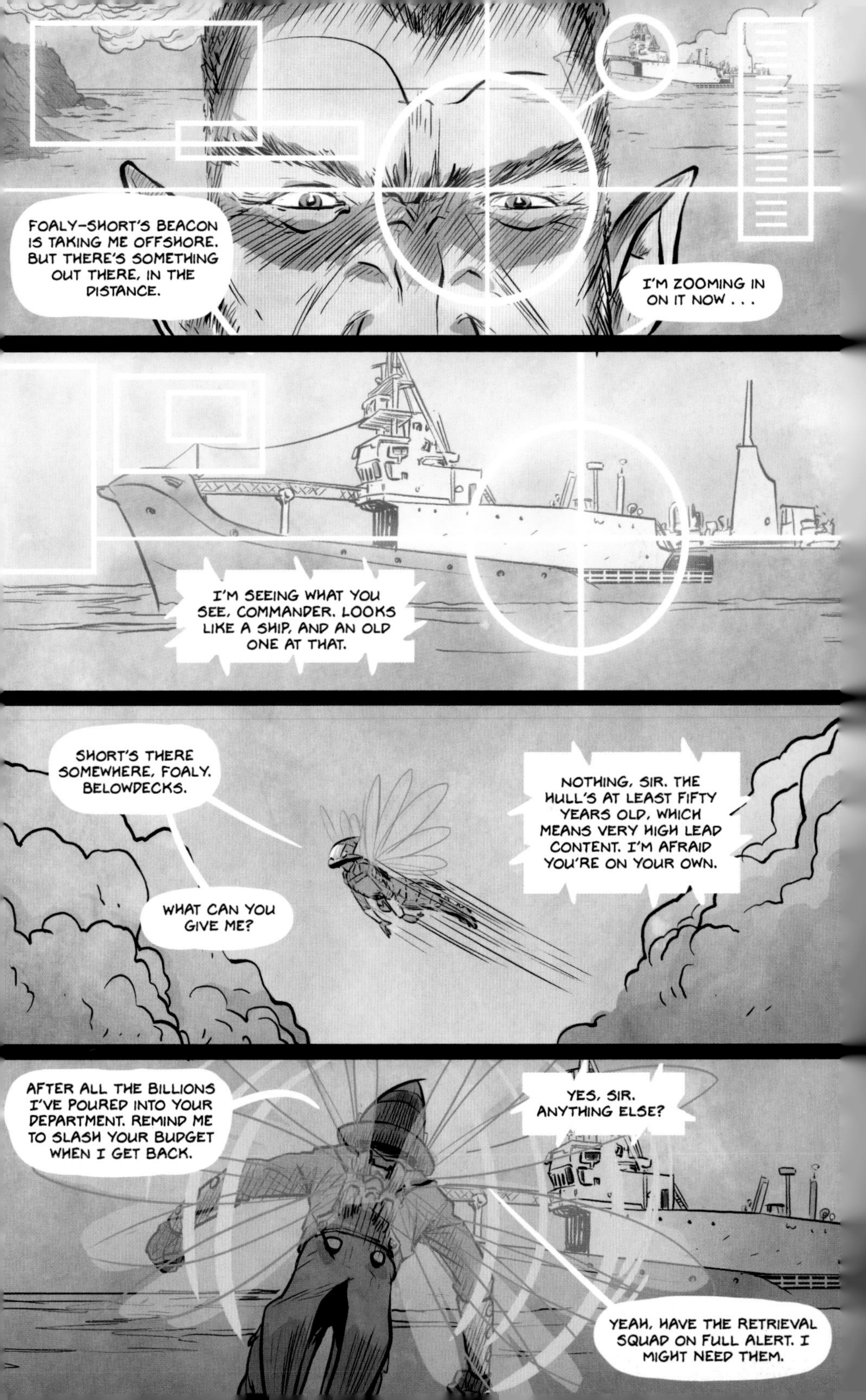
FOALY—SHORT'S BEACON IS TAKING ME OFFSHORE. BUT THERE'S SOMETHING OUT THERE, IN THE DISTANCE.
I'M ZOOMING IN ON IT NOW . . .
I'M SEEING WHAT YOU SEE, COMMANDER. LOOKS LIKE A SHIP, AND AN OLD ONE AT THAT.
SHORT'S THERE SOMEWHERE, FOALY. BELOWDECKS.
WHAT CAN YOU GIVE ME?
NOTHING, SIR. THE HULL'S AT LEAST FIFTY YEARS OLD, WHICH MEANS VERY HIGH LEAD CONTENT. I'M AFRAID YOU'RE ON YOUR OWN.
AFTER ALL THE BILLIONS I'VE POURED INTO YOUR DEPARTMENT. REMIND ME TO SLASH YOUR BUDGET WHEN I GET BACK.
YES, SIR. ANYTHING ELSE?
YEAH, HAVE THE RETRIEVAL SQUAD ON FULL ALERT. I MIGHT NEED THEM.

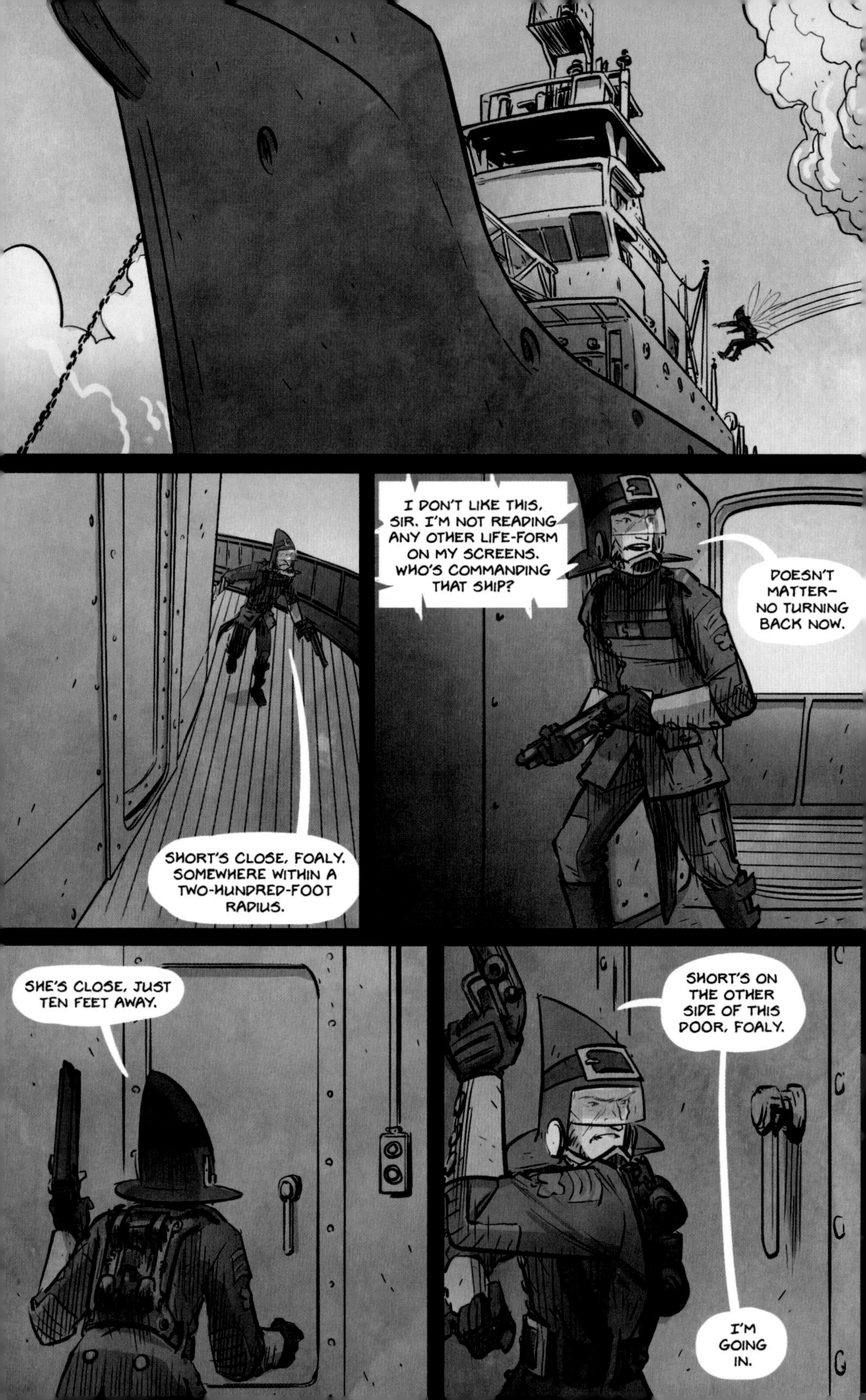
I DON'T LIKE THIS, SIR. I'M NOT READING ANY OTHER LIFE-FORM ON MY SCREENS. WHO'S COMMANDING THAT SHIP?
DOESN'T MATTER— NO TURNING BACK NOW.
SHORT'S CLOSE, FOALY. SOMEWHERE WITHIN A TWO-HUNDRED-FOOT RADIUS.
SHE'S CLOSE, JUST TEN FEET AWAY.
SHORT'S ON THE OTHER SIDE OF THIS DOOR, FOALY.
I'M GOING IN.

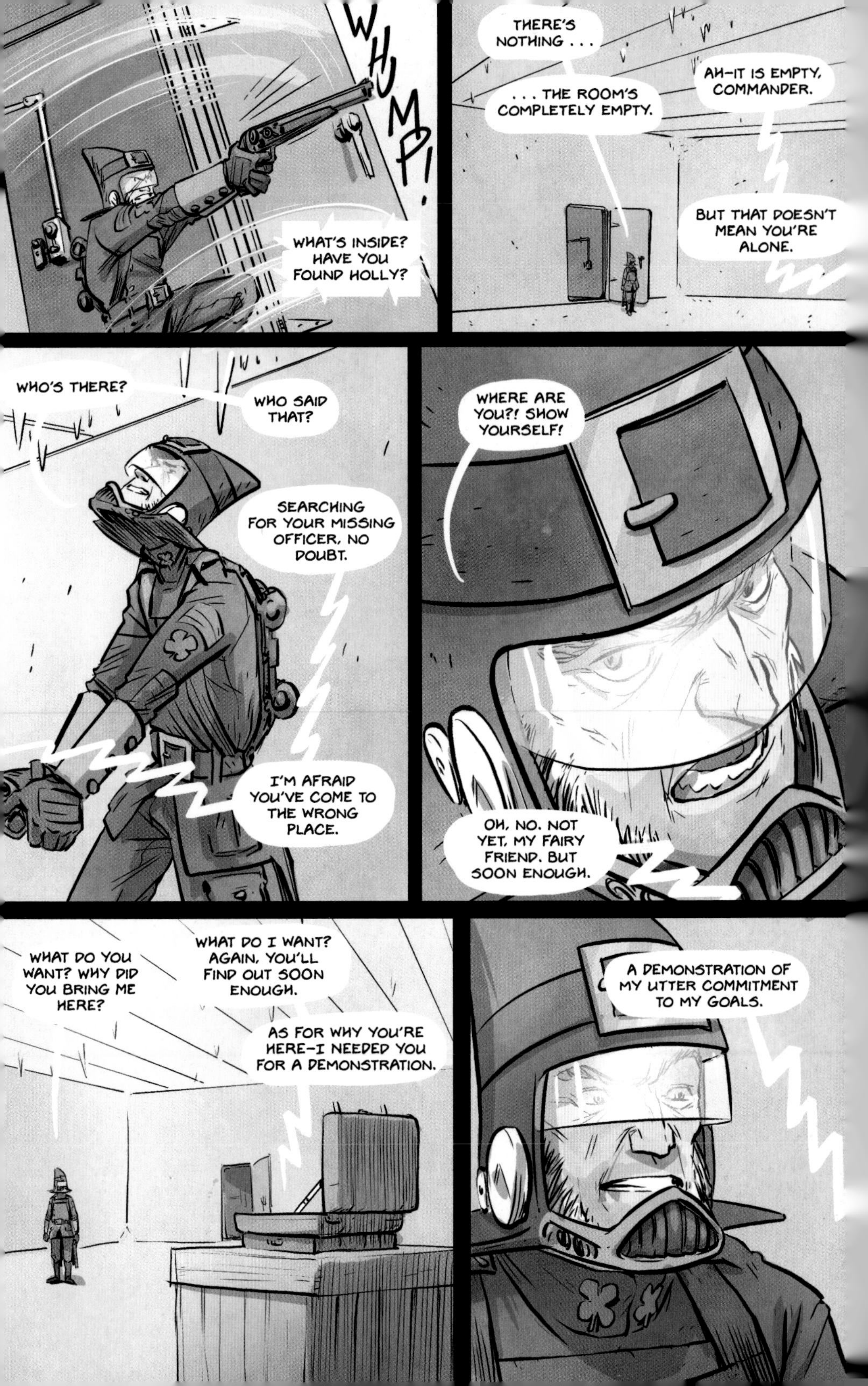
WHUMP!
WHAT'S INSIDE? HAVE YOU FOUND HOLLY?
THERE'S NOTHING . . .
. . . THE ROOM'S COMPLETELY EMPTY.
AH—IT IS EMPTY, COMMANDER.
BUT THAT DOESN'T MEAN YOU'RE ALONE.
WHO'S THERE?
WHO SAID THAT?
SEARCHING FOR YOUR MISSING OFFICER, NO DOUBT.
I'M AFRAID YOU'VE COME TO THE WRONG PLACE.
WHERE ARE YOU?! SHOW YOURSELF!
OH, NO. NOT YET, MY FAIRY FRIEND. BUT SOON ENOUGH.
WHAT DO YOU WANT? WHY DID YOU BRING ME HERE?
WHAT DO I WANT? AGAIN, YOU'LL FIND OUT SOON ENOUGH.
AS FOR WHY YOU'RE HERE—I NEEDED YOU FOR A DEMONSTRATION.
A DEMONSTRATION OF MY UTTER COMMITMENT TO MY GOALS.

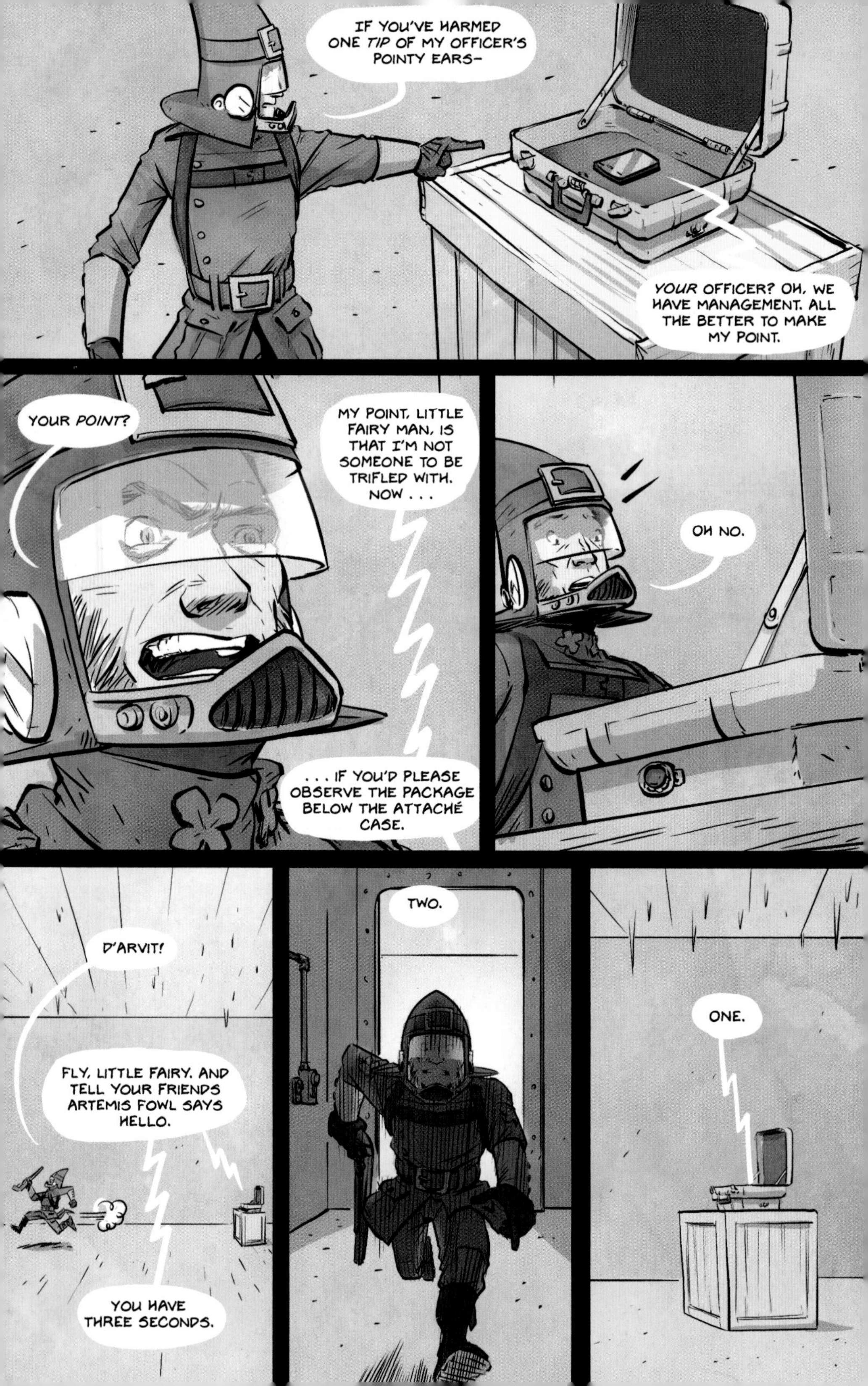
IF YOU'VE HARMED ONE *TIP* OF MY OFFICER'S POINTY EARS–
YOUR OFFICER? OH, WE HAVE MANAGEMENT. ALL THE BETTER TO MAKE MY POINT.
YOUR *POINT*?
MY POINT, LITTLE FAIRY MAN, IS THAT I'M NOT SOMEONE TO BE TRIFLED WITH. NOW . . .
. . . IF YOU'D PLEASE OBSERVE THE PACKAGE BELOW THE ATTACHÉ CASE.
OH NO.
D'ARVIT!
FLY, LITTLE FAIRY. AND TELL YOUR FRIENDS ARTEMIS FOWL SAYS HELLO.
YOU HAVE THREE SECONDS.
TWO.
ONE.

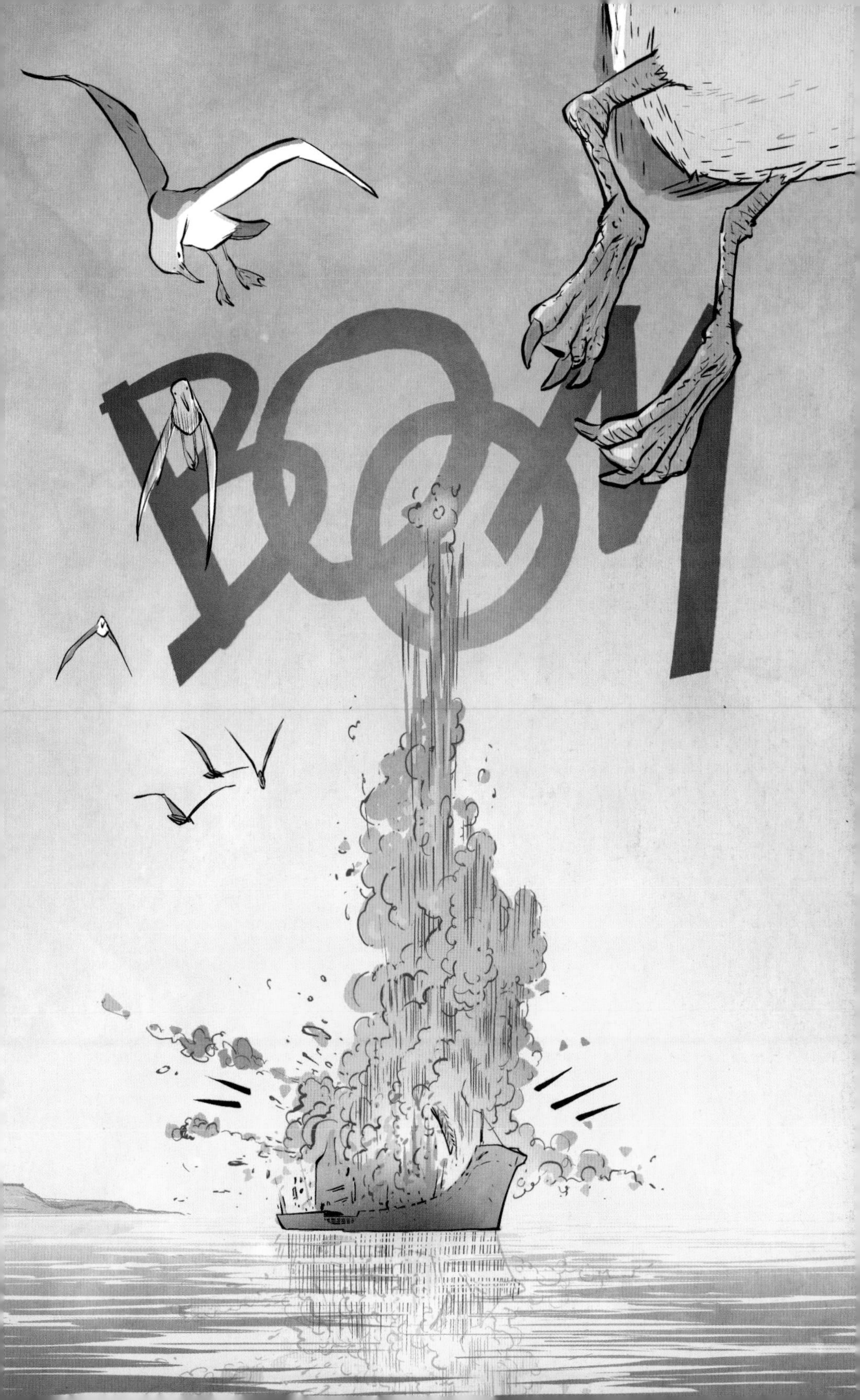
BOOM

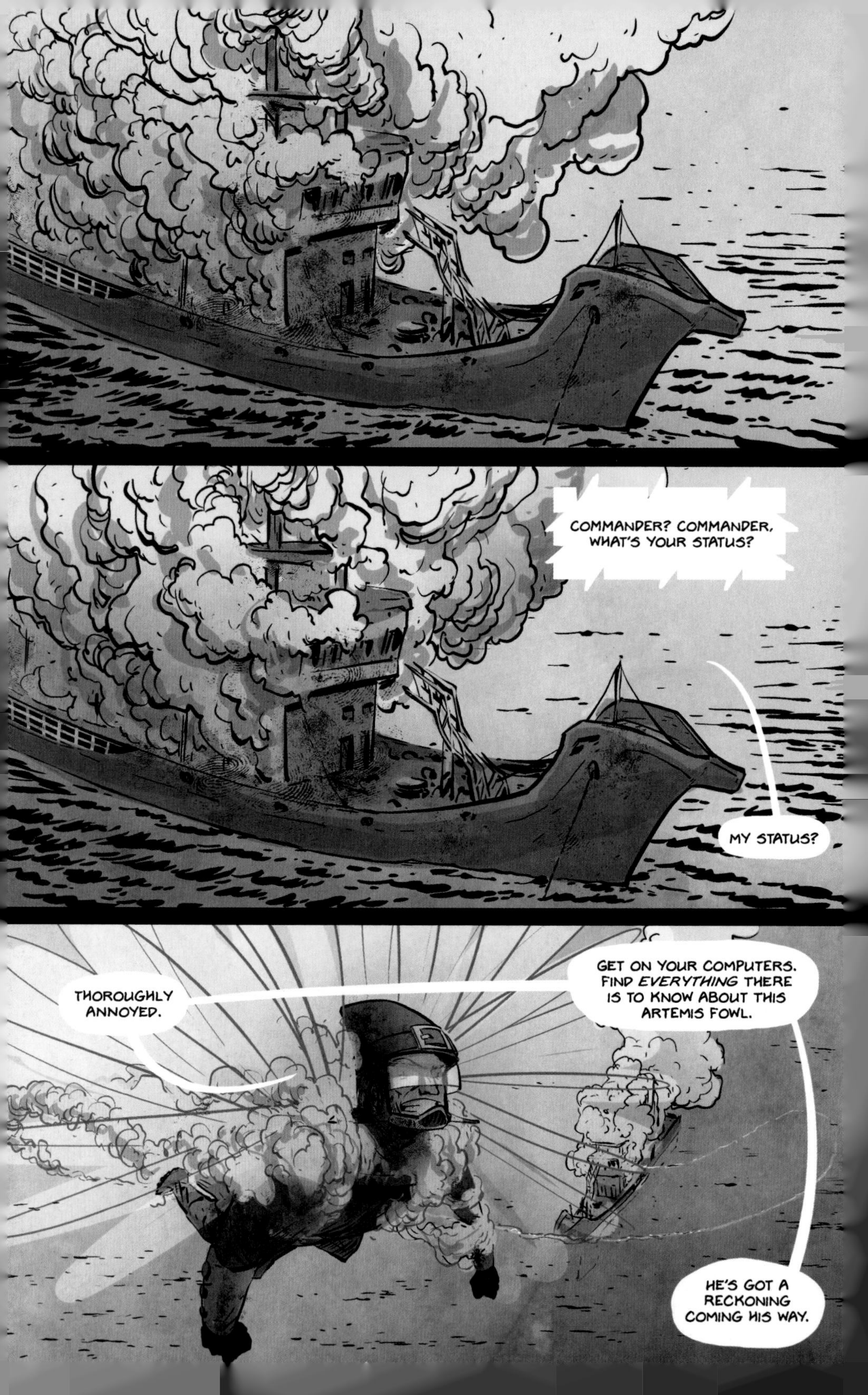
COMMANDER? COMMANDER, WHAT'S YOUR STATUS?
MY STATUS?
THOROUGHLY ANNOYED.
GET ON YOUR COMPUTERS. FIND *EVERYTHING* THERE IS TO KNOW ABOUT THIS ARTEMIS FOWL.
HE'S GOT A RECKONING COMING HIS WAY.

CHAPTER SIX

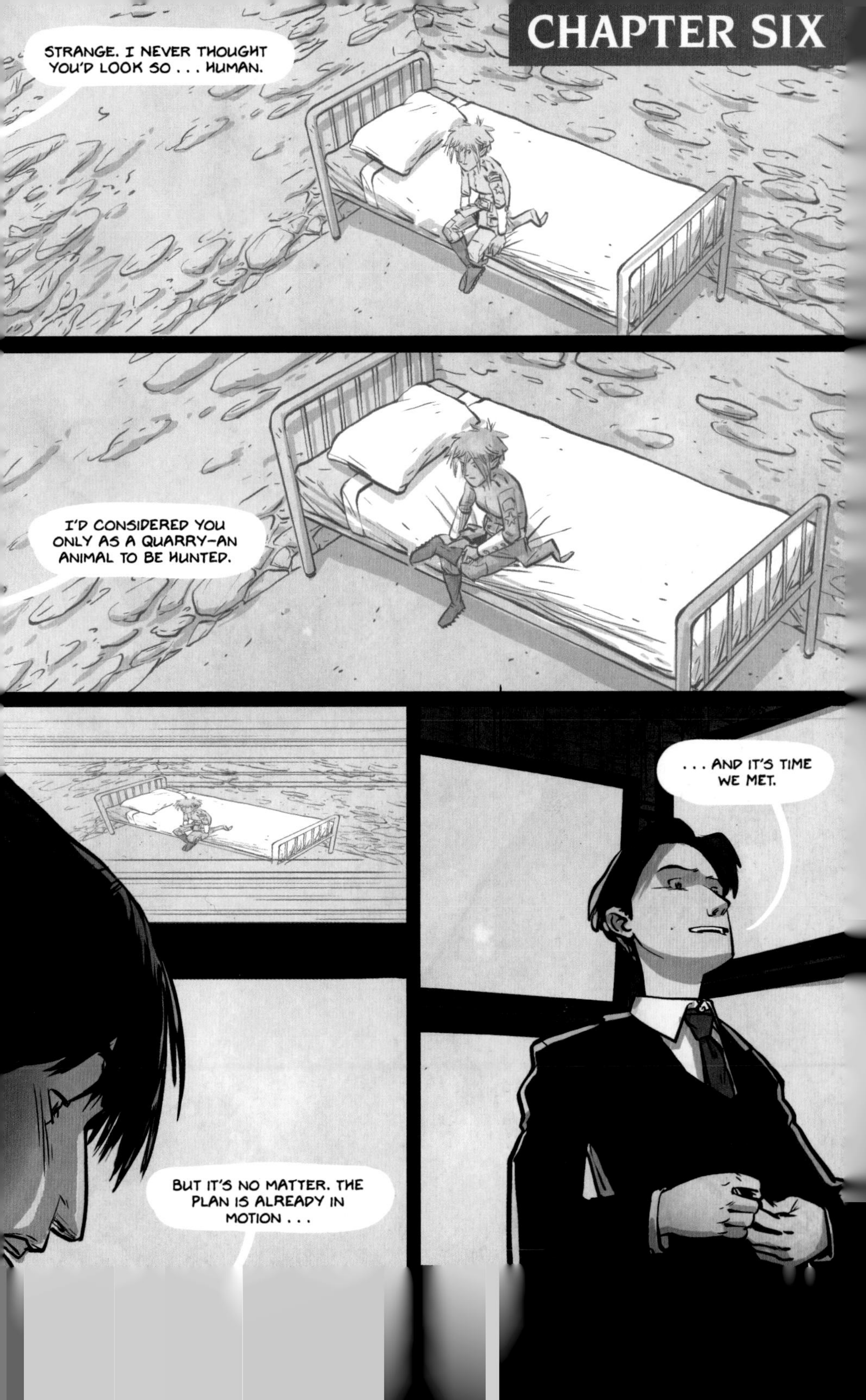

STRANGE. I NEVER THOUGHT YOU'D LOOK SO . . . HUMAN.
I'D CONSIDERED YOU ONLY AS A QUARRY—AN ANIMAL TO BE HUNTED.
BUT IT'S NO MATTER. THE PLAN IS ALREADY IN MOTION . . .
. . . AND IT'S TIME WE MET.

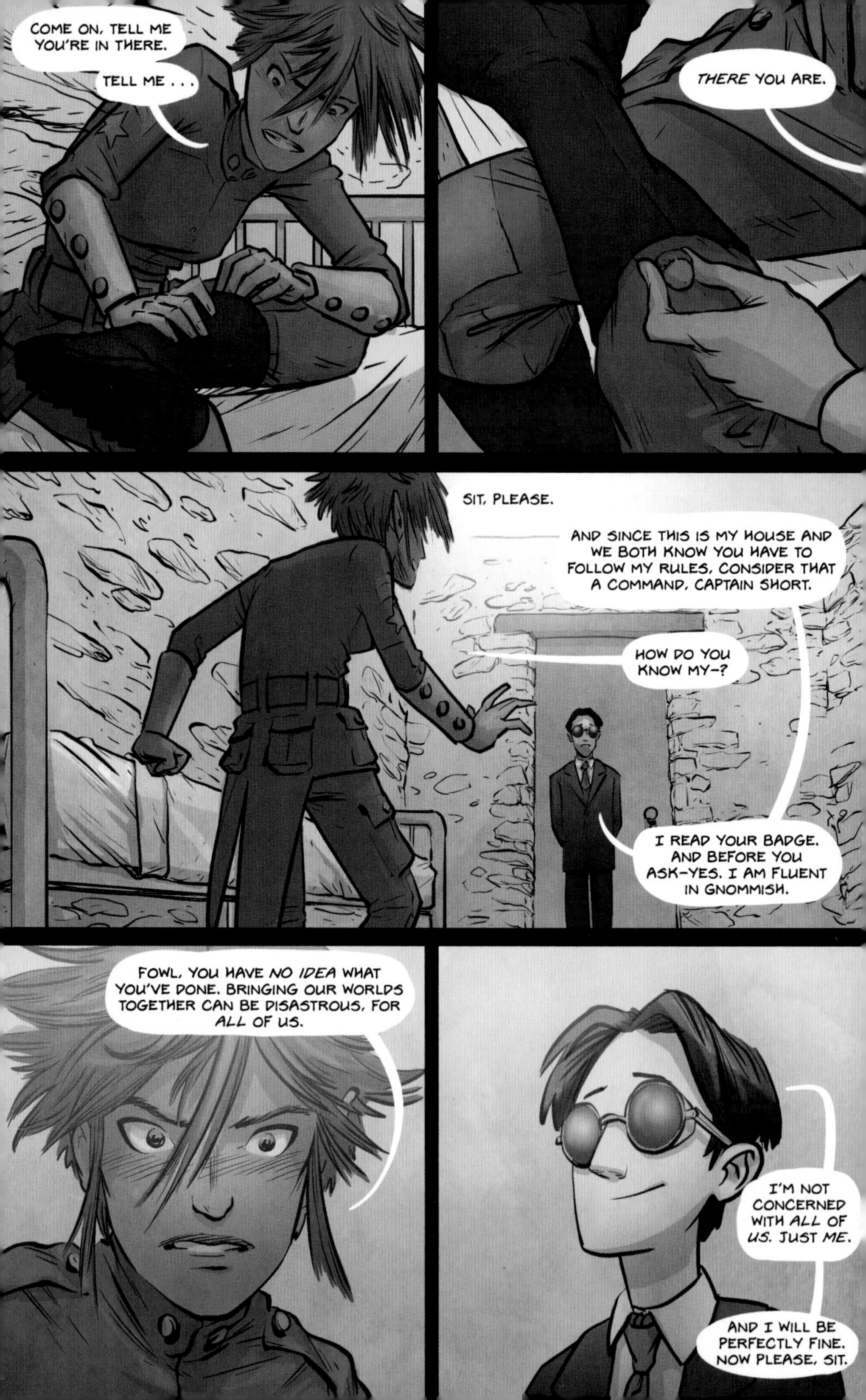
COME ON, TELL ME YOU'RE IN THERE.
TELL ME . . .
THERE YOU ARE.
SIT, PLEASE.
AND SINCE THIS IS MY HOUSE AND WE BOTH KNOW YOU HAVE TO FOLLOW MY RULES, CONSIDER THAT A COMMAND, CAPTAIN SHORT.
HOW DO YOU KNOW MY–?
I READ YOUR BADGE. AND BEFORE YOU ASK–YES. I AM FLUENT IN GNOMMISH.
FOWL, YOU HAVE *NO IDEA* WHAT YOU'VE DONE. BRINGING OUR WORLDS TOGETHER CAN BE DISASTROUS, FOR *ALL* OF US.
I'M NOT CONCERNED WITH *ALL OF US*. JUST *ME*.
AND I WILL BE PERFECTLY FINE. NOW PLEASE, SIT.

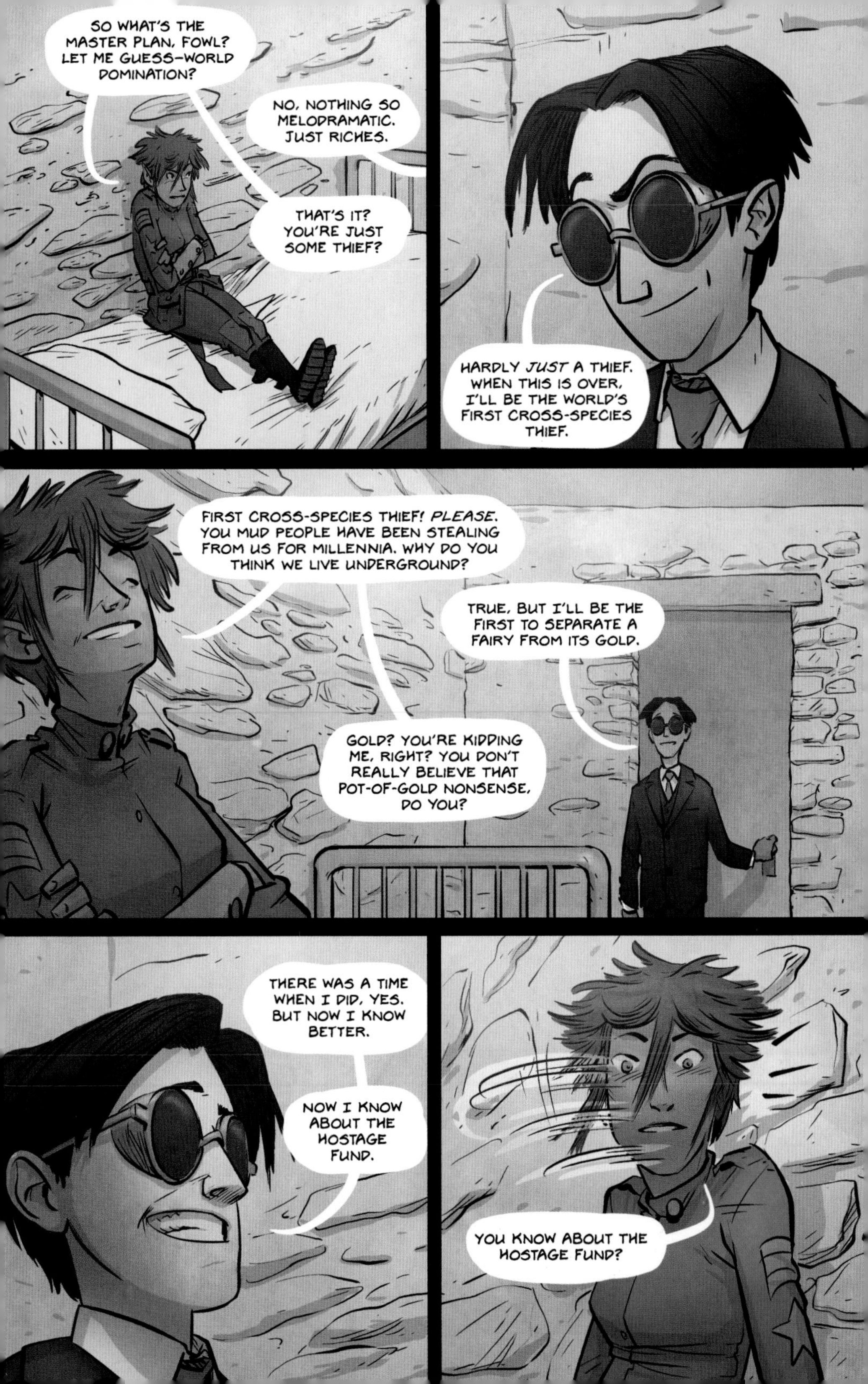
SO WHAT'S THE MASTER PLAN, FOWL? LET ME GUESS–WORLD DOMINATION?
NO, NOTHING SO MELODRAMATIC. JUST RICHES.
THAT'S IT? YOU'RE JUST SOME THIEF?
HARDLY *JUST* A THIEF. WHEN THIS IS OVER, I'LL BE THE WORLD'S FIRST CROSS-SPECIES THIEF.
FIRST CROSS-SPECIES THIEF! *PLEASE.* YOU MUD PEOPLE HAVE BEEN STEALING FROM US FOR MILLENNIA. WHY DO YOU THINK WE LIVE UNDERGROUND?
TRUE, BUT I'LL BE THE FIRST TO SEPARATE A FAIRY FROM ITS GOLD.
GOLD? YOU'RE KIDDING ME, RIGHT? YOU DON'T REALLY BELIEVE THAT POT-OF-GOLD NONSENSE, DO YOU?
THERE WAS A TIME WHEN I DID, YES. BUT NOW I KNOW BETTER.
NOW I KNOW ABOUT THE HOSTAGE FUND.
YOU KNOW ABOUT THE HOSTAGE FUND?

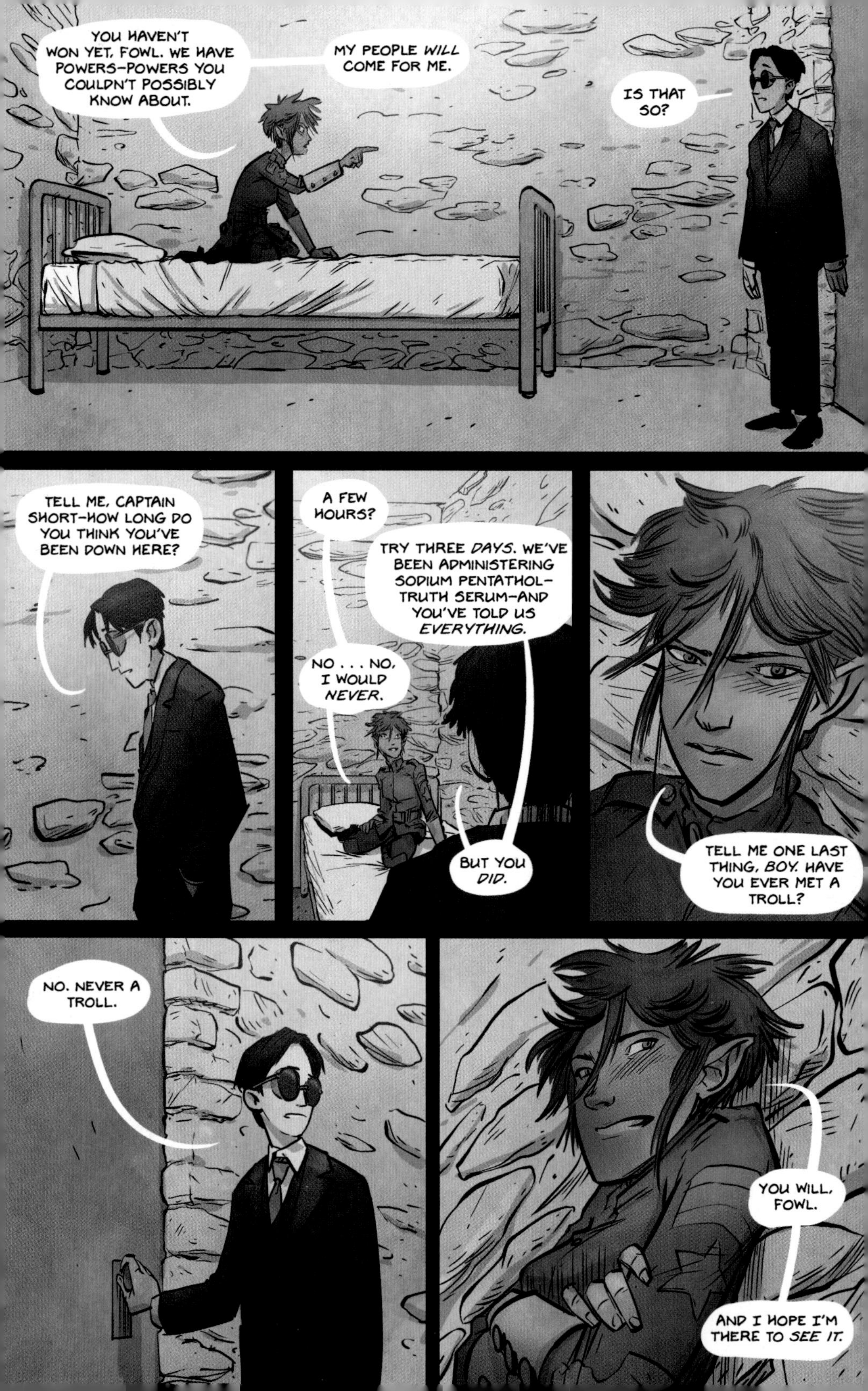
YOU HAVEN'T WON YET, FOWL. WE HAVE POWERS—POWERS YOU COULDN'T POSSIBLY KNOW ABOUT.
MY PEOPLE *WILL* COME FOR ME.
IS THAT SO?
TELL ME, CAPTAIN SHORT—HOW LONG DO YOU THINK YOU'VE BEEN DOWN HERE?
A FEW HOURS?
TRY THREE *DAYS*. WE'VE BEEN ADMINISTERING SODIUM PENTATHOL—TRUTH SERUM—AND YOU'VE TOLD US *EVERYTHING*.
NO . . . NO, I WOULD *NEVER*.
BUT YOU *DID*.
TELL ME ONE LAST THING, *BOY*. HAVE YOU EVER MET A TROLL?
NO. NEVER A TROLL.
YOU WILL, FOWL.
AND I HOPE I'M THERE TO *SEE IT*.

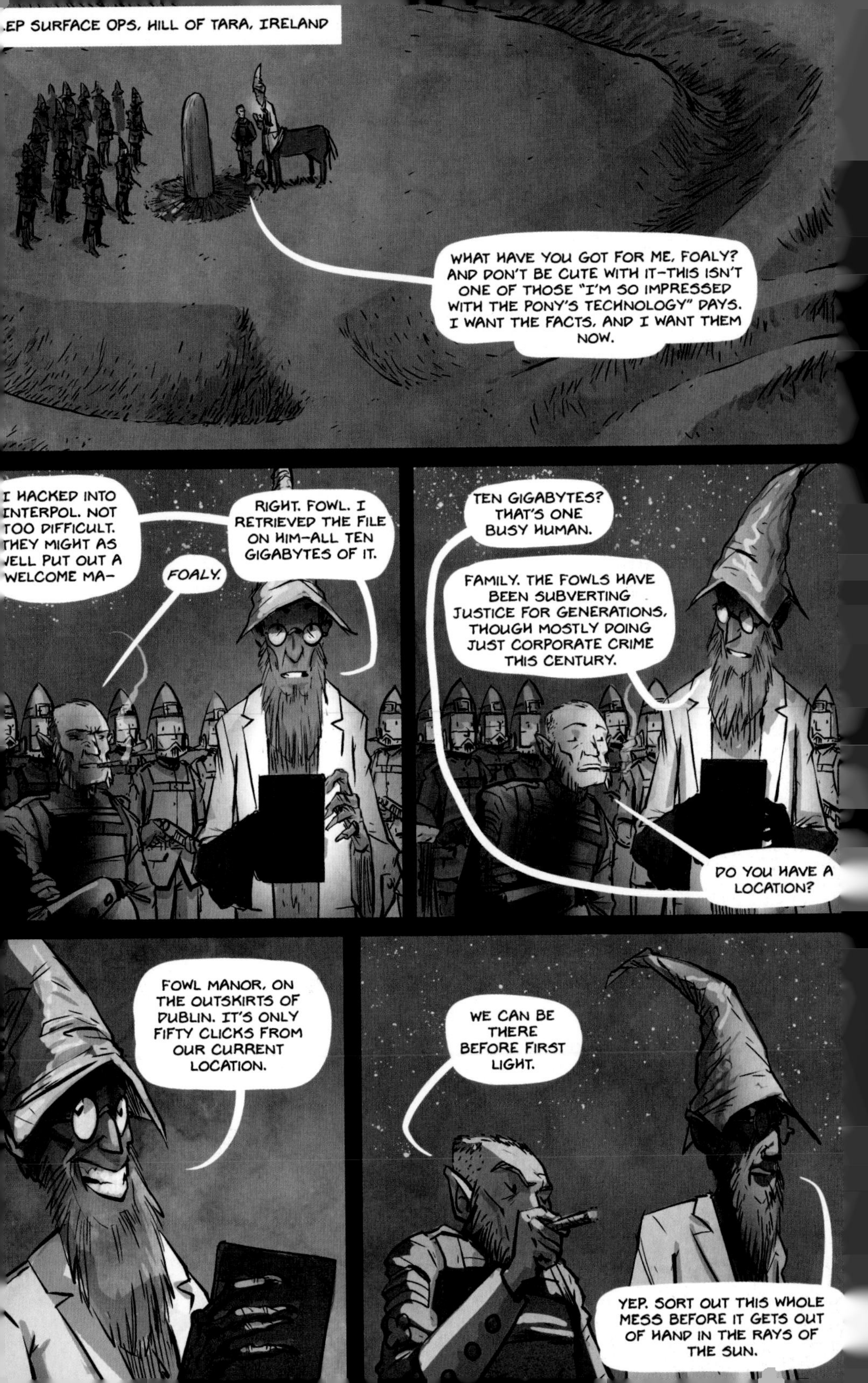

.EP SURFACE OPS, HILL OF TARA, IRELAND
WHAT HAVE YOU GOT FOR ME, FOALY? AND DON'T BE CUTE WITH IT—THIS ISN'T ONE OF THOSE "I'M SO IMPRESSED WITH THE PONY'S TECHNOLOGY" DAYS. I WANT THE FACTS, AND I WANT THEM NOW.
I HACKED INTO INTERPOL. NOT TOO DIFFICULT. THEY MIGHT AS VELL PUT OUT A WELCOME MA—
FOALY.
RIGHT. FOWL. I RETRIEVED THE FILE ON HIM—ALL TEN GIGABYTES OF IT.
TEN GIGABYTES? THAT'S ONE BUSY HUMAN.
FAMILY. THE FOWLS HAVE BEEN SUBVERTING JUSTICE FOR GENERATIONS, THOUGH MOSTLY DOING JUST CORPORATE CRIME THIS CENTURY.
DO YOU HAVE A LOCATION?
FOWL MANOR, ON THE OUTSKIRTS OF DUBLIN. IT'S ONLY FIFTY CLICKS FROM OUR CURRENT LOCATION.
WE CAN BE THERE BEFORE FIRST LIGHT.
YEP. SORT OUT THIS WHOLE MESS BEFORE IT GETS OUT OF HAND IN THE RAYS OF THE SUN.

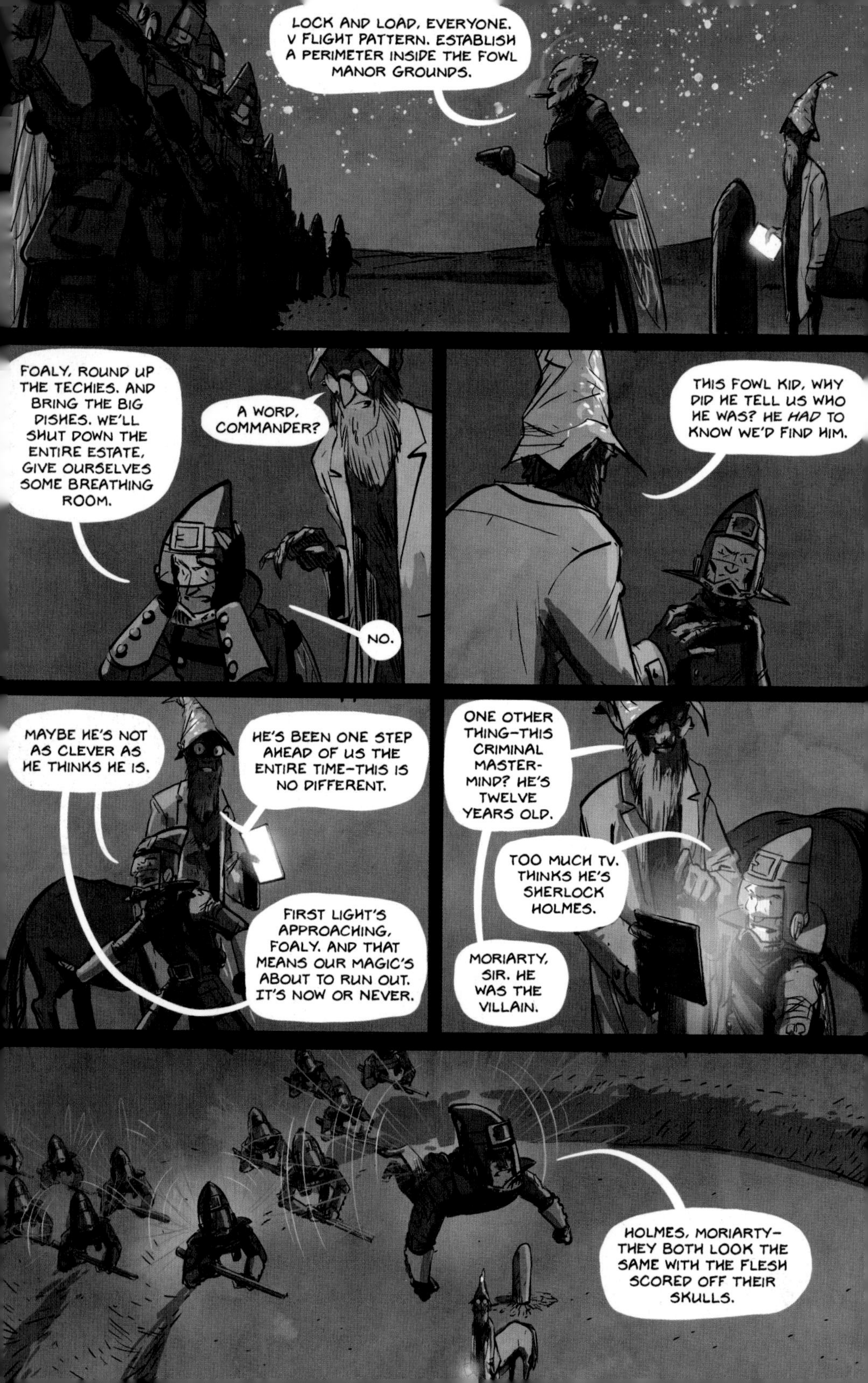
LOCK AND LOAD, EVERYONE. V FLIGHT PATTERN. ESTABLISH A PERIMETER INSIDE THE FOWL MANOR GROUNDS.
FOALY, ROUND UP THE TECHIES. AND BRING THE BIG DISHES. WE'LL SHUT DOWN THE ENTIRE ESTATE, GIVE OURSELVES SOME BREATHING ROOM.
A WORD, COMMANDER?
NO.
THIS FOWL KID, WHY DID HE TELL US WHO HE WAS? HE *HAD* TO KNOW WE'D FIND HIM.
MAYBE HE'S NOT AS CLEVER AS HE THINKS HE IS.
HE'S BEEN ONE STEP AHEAD OF US THE ENTIRE TIME—THIS IS NO DIFFERENT.
FIRST LIGHT'S APPROACHING, FOALY. AND THAT MEANS OUR MAGIC'S ABOUT TO RUN OUT. IT'S NOW OR NEVER.
ONE OTHER THING—THIS CRIMINAL MASTER-MIND? HE'S TWELVE YEARS OLD.
TOO MUCH TV. THINKS HE'S SHERLOCK HOLMES.
MORIARTY, SIR. HE WAS THE VILLAIN.
HOLMES, MORIARTY—THEY BOTH LOOK THE SAME WITH THE FLESH SCORED OFF THEIR SKULLS.

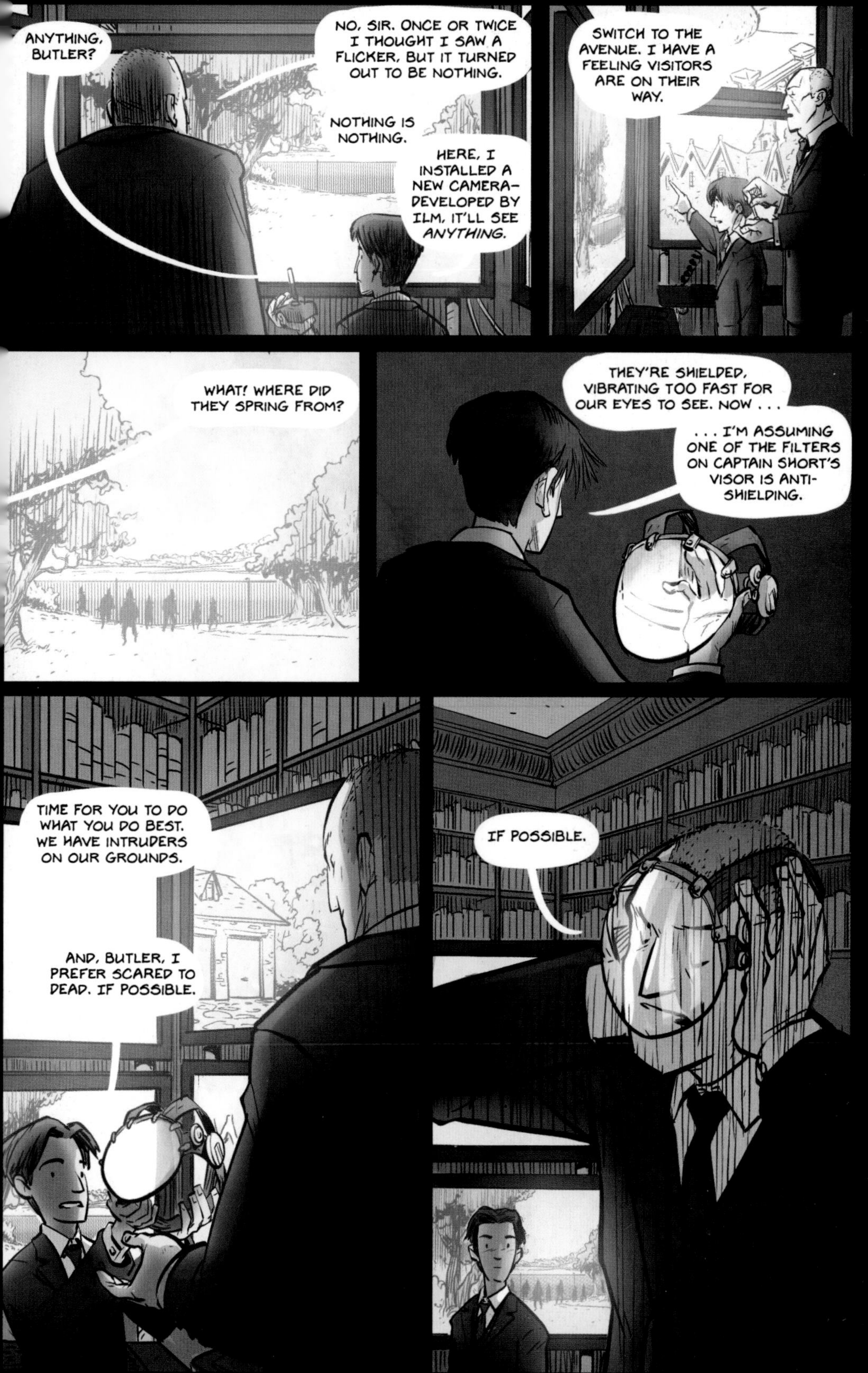
ANYTHING, BUTLER?
NO, SIR. ONCE OR TWICE I THOUGHT I SAW A FLICKER, BUT IT TURNED OUT TO BE NOTHING.
NOTHING IS NOTHING.
HERE, I INSTALLED A NEW CAMERA— DEVELOPED BY ILM, IT'LL SEE *ANYTHING*.
SWITCH TO THE AVENUE. I HAVE A FEELING VISITORS ARE ON THEIR WAY.
WHAT! WHERE DID THEY SPRING FROM?
THEY'RE SHIELDED, VIBRATING TOO FAST FOR OUR EYES TO SEE. NOW . . .
. . . I'M ASSUMING ONE OF THE FILTERS ON CAPTAIN SHORT'S VISOR IS ANTI-SHIELDING.
TIME FOR YOU TO DO WHAT YOU DO BEST. WE HAVE INTRUDERS ON OUR GROUNDS.
AND, BUTLER, I PREFER SCARED TO DEAD. IF POSSIBLE.
IF POSSIBLE.

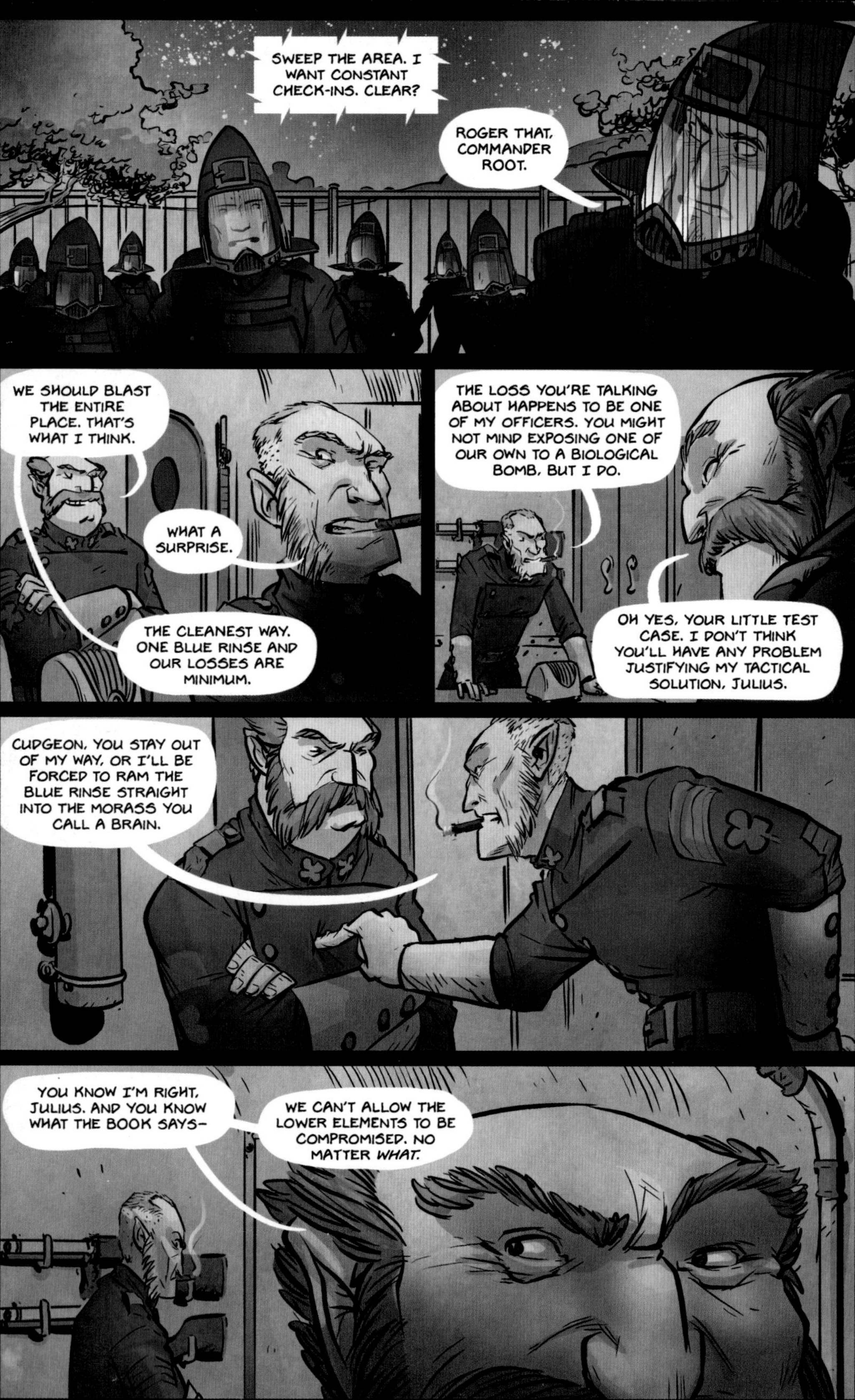
SWEEP THE AREA. I WANT CONSTANT CHECK-INS. CLEAR?
ROGER THAT, COMMANDER ROOT.
WE SHOULD BLAST THE ENTIRE PLACE. THAT'S WHAT I THINK.
WHAT A SURPRISE.
THE CLEANEST WAY. ONE BLUE RINSE AND OUR LOSSES ARE MINIMUM.
THE LOSS YOU'RE TALKING ABOUT HAPPENS TO BE ONE OF MY OFFICERS. YOU MIGHT NOT MIND EXPOSING ONE OF OUR OWN TO A BIOLOGICAL BOMB, BUT I DO.
OH YES, YOUR LITTLE TEST CASE. I DON'T THINK YOU'LL HAVE ANY PROBLEM JUSTIFYING MY TACTICAL SOLUTION, JULIUS.
CUDGEON, YOU STAY OUT OF MY WAY, OR I'LL BE FORCED TO RAM THE BLUE RINSE STRAIGHT INTO THE MORASS YOU CALL A BRAIN.
YOU KNOW I'M RIGHT, JULIUS. AND YOU KNOW WHAT THE BOOK SAYS–
WE CAN'T ALLOW THE LOWER ELEMENTS TO BE COMPROMISED. NO MATTER *WHAT.*

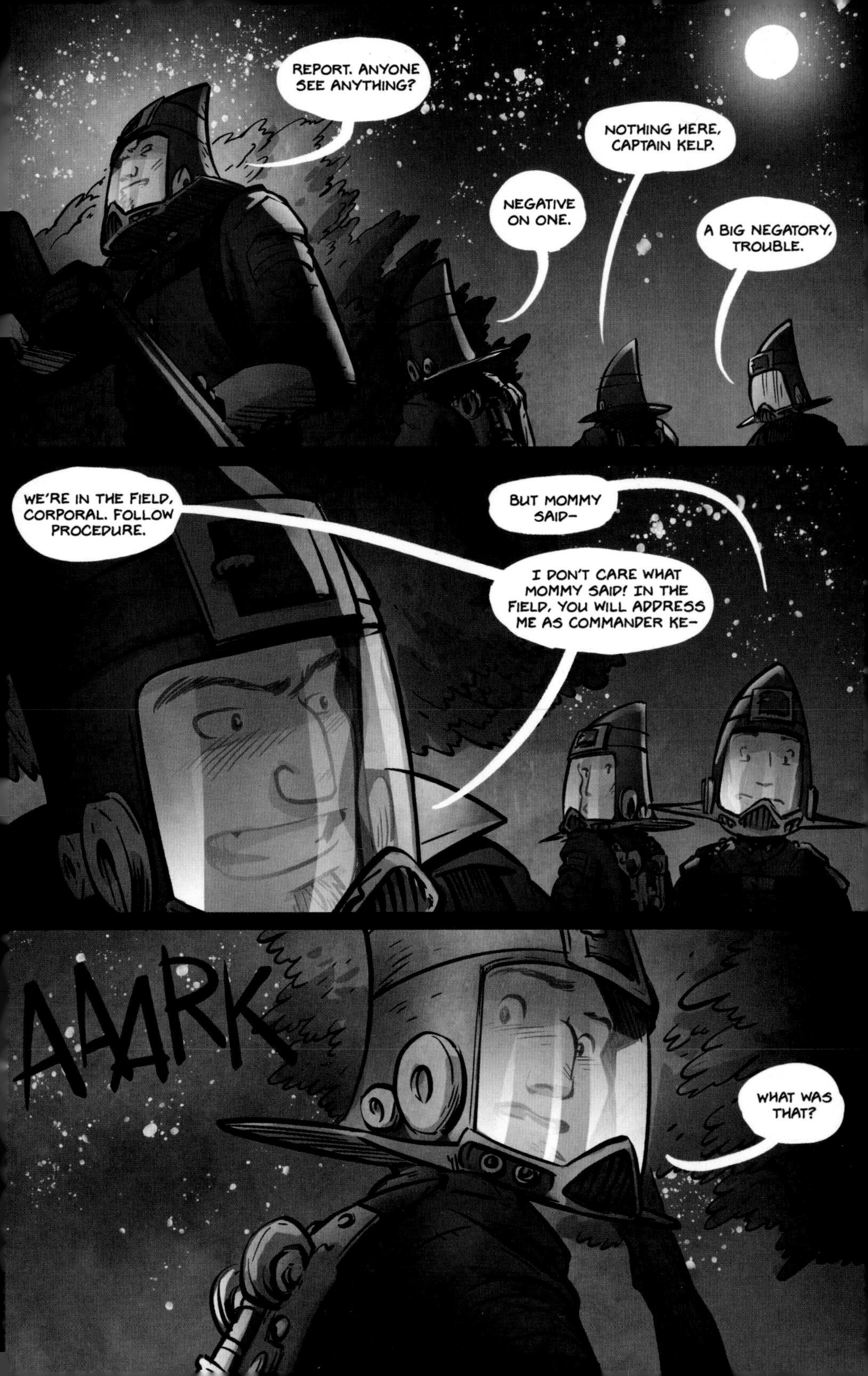
REPORT. ANYONE SEE ANYTHING?
NEGATIVE ON ONE.
NOTHING HERE, CAPTAIN KELP.
A BIG NEGATORY, TROUBLE.
WE'RE IN THE FIELD, CORPORAL. FOLLOW PROCEDURE.
BUT MOMMY SAID–
I DON'T CARE WHAT MOMMY SAID! IN THE FIELD, YOU WILL ADDRESS ME AS COMMANDER KE–
AAARK
WHAT WAS THAT?

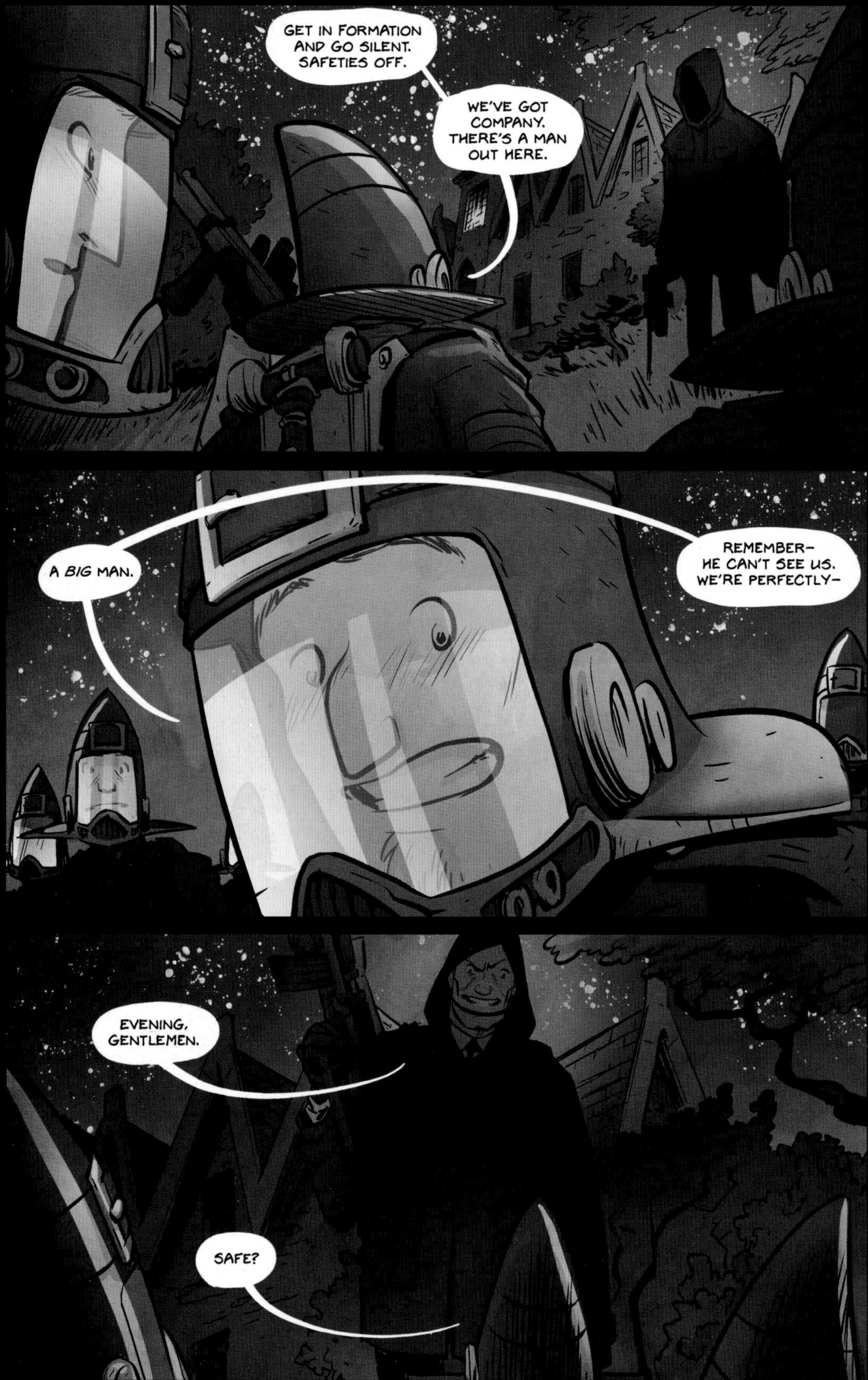
GET IN FORMATION AND GO SILENT. SAFETIES OFF.
WE'VE GOT COMPANY. THERE'S A MAN OUT HERE.
A *BIG* MAN.
REMEMBER– HE CAN'T SEE US. WE'RE PERFECTLY–
EVENING, GENTLEMEN.
SAFE?

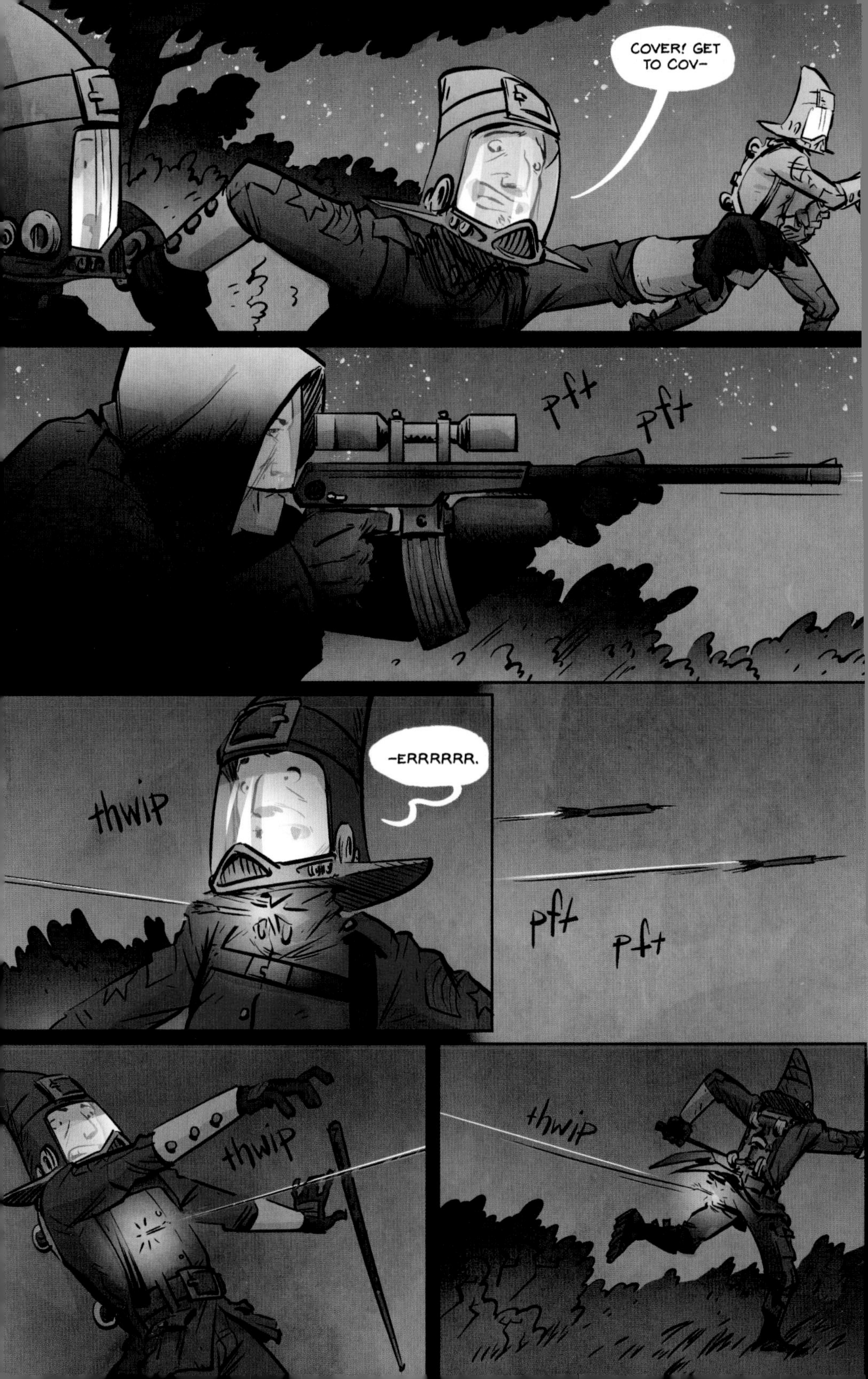
COVER! GET TO COV-
pft
pft
thwip
-ERRRRRR.
pft
pft
thwip
thwip

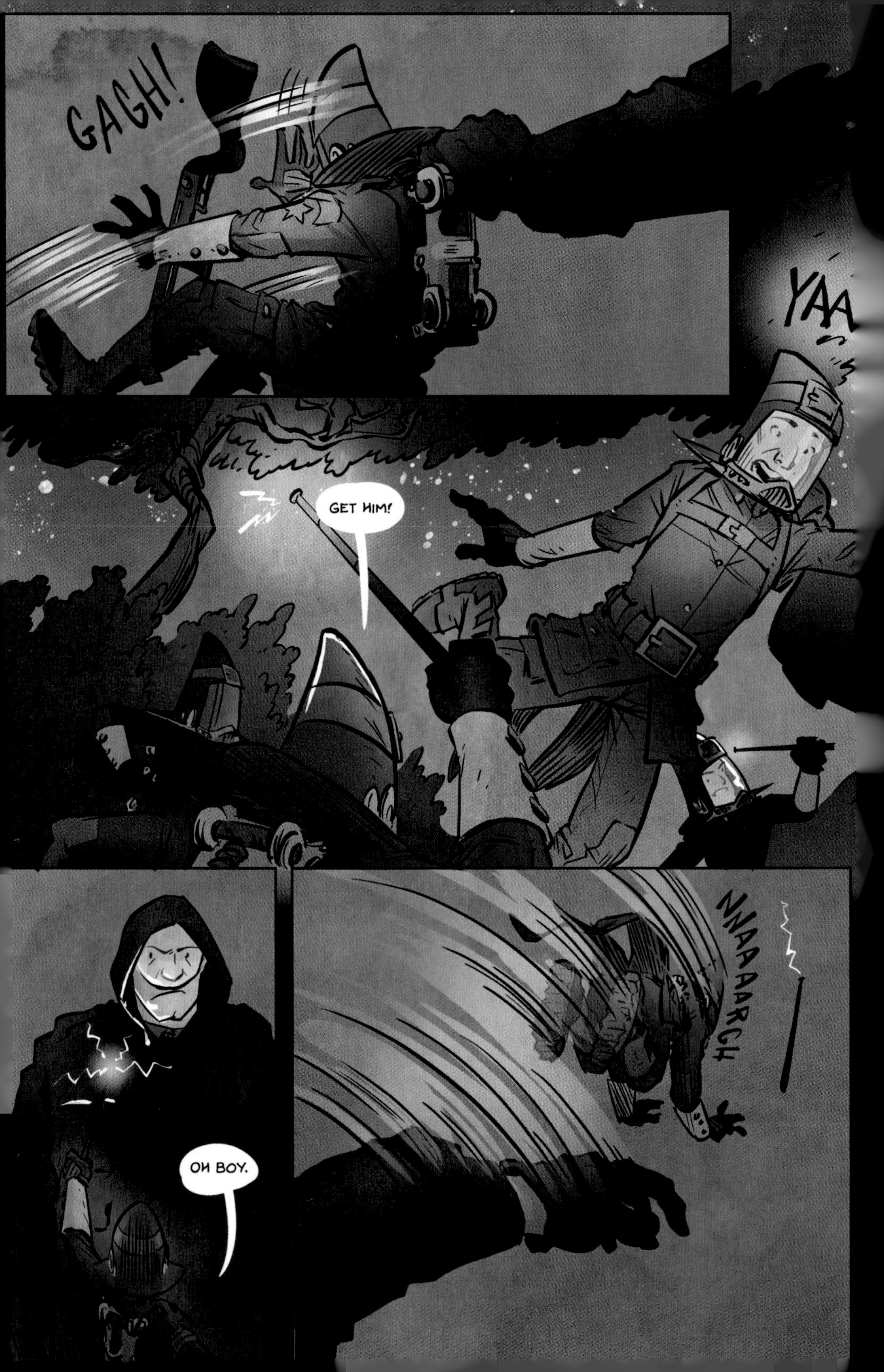
GAGH!
YAA
GET HIM!
OH BOY.
NNAAAAARCH

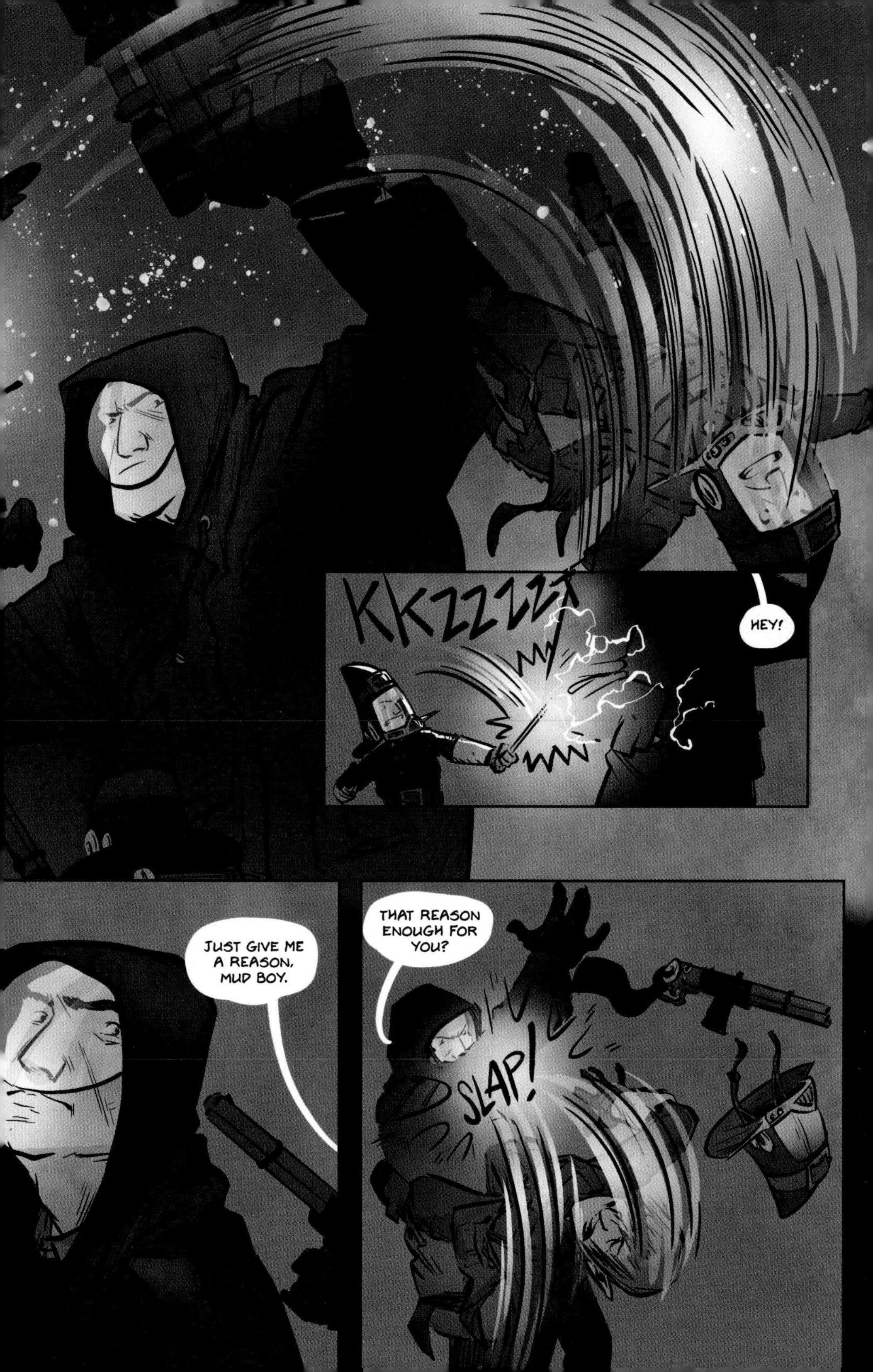
KKZZZZZT
HEY!
JUST GIVE ME A REASON, MUD BOY.
THAT REASON ENOUGH FOR YOU?
SLAP!

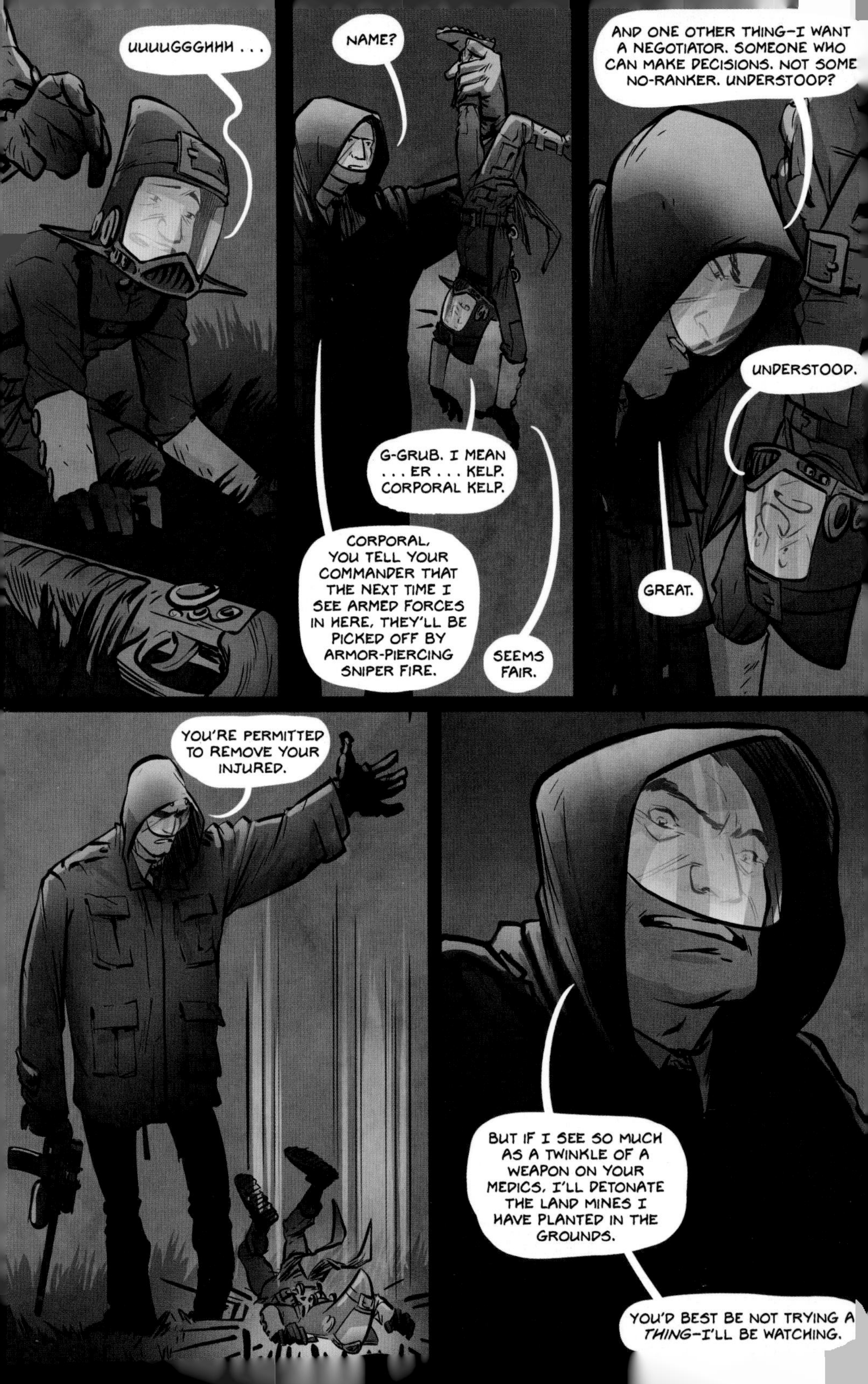
UUUUGGGHHH . . .
NAME?
G-GRUB. I MEAN . . . ER . . . KELP. CORPORAL KELP.
CORPORAL, YOU TELL YOUR COMMANDER THAT THE NEXT TIME I SEE ARMED FORCES IN HERE, THEY'LL BE PICKED OFF BY ARMOR-PIERCING SNIPER FIRE.
SEEMS FAIR.
AND ONE OTHER THING—I WANT A NEGOTIATOR. SOMEONE WHO CAN MAKE DECISIONS. NOT SOME NO-RANKER. UNDERSTOOD?
UNDERSTOOD.
GREAT.
YOU'RE PERMITTED TO REMOVE YOUR INJURED.
BUT IF I SEE SO MUCH AS A TWINKLE OF A WEAPON ON YOUR MEDICS, I'LL DETONATE THE LAND MINES I HAVE PLANTED IN THE GROUNDS.
YOU'D BEST BE NOT TRYING A *THING*—I'LL BE WATCHING.

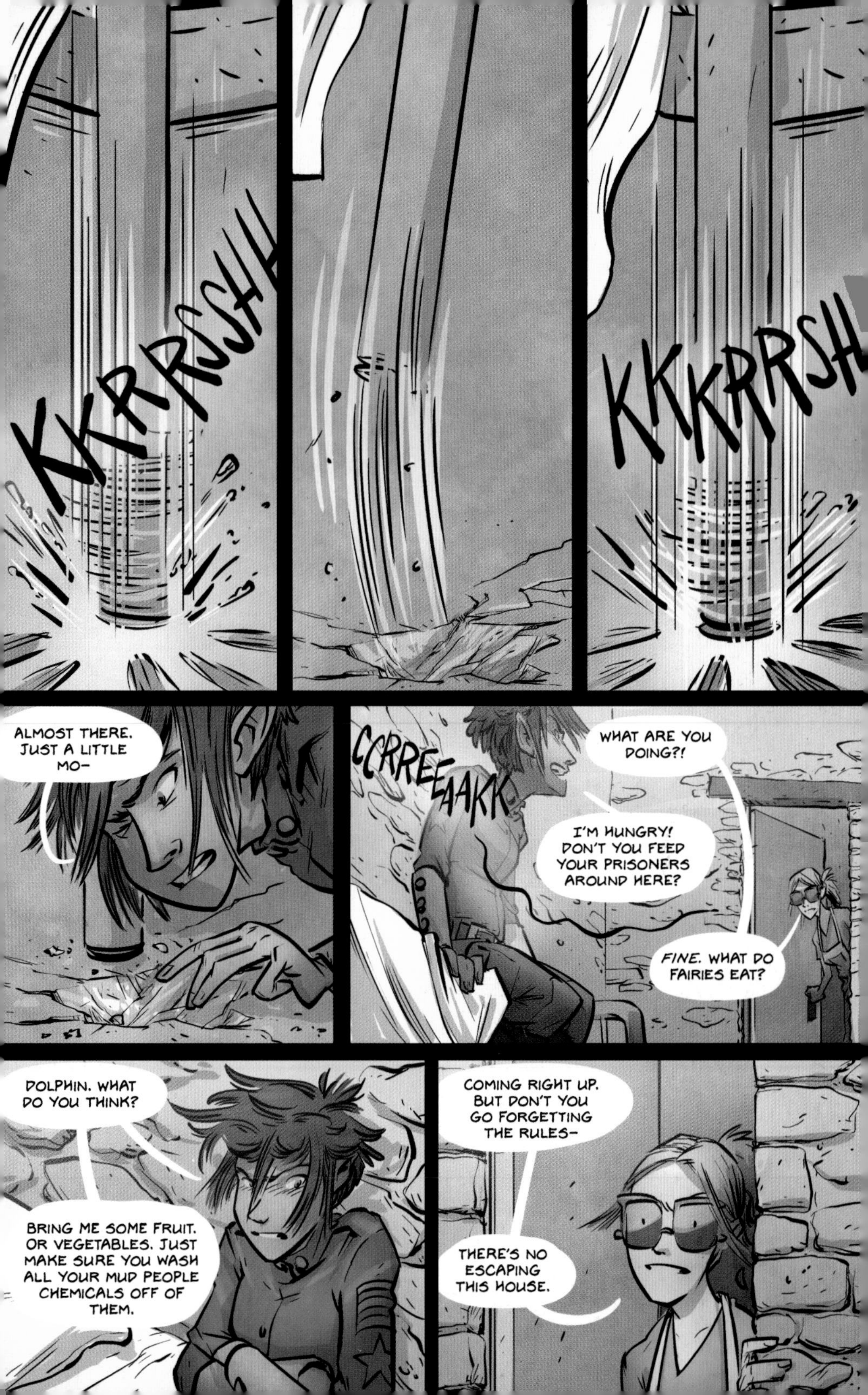
KKRRSHH
KKKRRSH
ALMOST THERE. JUST A LITTLE MO–
CCRREEAAKK
WHAT ARE YOU DOING?!
I'M HUNGRY! DON'T YOU FEED YOUR PRISONERS AROUND HERE?
FINE. WHAT DO FAIRIES EAT?
DOLPHIN. WHAT DO YOU THINK?
BRING ME SOME FRUIT. OR VEGETABLES. JUST MAKE SURE YOU WASH ALL YOUR MUD PEOPLE CHEMICALS OFF OF THEM.
COMING RIGHT UP. BUT DON'T YOU GO FORGETTING THE RULES–
THERE'S NO ESCAPING THIS HOUSE.

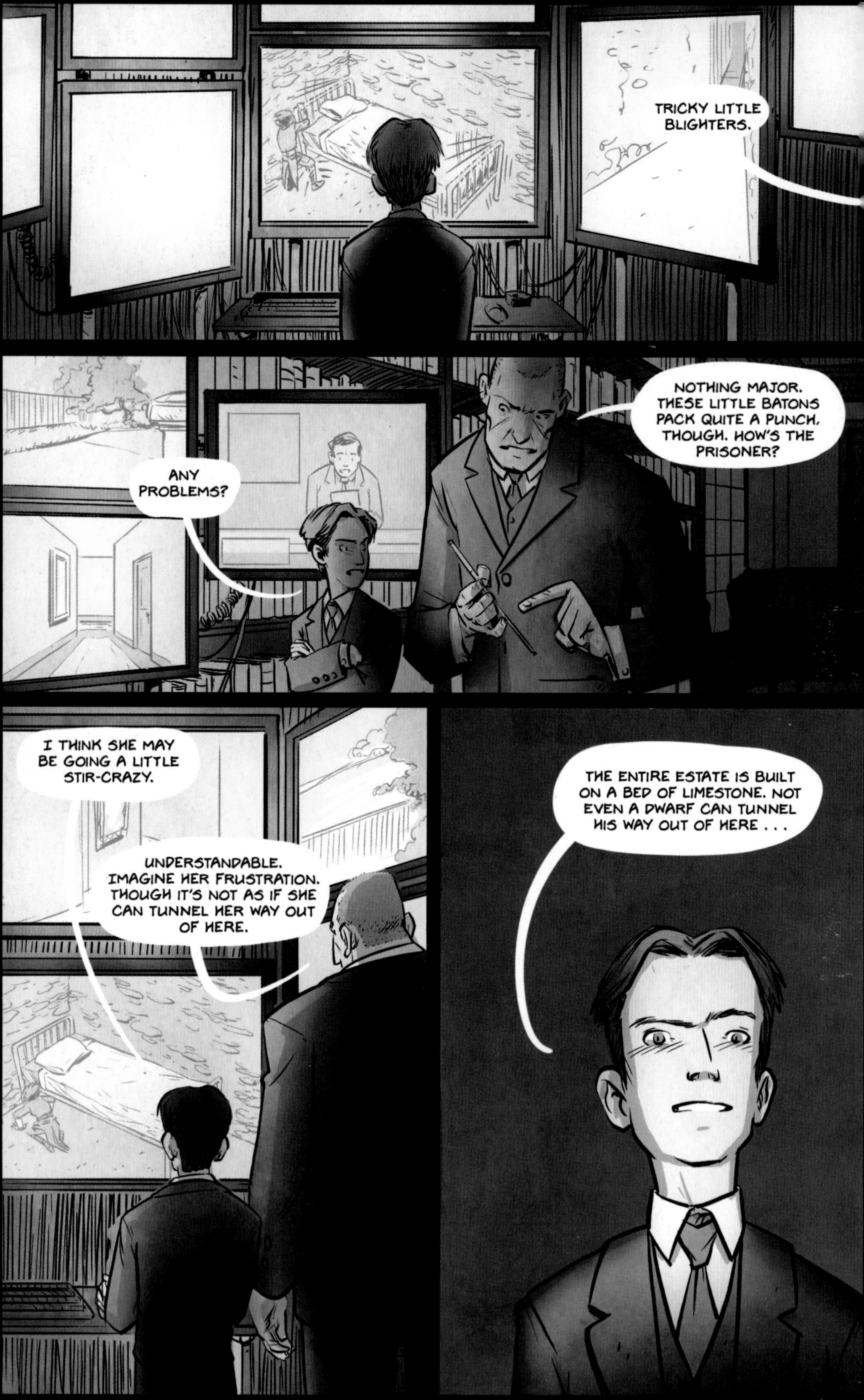
TRICKY LITTLE BLIGHTERS.
ANY PROBLEMS?
NOTHING MAJOR. THESE LITTLE BATONS PACK QUITE A PUNCH, THOUGH. HOW'S THE PRISONER?
I THINK SHE MAY BE GOING A LITTLE STIR-CRAZY.
UNDERSTANDABLE. IMAGINE HER FRUSTRATION. THOUGH IT'S NOT AS IF SHE CAN TUNNEL HER WAY OUT OF HERE.
THE ENTIRE ESTATE IS BUILT ON A BED OF LIMESTONE. NOT EVEN A DWARF CAN TUNNEL HIS WAY OUT OF HERE . . .

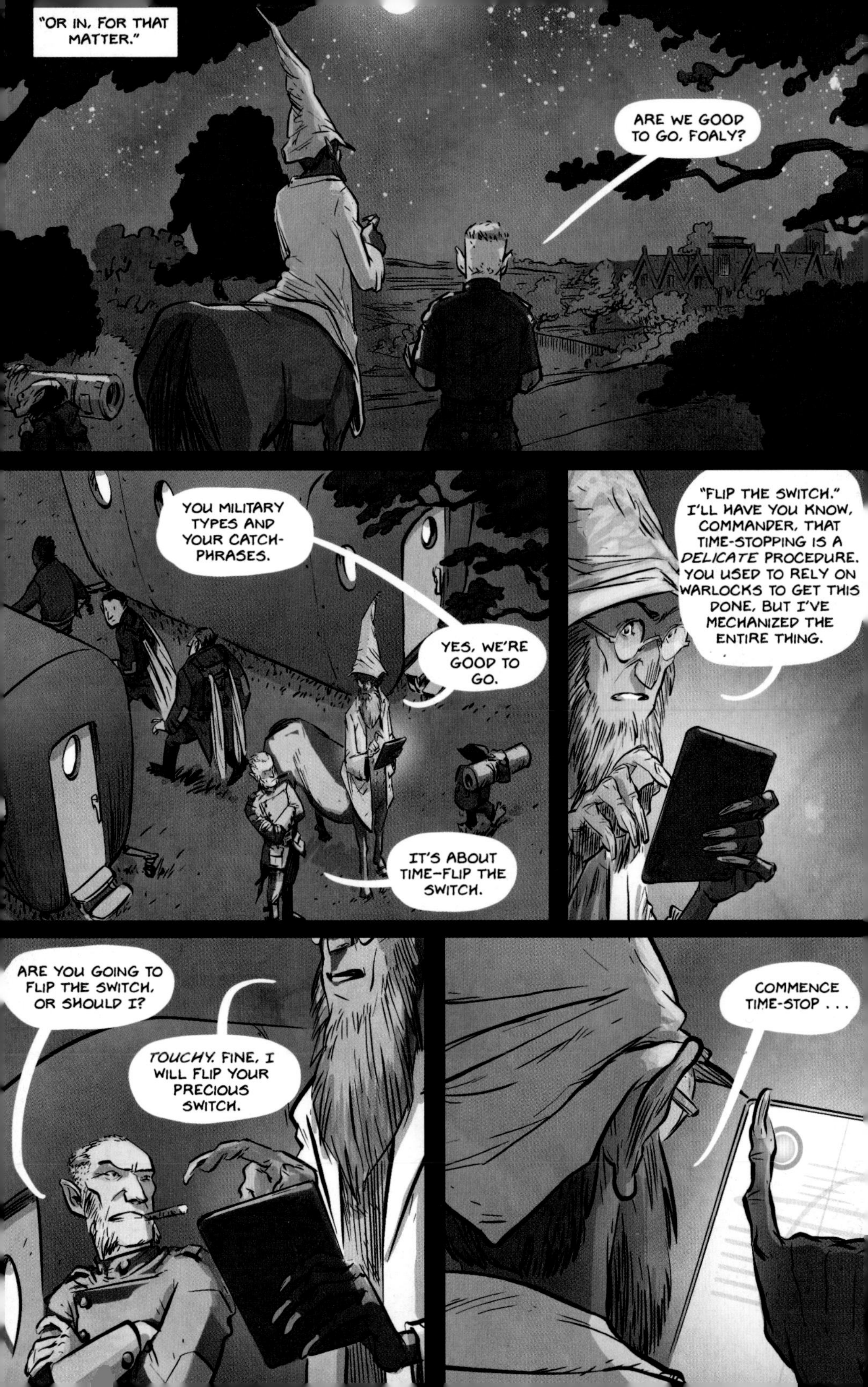
"OR IN, FOR THAT MATTER."
ARE WE GOOD TO GO, FOALY?
YOU MILITARY TYPES AND YOUR CATCH-PHRASES.
YES, WE'RE GOOD TO GO.
IT'S ABOUT TIME—FLIP THE SWITCH.
"FLIP THE SWITCH." I'LL HAVE YOU KNOW, COMMANDER, THAT TIME-STOPPING IS A *DELICATE* PROCEDURE. YOU USED TO RELY ON WARLOCKS TO GET THIS DONE, BUT I'VE MECHANIZED THE ENTIRE THING.
ARE YOU GOING TO FLIP THE SWITCH, OR SHOULD I?
TOUCHY. FINE, I WILL FLIP YOUR PRECIOUS SWITCH.
COMMENCE TIME-STOP . . .

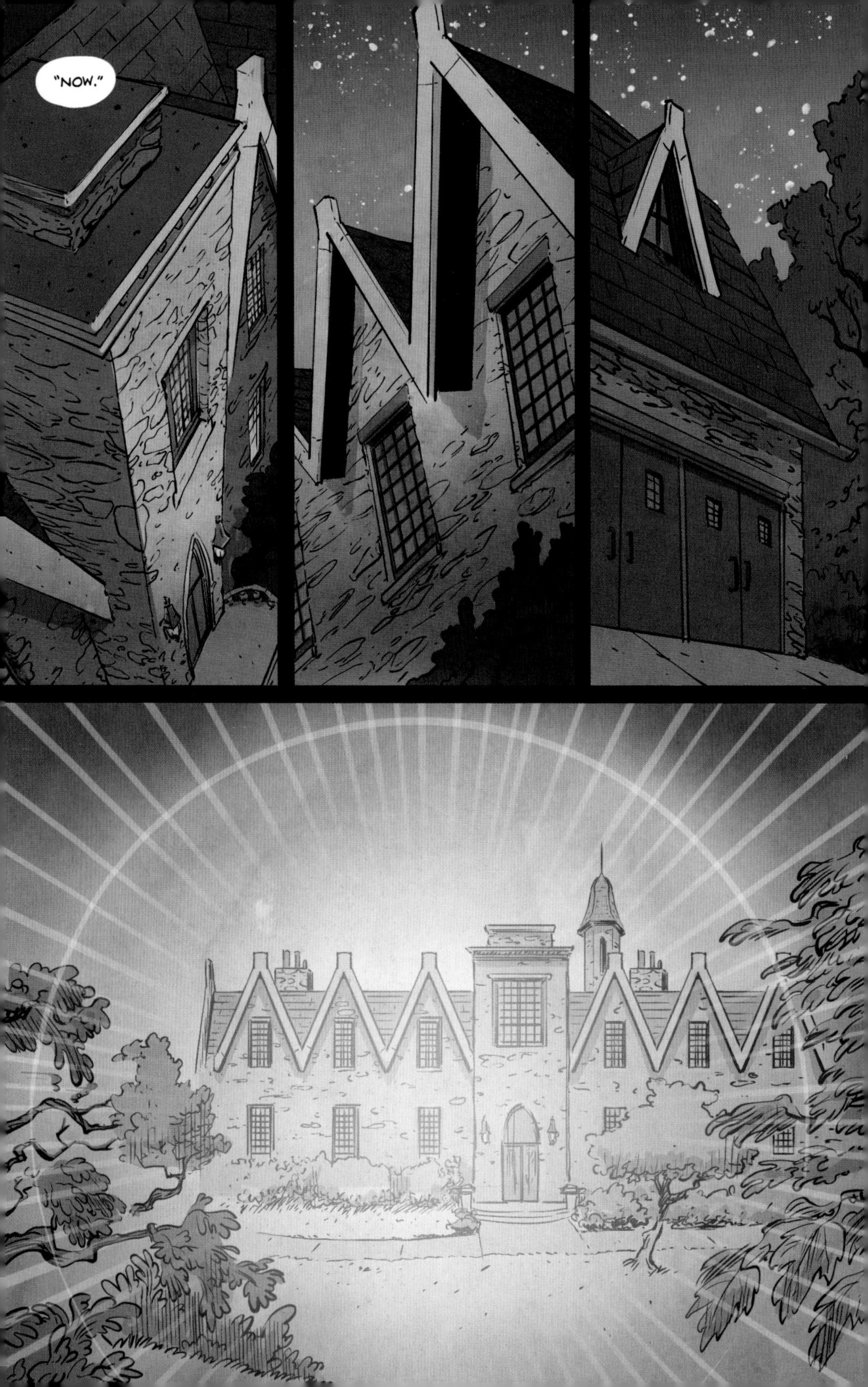
"NOW."

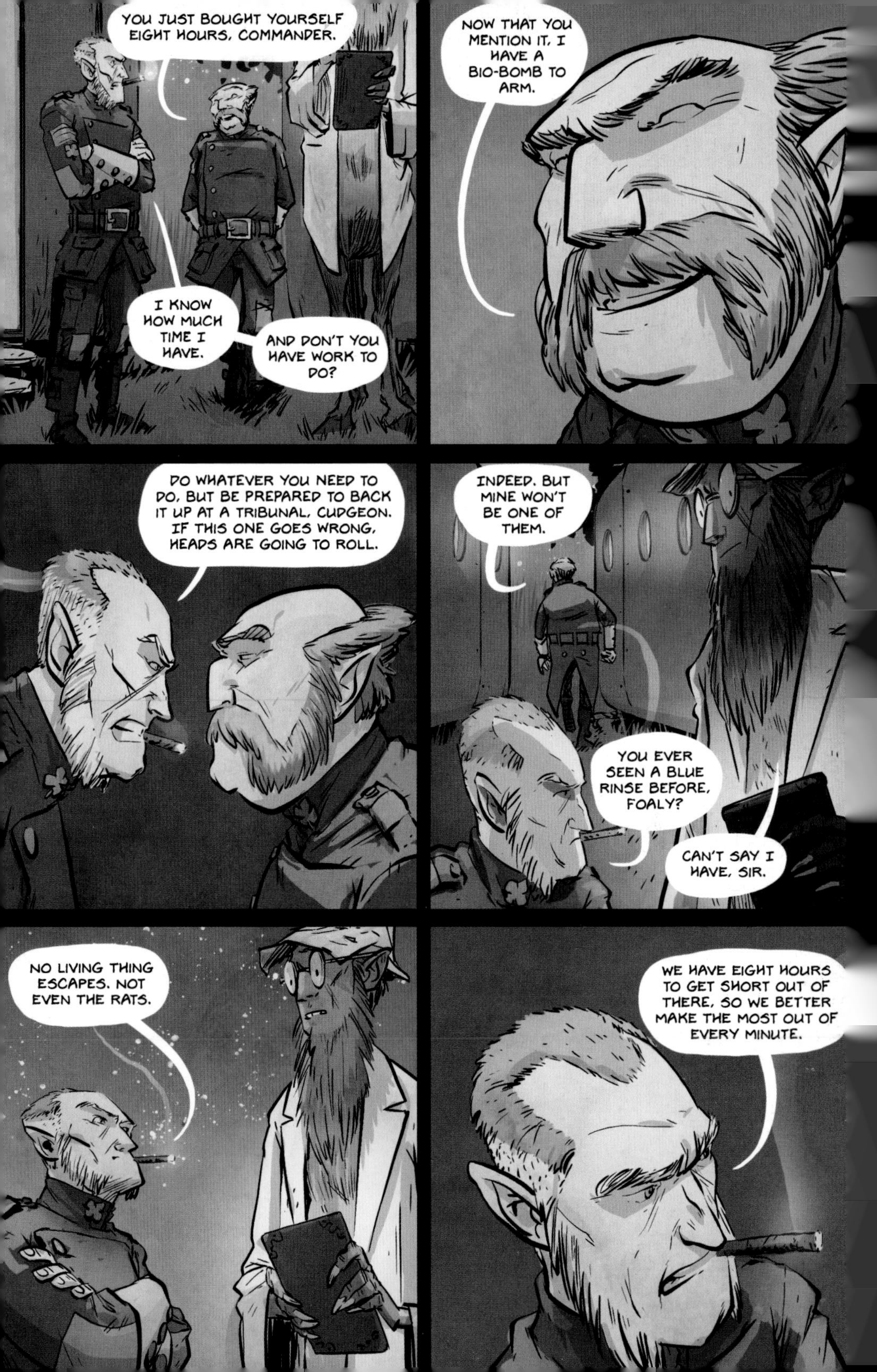
YOU JUST BOUGHT YOURSELF EIGHT HOURS, COMMANDER.
I KNOW HOW MUCH TIME I HAVE.
AND DON'T YOU HAVE WORK TO DO?
NOW THAT YOU MENTION IT, I HAVE A BIO-BOMB TO ARM.
DO WHATEVER YOU NEED TO DO, BUT BE PREPARED TO BACK IT UP AT A TRIBUNAL, CUDGEON. IF THIS ONE GOES WRONG, HEADS ARE GOING TO ROLL.
INDEED. BUT MINE WON'T BE ONE OF THEM.
YOU EVER SEEN A BLUE RINSE BEFORE, FOALY?
CAN'T SAY I HAVE, SIR.
NO LIVING THING ESCAPES. NOT EVEN THE RATS.
WE HAVE EIGHT HOURS TO GET SHORT OUT OF THERE, SO WE BETTER MAKE THE MOST OUT OF EVERY MINUTE.

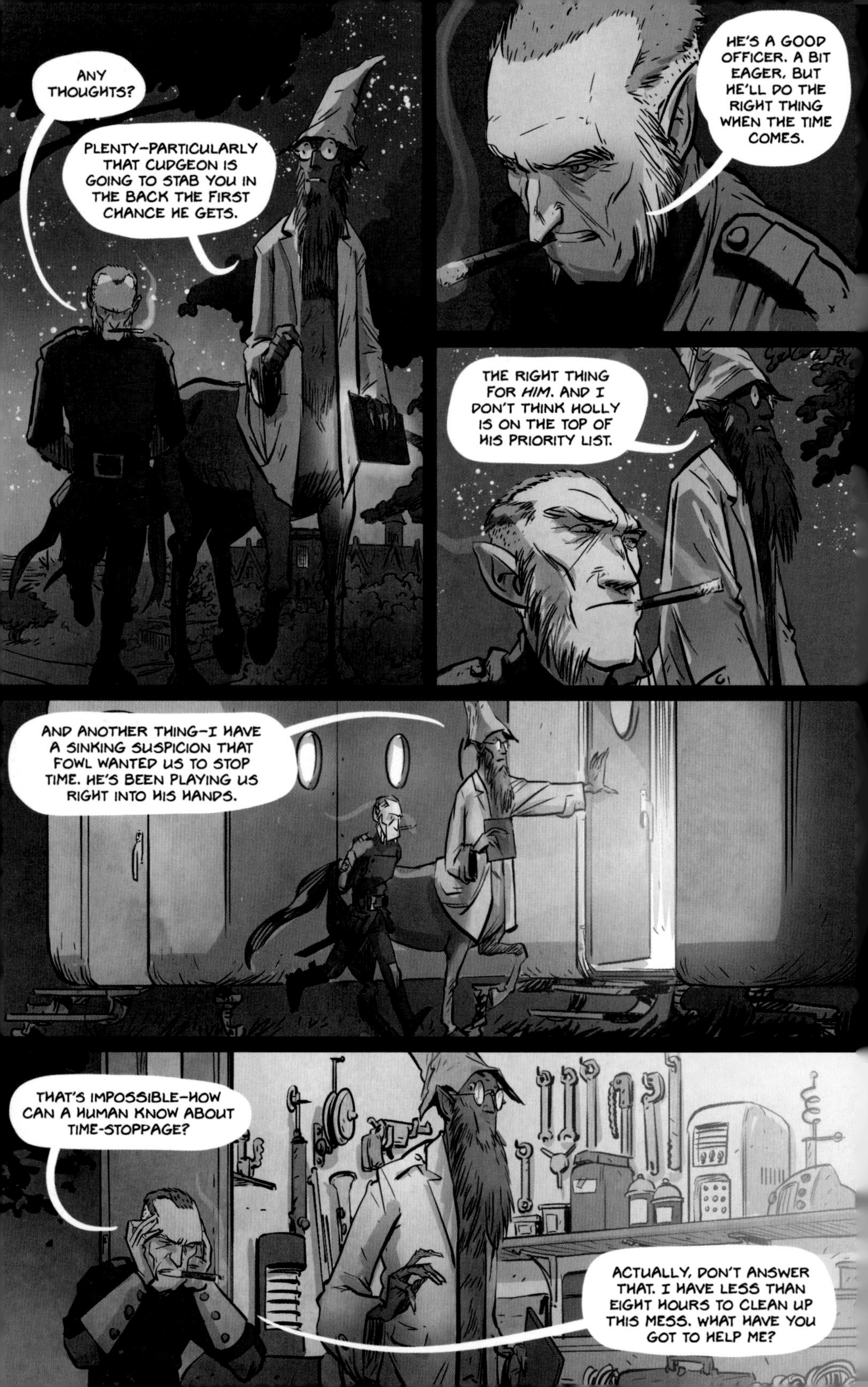
ANY THOUGHTS?
PLENTY—PARTICULARLY THAT CUDGEON IS GOING TO STAB YOU IN THE BACK THE FIRST CHANCE HE GETS.
HE'S A GOOD OFFICER. A BIT EAGER, BUT HE'LL DO THE RIGHT THING WHEN THE TIME COMES.
THE RIGHT THING FOR *HIM*. AND I DON'T THINK HOLLY IS ON THE TOP OF HIS PRIORITY LIST.
AND ANOTHER THING—I HAVE A SINKING SUSPICION THAT FOWL WANTED US TO STOP TIME. HE'S BEEN PLAYING US RIGHT INTO HIS HANDS.
THAT'S IMPOSSIBLE—HOW CAN A HUMAN KNOW ABOUT TIME-STOPPAGE?
ACTUALLY, DON'T ANSWER THAT. I HAVE LESS THAN EIGHT HOURS TO CLEAN UP THIS MESS. WHAT HAVE YOU GOT TO HELP ME?

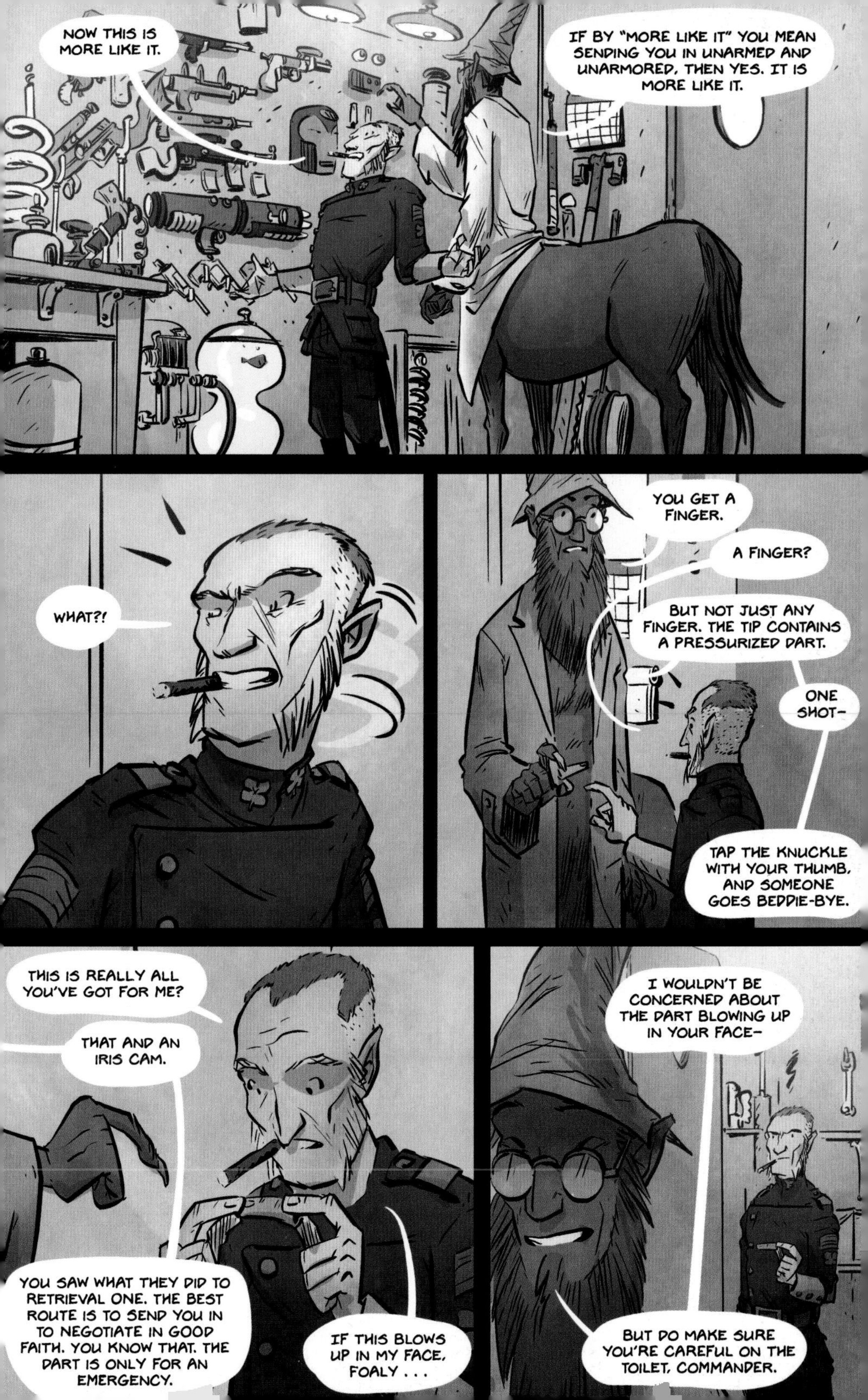
NOW THIS IS MORE LIKE IT.
IF BY "MORE LIKE IT" YOU MEAN SENDING YOU IN UNARMED AND UNARMORED, THEN YES. IT IS MORE LIKE IT.
WHAT?!
YOU GET A FINGER.
A FINGER?
BUT NOT JUST ANY FINGER. THE TIP CONTAINS A PRESSURIZED DART.
ONE SHOT-
TAP THE KNUCKLE WITH YOUR THUMB, AND SOMEONE GOES BEDDIE-BYE.
THIS IS REALLY ALL YOU'VE GOT FOR ME?
THAT AND AN IRIS CAM.
YOU SAW WHAT THEY DID TO RETRIEVAL ONE. THE BEST ROUTE IS TO SEND YOU IN TO NEGOTIATE IN GOOD FAITH. YOU KNOW THAT. THE DART IS ONLY FOR AN EMERGENCY.
IF THIS BLOWS UP IN MY FACE, FOALY . . .
I WOULDN'T BE CONCERNED ABOUT THE DART BLOWING UP IN YOUR FACE-
BUT DO MAKE SURE YOU'RE CAREFUL ON THE TOILET, COMMANDER.

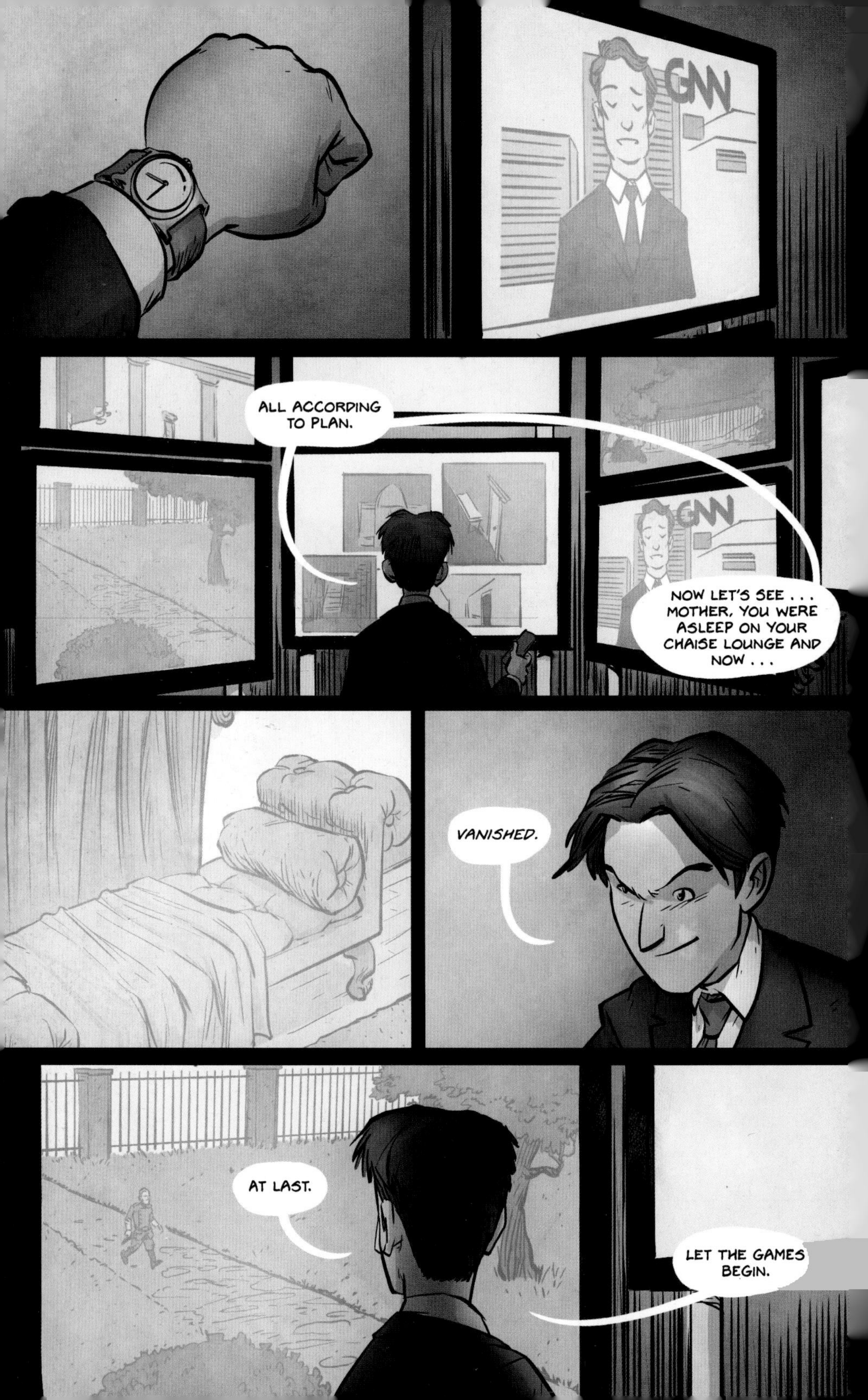
GNN
ALL ACCORDING TO PLAN.
NOW LET'S SEE . . . MOTHER, YOU WERE ASLEEP ON YOUR CHAISE LOUNGE AND NOW . . .
VANISHED.
AT LAST.
LET THE GAMES BEGIN.

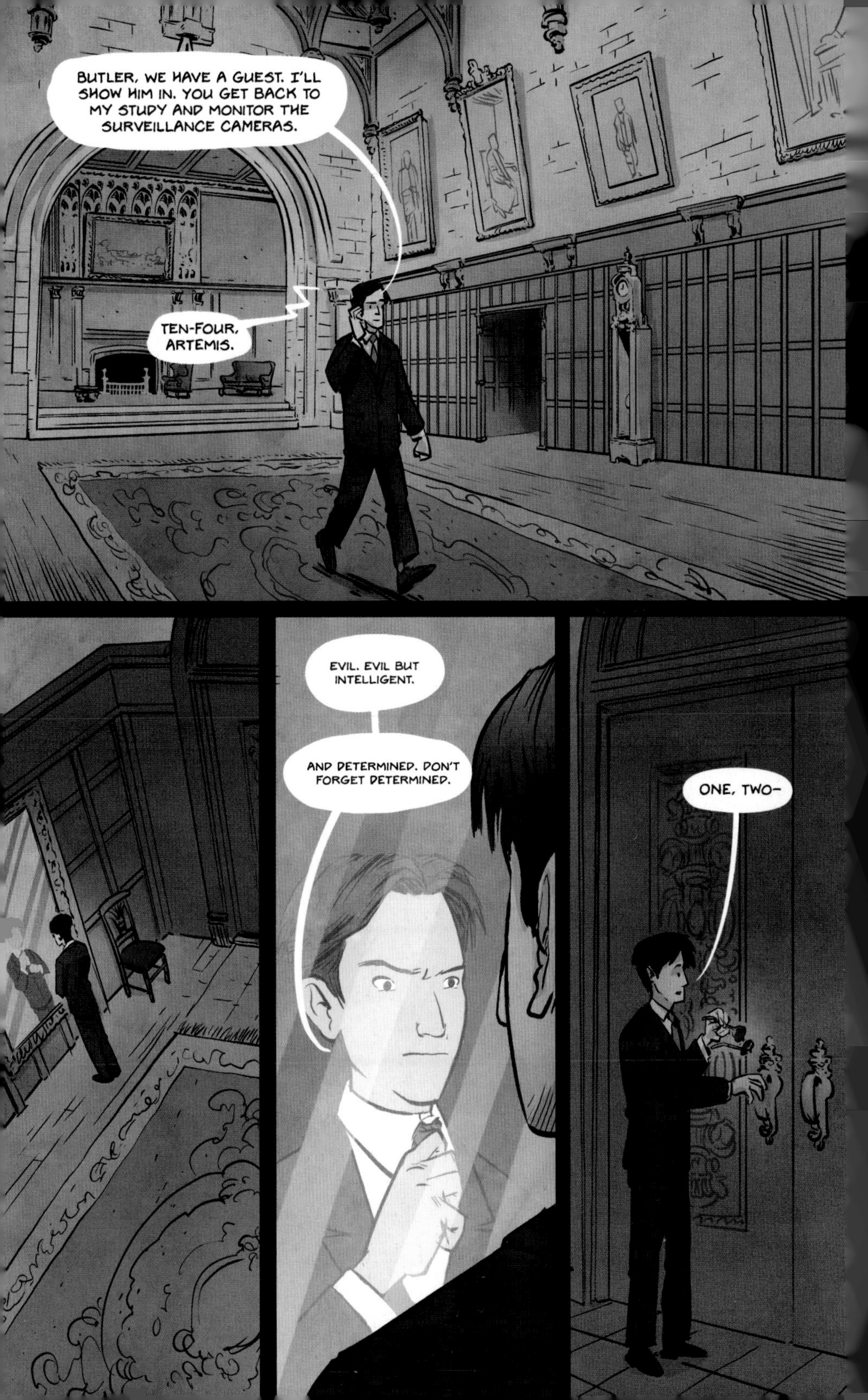
BUTLER, WE HAVE A GUEST. I'LL SHOW HIM IN. YOU GET BACK TO MY STUDY AND MONITOR THE SURVEILLANCE CAMERAS.
TEN-FOUR, ARTEMIS.
EVIL. EVIL BUT INTELLIGENT.
AND DETERMINED. DON'T FORGET DETERMINED.
ONE, TWO-

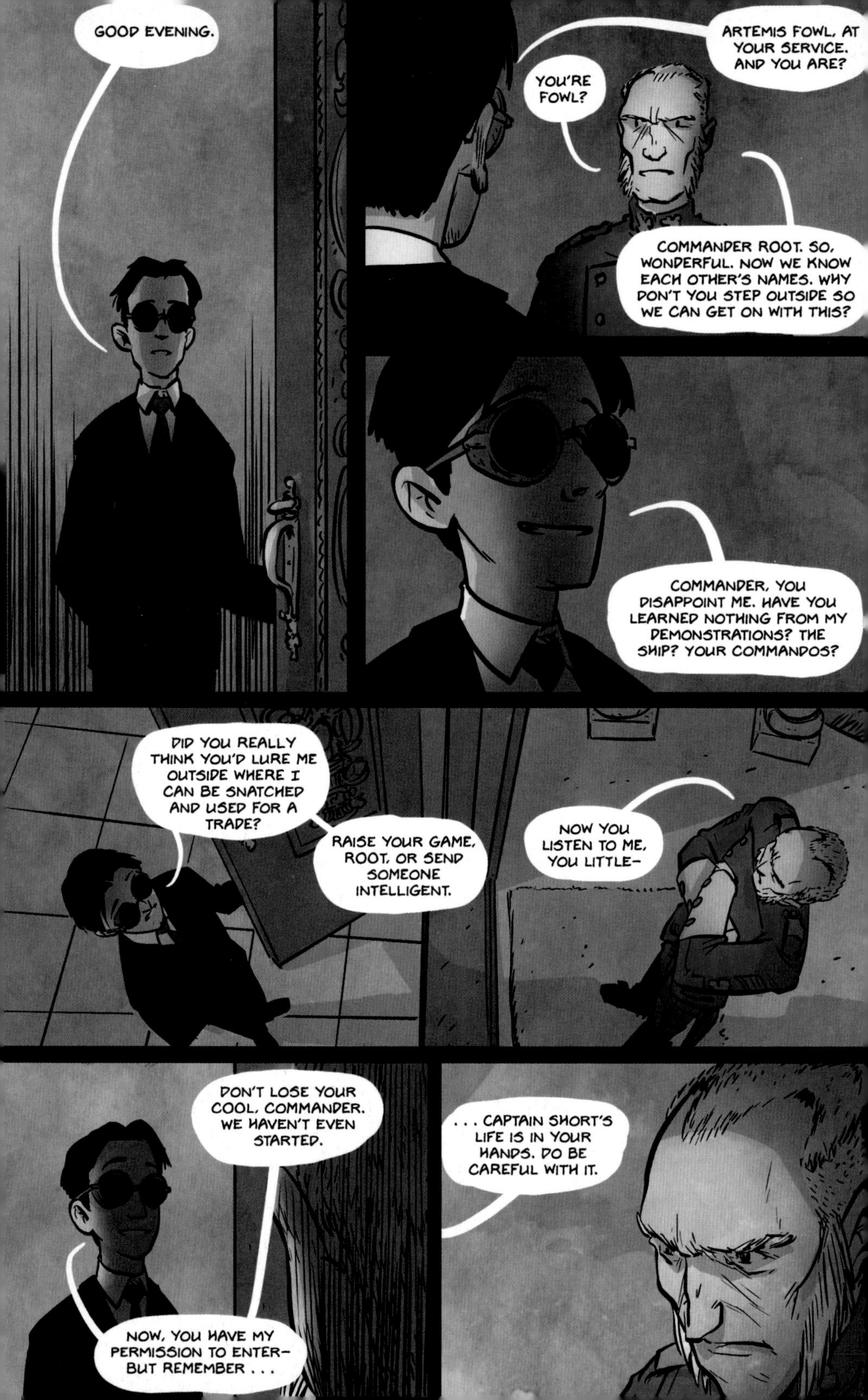
GOOD EVENING.
ARTEMIS FOWL, AT YOUR SERVICE. AND YOU ARE?
YOU'RE FOWL?
COMMANDER ROOT. SO, WONDERFUL. NOW WE KNOW EACH OTHER'S NAMES. WHY DON'T YOU STEP OUTSIDE SO WE CAN GET ON WITH THIS?
COMMANDER, YOU DISAPPOINT ME. HAVE YOU LEARNED NOTHING FROM MY DEMONSTRATIONS? THE SHIP? YOUR COMMANDOS?
DID YOU REALLY THINK YOU'D LURE ME OUTSIDE WHERE I CAN BE SNATCHED AND USED FOR A TRADE?
RAISE YOUR GAME, ROOT, OR SEND SOMEONE INTELLIGENT.
NOW YOU LISTEN TO ME, YOU LITTLE–
DON'T LOSE YOUR COOL, COMMANDER. WE HAVEN'T EVEN STARTED.
NOW, YOU HAVE MY PERMISSION TO ENTER– BUT REMEMBER . . .
. . . CAPTAIN SHORT'S LIFE IS IN YOUR HANDS. DO BE CAREFUL WITH IT.

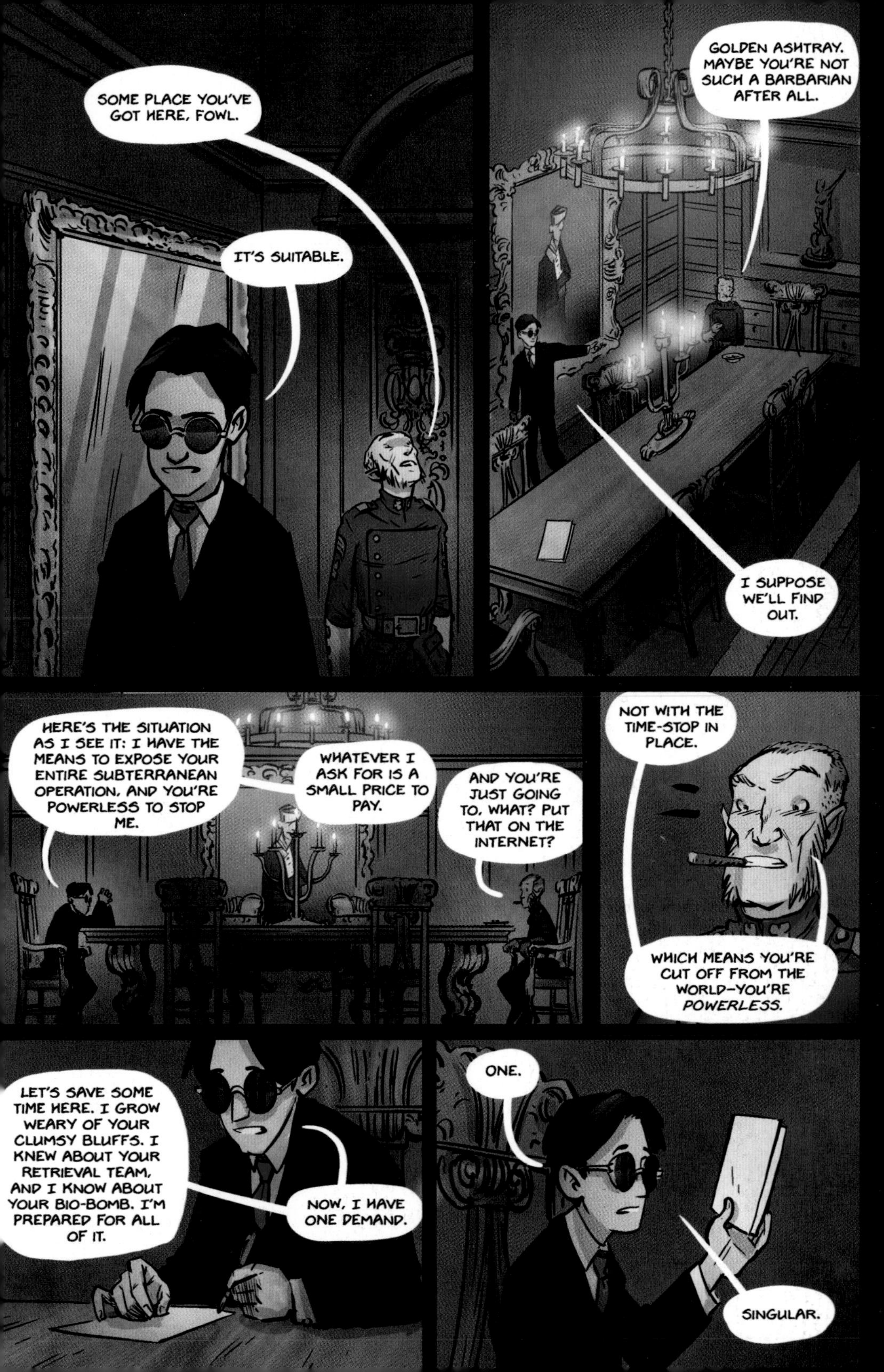
SOME PLACE YOU'VE GOT HERE, FOWL.
IT'S SUITABLE.
GOLDEN ASHTRAY. MAYBE YOU'RE NOT SUCH A BARBARIAN AFTER ALL.
I SUPPOSE WE'LL FIND OUT.
HERE'S THE SITUATION AS I SEE IT: I HAVE THE MEANS TO EXPOSE YOUR ENTIRE SUBTERRANEAN OPERATION, AND YOU'RE POWERLESS TO STOP ME.
WHATEVER I ASK FOR IS A SMALL PRICE TO PAY.
AND YOU'RE JUST GOING TO, WHAT? PUT THAT ON THE INTERNET?
NOT WITH THE TIME-STOP IN PLACE.
WHICH MEANS YOU'RE CUT OFF FROM THE WORLD—YOU'RE *POWERLESS.*
LET'S SAVE SOME TIME HERE. I GROW WEARY OF YOUR CLUMSY BLUFFS. I KNEW ABOUT YOUR RETRIEVAL TEAM, AND I KNOW ABOUT YOUR BIO-BOMB. I'M PREPARED FOR ALL OF IT.
NOW, I HAVE ONE DEMAND.
ONE.
SINGULAR.

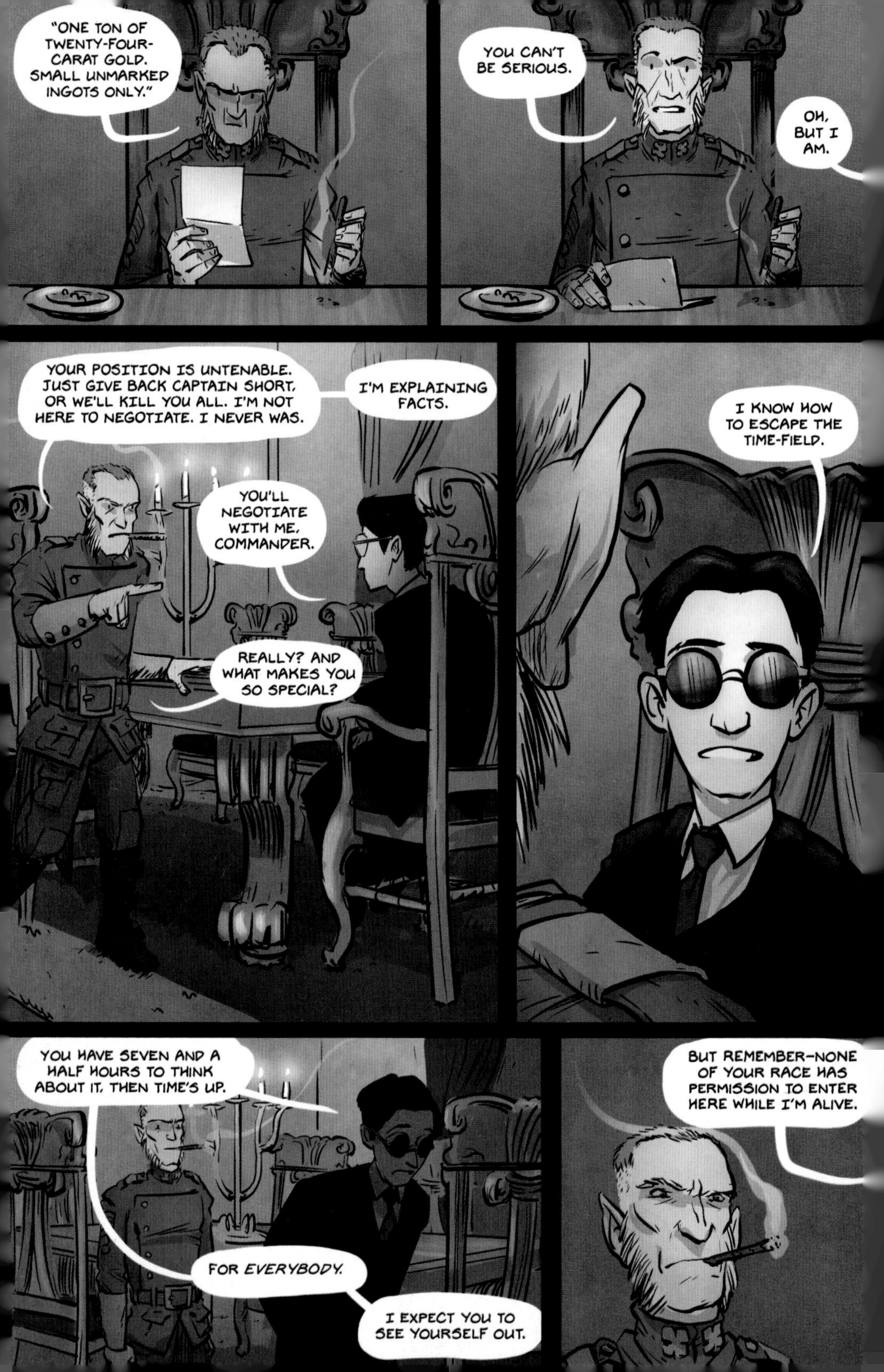
"ONE TON OF TWENTY-FOUR-CARAT GOLD. SMALL UNMARKED INGOTS ONLY."
YOU CAN'T BE SERIOUS.
OH, BUT I AM.
YOUR POSITION IS UNTENABLE. JUST GIVE BACK CAPTAIN SHORT, OR WE'LL KILL YOU ALL. I'M NOT HERE TO NEGOTIATE. I NEVER WAS.
I'M EXPLAINING FACTS.
YOU'LL NEGOTIATE WITH ME, COMMANDER.
REALLY? AND WHAT MAKES YOU SO SPECIAL?
I KNOW HOW TO ESCAPE THE TIME-FIELD.
YOU HAVE SEVEN AND A HALF HOURS TO THINK ABOUT IT, THEN TIME'S UP.
FOR *EVERYBODY.*
I EXPECT YOU TO SEE YOURSELF OUT.
BUT REMEMBER—NONE OF YOUR RACE HAS PERMISSION TO ENTER HERE WHILE I'M ALIVE.

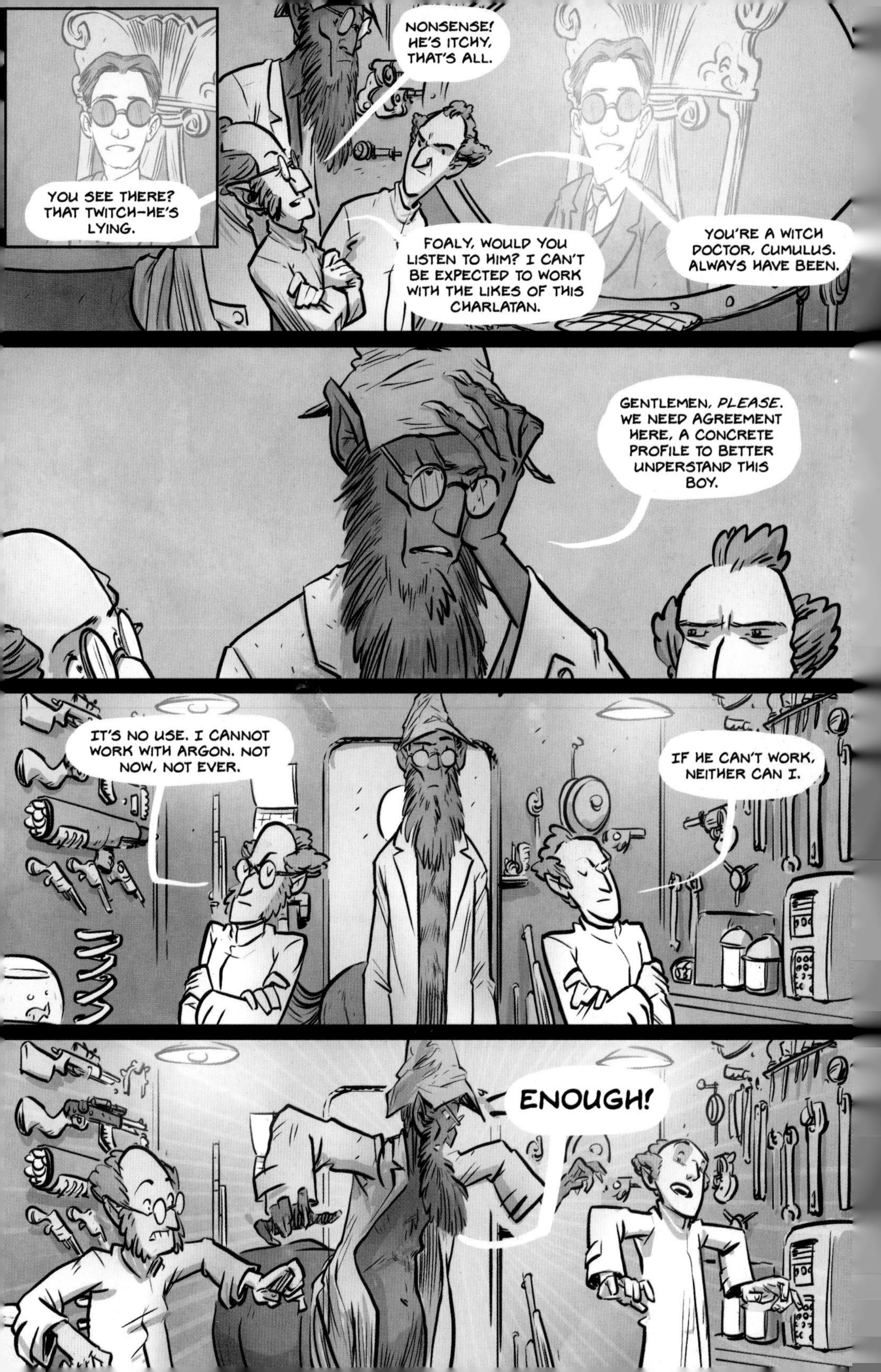
YOU SEE THERE? THAT TWITCH—HE'S LYING.
NONSENSE! HE'S ITCHY, THAT'S ALL.
FOALY, WOULD YOU LISTEN TO HIM? I CAN'T BE EXPECTED TO WORK WITH THE LIKES OF THIS CHARLATAN.
YOU'RE A WITCH DOCTOR, CUMULUS. ALWAYS HAVE BEEN.
GENTLEMEN, *PLEASE*. WE NEED AGREEMENT HERE, A CONCRETE PROFILE TO BETTER UNDERSTAND THIS BOY.
IT'S NO USE. I CANNOT WORK WITH ARGON. NOT NOW, NOT EVER.
IF HE CAN'T WORK, NEITHER CAN I.
ENOUGH!

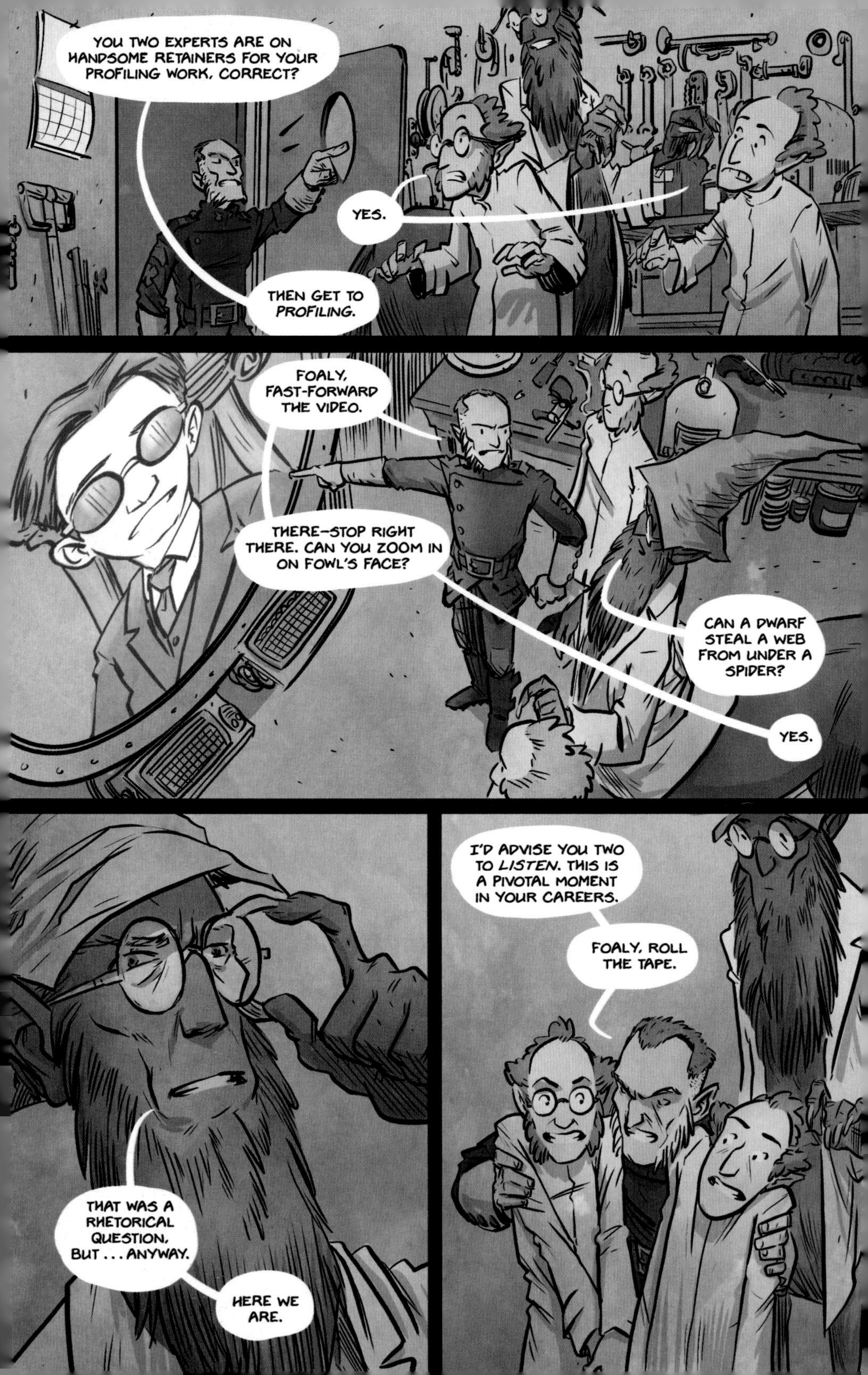
YOU TWO EXPERTS ARE ON HANDSOME RETAINERS FOR YOUR PROFILING WORK, CORRECT?
YES.
THEN GET TO *PROFILING*.
FOALY, FAST-FORWARD THE VIDEO.
THERE—STOP RIGHT THERE. CAN YOU ZOOM IN ON FOWL'S FACE?
CAN A DWARF STEAL A WEB FROM UNDER A SPIDER?
YES.
THAT WAS A RHETORICAL QUESTION, BUT . . . ANYWAY.
HERE WE ARE.
I'D ADVISE YOU TWO TO *LISTEN*. THIS IS A PIVOTAL MOMENT IN YOUR CAREERS.
FOALY, ROLL THE TAPE.

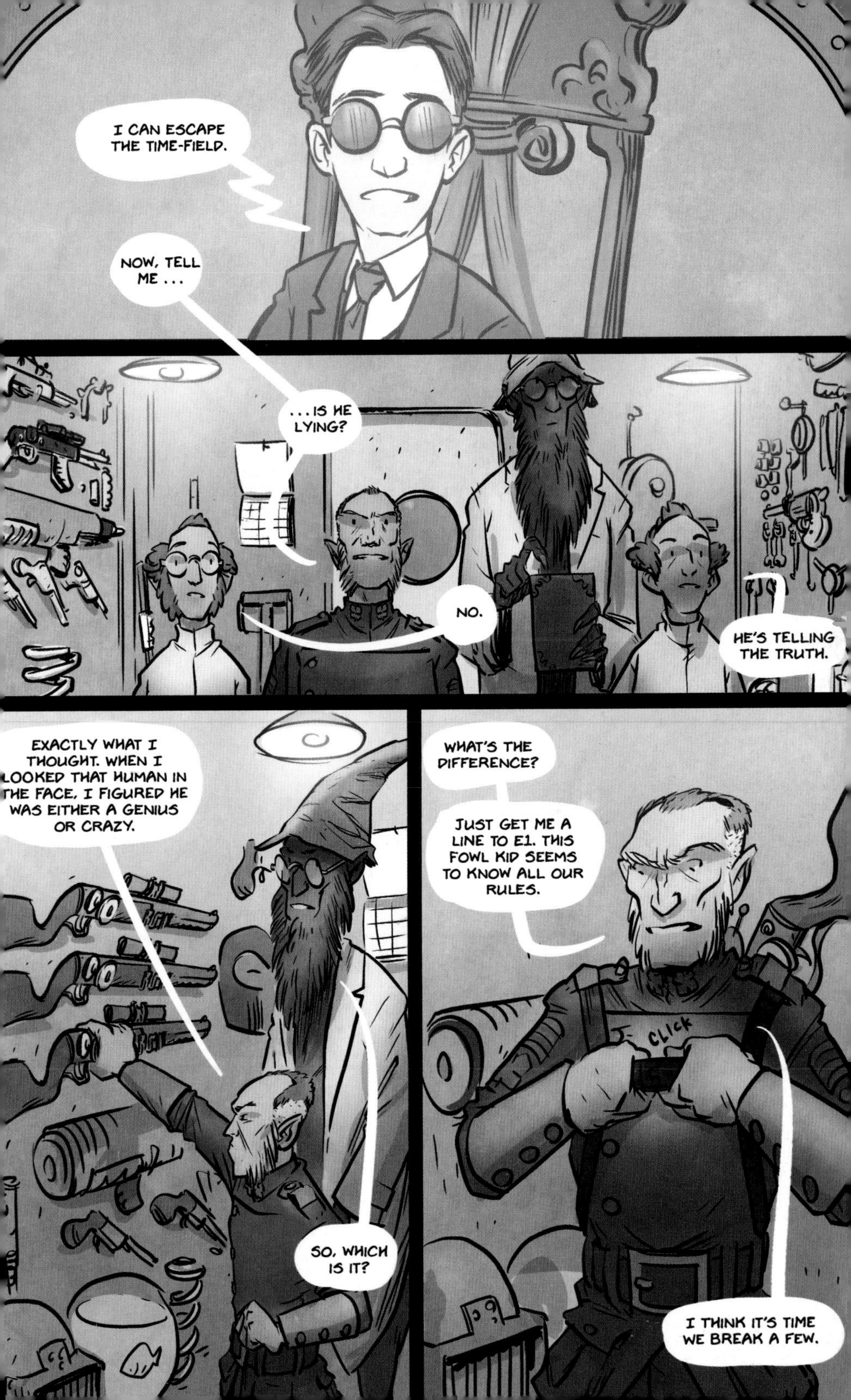
I CAN ESCAPE THE TIME-FIELD.
NOW, TELL ME . . .
. . . IS HE LYING?
NO.
HE'S TELLING THE TRUTH.
EXACTLY WHAT I THOUGHT. WHEN I LOOKED THAT HUMAN IN THE FACE, I FIGURED HE WAS EITHER A GENIUS OR CRAZY.
SO, WHICH IS IT?
WHAT'S THE DIFFERENCE?
JUST GET ME A LINE TO E1. THIS FOWL KID SEEMS TO KNOW ALL OUR RULES.
CLICK
I THINK IT'S TIME WE BREAK A FEW.

CHAPTER SEVEN

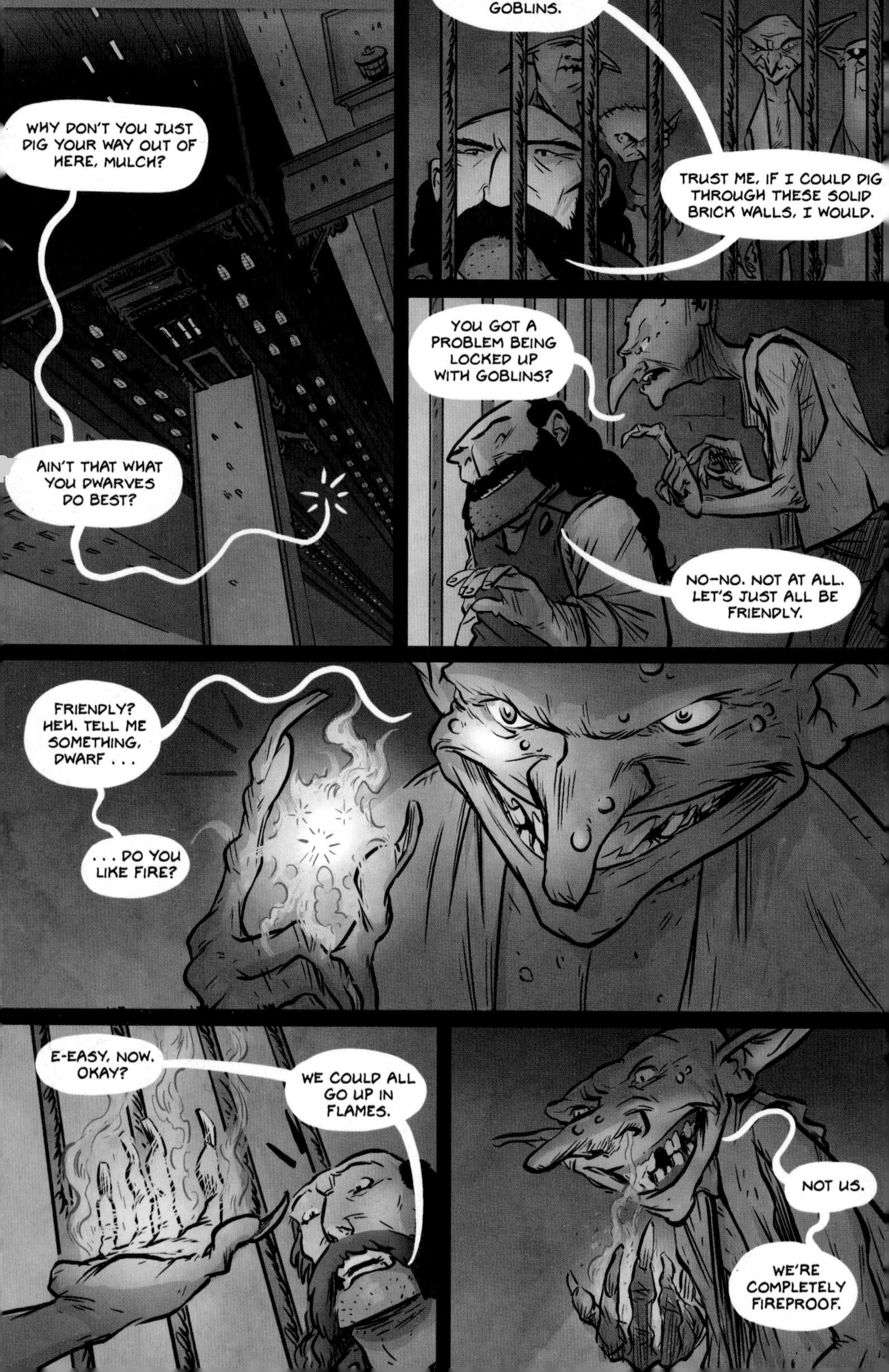
WHY DON'T YOU JUST DIG YOUR WAY OUT OF HERE, MULCH?
AIN'T THAT WHAT YOU DWARVES DO BEST?
I'M LOCKED UP IN A CELL WITH FOUR GOBLINS.
TRUST ME, IF I COULD DIG THROUGH THESE SOLID BRICK WALLS, I WOULD.
YOU GOT A PROBLEM BEING LOCKED UP WITH GOBLINS?
NO-NO. NOT AT ALL. LET'S JUST ALL BE FRIENDLY.
FRIENDLY? HEH. TELL ME SOMETHING, DWARF . . .
. . . DO YOU LIKE FIRE?
E-EASY, NOW. OKAY?
WE COULD ALL GO UP IN FLAMES.
NOT US.
WE'RE COMPLETELY FIREPROOF.

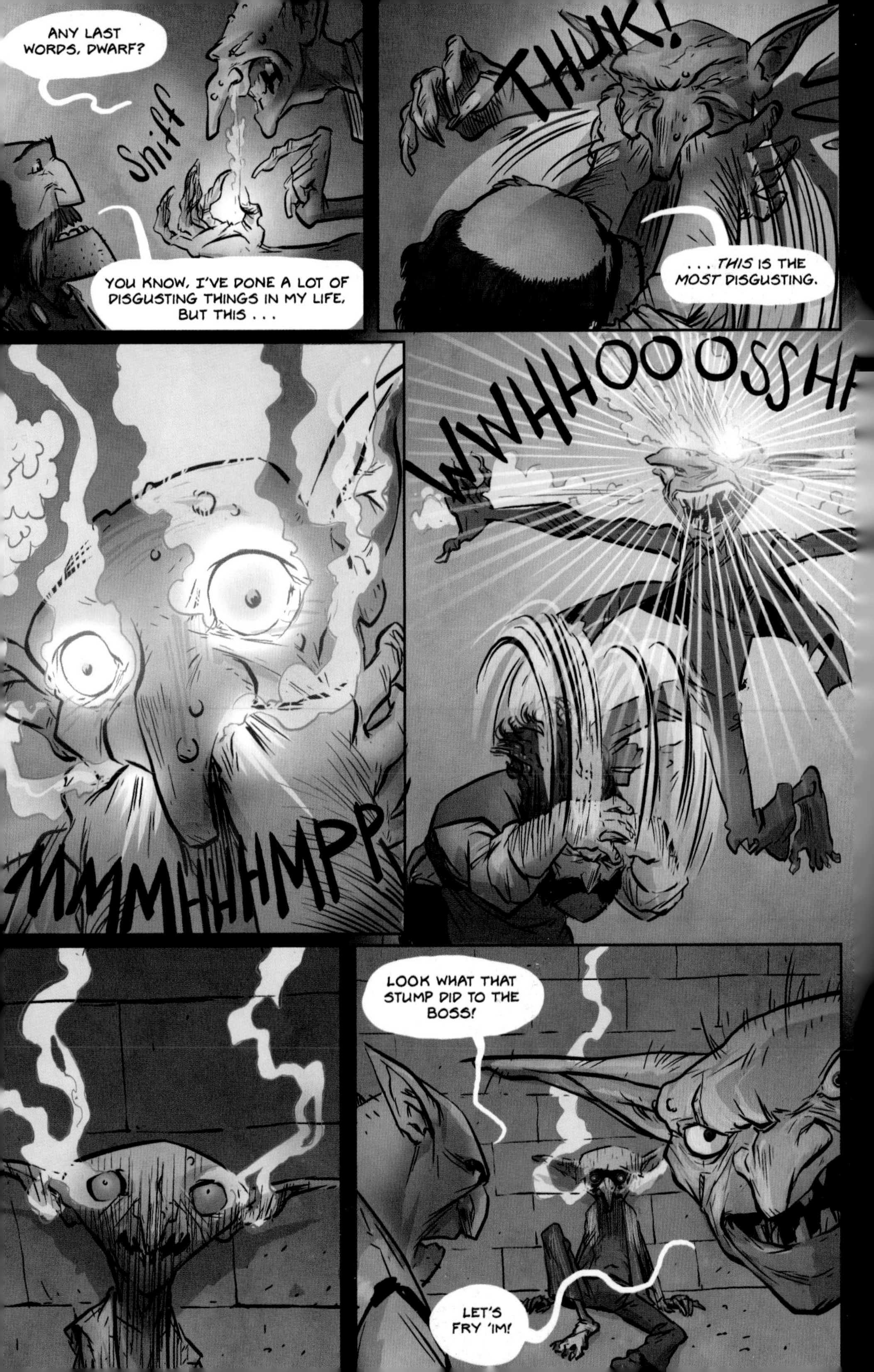
ANY LAST WORDS, DWARF?
Sniff
YOU KNOW, I'VE DONE A LOT OF DISGUSTING THINGS IN MY LIFE, BUT THIS . . .
THUK!
. . . *THIS* IS THE *MOST* DISGUSTING.
MMMHHHMPP
WWHHOOOSSH
LOOK WHAT THAT STUMP DID TO THE BOSS!
LET'S FRY 'IM!

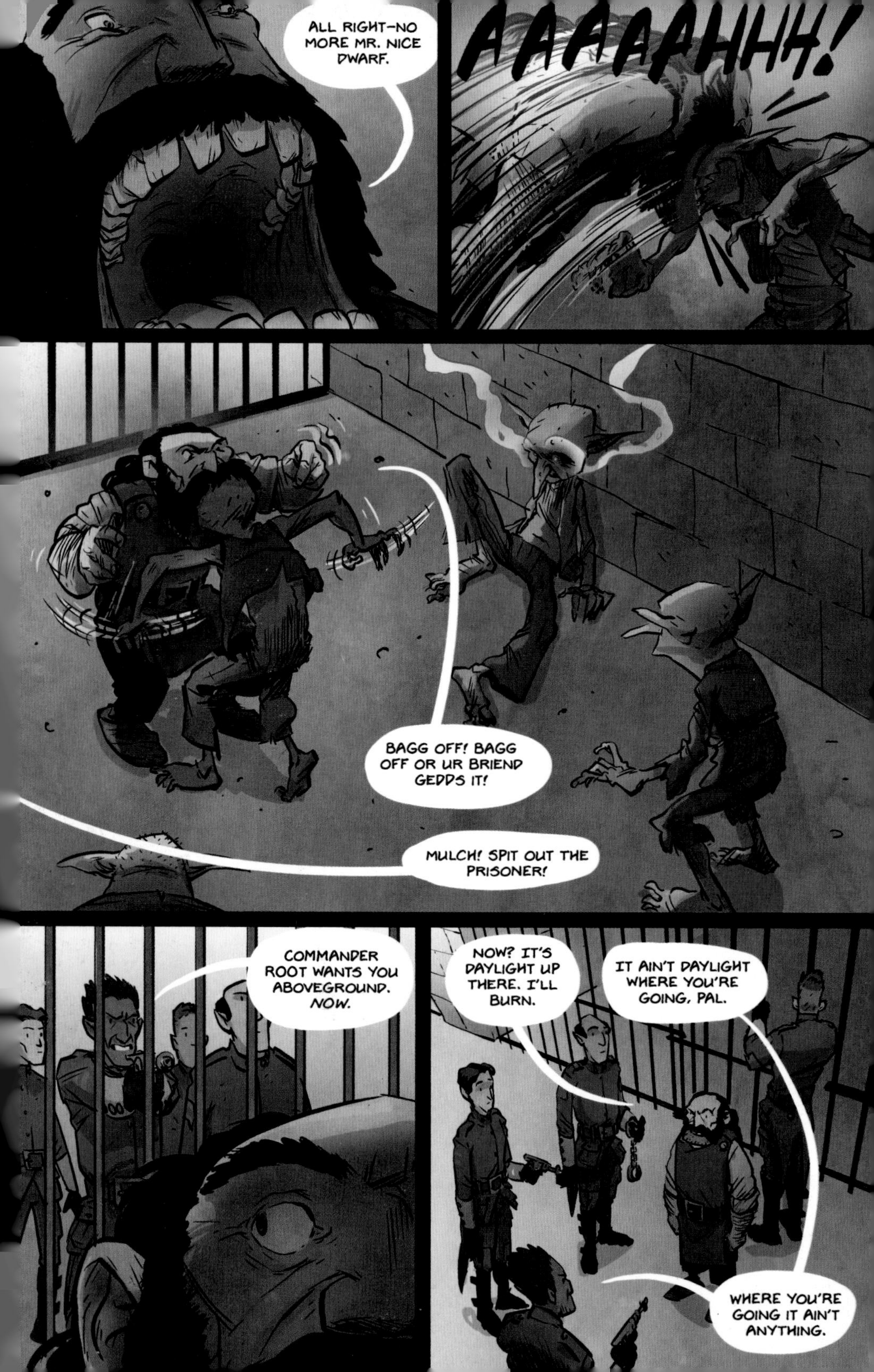
ALL RIGHT—NO MORE MR. NICE DWARF.
AAAAAHHH!
BAGG OFF! BAGG OFF OR UR BRIEND GEDDS IT!
MULCH! SPIT OUT THE PRISONER!
COMMANDER ROOT WANTS YOU ABOVEGROUND. *NOW.*
NOW? IT'S DAYLIGHT UP THERE. I'LL BURN.
IT AIN'T DAYLIGHT WHERE YOU'RE GOING, PAL.
WHERE YOU'RE GOING IT AIN'T ANYTHING.

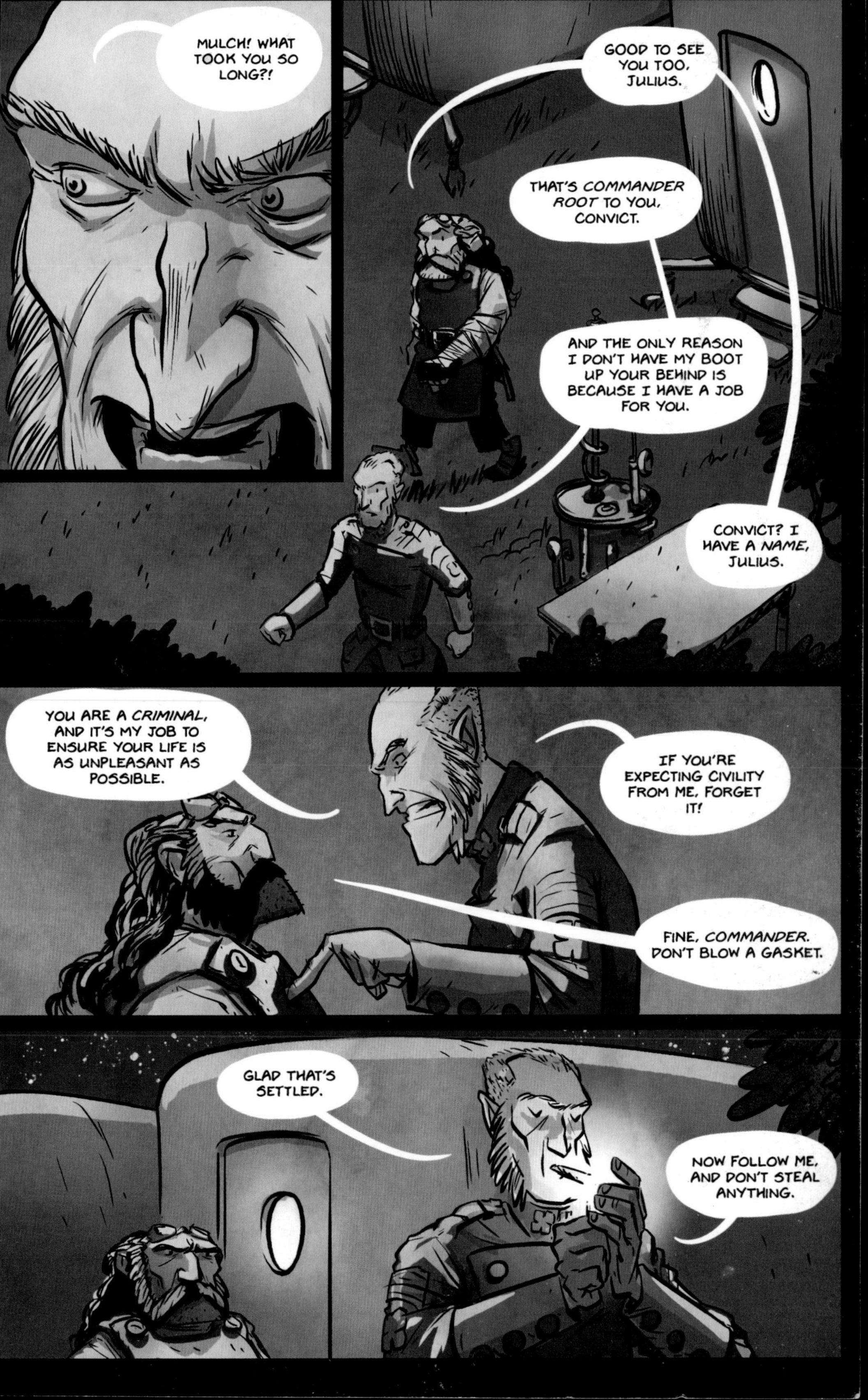
MULCH! WHAT TOOK YOU SO LONG?!
GOOD TO SEE YOU TOO, JULIUS.
THAT'S *COMMANDER ROOT* TO YOU, CONVICT.
AND THE ONLY REASON I DON'T HAVE MY BOOT UP YOUR BEHIND IS BECAUSE I HAVE A JOB FOR YOU.
CONVICT? I HAVE A *NAME*, JULIUS.
YOU ARE A *CRIMINAL*, AND IT'S MY JOB TO ENSURE YOUR LIFE IS AS UNPLEASANT AS POSSIBLE.
IF YOU'RE EXPECTING CIVILITY FROM ME, FORGET IT!
FINE, *COMMANDER*. DON'T BLOW A GASKET.
GLAD THAT'S SETTLED.
NOW FOLLOW ME, AND DON'T STEAL ANYTHING.

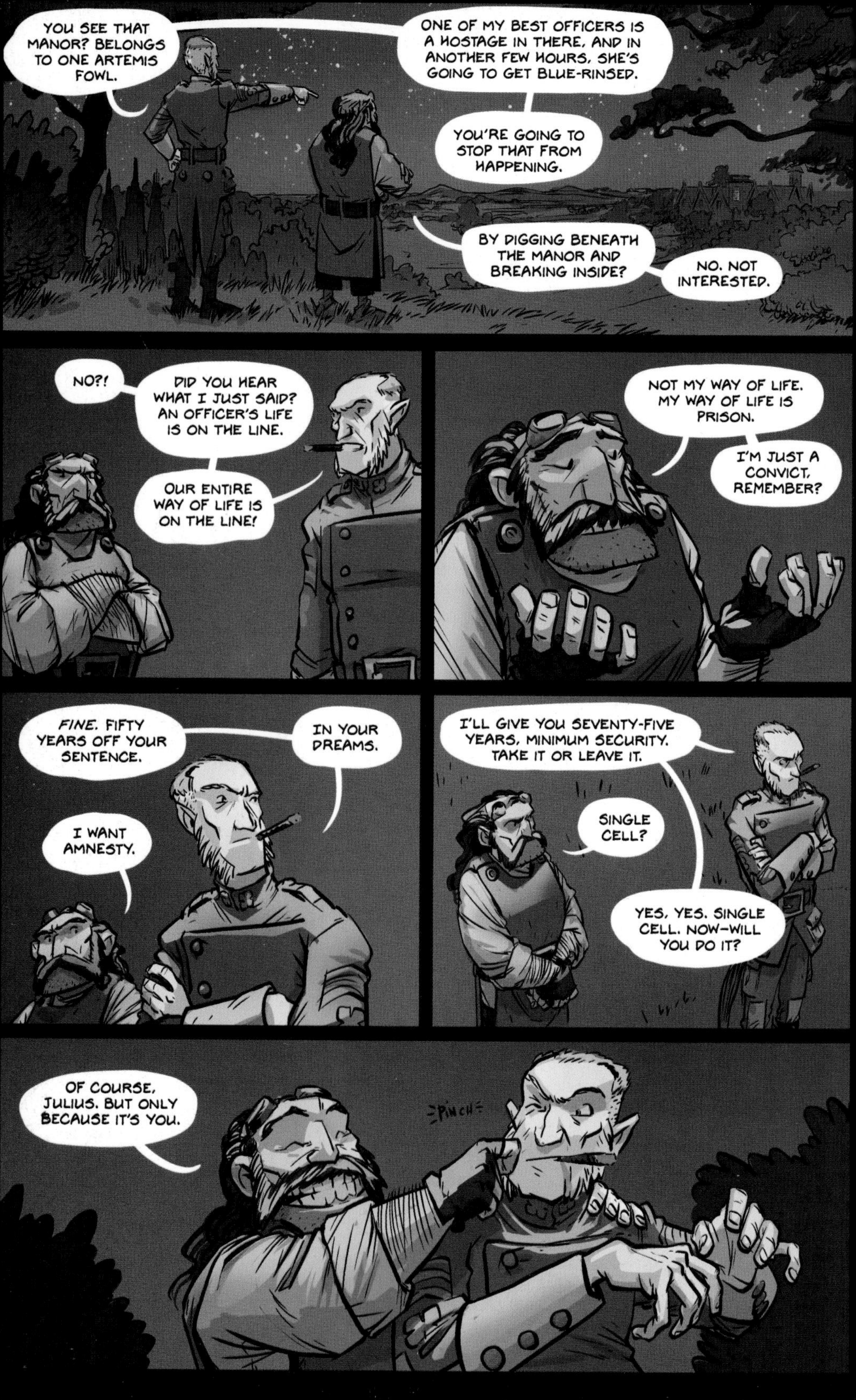
YOU SEE THAT MANOR? BELONGS TO ONE ARTEMIS FOWL.
ONE OF MY BEST OFFICERS IS A HOSTAGE IN THERE, AND IN ANOTHER FEW HOURS, SHE'S GOING TO GET BLUE-RINSED.
YOU'RE GOING TO STOP THAT FROM HAPPENING.
BY DIGGING BENEATH THE MANOR AND BREAKING INSIDE?
NO. NOT INTERESTED.
NO?!
DID YOU HEAR WHAT I JUST SAID? AN OFFICER'S LIFE IS ON THE LINE.
OUR ENTIRE WAY OF LIFE IS ON THE LINE!
NOT MY WAY OF LIFE. MY WAY OF LIFE IS PRISON.
I'M JUST A CONVICT, REMEMBER?
I WANT AMNESTY.
IN YOUR DREAMS.
FINE. FIFTY YEARS OFF YOUR SENTENCE.
I'LL GIVE YOU SEVENTY-FIVE YEARS, MINIMUM SECURITY. TAKE IT OR LEAVE IT.
SINGLE CELL?
YES, YES. SINGLE CELL. NOW—WILL YOU DO IT?
OF COURSE, JULIUS. BUT ONLY BECAUSE IT'S YOU.
PINCH

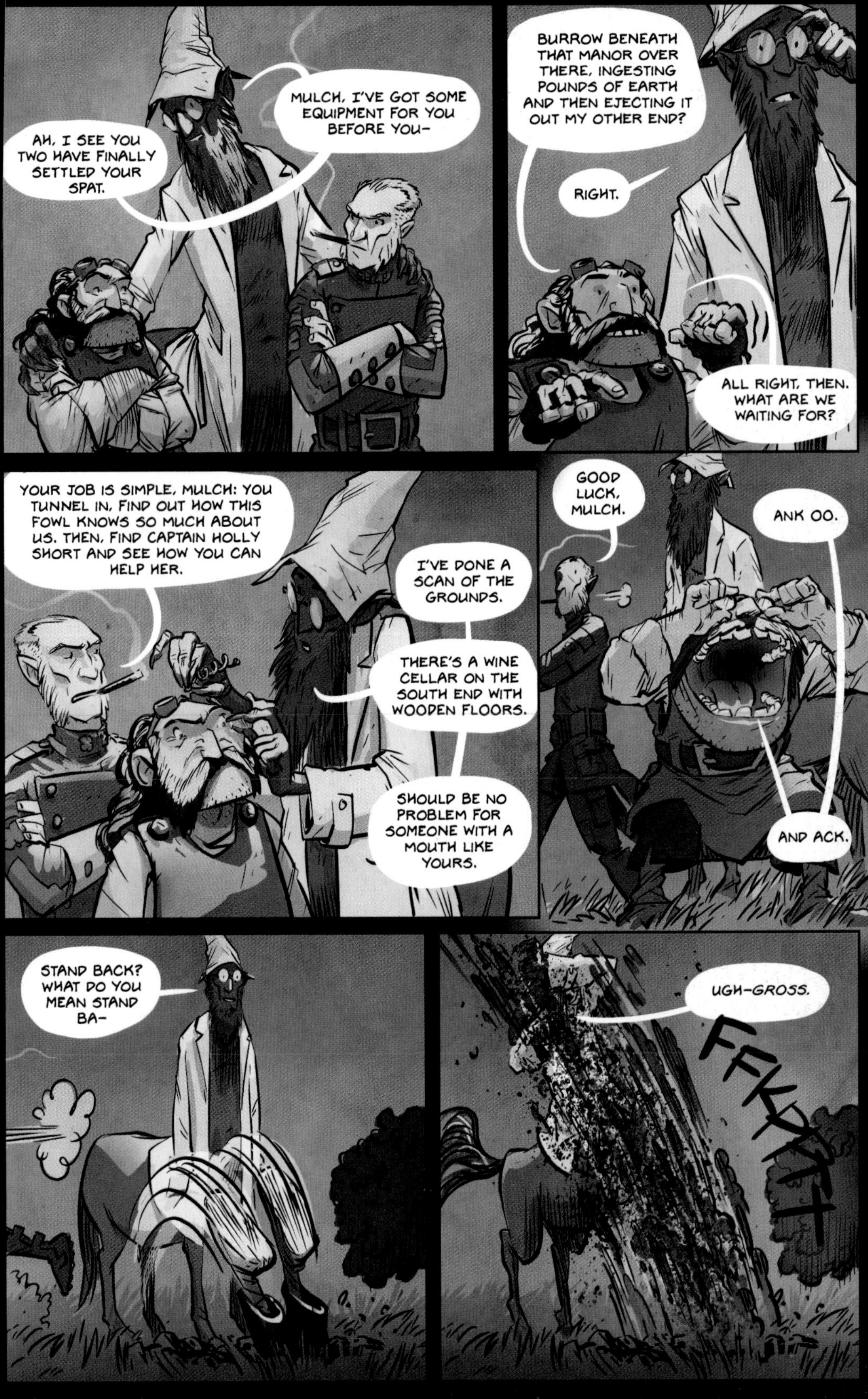

AH, I SEE YOU TWO HAVE FINALLY SETTLED YOUR SPAT.
MULCH, I'VE GOT SOME EQUIPMENT FOR YOU BEFORE YOU-
BURROW BENEATH THAT MANOR OVER THERE, INGESTING POUNDS OF EARTH AND THEN EJECTING IT OUT MY OTHER END?
RIGHT.
ALL RIGHT, THEN. WHAT ARE WE WAITING FOR?
YOUR JOB IS SIMPLE, MULCH: YOU TUNNEL IN, FIND OUT HOW THIS FOWL KNOWS SO MUCH ABOUT US. THEN, FIND CAPTAIN HOLLY SHORT AND SEE HOW YOU CAN HELP HER.
I'VE DONE A SCAN OF THE GROUNDS.
THERE'S A WINE CELLAR ON THE SOUTH END WITH WOODEN FLOORS.
SHOULD BE NO PROBLEM FOR SOMEONE WITH A MOUTH LIKE YOURS.
GOOD LUCK, MULCH.
ANK OO.
AND ACK.
STAND BACK? WHAT DO YOU MEAN STAND BA-
UGH-GROSS.
FFKKTTT

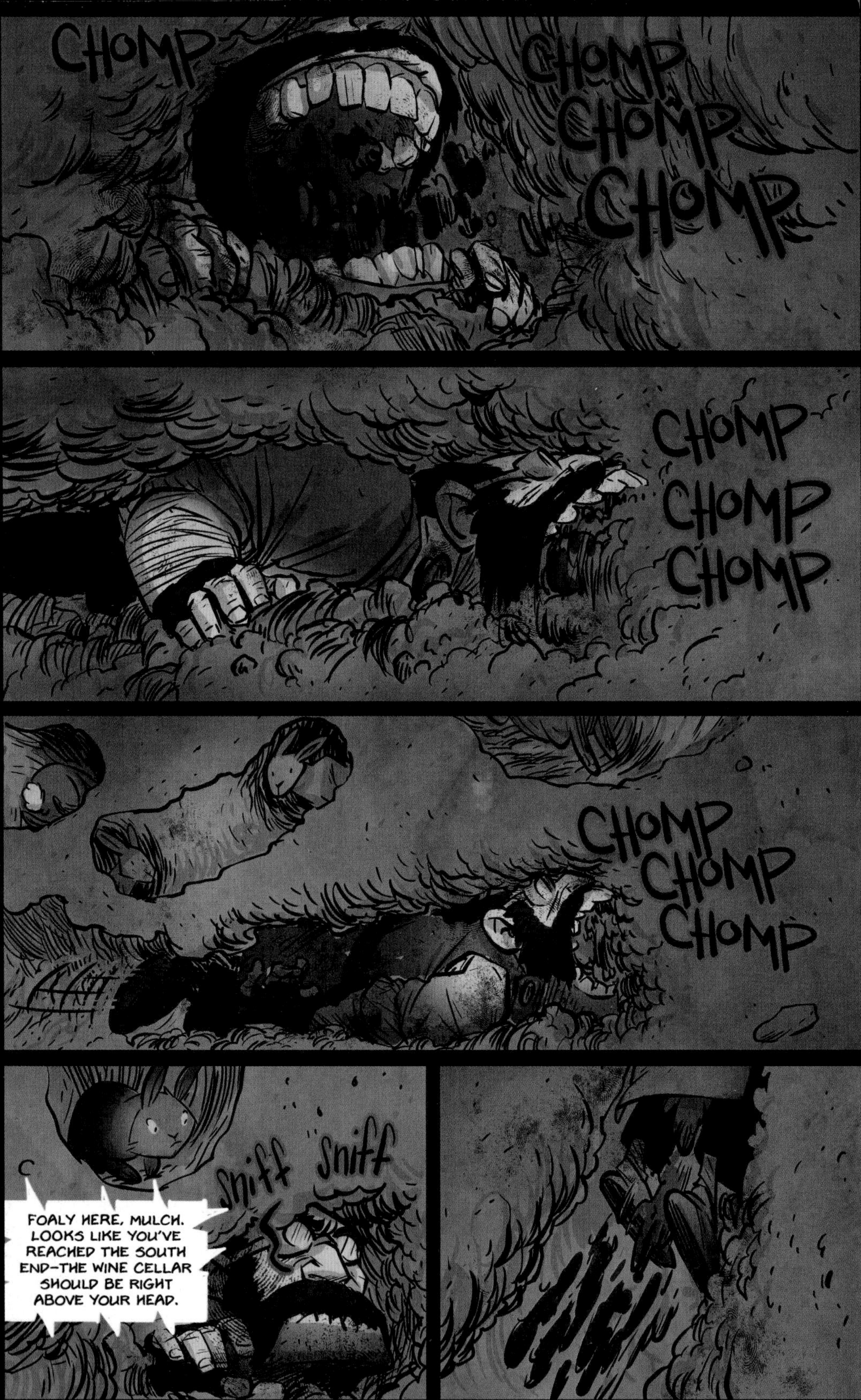
CHOMP
CHOMP
CHOMP
CHOMP
CHOMP
CHOMP
CHOMP
CHOMP
CHOMP
CHOMP
Sniff Sniff
FOALY HERE, MULCH. LOOKS LIKE YOU'VE REACHED THE SOUTH END—THE WINE CELLAR SHOULD BE RIGHT ABOVE YOUR HEAD.

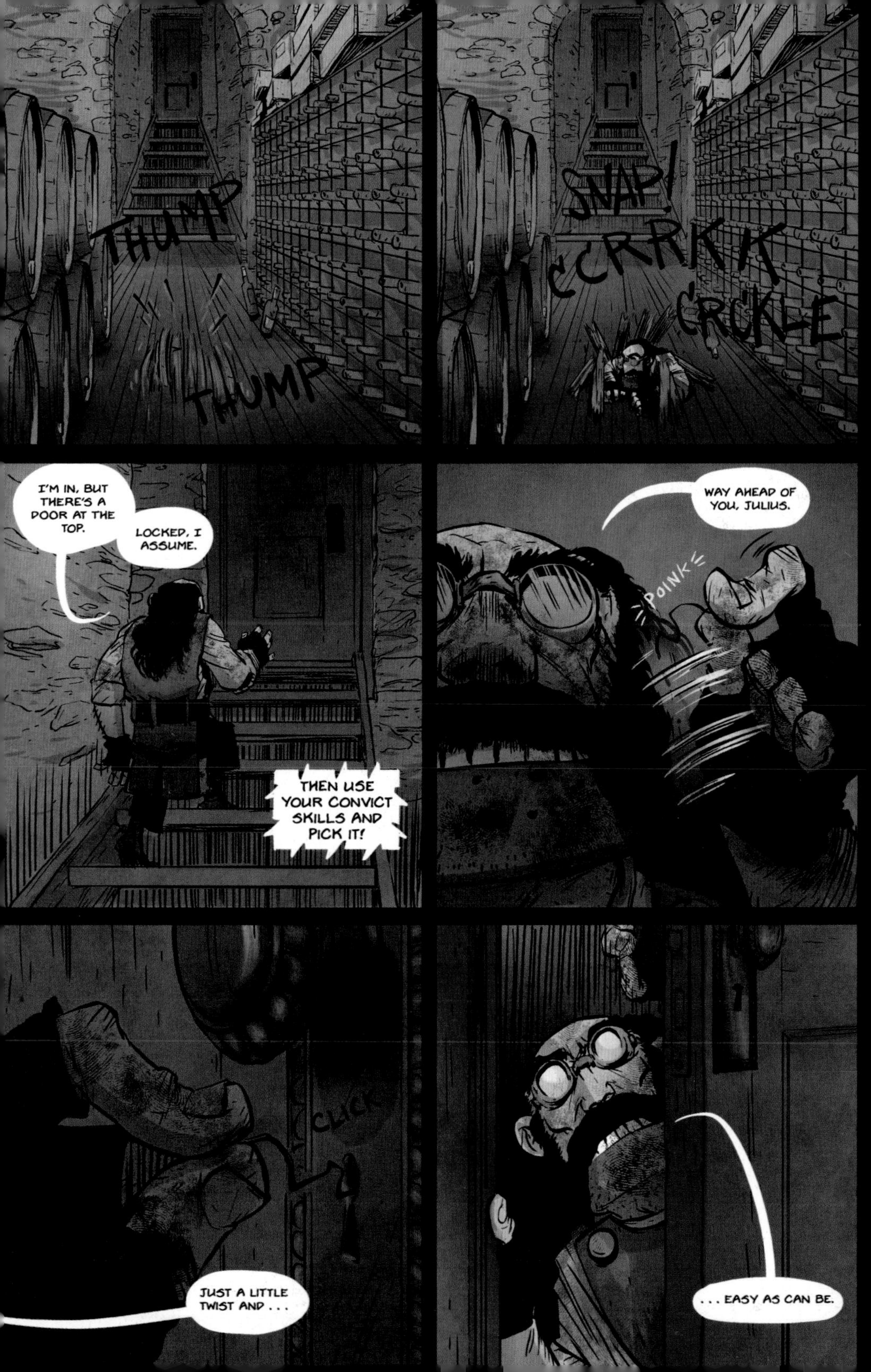
THUMP
THUMP
SNAP!
CCRRKKK
CRCKLE
I'M IN, BUT THERE'S A DOOR AT THE TOP.
LOCKED, I ASSUME.
THEN USE YOUR CONVICT SKILLS AND PICK IT!
WAY AHEAD OF YOU, JULIUS.
POINK
CLICK
JUST A LITTLE TWIST AND . . .
. . . EASY AS CAN BE.

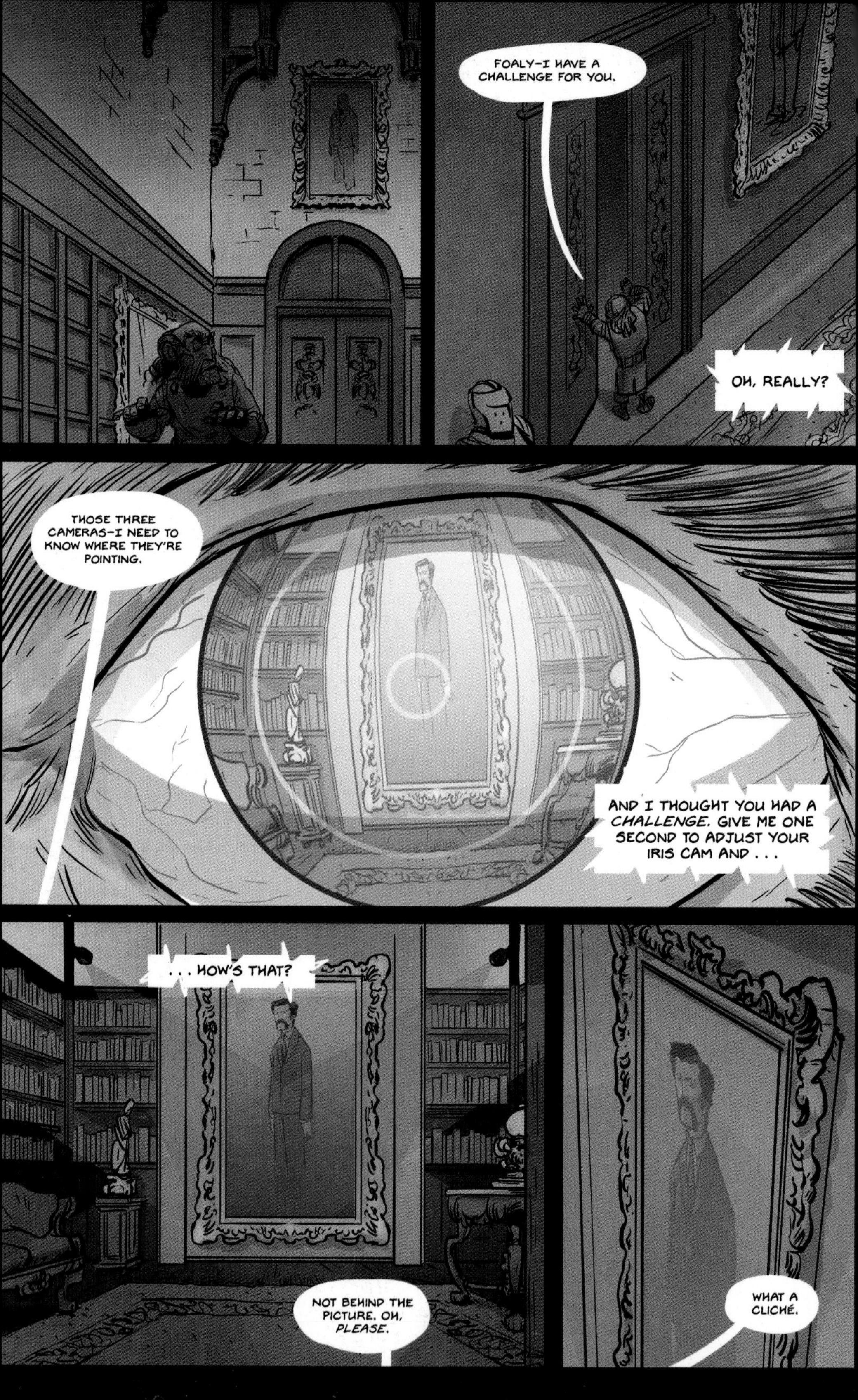
FOALY—I HAVE A CHALLENGE FOR YOU.
OH, REALLY?
THOSE THREE CAMERAS—I NEED TO KNOW WHERE THEY'RE POINTING.
AND I THOUGHT YOU HAD A *CHALLENGE*. GIVE ME ONE SECOND TO ADJUST YOUR IRIS CAM AND . . .
. . . HOW'S THAT?
NOT BEHIND THE PICTURE. OH, *PLEASE*.
WHAT A CLICHÉ.

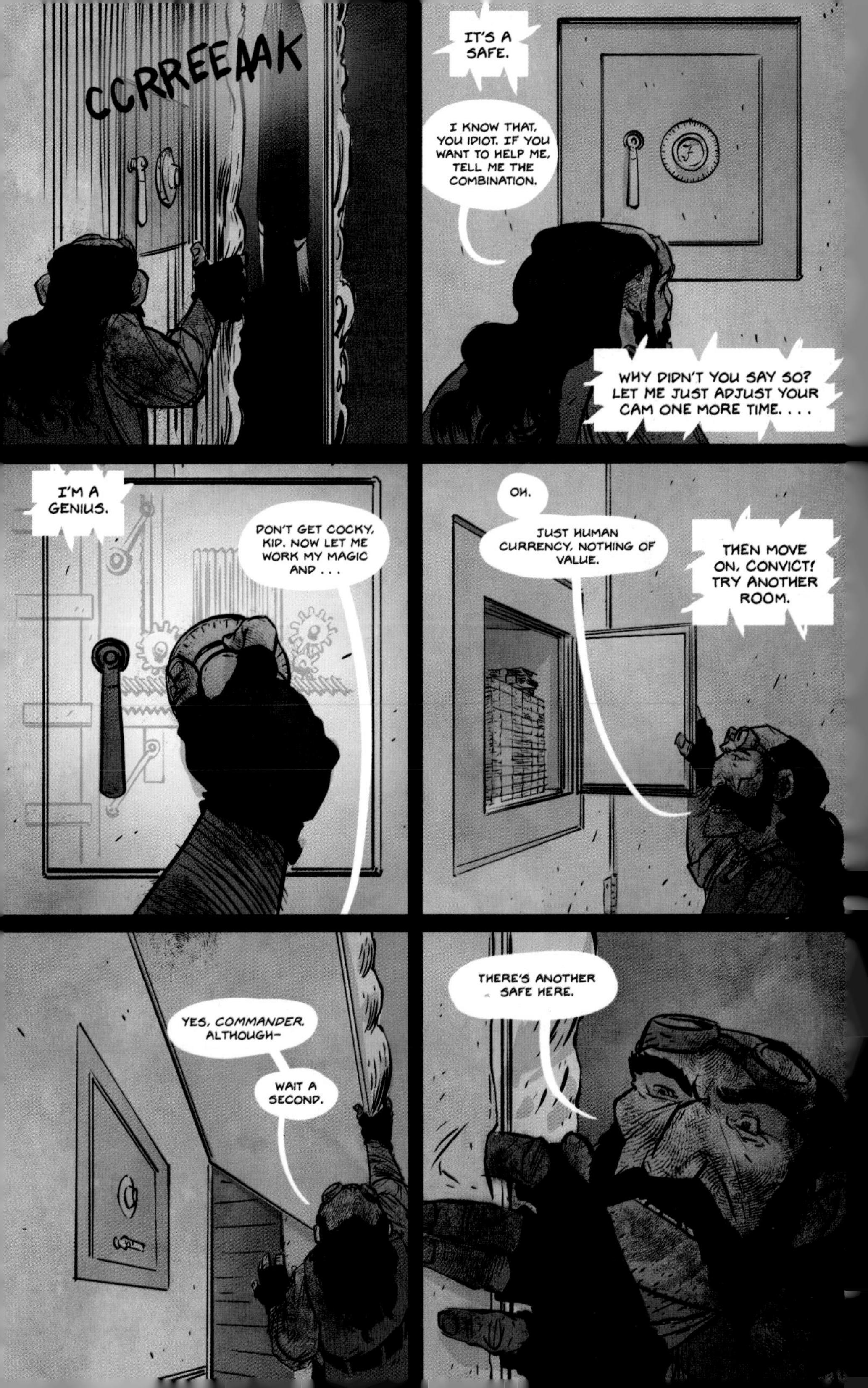
CCRREEAAK
IT'S A SAFE.
I KNOW THAT, YOU IDIOT. IF YOU WANT TO HELP ME, TELL ME THE COMBINATION.
WHY DIDN'T YOU SAY SO? LET ME JUST ADJUST YOUR CAM ONE MORE TIME. . . .
I'M A GENIUS.
DON'T GET COCKY, KID. NOW LET ME WORK MY MAGIC AND . . .
OH.
JUST HUMAN CURRENCY, NOTHING OF VALUE.
THEN MOVE ON, CONVICT! TRY ANOTHER ROOM.
YES, COMMANDER. ALTHOUGH–
WAIT A SECOND.
THERE'S ANOTHER SAFE HERE.

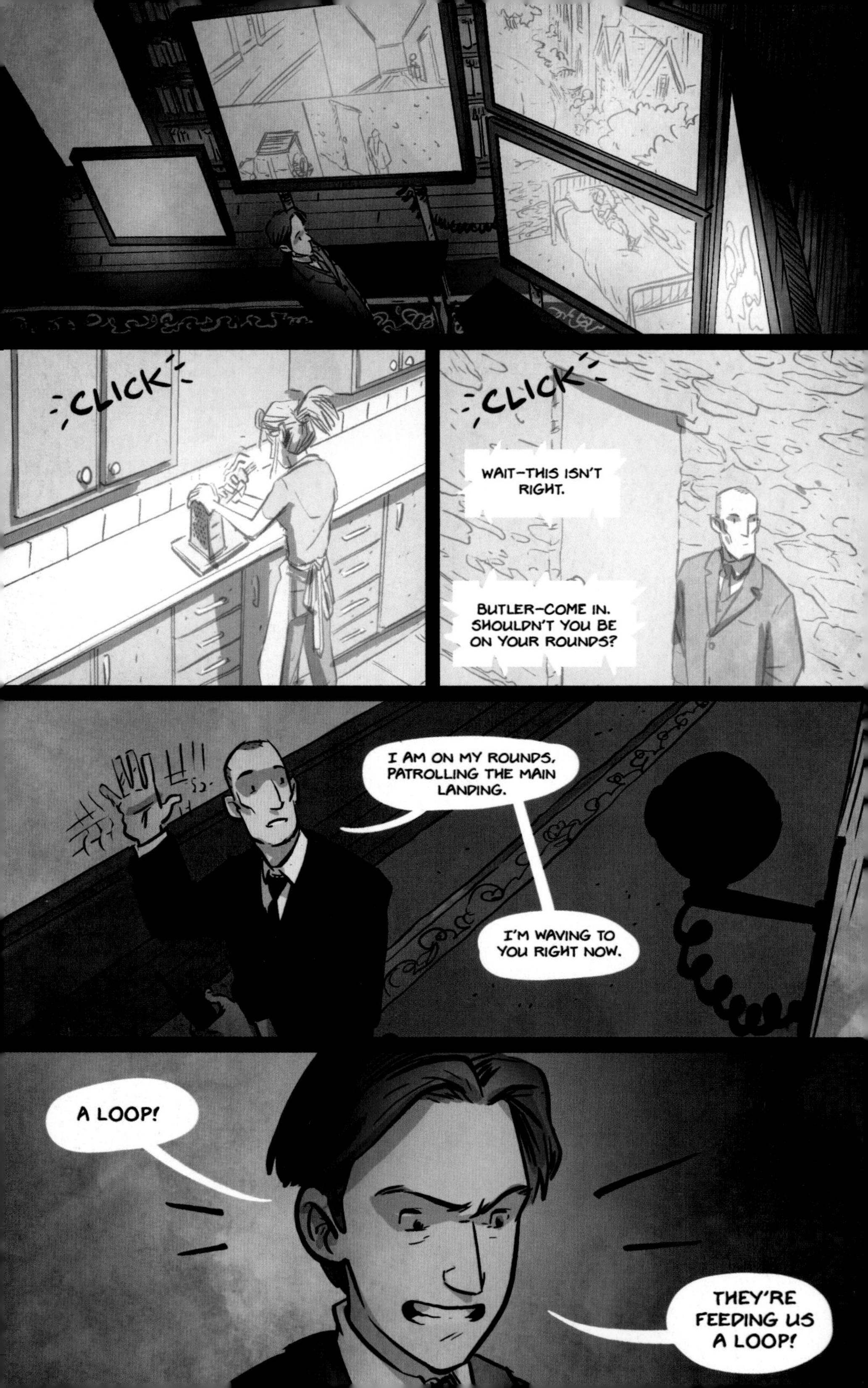
CLICK
CLICK
WAIT—THIS ISN'T RIGHT.
BUTLER—COME IN. SHOULDN'T YOU BE ON YOUR ROUNDS?
I AM ON MY ROUNDS, PATROLLING THE MAIN LANDING.
I'M WAVING TO YOU RIGHT NOW.
A LOOP!
THEY'RE FEEDING US A LOOP!

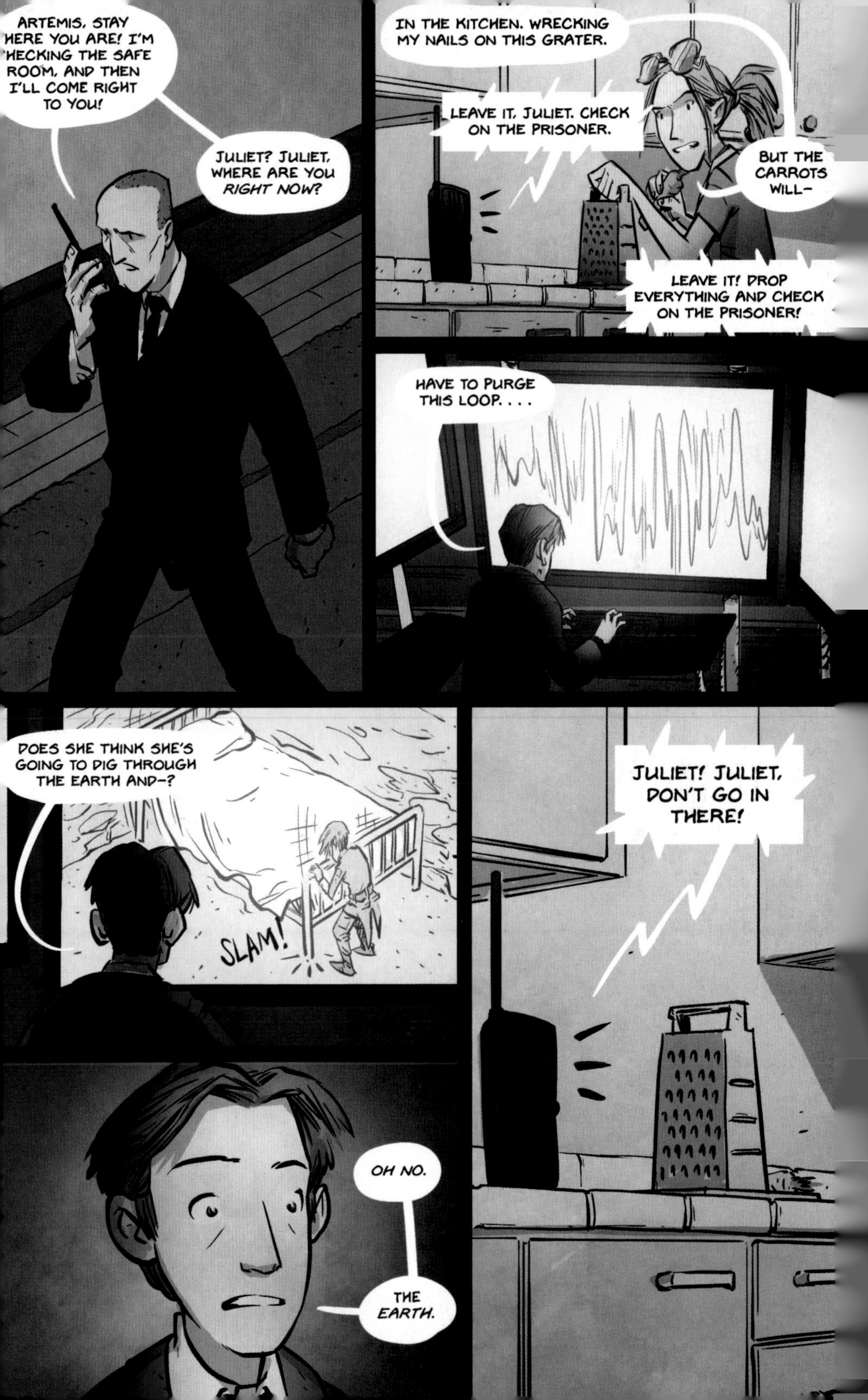
ARTEMIS, STAY HERE YOU ARE! I'M CHECKING THE SAFE ROOM, AND THEN I'LL COME RIGHT TO YOU!
JULIET? JULIET, WHERE ARE YOU *RIGHT NOW*?
IN THE KITCHEN. WRECKING MY NAILS ON THIS GRATER.
LEAVE IT, JULIET. CHECK ON THE PRISONER.
BUT THE CARROTS WILL—
LEAVE IT! DROP EVERYTHING AND CHECK ON THE PRISONER!
HAVE TO PURGE THIS LOOP. . . .
DOES SHE THINK SHE'S GOING TO DIG THROUGH THE EARTH AND—?
SLAM!
OH NO.
THE *EARTH*.
JULIET! JULIET, DON'T GO IN THERE!

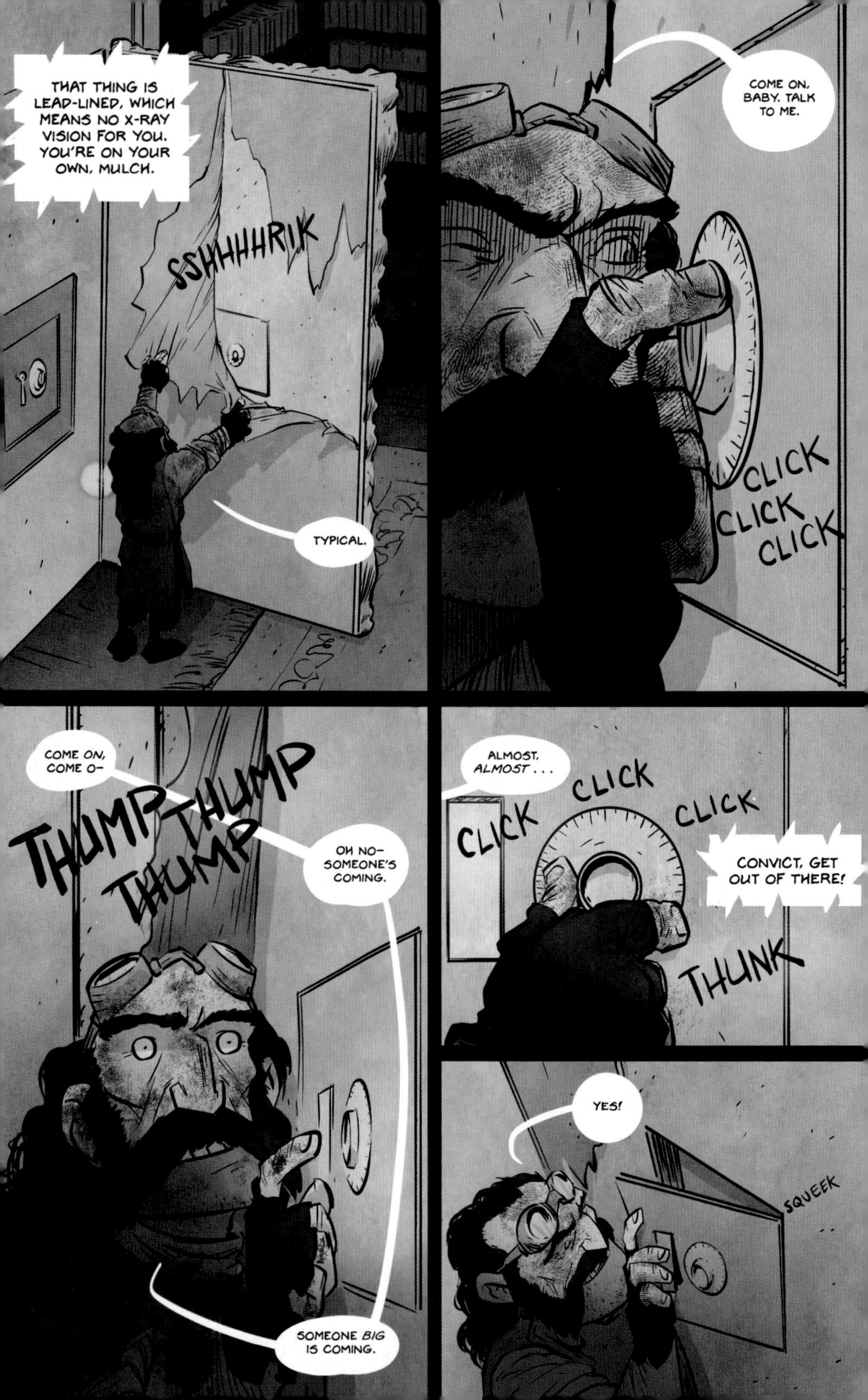
THAT THING IS LEAD-LINED, WHICH MEANS NO X-RAY VISION FOR YOU. YOU'RE ON YOUR OWN, MULCH.
SSHHHHRIK
TYPICAL.
COME ON, BABY. TALK TO ME.
CLICK
CLICK
CLICK
COME ON, COME O-
THUMP
THUMP
THUMP
OH NO- SOMEONE'S COMING.
SOMEONE *BIG* IS COMING.
ALMOST, *ALMOST* . . .
CLICK
CLICK
CLICK
CONVICT, GET OUT OF THERE!
THUNK
YES!
SQUEEK

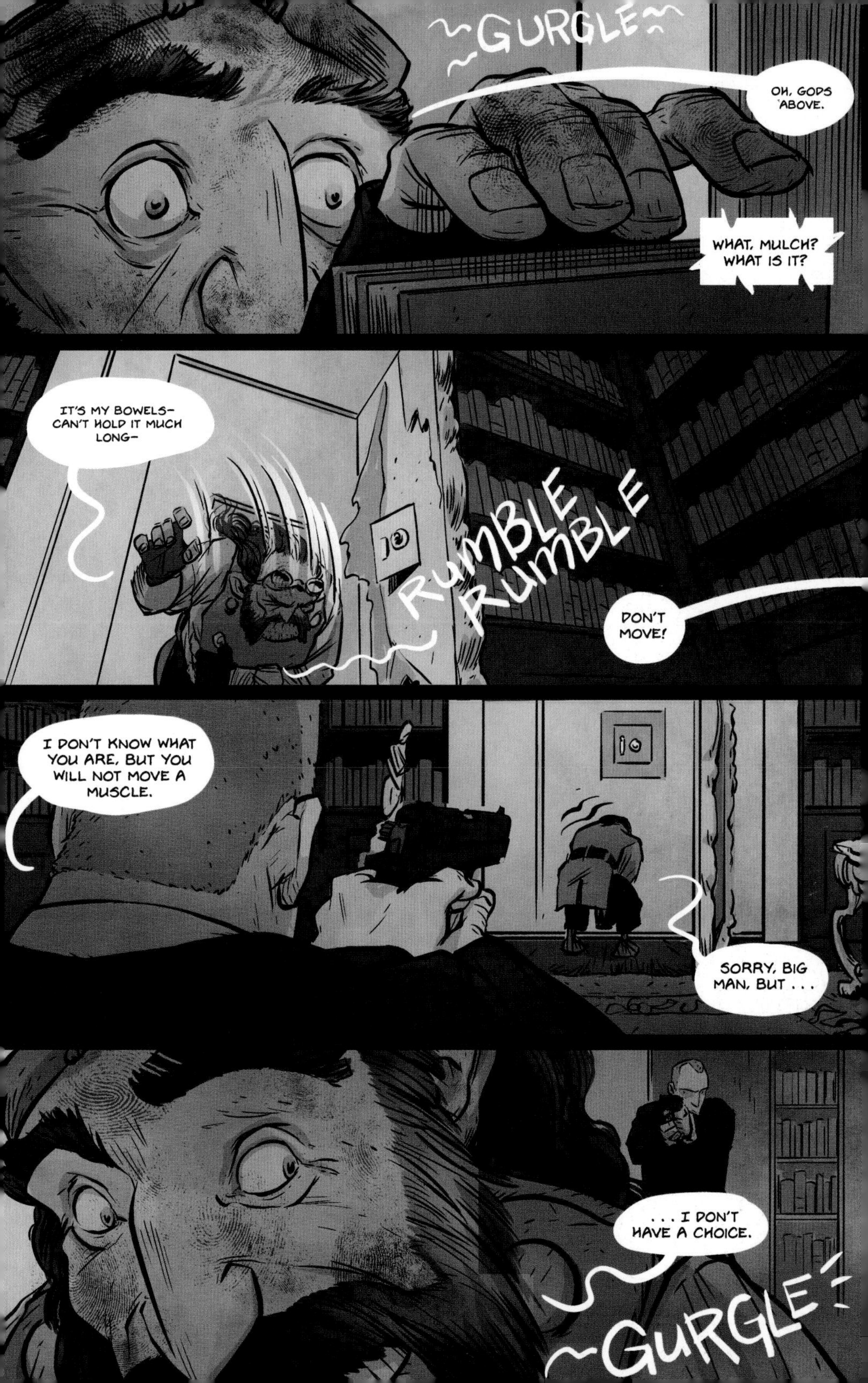
~GURGLE~
OH, GODS ABOVE.
WHAT, MULCH? WHAT IS IT?
IT'S MY BOWELS— CAN'T HOLD IT MUCH LONG—
RUMBLE RUMBLE
DON'T MOVE!
I DON'T KNOW WHAT YOU ARE, BUT YOU WILL NOT MOVE A MUSCLE.
SORRY, BIG MAN, BUT . . .
. . . I DON'T HAVE A CHOICE.
~GURGLE~

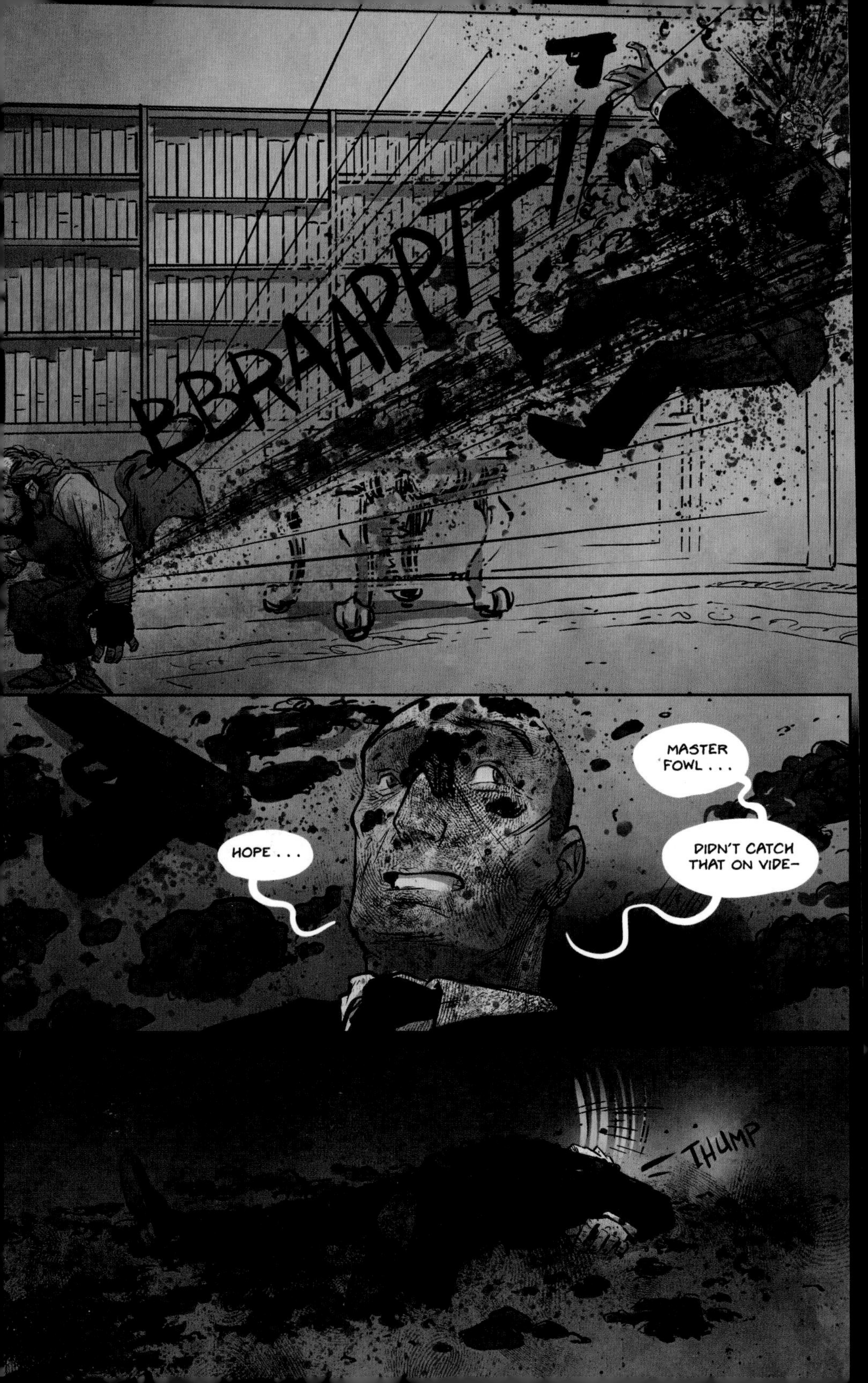
BBRAAPPTT!!
MASTER FOWL . . .
HOPE . . .
DIDN'T CATCH THAT ON VIDE–
THUMP

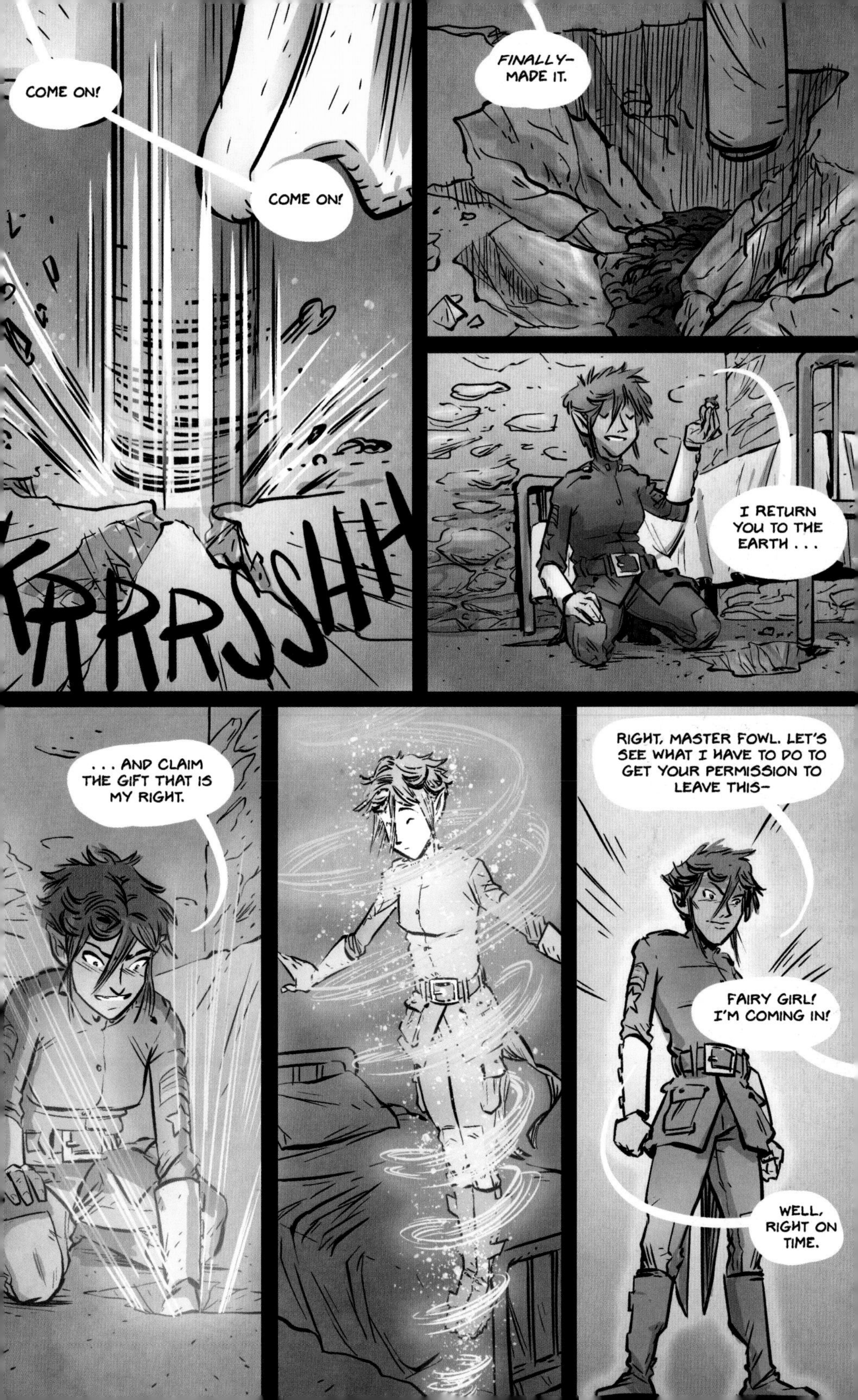
COME ON!
COME ON!
KRRRSSHH
FINALLY-
MADE IT.
I RETURN YOU TO THE EARTH . . .
. . . AND CLAIM THE GIFT THAT IS MY RIGHT.
RIGHT, MASTER FOWL. LET'S SEE WHAT I HAVE TO DO TO GET YOUR PERMISSION TO LEAVE THIS-
FAIRY GIRL! I'M COMING IN!
WELL, RIGHT ON TIME.

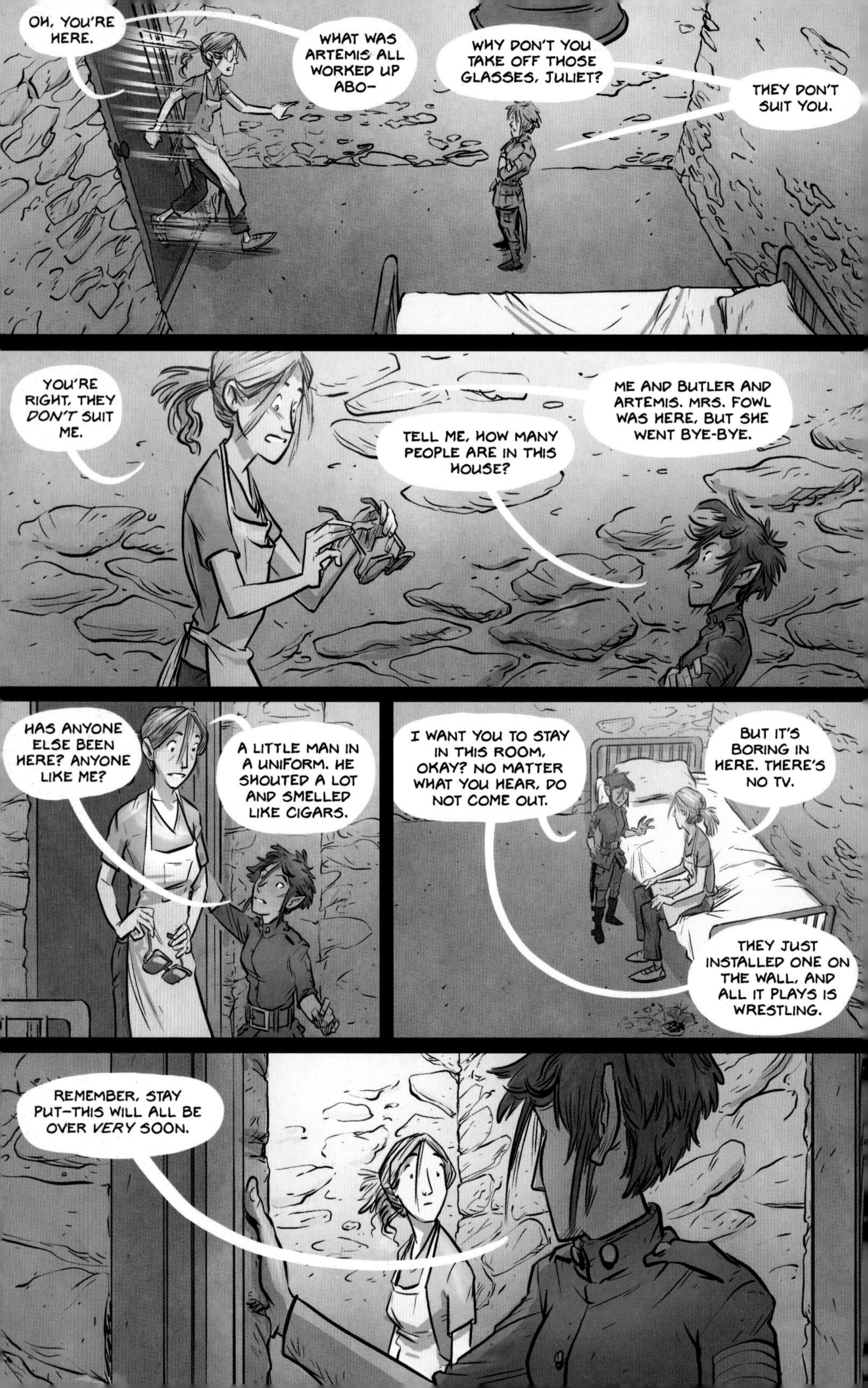
OH, YOU'RE HERE.
WHAT WAS ARTEMIS ALL WORKED UP ABO–
WHY DON'T YOU TAKE OFF THOSE GLASSES, JULIET?
THEY DON'T SUIT YOU.
YOU'RE RIGHT, THEY *DON'T* SUIT ME.
TELL ME, HOW MANY PEOPLE ARE IN THIS HOUSE?
ME AND BUTLER AND ARTEMIS. MRS. FOWL WAS HERE, BUT SHE WENT BYE-BYE.
HAS ANYONE ELSE BEEN HERE? ANYONE LIKE ME?
A LITTLE MAN IN A UNIFORM. HE SHOUTED A LOT AND SMELLED LIKE CIGARS.
I WANT YOU TO STAY IN THIS ROOM, OKAY? NO MATTER WHAT YOU HEAR, DO NOT COME OUT.
BUT IT'S BORING IN HERE. THERE'S NO TV.
THEY JUST INSTALLED ONE ON THE WALL, AND ALL IT PLAYS IS WRESTLING.
REMEMBER, STAY PUT–THIS WILL ALL BE OVER *VERY* SOON.

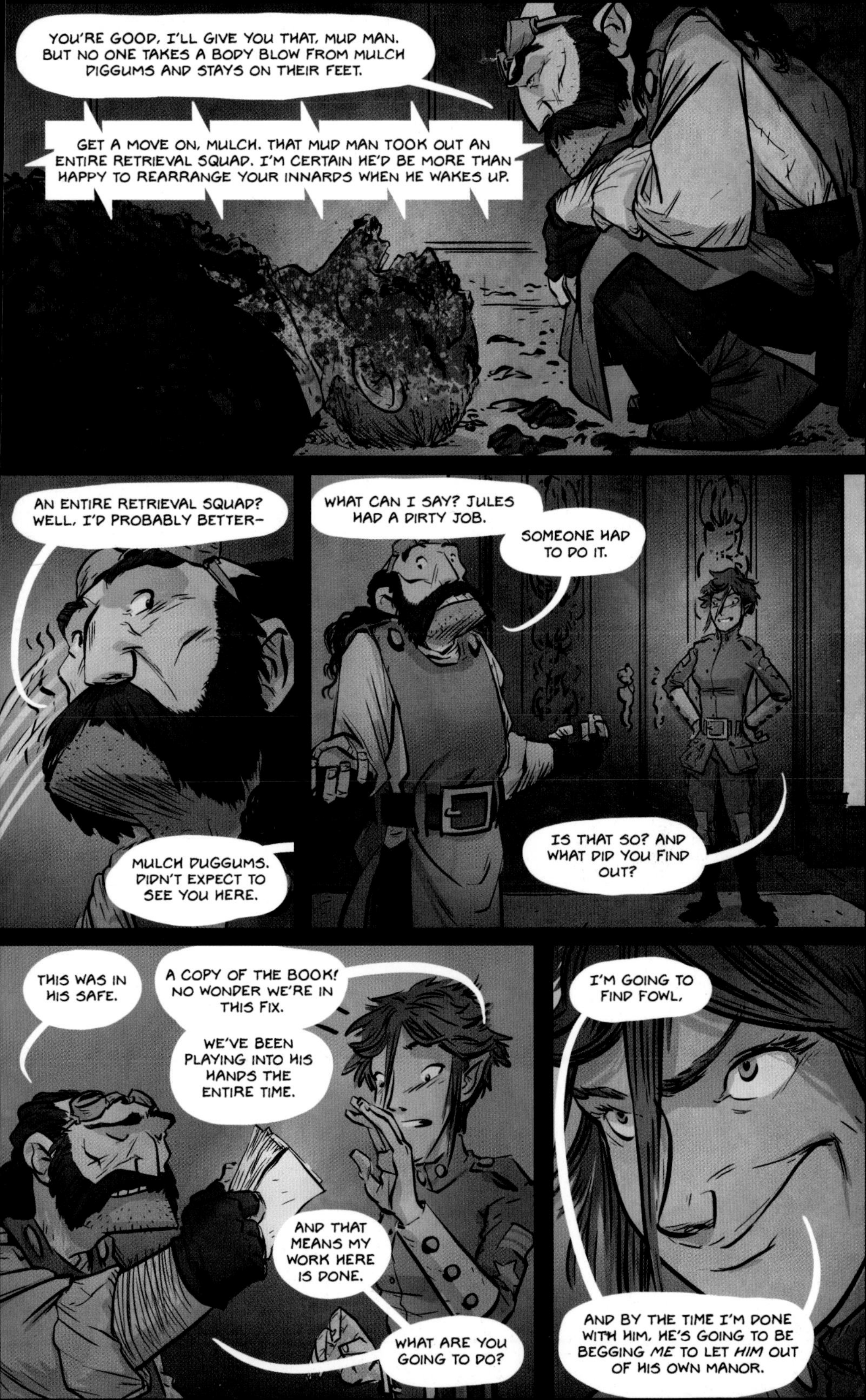
YOU'RE GOOD, I'LL GIVE YOU THAT, MUD MAN. BUT NO ONE TAKES A BODY BLOW FROM MULCH DIGGUMS AND STAYS ON THEIR FEET.
GET A MOVE ON, MULCH. THAT MUD MAN TOOK OUT AN ENTIRE RETRIEVAL SQUAD. I'M CERTAIN HE'D BE MORE THAN HAPPY TO REARRANGE YOUR INNARDS WHEN HE WAKES UP.
AN ENTIRE RETRIEVAL SQUAD? WELL, I'D PROBABLY BETTER-
MULCH DUGGUMS. DIDN'T EXPECT TO SEE YOU HERE.
WHAT CAN I SAY? JULES HAD A DIRTY JOB.
SOMEONE HAD TO DO IT.
IS THAT SO? AND WHAT DID YOU FIND OUT?
THIS WAS IN HIS SAFE.
A COPY OF THE BOOK! NO WONDER WE'RE IN THIS FIX.
WE'VE BEEN PLAYING INTO HIS HANDS THE ENTIRE TIME.
AND THAT MEANS MY WORK HERE IS DONE.
WHAT ARE YOU GOING TO DO?
I'M GOING TO FIND FOWL,
AND BY THE TIME I'M DONE WITH HIM, HE'S GOING TO BE BEGGING *ME* TO LET *HIM* OUT OF HIS OWN MANOR.

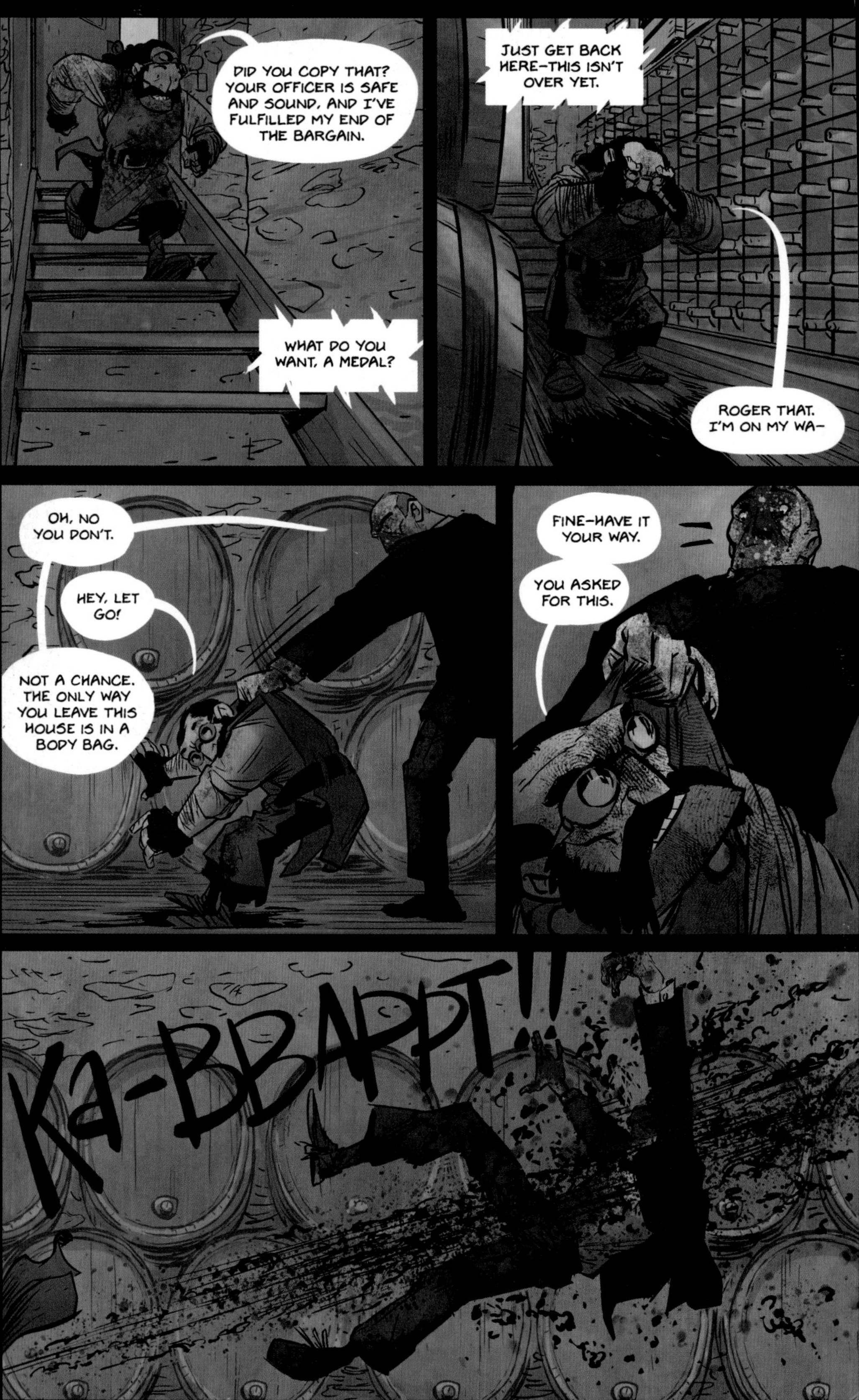
DID YOU COPY THAT? YOUR OFFICER IS SAFE AND SOUND, AND I'VE FULFILLED MY END OF THE BARGAIN.
WHAT DO YOU WANT, A MEDAL?
JUST GET BACK HERE—THIS ISN'T OVER YET.
ROGER THAT. I'M ON MY WA—
OH, NO YOU DON'T.
HEY, LET GO!
NOT A CHANCE. THE ONLY WAY YOU LEAVE THIS HOUSE IS IN A BODY BAG.
FINE—HAVE IT YOUR WAY.
YOU ASKED FOR THIS.
KA-BBAPPT!!

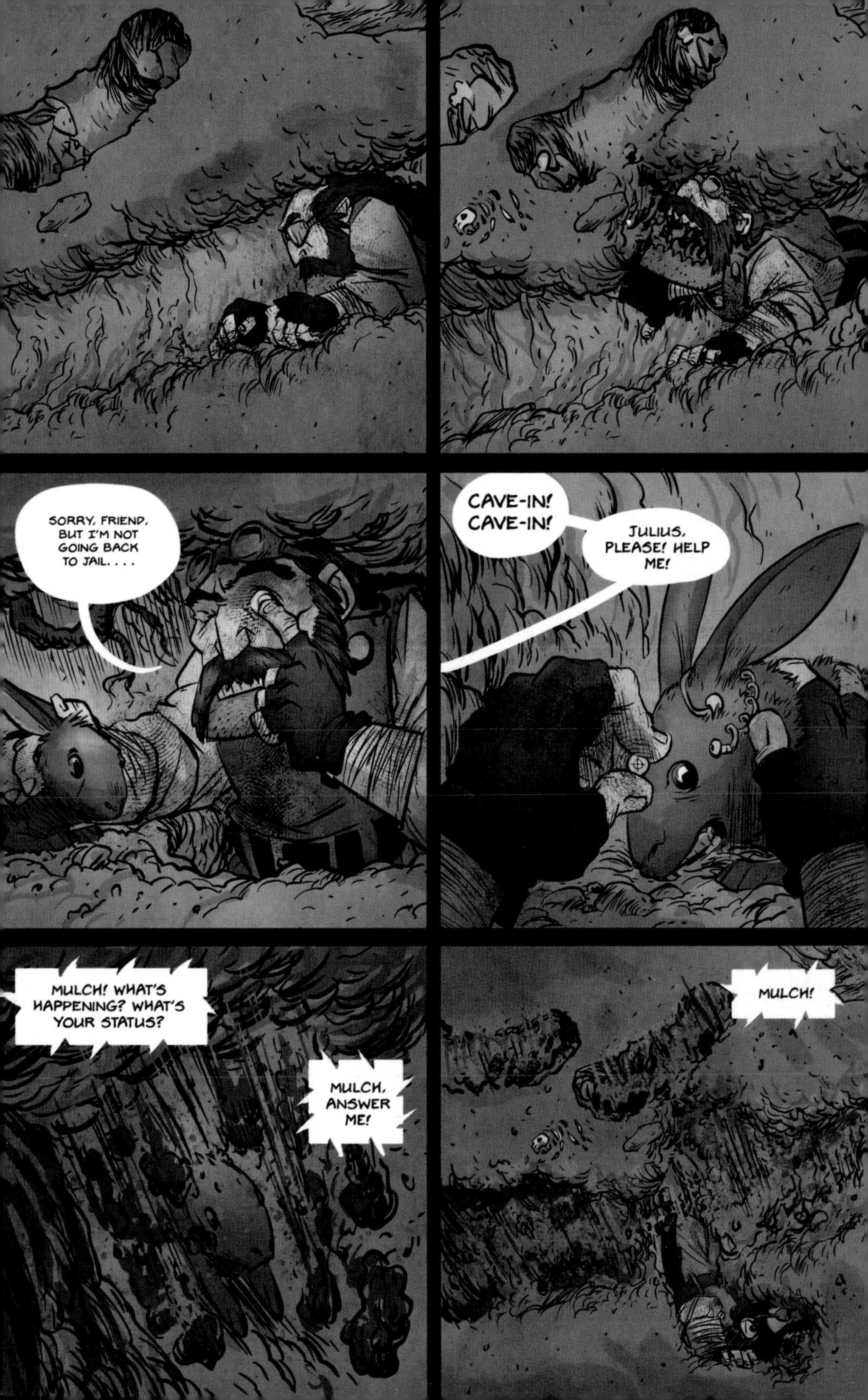
SORRY, FRIEND, BUT I'M NOT GOING BACK TO JAIL. . . .
CAVE-IN! CAVE-IN!
JULIUS, PLEASE! HELP ME!
MULCH! WHAT'S HAPPENING? WHAT'S YOUR STATUS?
MULCH, ANSWER ME!
MULCH!

CHAPTER EIGHT

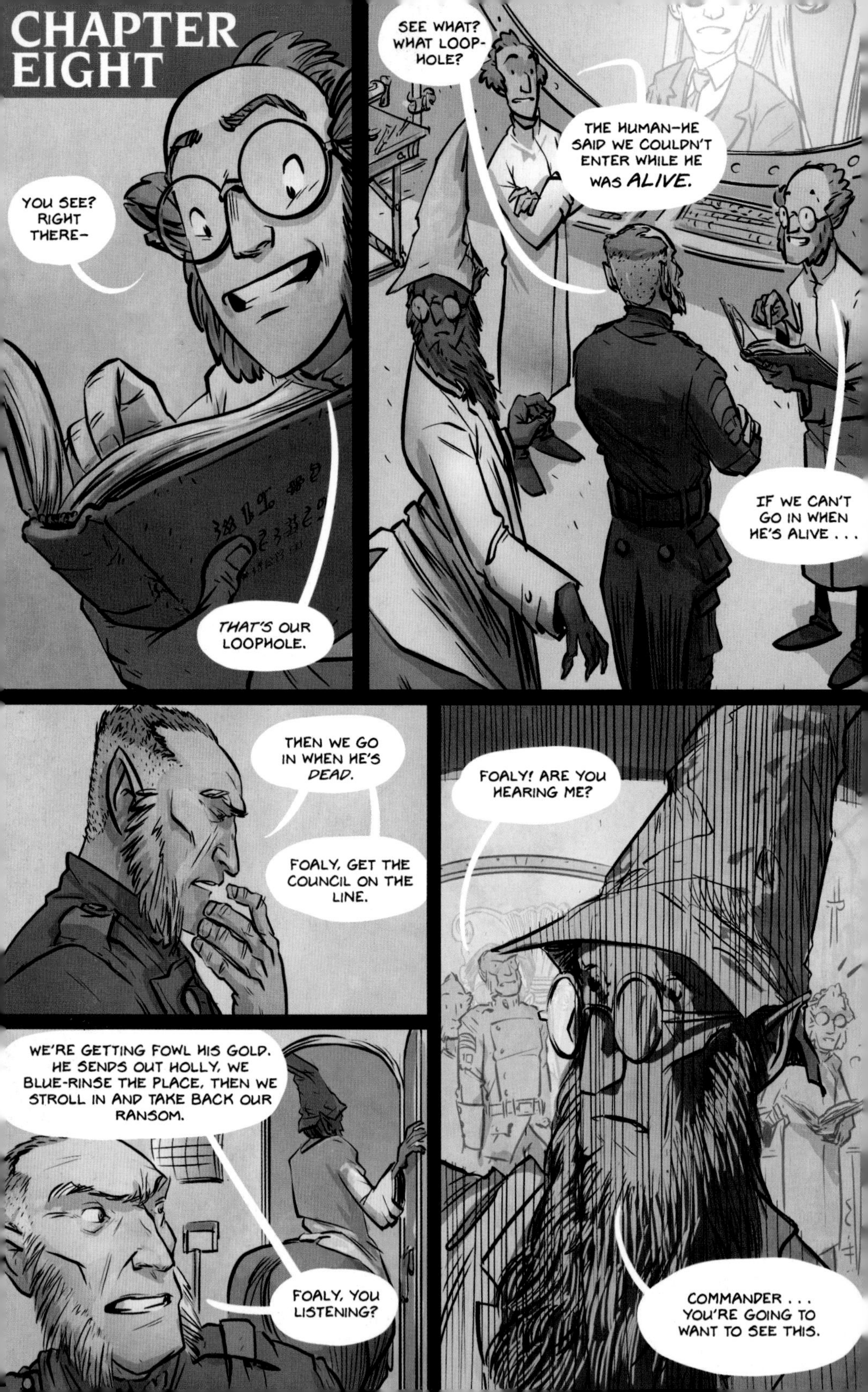

YOU SEE? RIGHT THERE–
THAT'S OUR LOOPHOLE.
SEE WHAT? WHAT LOOP-HOLE?
THE HUMAN–HE SAID WE COULDN'T ENTER WHILE HE WAS *ALIVE.*
IF WE CAN'T GO IN WHEN HE'S ALIVE . . .
THEN WE GO IN WHEN HE'S *DEAD.*
FOALY, GET THE COUNCIL ON THE LINE.
WE'RE GETTING FOWL HIS GOLD. HE SENDS OUT HOLLY, WE BLUE-RINSE THE PLACE, THEN WE STROLL IN AND TAKE BACK OUR RANSOM.
FOALY, YOU LISTENING?
FOALY! ARE YOU HEARING ME?
COMMANDER . . . YOU'RE GOING TO WANT TO SEE THIS.

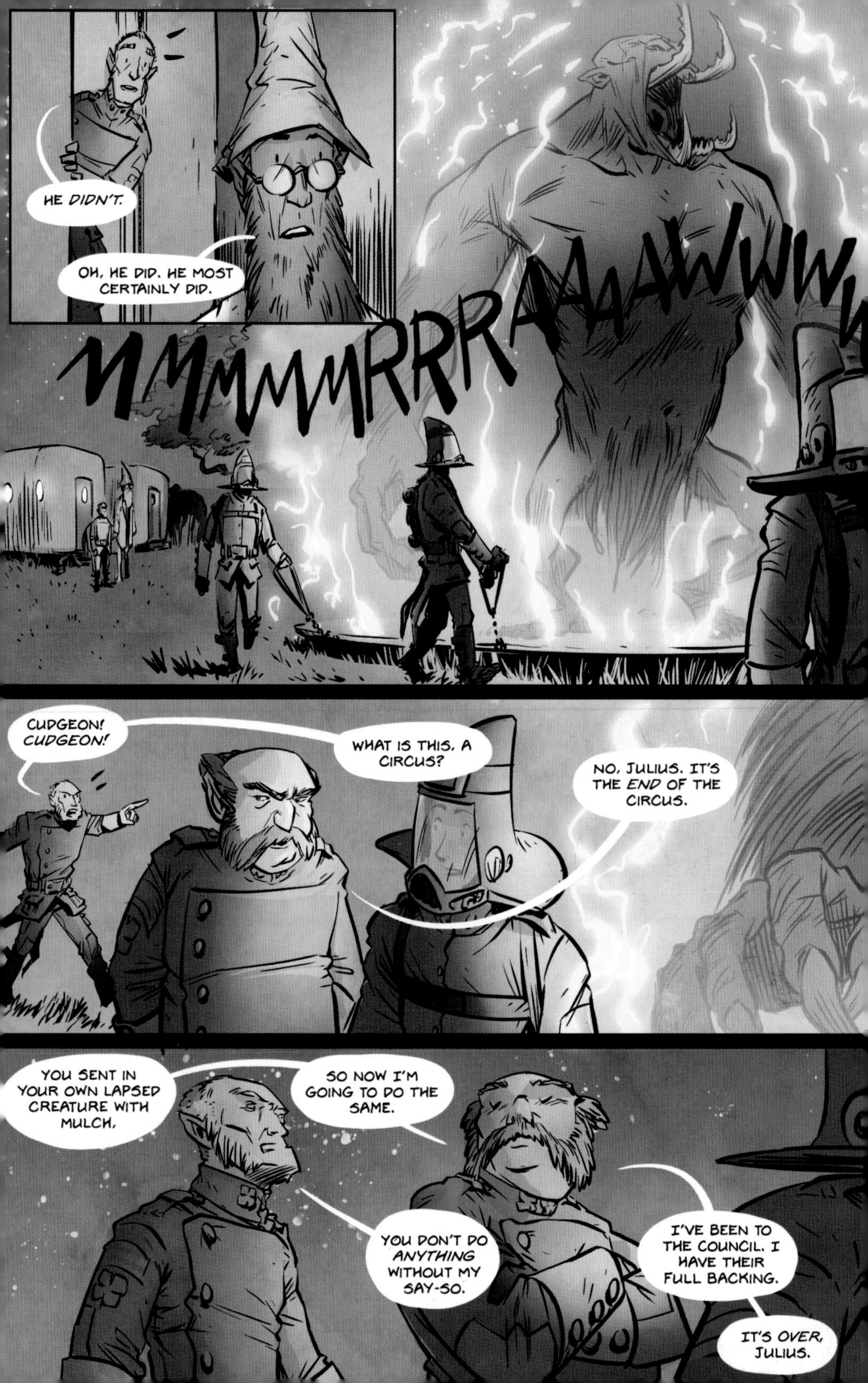
HE *DIDN'T.*
OH, HE DID. HE MOST CERTAINLY DID.
MMMMMRRRRAAAAAWWWWW
CUDGEON! *CUDGEON!*
WHAT IS THIS, A CIRCUS?
NO, JULIUS. IT'S THE *END* OF THE CIRCUS.
YOU SENT IN YOUR OWN LAPSED CREATURE WITH MULCH,
SO NOW I'M GOING TO DO THE SAME.
YOU DON'T DO *ANYTHING* WITHOUT MY SAY-SO.
I'VE BEEN TO THE COUNCIL. I HAVE THEIR FULL BACKING.
IT'S *OVER,* JULIUS.

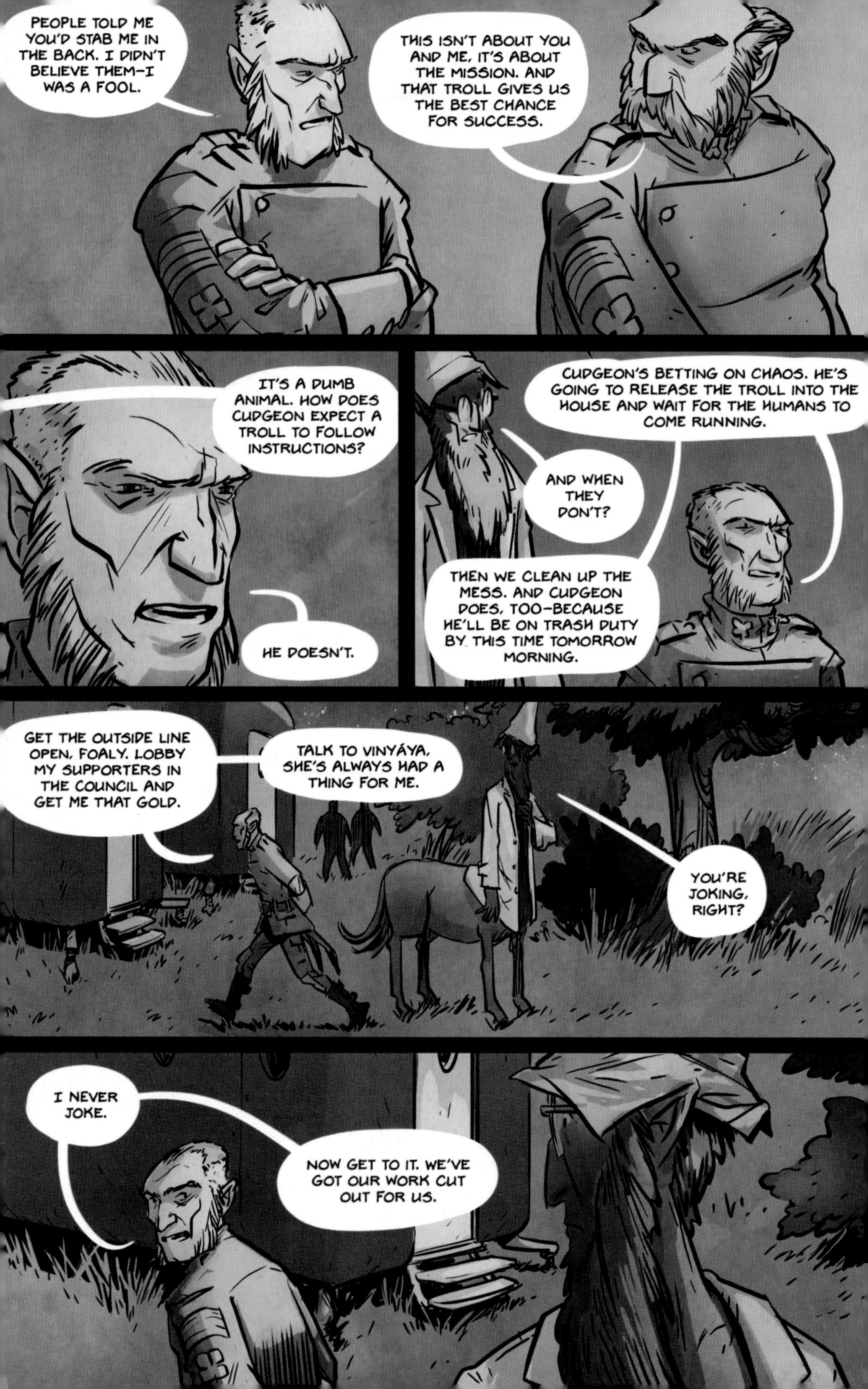
PEOPLE TOLD ME YOU'D STAB ME IN THE BACK. I DIDN'T BELIEVE THEM—I WAS A FOOL.
THIS ISN'T ABOUT YOU AND ME, IT'S ABOUT THE MISSION. AND THAT TROLL GIVES US THE BEST CHANCE FOR SUCCESS.
IT'S A DUMB ANIMAL. HOW DOES CUDGEON EXPECT A TROLL TO FOLLOW INSTRUCTIONS?
HE DOESN'T.
CUDGEON'S BETTING ON CHAOS. HE'S GOING TO RELEASE THE TROLL INTO THE HOUSE AND WAIT FOR THE HUMANS TO COME RUNNING.
AND WHEN THEY DON'T?
THEN WE CLEAN UP THE MESS. AND CUDGEON DOES, TOO—BECAUSE HE'LL BE ON TRASH DUTY BY THIS TIME TOMORROW MORNING.
GET THE OUTSIDE LINE OPEN, FOALY. LOBBY MY SUPPORTERS IN THE COUNCIL AND GET ME THAT GOLD.
TALK TO VINYÁYA, SHE'S ALWAYS HAD A THING FOR ME.
YOU'RE JOKING, RIGHT?
I NEVER JOKE.
NOW GET TO IT. WE'VE GOT OUR WORK CUT OUT FOR US.

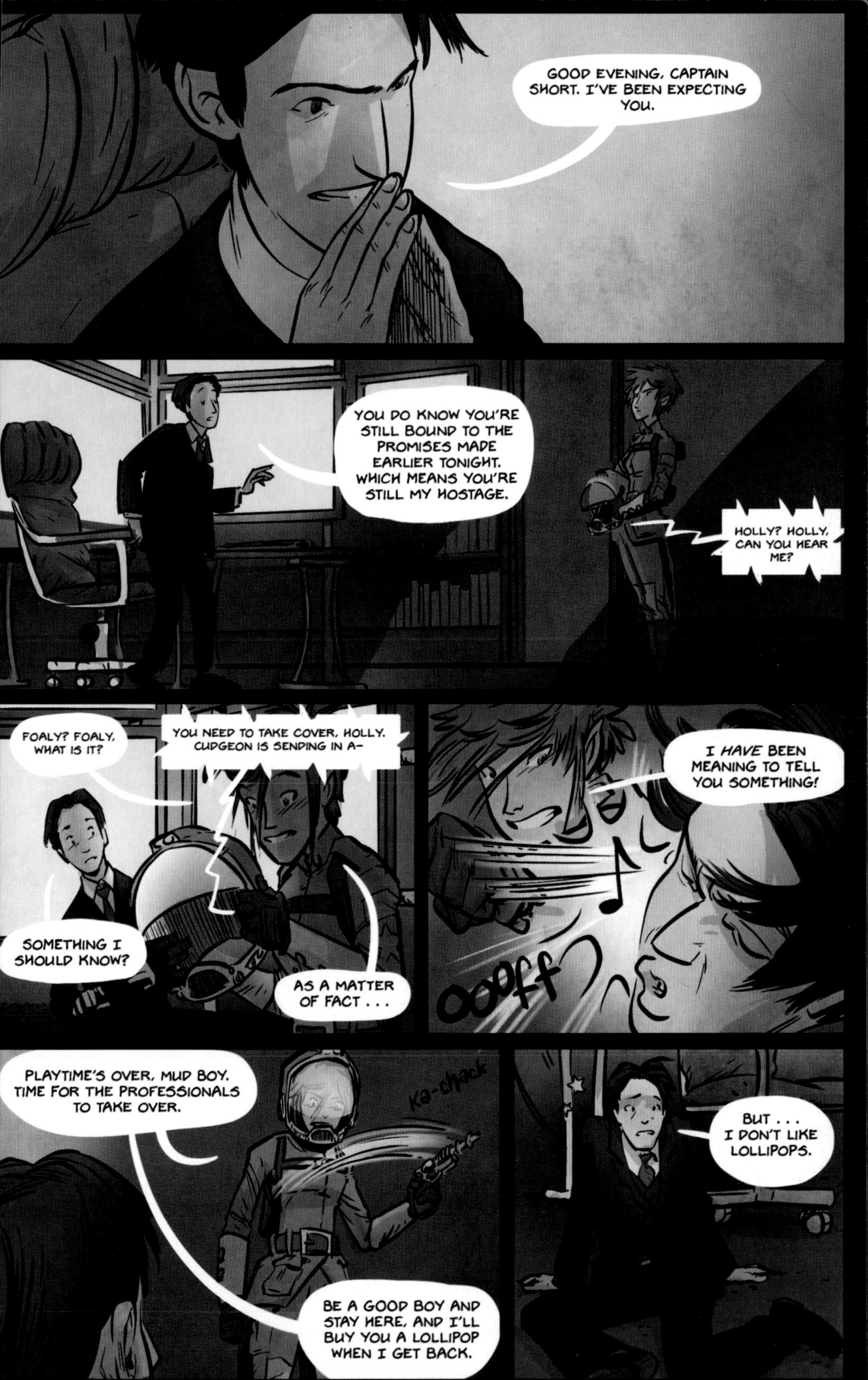
GOOD EVENING, CAPTAIN SHORT. I'VE BEEN EXPECTING YOU.
YOU DO KNOW YOU'RE STILL BOUND TO THE PROMISES MADE EARLIER TONIGHT. WHICH MEANS YOU'RE STILL MY HOSTAGE.
HOLLY? HOLLY, CAN YOU HEAR ME?
FOALY? FOALY, WHAT IS IT?
YOU NEED TO TAKE COVER, HOLLY. CUDGEON IS SENDING IN A–
SOMETHING I SHOULD KNOW?
AS A MATTER OF FACT . . .
I *HAVE* BEEN MEANING TO TELL YOU SOMETHING!
OOOFF
PLAYTIME'S OVER, MUD BOY. TIME FOR THE PROFESSIONALS TO TAKE OVER.
KA-CHACK
BE A GOOD BOY AND STAY HERE, AND I'LL BUY YOU A LOLLIPOP WHEN I GET BACK.
BUT . . . I DON'T LIKE LOLLIPOPS.

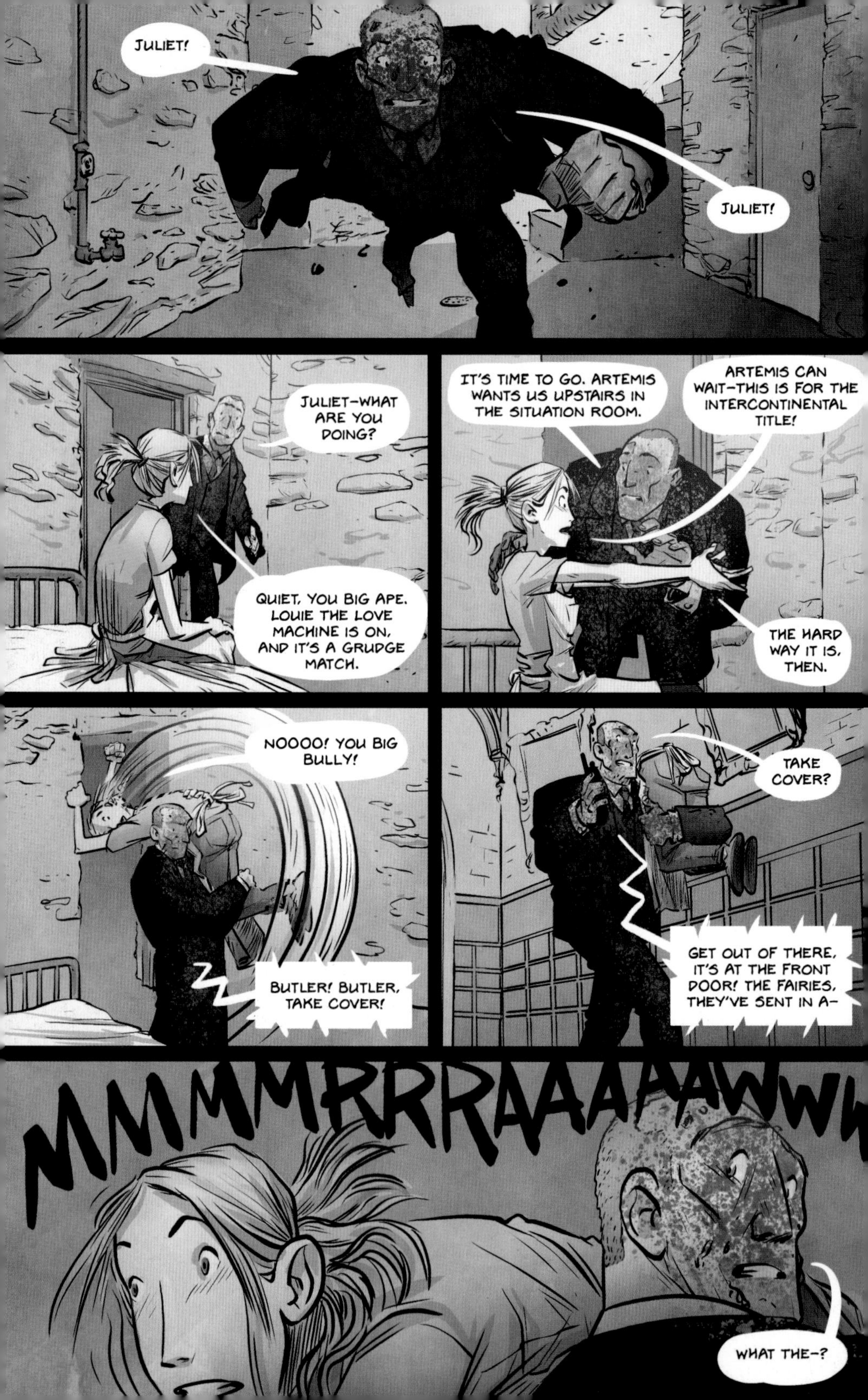
JULIET!
JULIET!
JULIET–WHAT ARE YOU DOING?
QUIET, YOU BIG APE. LOUIE THE LOVE MACHINE IS ON, AND IT'S A GRUDGE MATCH.
IT'S TIME TO GO. ARTEMIS WANTS US UPSTAIRS IN THE SITUATION ROOM.
ARTEMIS CAN WAIT–THIS IS FOR THE INTERCONTINENTAL TITLE!
THE HARD WAY IT IS, THEN.
NOOOO! YOU BIG BULLY!
BUTLER! BUTLER, TAKE COVER!
TAKE COVER?
GET OUT OF THERE, IT'S AT THE FRONT DOOR! THE FAIRIES, THEY'VE SENT IN A–
MMMMRRRAAAAAWW
WHAT THE–?

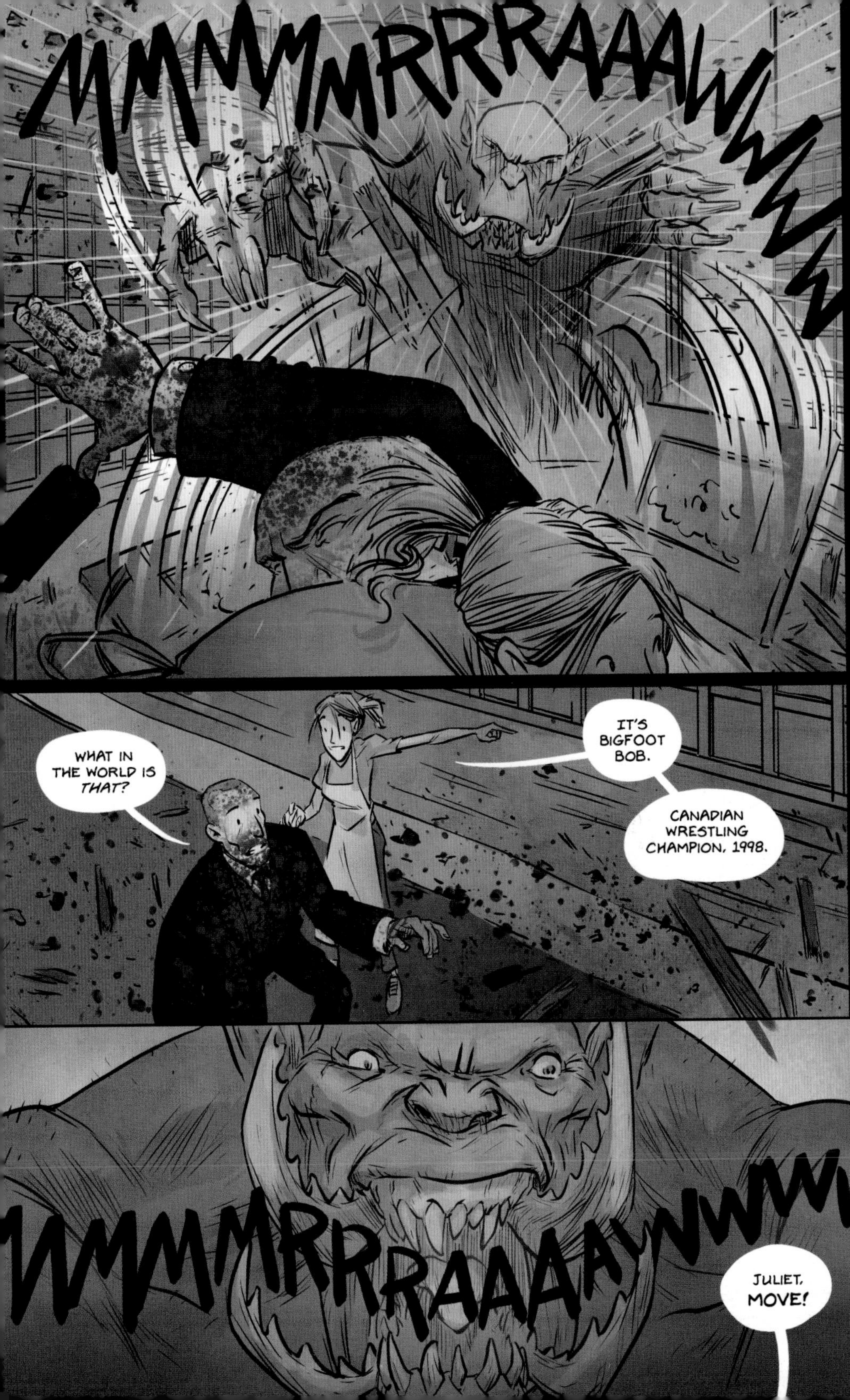
MMMMMRRRAAAWWWW
WHAT IN THE WORLD IS *THAT?*
IT'S BIGFOOT BOB.
CANADIAN WRESTLING CHAMPION, 1998.
MMMMRRRAAAAWWWW
JULIET, **MOVE!**

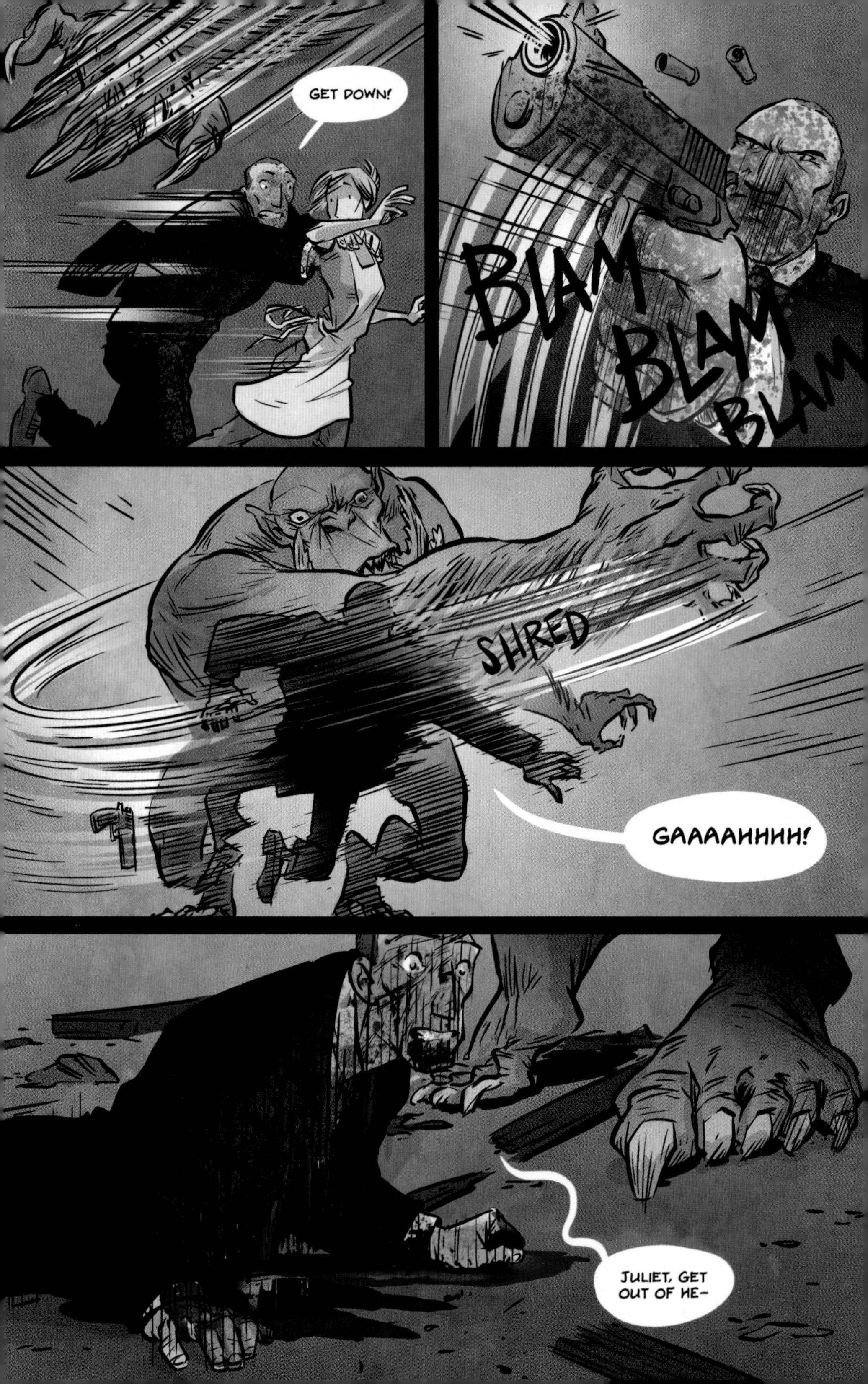
GET DOWN!
BLAM
BLAM
BLAM
SHRED
GAAAAHHHH!
JULIET, GET OUT OF HE–

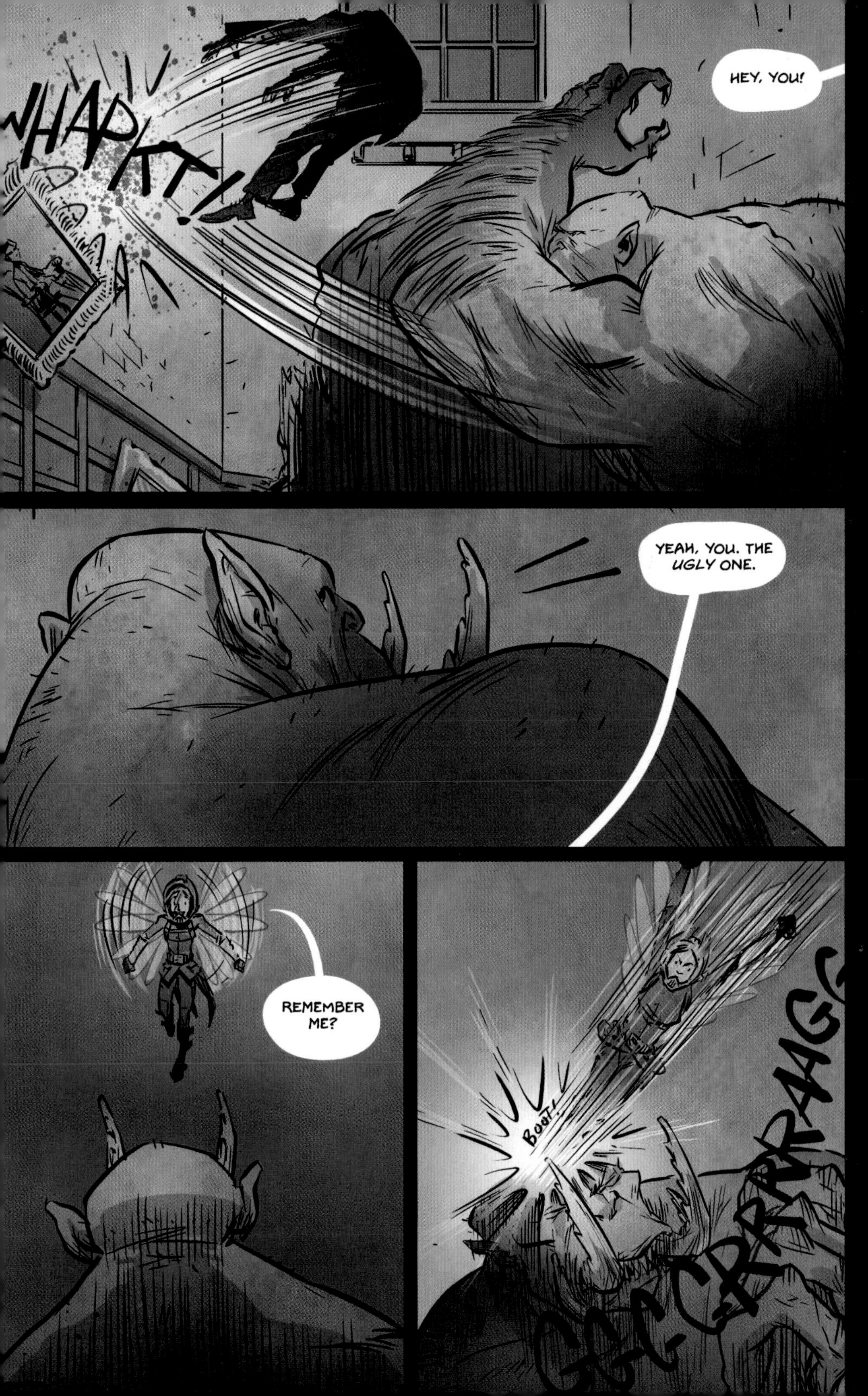
WHAPKT!!
HEY, YOU!
YEAH, YOU. THE UGLY ONE.
REMEMBER ME?
BOOT!
GGGCRRRAAGG

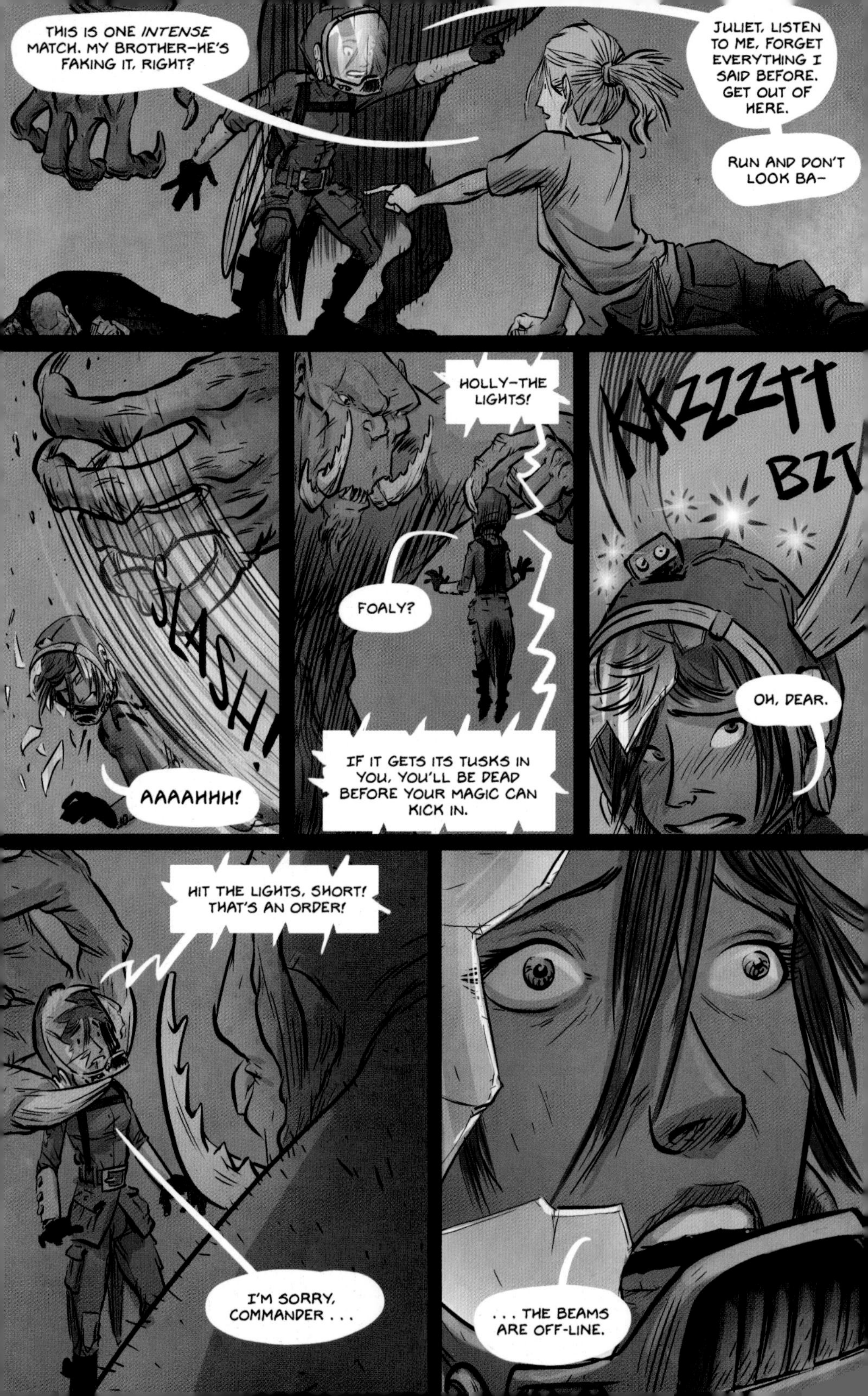
THIS IS ONE *INTENSE* MATCH. MY BROTHER—HE'S FAKING IT, RIGHT?
JULIET, LISTEN TO ME, FORGET EVERYTHING I SAID BEFORE. GET OUT OF HERE.
RUN AND DON'T LOOK BA—
SLASH!
AAAAHHH!
HOLLY—THE LIGHTS!
FOALY?
IF IT GETS ITS TUSKS IN YOU, YOU'LL BE DEAD BEFORE YOUR MAGIC CAN KICK IN.
KKZZZTT
BZT
OH, DEAR.
HIT THE LIGHTS, SHORT! THAT'S AN ORDER!
I'M SORRY, COMMANDER . . .
. . . THE BEAMS ARE OFF-LINE.

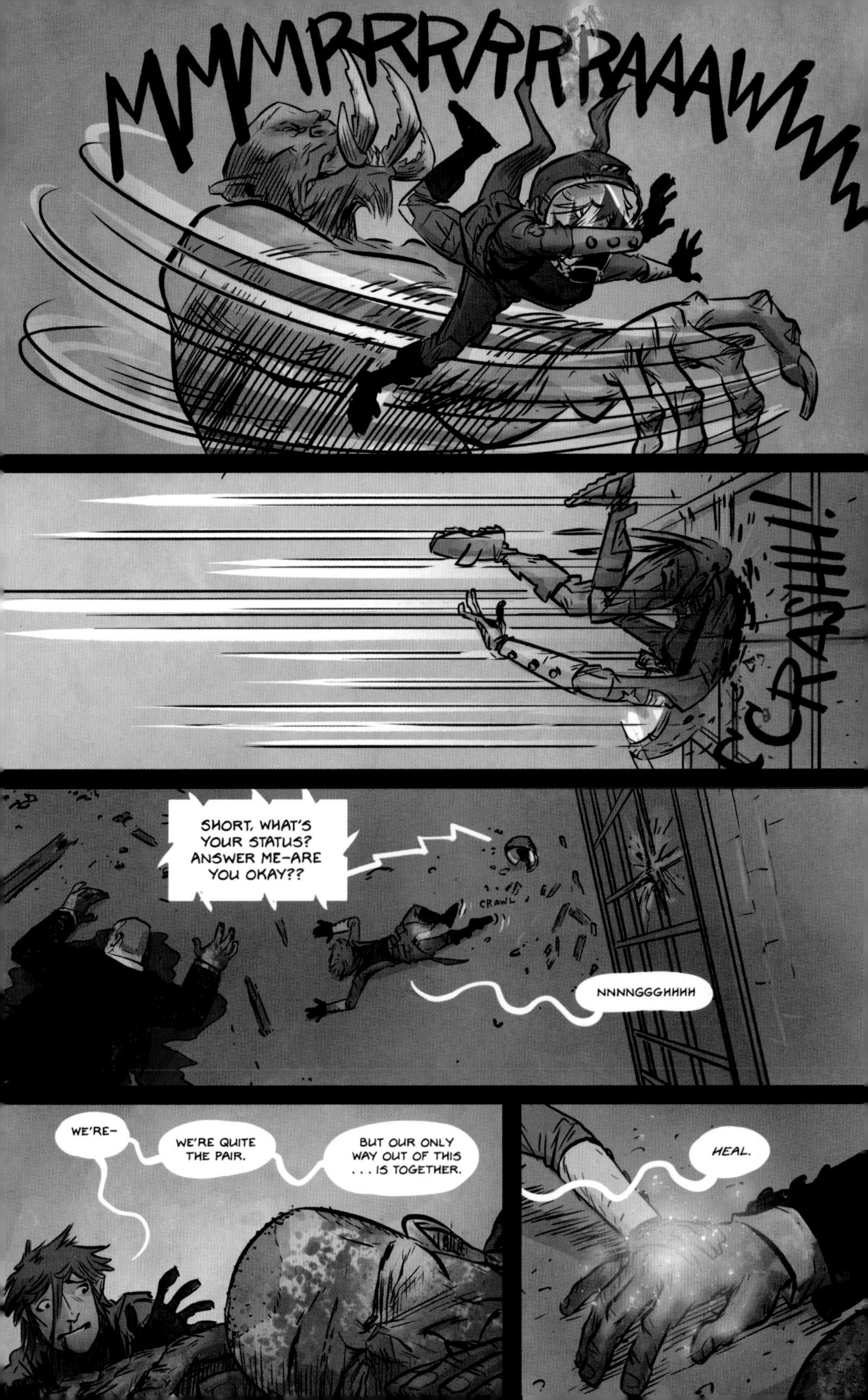

MMMRRRRRRAAAWW
CRASHH!!
SHORT, WHAT'S YOUR STATUS? ANSWER ME–ARE YOU OKAY??
CRAWL
NNNNGGGHHHH
WE'RE–
WE'RE QUITE THE PAIR.
BUT OUR ONLY WAY OUT OF THIS . . . IS TOGETHER.
HEAL.

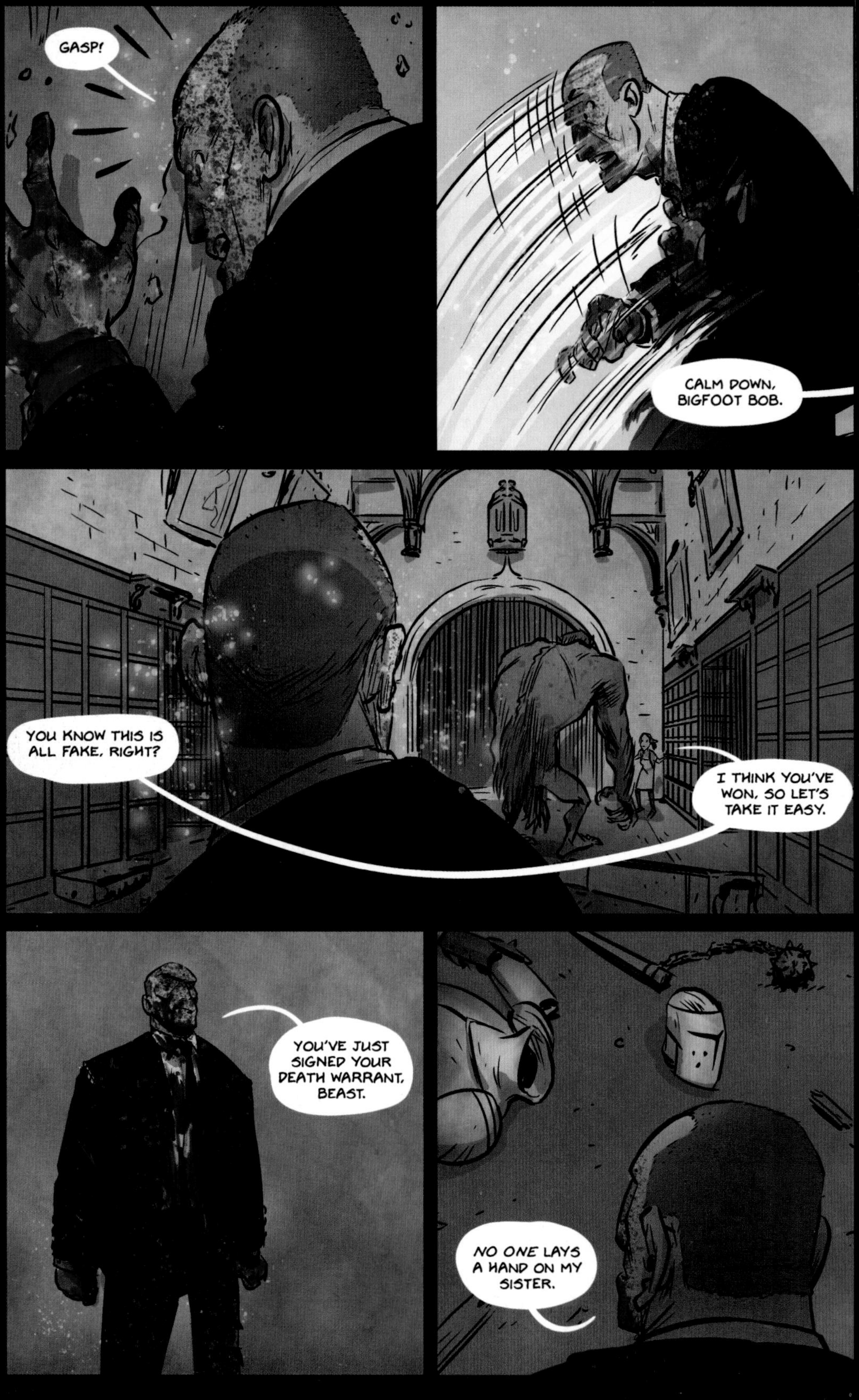
GASP!
CALM DOWN, BIGFOOT BOB.
YOU KNOW THIS IS ALL FAKE, RIGHT?
I THINK YOU'VE WON, SO LET'S TAKE IT EASY.
YOU'VE JUST SIGNED YOUR DEATH WARRANT, BEAST.
NO ONE LAYS A HAND ON MY SISTER.

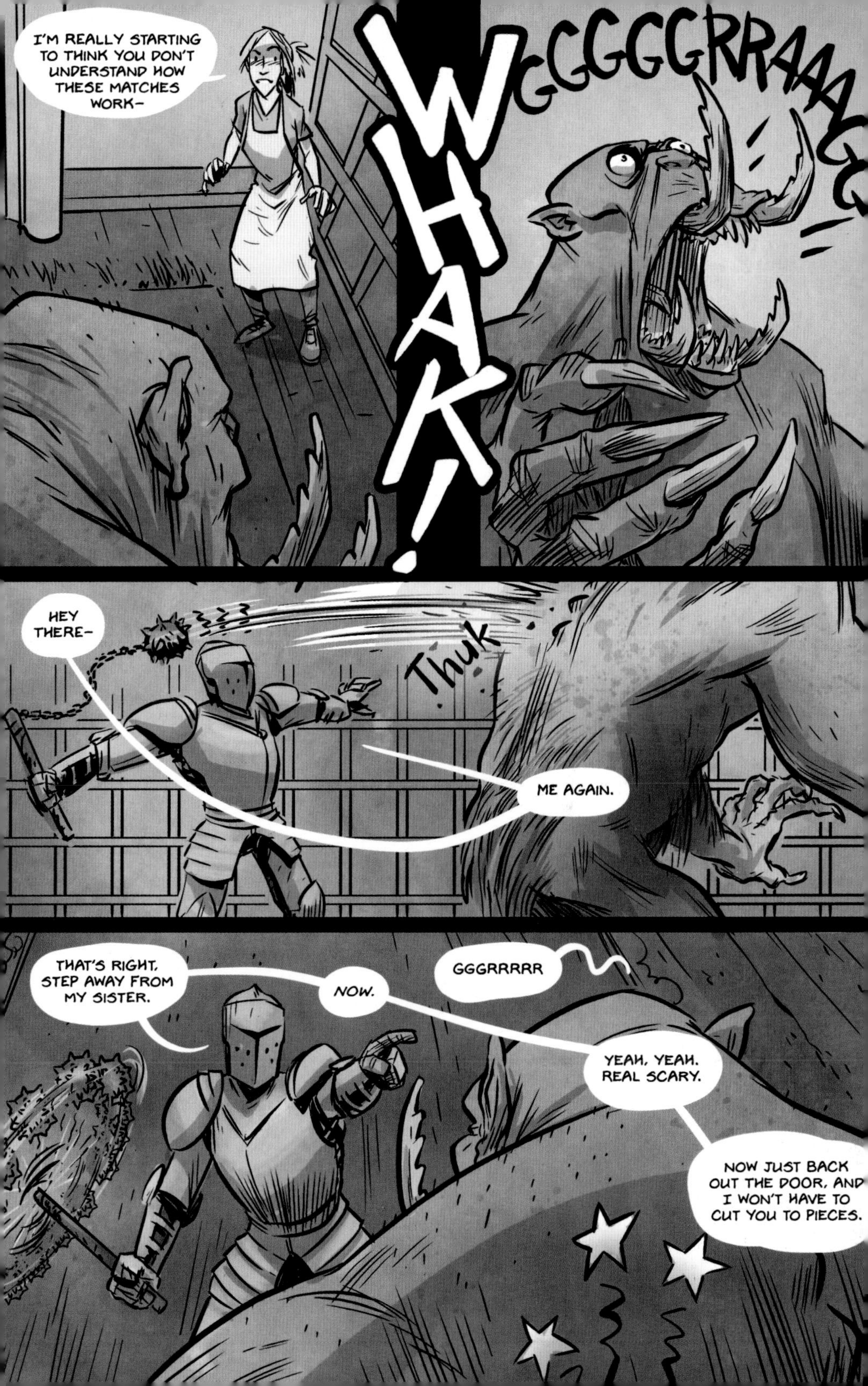
I'M REALLY STARTING TO THINK YOU DON'T UNDERSTAND HOW THESE MATCHES WORK-
WHAK!
WGGGGGRRAAAGG
HEY THERE-
Thuk
ME AGAIN.
THAT'S RIGHT, STEP AWAY FROM MY SISTER.
NOW.
GGGRRRRR
YEAH, YEAH. REAL SCARY.
NOW JUST BACK OUT THE DOOR, AND I WON'T HAVE TO CUT YOU TO PIECES.

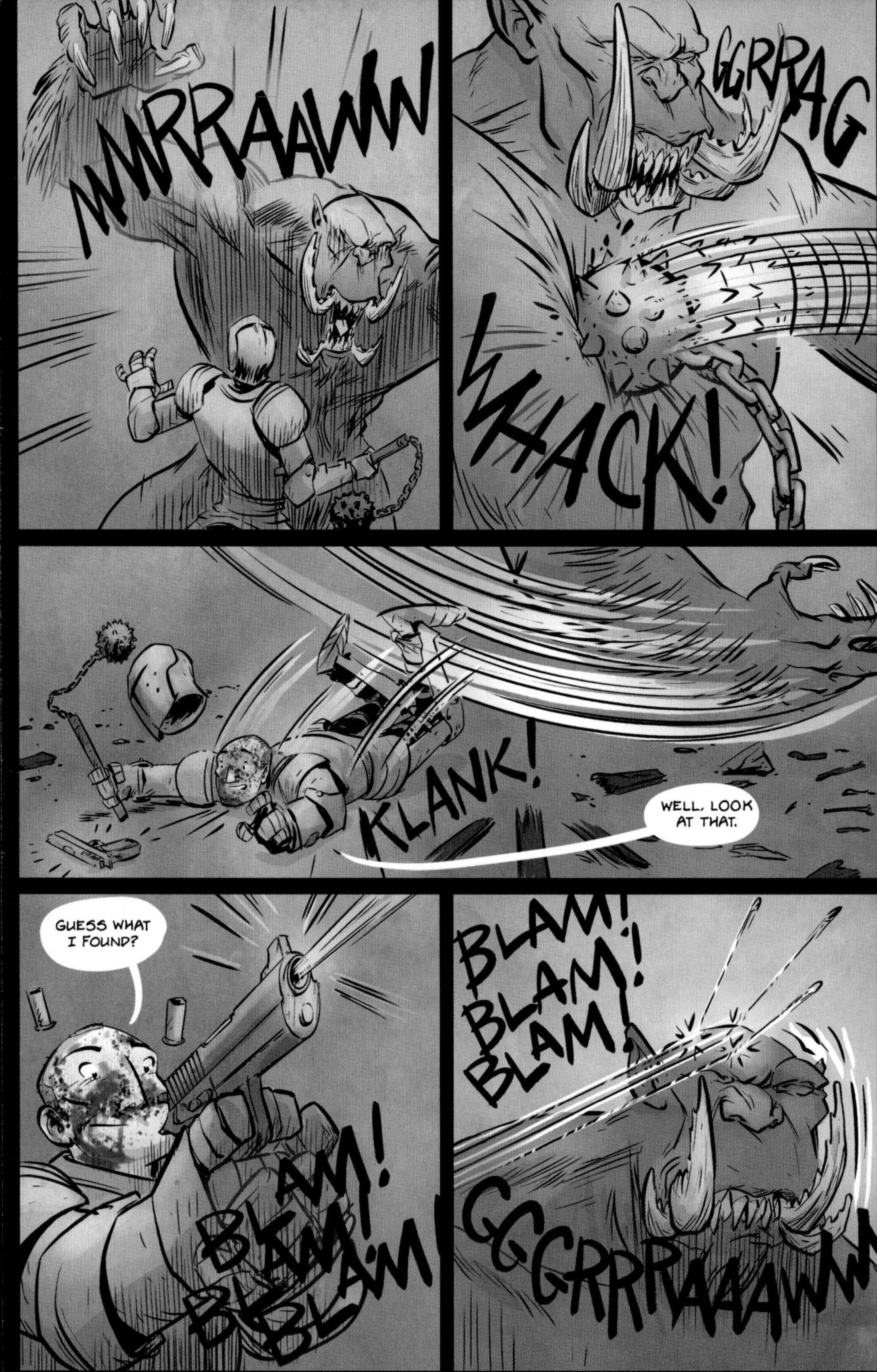
MMRRAAWW
GGRRAG
WHACK!
KLANK!
WELL, LOOK AT THAT.
GUESS WHAT I FOUND?
BLAM!
BLAM!
BLAM!
BLAM!
BLAM!
BLAM!
GGGRRRAAAWW

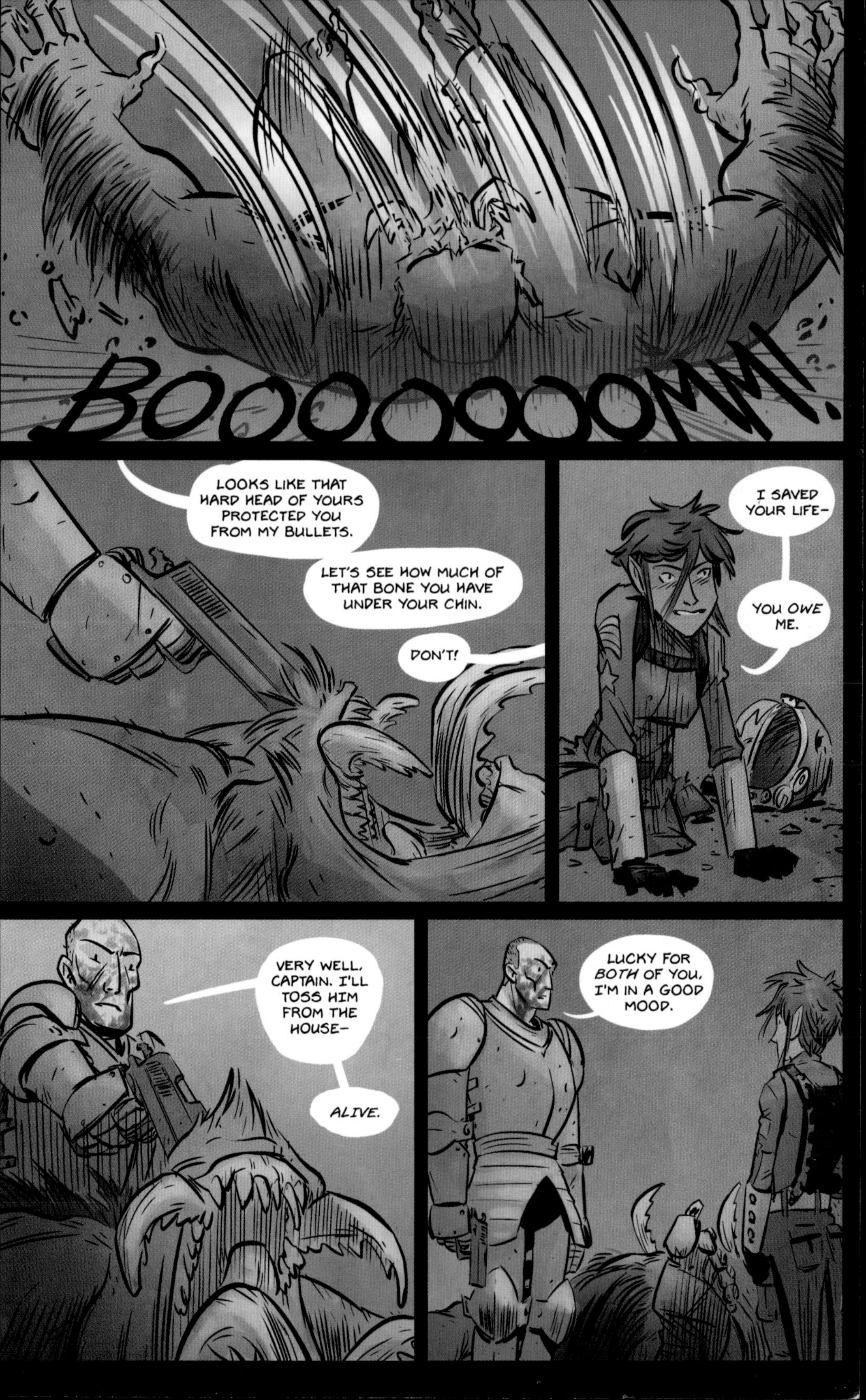
BOOOOOOOM!
LOOKS LIKE THAT HARD HEAD OF YOURS PROTECTED YOU FROM MY BULLETS.
LET'S SEE HOW MUCH OF THAT BONE YOU HAVE UNDER YOUR CHIN.
DON'T!
I SAVED YOUR LIFE-
YOU *OWE* ME.
VERY WELL, CAPTAIN. I'LL TOSS HIM FROM THE HOUSE-
ALIVE.
LUCKY FOR *BOTH* OF YOU, I'M IN A GOOD MOOD.

CHAPTER NINE

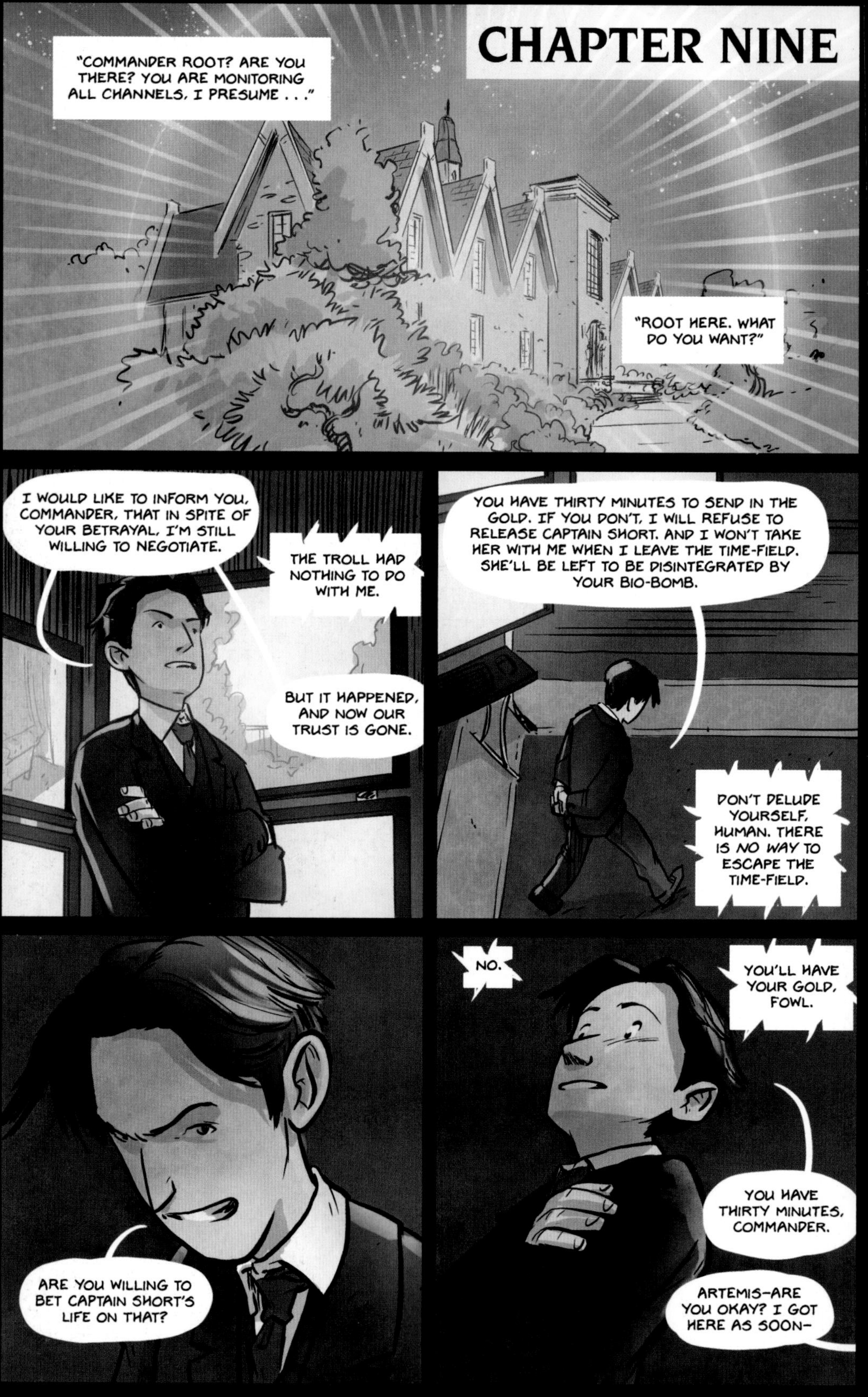
"COMMANDER ROOT? ARE YOU THERE? YOU ARE MONITORING ALL CHANNELS, I PRESUME . . ."
"ROOT HERE. WHAT DO YOU WANT?"
I WOULD LIKE TO INFORM YOU, COMMANDER, THAT IN SPITE OF YOUR BETRAYAL, I'M STILL WILLING TO NEGOTIATE.
THE TROLL HAD NOTHING TO DO WITH ME.
BUT IT HAPPENED, AND NOW OUR TRUST IS GONE.
YOU HAVE THIRTY MINUTES TO SEND IN THE GOLD. IF YOU DON'T, I WILL REFUSE TO RELEASE CAPTAIN SHORT. AND I WON'T TAKE HER WITH ME WHEN I LEAVE THE TIME-FIELD. SHE'LL BE LEFT TO BE DISINTEGRATED BY YOUR BIO-BOMB.
DON'T DELUDE YOURSELF, HUMAN. THERE IS NO WAY TO ESCAPE THE TIME-FIELD.
ARE YOU WILLING TO BET CAPTAIN SHORT'S LIFE ON THAT?
NO.
YOU'LL HAVE YOUR GOLD, FOWL.
YOU HAVE THIRTY MINUTES, COMMANDER.
ARTEMIS—ARE YOU OKAY? I GOT HERE AS SOON—

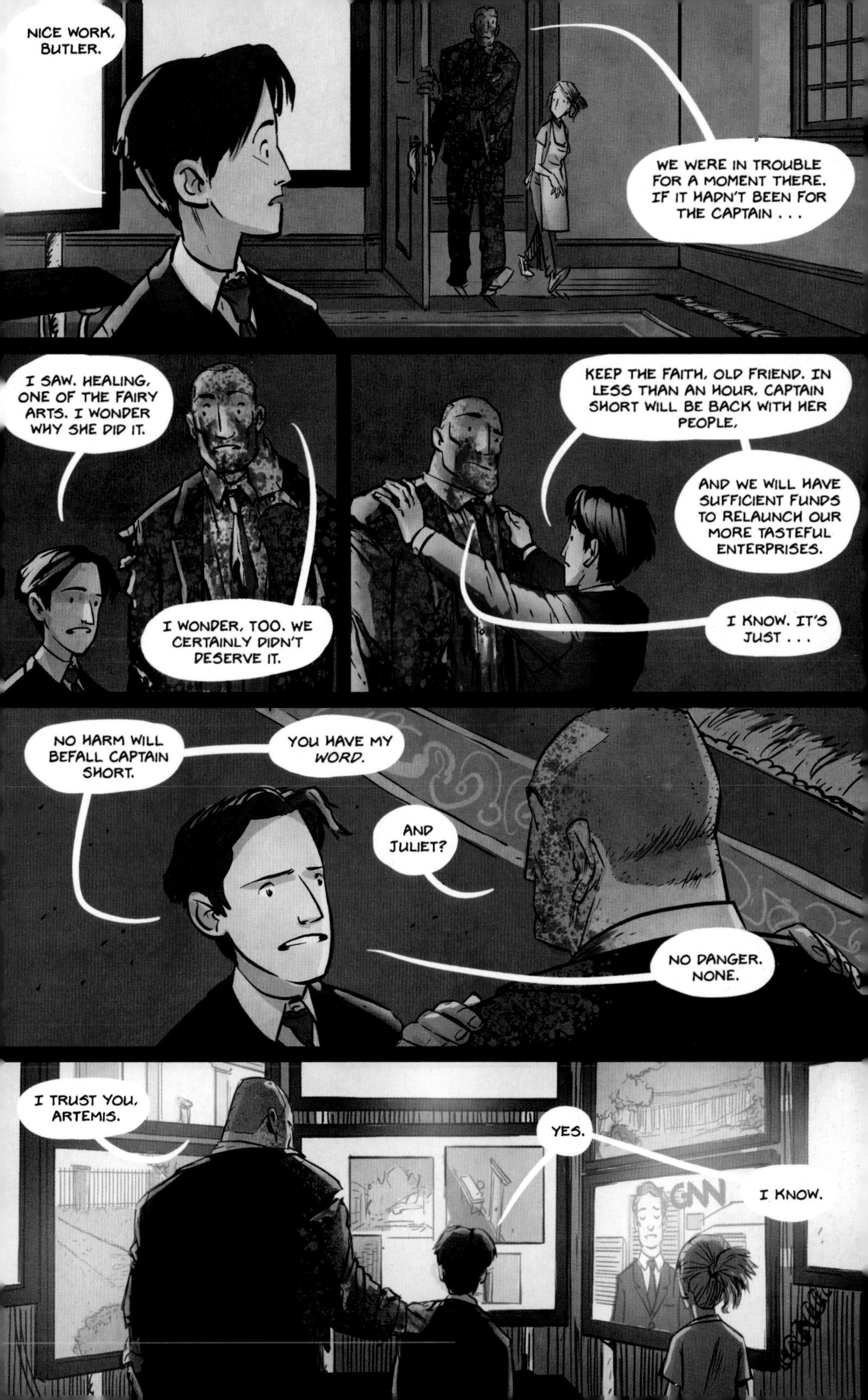
NICE WORK, BUTLER.
WE WERE IN TROUBLE FOR A MOMENT THERE. IF IT HADN'T BEEN FOR THE CAPTAIN . . .
I SAW. HEALING, ONE OF THE FAIRY ARTS. I WONDER WHY SHE DID IT.
I WONDER, TOO. WE CERTAINLY DIDN'T DESERVE IT.
KEEP THE FAITH, OLD FRIEND. IN LESS THAN AN HOUR, CAPTAIN SHORT WILL BE BACK WITH HER PEOPLE,
AND WE WILL HAVE SUFFICIENT FUNDS TO RELAUNCH OUR MORE TASTEFUL ENTERPRISES.
I KNOW. IT'S JUST . . .
NO HARM WILL BEFALL CAPTAIN SHORT.
YOU HAVE MY *WORD.*
AND JULIET?
NO DANGER. NONE.
I TRUST YOU, ARTEMIS.
YES.
I KNOW.

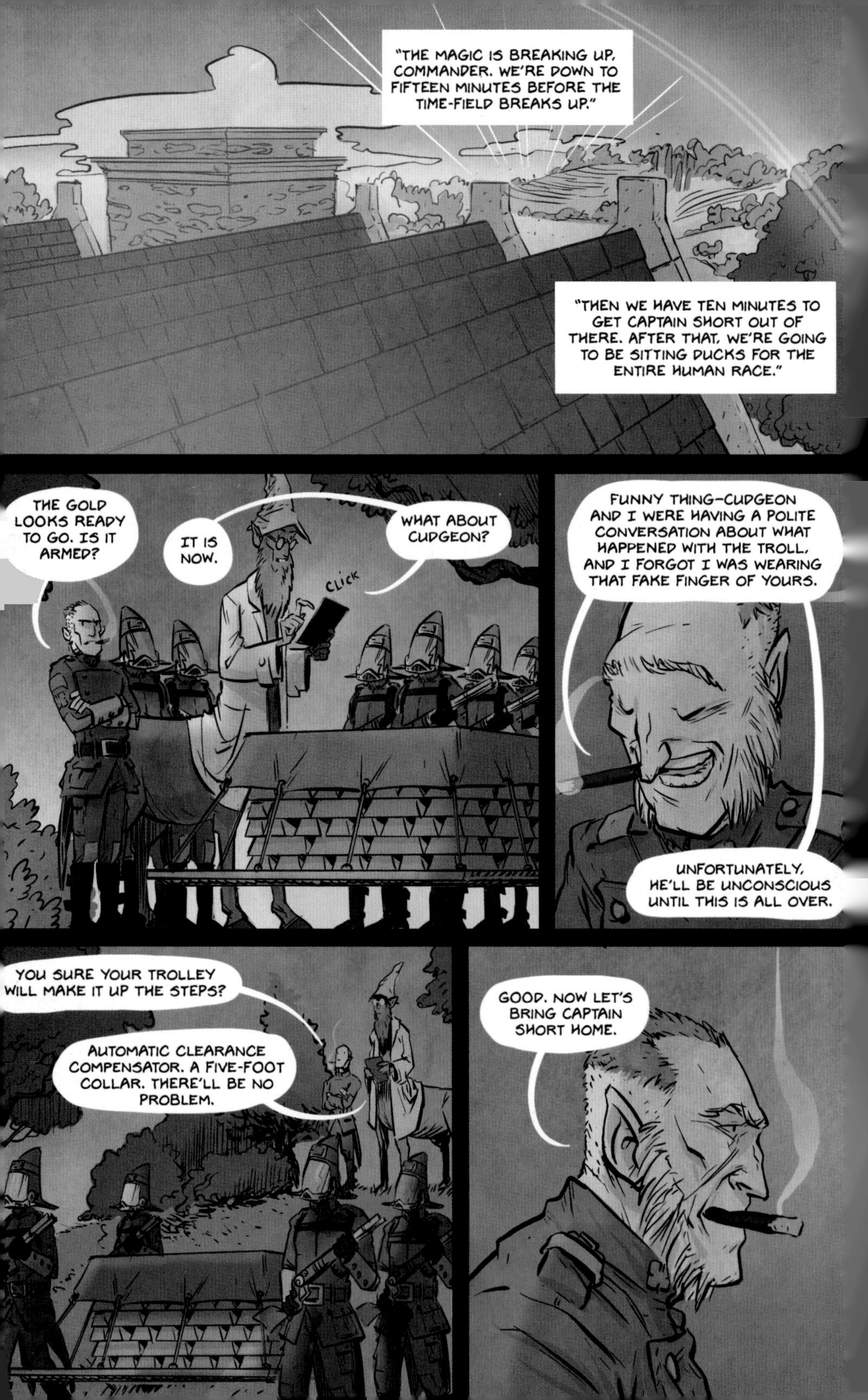
"THE MAGIC IS BREAKING UP, COMMANDER. WE'RE DOWN TO FIFTEEN MINUTES BEFORE THE TIME-FIELD BREAKS UP."
"THEN WE HAVE TEN MINUTES TO GET CAPTAIN SHORT OUT OF THERE. AFTER THAT, WE'RE GOING TO BE SITTING DUCKS FOR THE ENTIRE HUMAN RACE."
THE GOLD LOOKS READY TO GO. IS IT ARMED?
IT IS NOW.
CLICK
WHAT ABOUT CUDGEON?
FUNNY THING—CUDGEON AND I WERE HAVING A POLITE CONVERSATION ABOUT WHAT HAPPENED WITH THE TROLL, AND I FORGOT I WAS WEARING THAT FAKE FINGER OF YOURS.
UNFORTUNATELY, HE'LL BE UNCONSCIOUS UNTIL THIS IS ALL OVER.
YOU SURE YOUR TROLLEY WILL MAKE IT UP THE STEPS?
AUTOMATIC CLEARANCE COMPENSATOR. A FIVE-FOOT COLLAR. THERE'LL BE NO PROBLEM.
GOOD. NOW LET'S BRING CAPTAIN SHORT HOME.

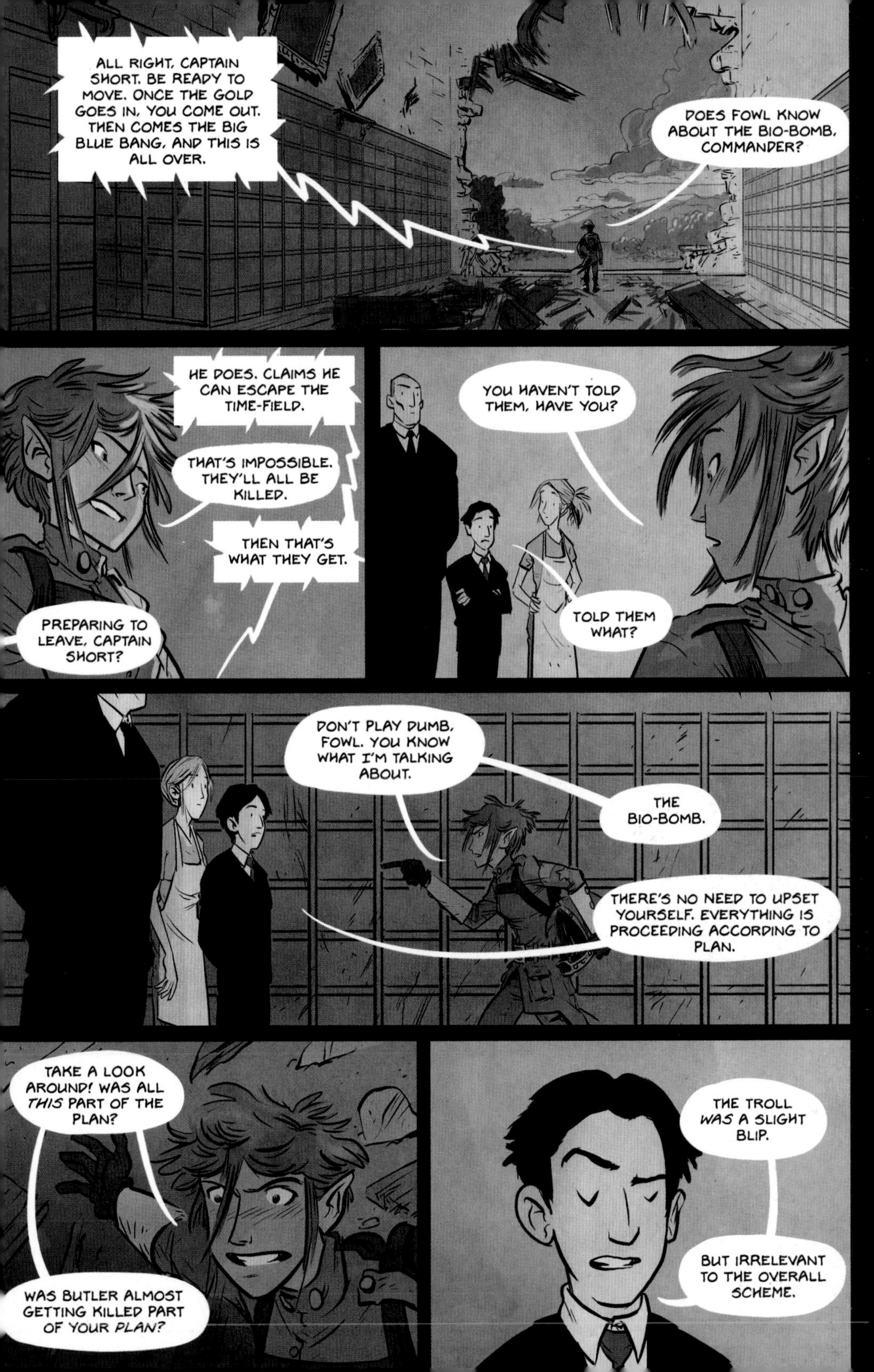
ALL RIGHT, CAPTAIN SHORT. BE READY TO MOVE. ONCE THE GOLD GOES IN, YOU COME OUT. THEN COMES THE BIG BLUE BANG, AND THIS IS ALL OVER.
DOES FOWL KNOW ABOUT THE BIO-BOMB, COMMANDER?
HE DOES. CLAIMS HE CAN ESCAPE THE TIME-FIELD.
THAT'S IMPOSSIBLE. THEY'LL ALL BE KILLED.
THEN THAT'S WHAT THEY GET.
PREPARING TO LEAVE, CAPTAIN SHORT?
YOU HAVEN'T TOLD THEM, HAVE YOU?
TOLD THEM WHAT?
DON'T PLAY DUMB, FOWL. YOU KNOW WHAT I'M TALKING ABOUT.
THE BIO-BOMB.
THERE'S NO NEED TO UPSET YOURSELF. EVERYTHING IS PROCEEDING ACCORDING TO PLAN.
TAKE A LOOK AROUND! WAS ALL *THIS* PART OF THE PLAN?
WAS BUTLER ALMOST GETTING KILLED PART OF YOUR *PLAN?*
THE TROLL *WAS* A SLIGHT BLIP.
BUT IRRELEVANT TO THE OVERALL SCHEME.

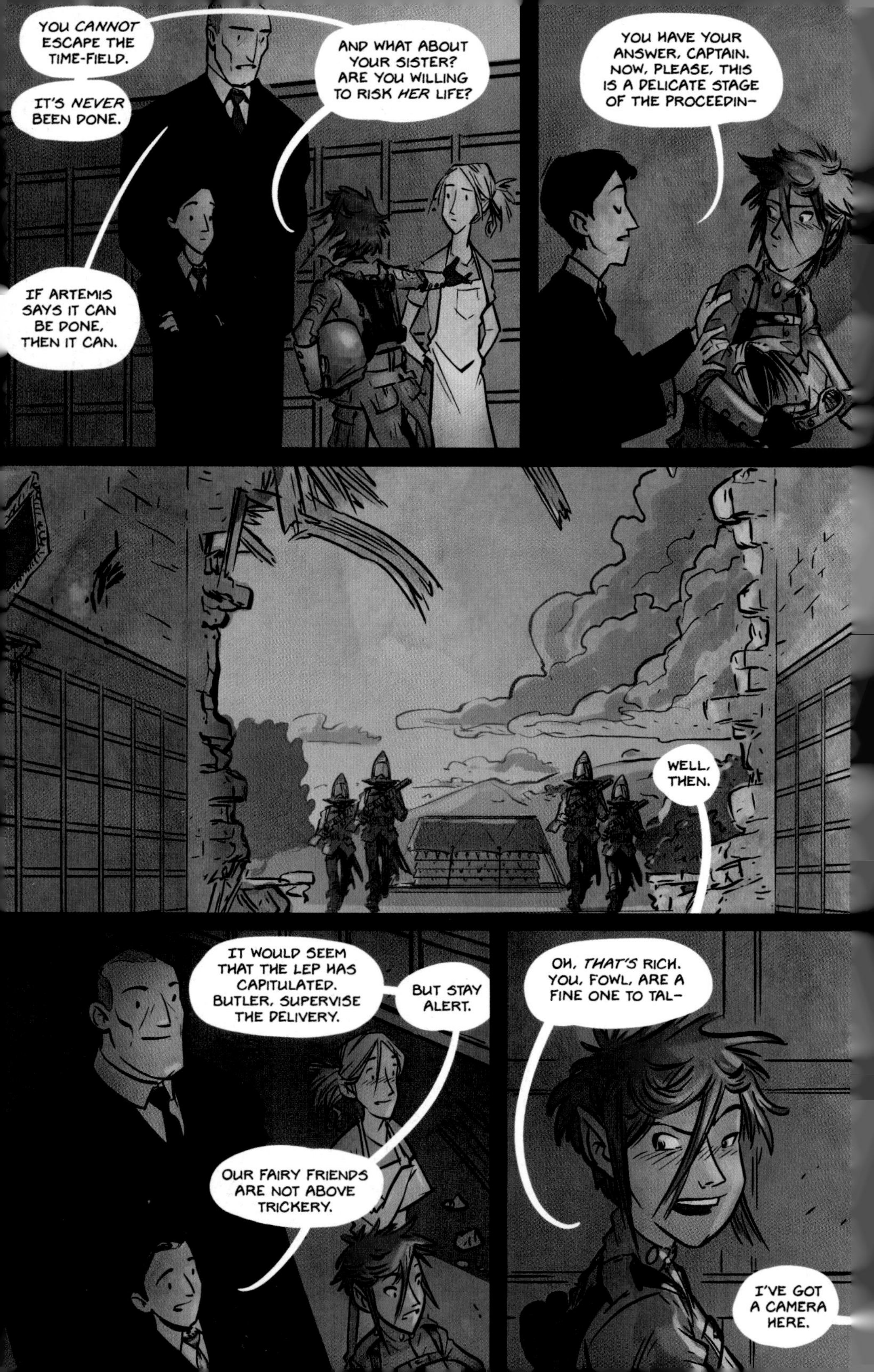
YOU CANNOT ESCAPE THE TIME-FIELD.
IT'S NEVER BEEN DONE.
IF ARTEMIS SAYS IT CAN BE DONE, THEN IT CAN.
AND WHAT ABOUT YOUR SISTER? ARE YOU WILLING TO RISK HER LIFE?
YOU HAVE YOUR ANSWER, CAPTAIN. NOW, PLEASE, THIS IS A DELICATE STAGE OF THE PROCEEDIN–
WELL, THEN.
IT WOULD SEEM THAT THE LEP HAS CAPITULATED. BUTLER, SUPERVISE THE DELIVERY.
BUT STAY ALERT.
OUR FAIRY FRIENDS ARE NOT ABOVE TRICKERY.
OH, THAT'S RICH. YOU, FOWL, ARE A FINE ONE TO TAL–
I'VE GOT A CAMERA HERE.

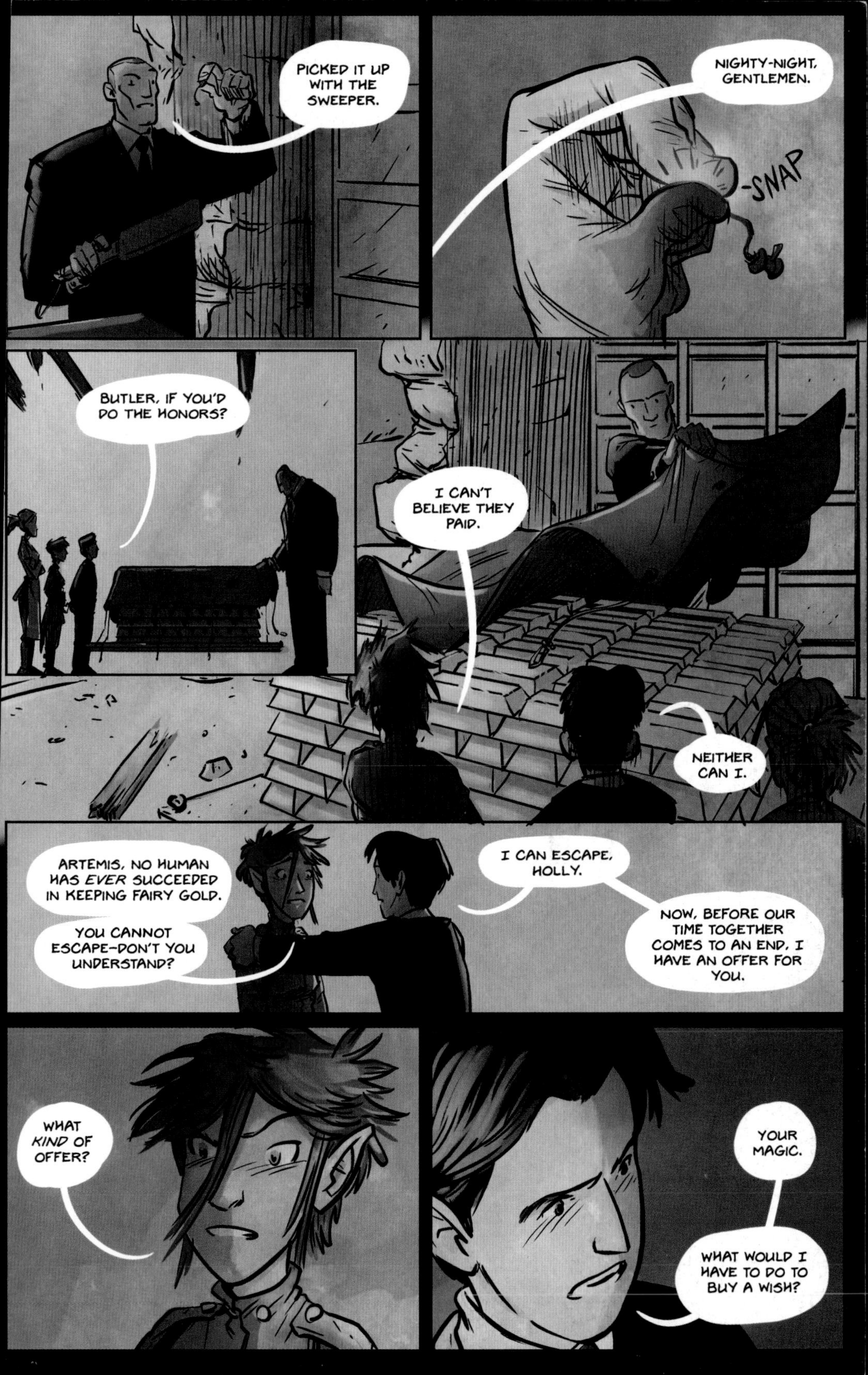
PICKED IT UP WITH THE SWEEPER.
NIGHTY-NIGHT, GENTLEMEN.
-SNAP
BUTLER, IF YOU'D DO THE HONORS?
I CAN'T BELIEVE THEY PAID.
NEITHER CAN I.
ARTEMIS, NO HUMAN HAS *EVER* SUCCEEDED IN KEEPING FAIRY GOLD.
YOU CANNOT ESCAPE—DON'T YOU UNDERSTAND?
I CAN ESCAPE, HOLLY.
NOW, BEFORE OUR TIME TOGETHER COMES TO AN END, I HAVE AN OFFER FOR YOU.
WHAT *KIND* OF OFFER?
YOUR MAGIC.
WHAT WOULD I HAVE TO DO TO BUY A WISH?

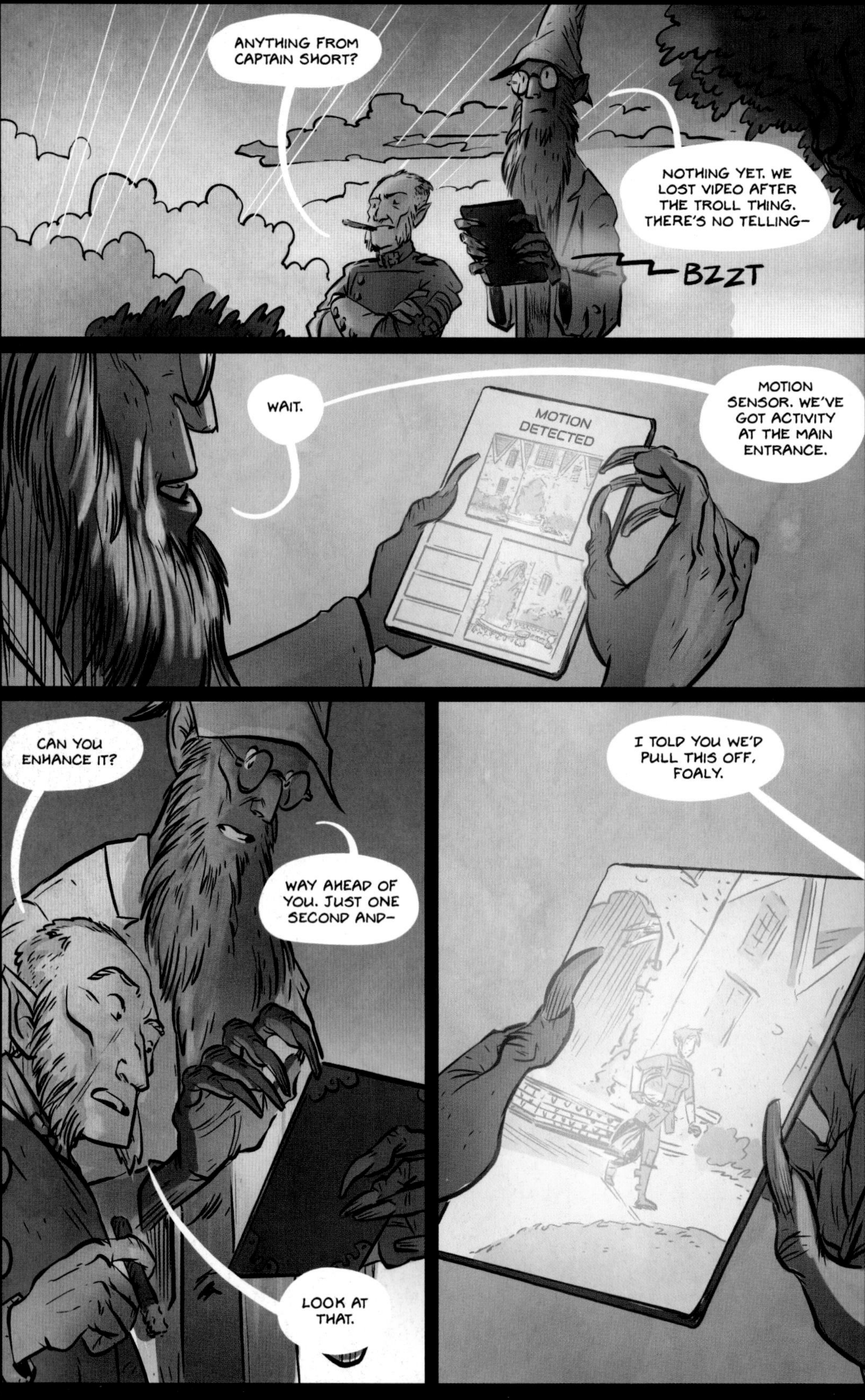
ANYTHING FROM CAPTAIN SHORT?
NOTHING YET. WE LOST VIDEO AFTER THE TROLL THING. THERE'S NO TELLING–
BZZT
WAIT.
MOTION SENSOR. WE'VE GOT ACTIVITY AT THE MAIN ENTRANCE.
MOTION DETECTED
CAN YOU ENHANCE IT?
WAY AHEAD OF YOU. JUST ONE SECOND AND–
LOOK AT THAT.
I TOLD YOU WE'D PULL THIS OFF, FOALY.

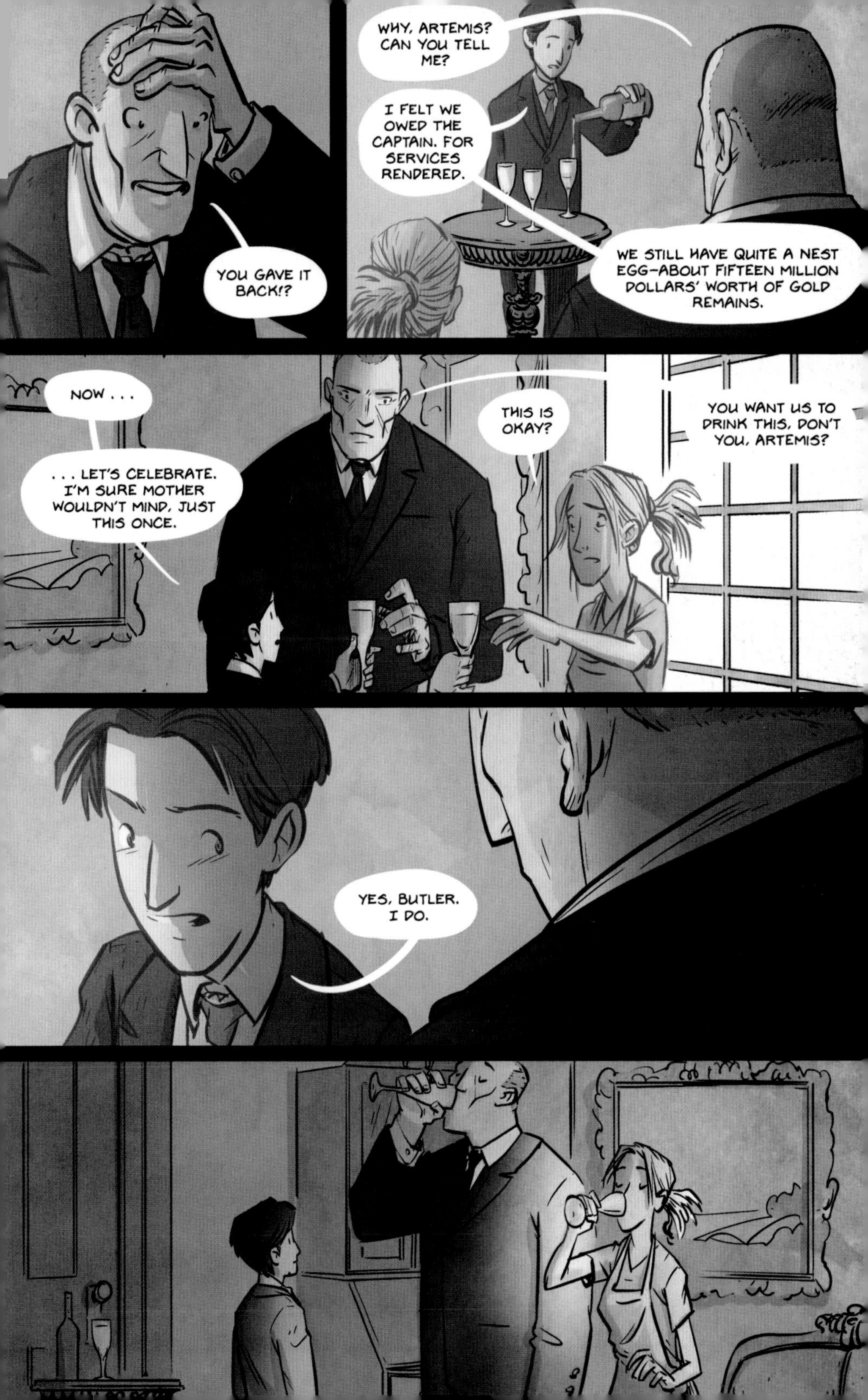
YOU GAVE IT BACK!?
WHY, ARTEMIS? CAN YOU TELL ME?
I FELT WE OWED THE CAPTAIN. FOR SERVICES RENDERED.
WE STILL HAVE QUITE A NEST EGG—ABOUT FIFTEEN MILLION DOLLARS' WORTH OF GOLD REMAINS.
NOW . . .
. . . LET'S CELEBRATE. I'M SURE MOTHER WOULDN'T MIND, JUST THIS ONCE.
THIS IS OKAY?
YOU WANT US TO DRINK THIS, DON'T YOU, ARTEMIS?
YES, BUTLER. I DO.

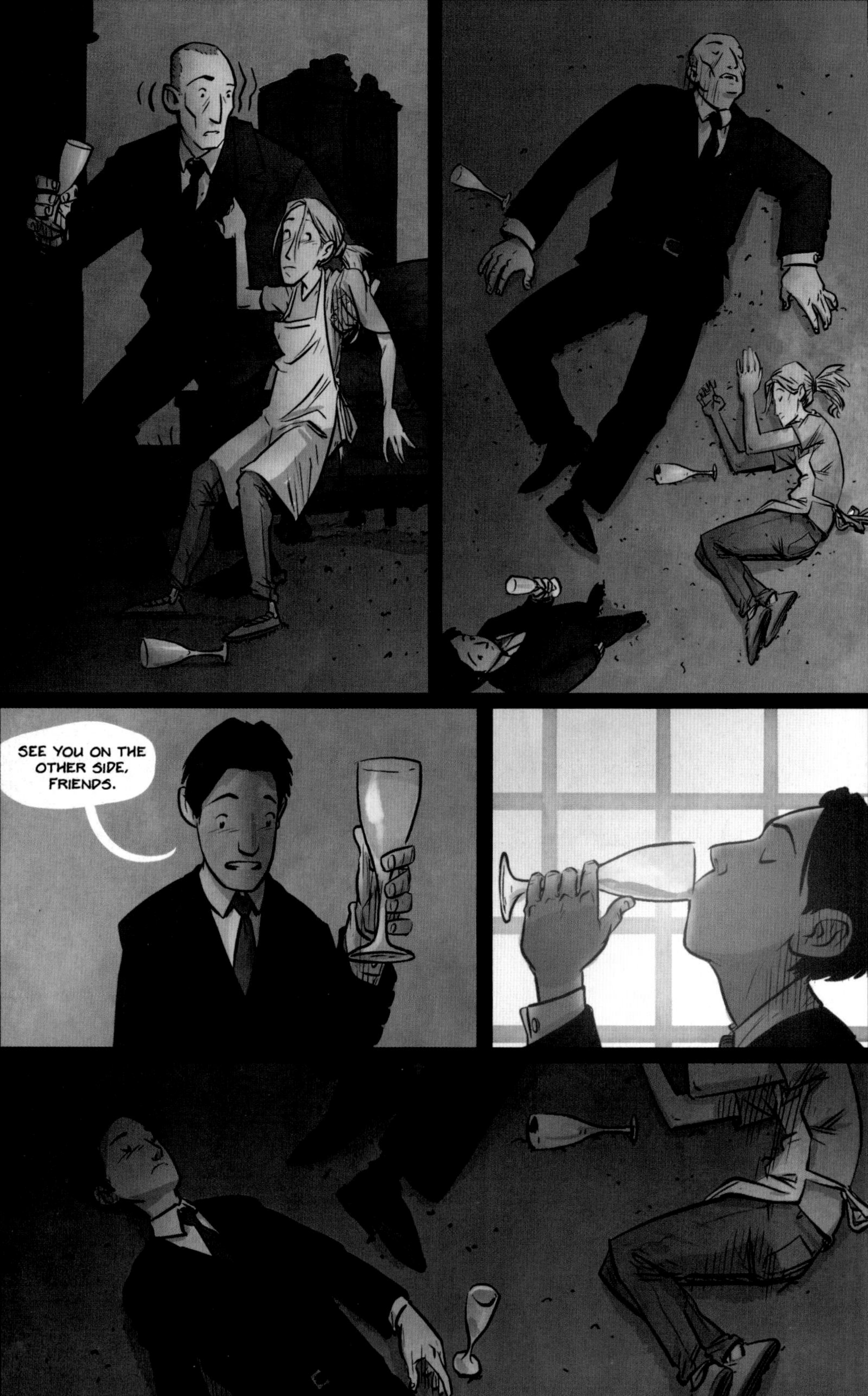
SEE YOU ON THE OTHER SIDE, FRIENDS.

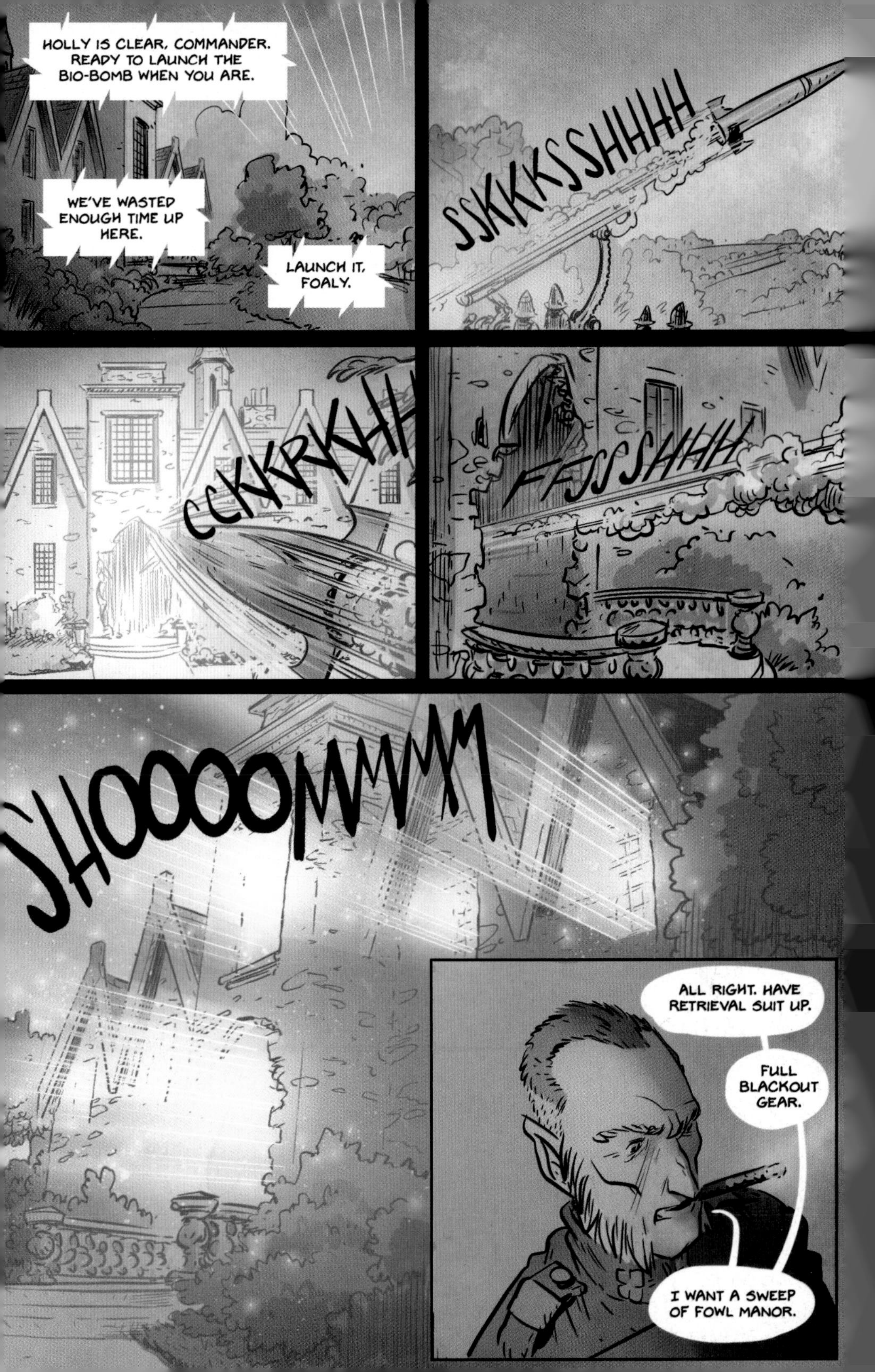
HOLLY IS CLEAR, COMMANDER. READY TO LAUNCH THE BIO-BOMB WHEN YOU ARE.
WE'VE WASTED ENOUGH TIME UP HERE.
LAUNCH IT, FOALY.
SSKKKSSHHHH
CCKKRKHH
FFSSSHHH
SHOOOOMMMM
ALL RIGHT. HAVE RETRIEVAL SUIT UP.
FULL BLACKOUT GEAR.
I WANT A SWEEP OF FOWL MANOR.

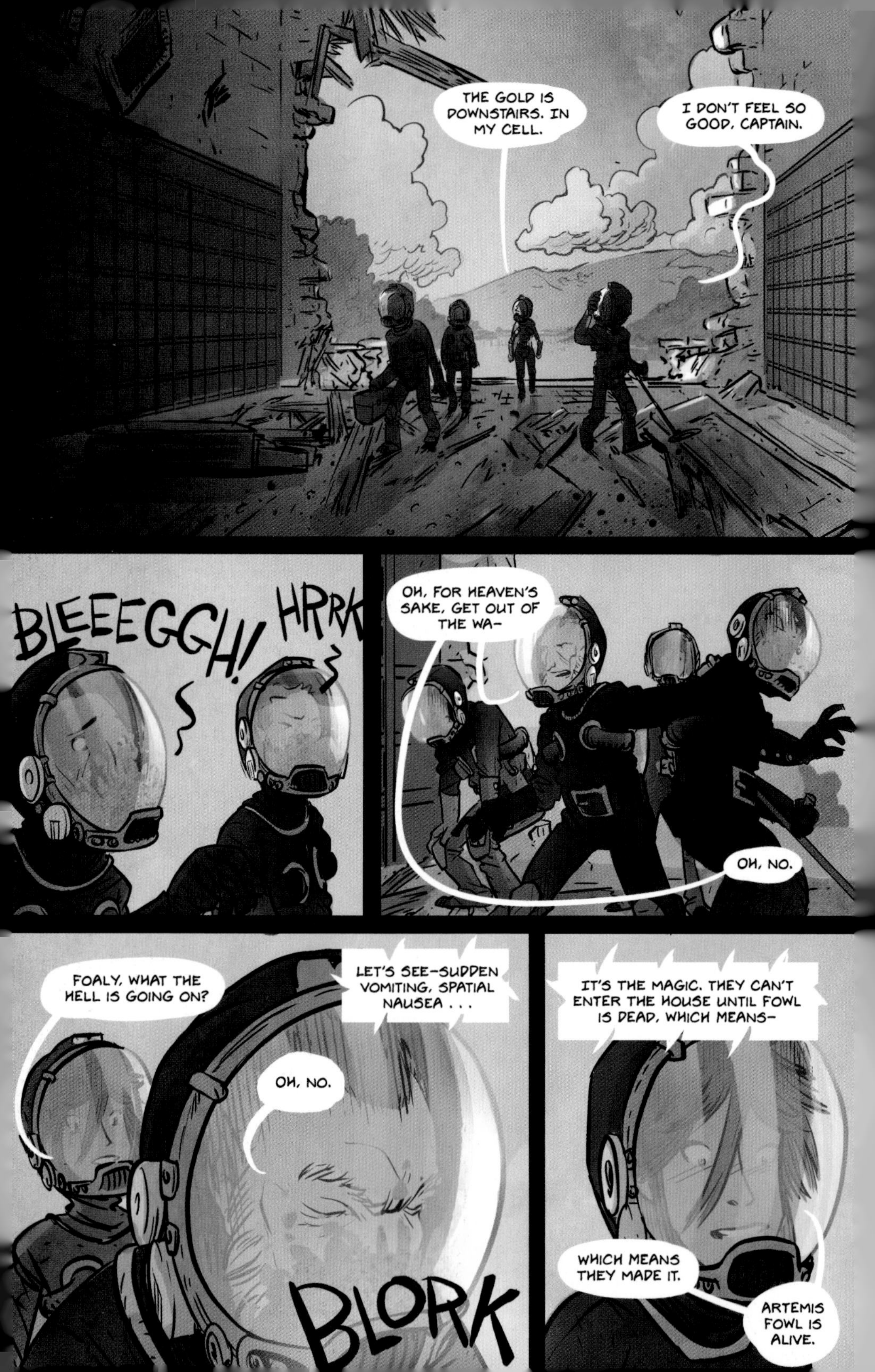
THE GOLD IS DOWNSTAIRS. IN MY CELL.
I DON'T FEEL SO GOOD, CAPTAIN.
BLEEEGGH!
HRRK
OH, FOR HEAVEN'S SAKE, GET OUT OF THE WA-
OH, NO.
FOALY, WHAT THE HELL IS GOING ON?
LET'S SEE-SUDDEN VOMITING, SPATIAL NAUSEA . . .
OH, NO.
BLORK
IT'S THE MAGIC. THEY CAN'T ENTER THE HOUSE UNTIL FOWL IS DEAD, WHICH MEANS-
WHICH MEANS THEY MADE IT.
ARTEMIS FOWL IS ALIVE.

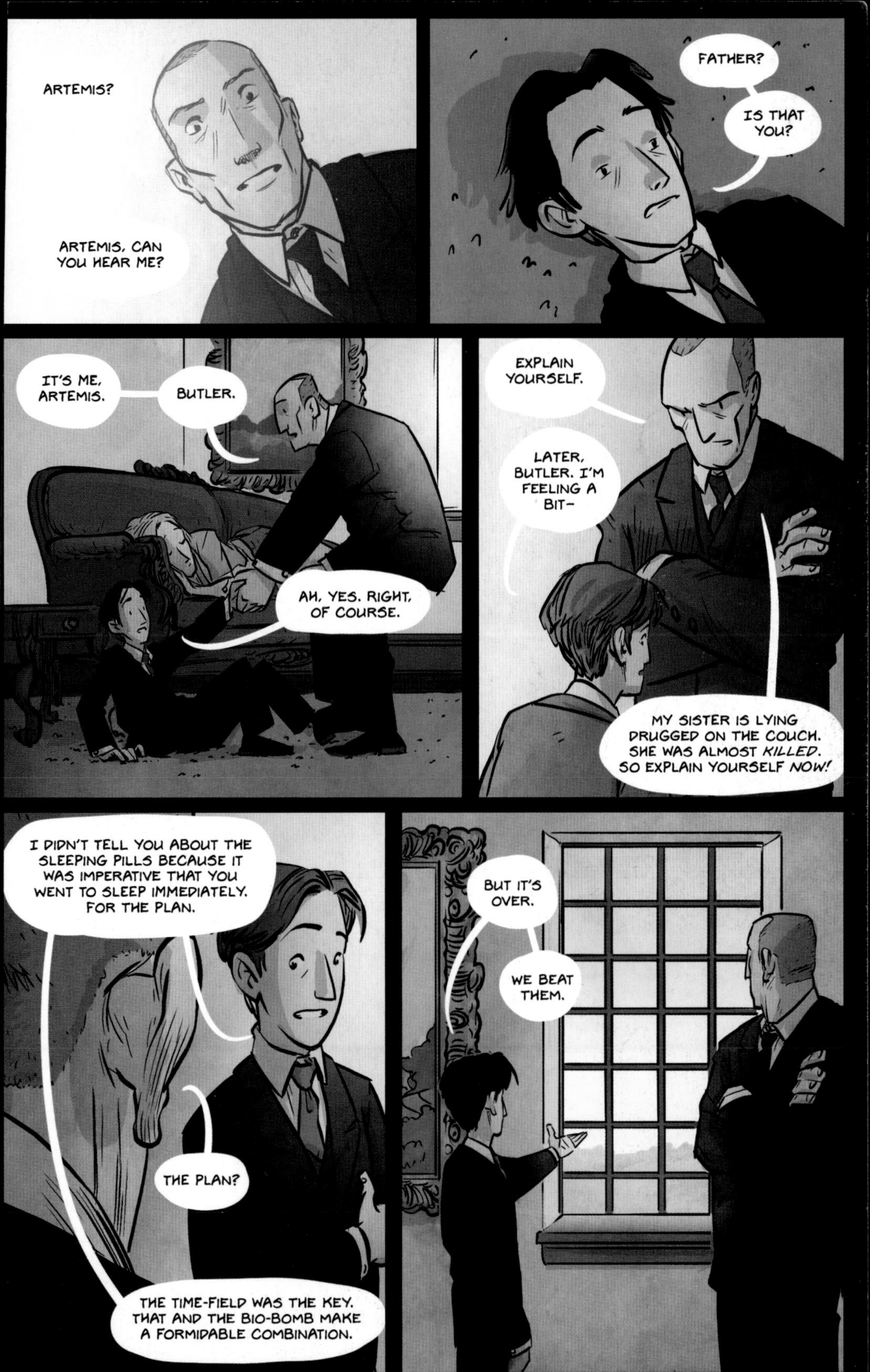
ARTEMIS?
ARTEMIS, CAN YOU HEAR ME?
FATHER?
IS THAT YOU?
IT'S ME, ARTEMIS.
BUTLER.
AH, YES. RIGHT, OF COURSE.
EXPLAIN YOURSELF.
LATER, BUTLER. I'M FEELING A BIT-
MY SISTER IS LYING DRUGGED ON THE COUCH. SHE WAS ALMOST *KILLED*. SO EXPLAIN YOURSELF *NOW!*
I DIDN'T TELL YOU ABOUT THE SLEEPING PILLS BECAUSE IT WAS IMPERATIVE THAT YOU WENT TO SLEEP IMMEDIATELY. FOR THE PLAN.
THE PLAN?
THE TIME-FIELD WAS THE KEY. THAT AND THE BIO-BOMB MAKE A FORMIDABLE COMBINATION.
BUT IT'S OVER.
WE BEAT THEM.

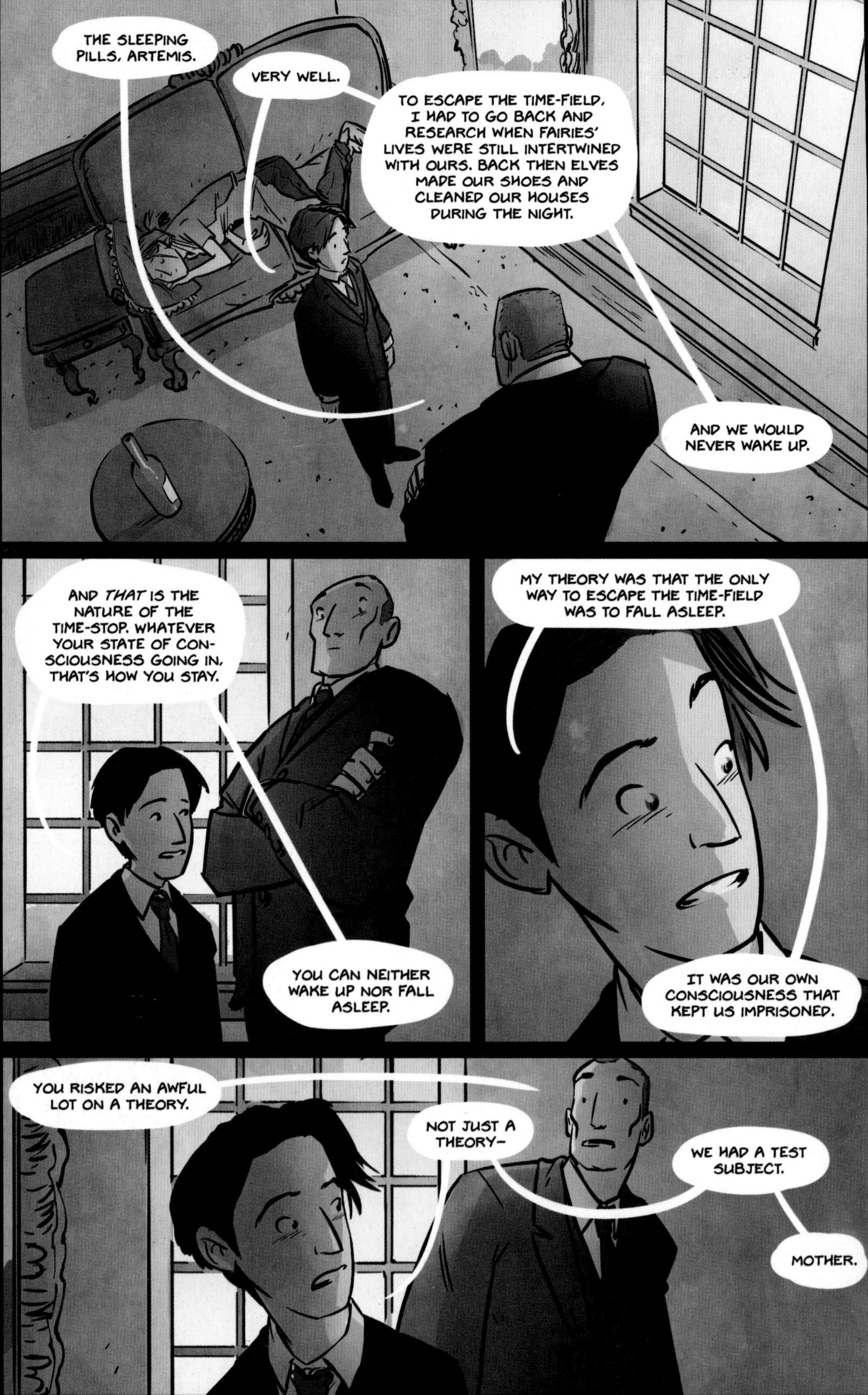
THE SLEEPING PILLS, ARTEMIS.
VERY WELL.
TO ESCAPE THE TIME-FIELD, I HAD TO GO BACK AND RESEARCH WHEN FAIRIES' LIVES WERE STILL INTERTWINED WITH OURS. BACK THEN ELVES MADE OUR SHOES AND CLEANED OUR HOUSES DURING THE NIGHT.
AND WE WOULD NEVER WAKE UP.
AND *THAT* IS THE NATURE OF THE TIME-STOP. WHATEVER YOUR STATE OF CONSCIOUSNESS GOING IN, THAT'S HOW YOU STAY.
YOU CAN NEITHER WAKE UP NOR FALL ASLEEP.
MY THEORY WAS THAT THE ONLY WAY TO ESCAPE THE TIME-FIELD WAS TO FALL ASLEEP.
IT WAS OUR OWN CONSCIOUSNESS THAT KEPT US IMPRISONED.
YOU RISKED AN AWFUL LOT ON A THEORY.
NOT JUST A THEORY—
WE HAD A TEST SUBJECT.
MOTHER.

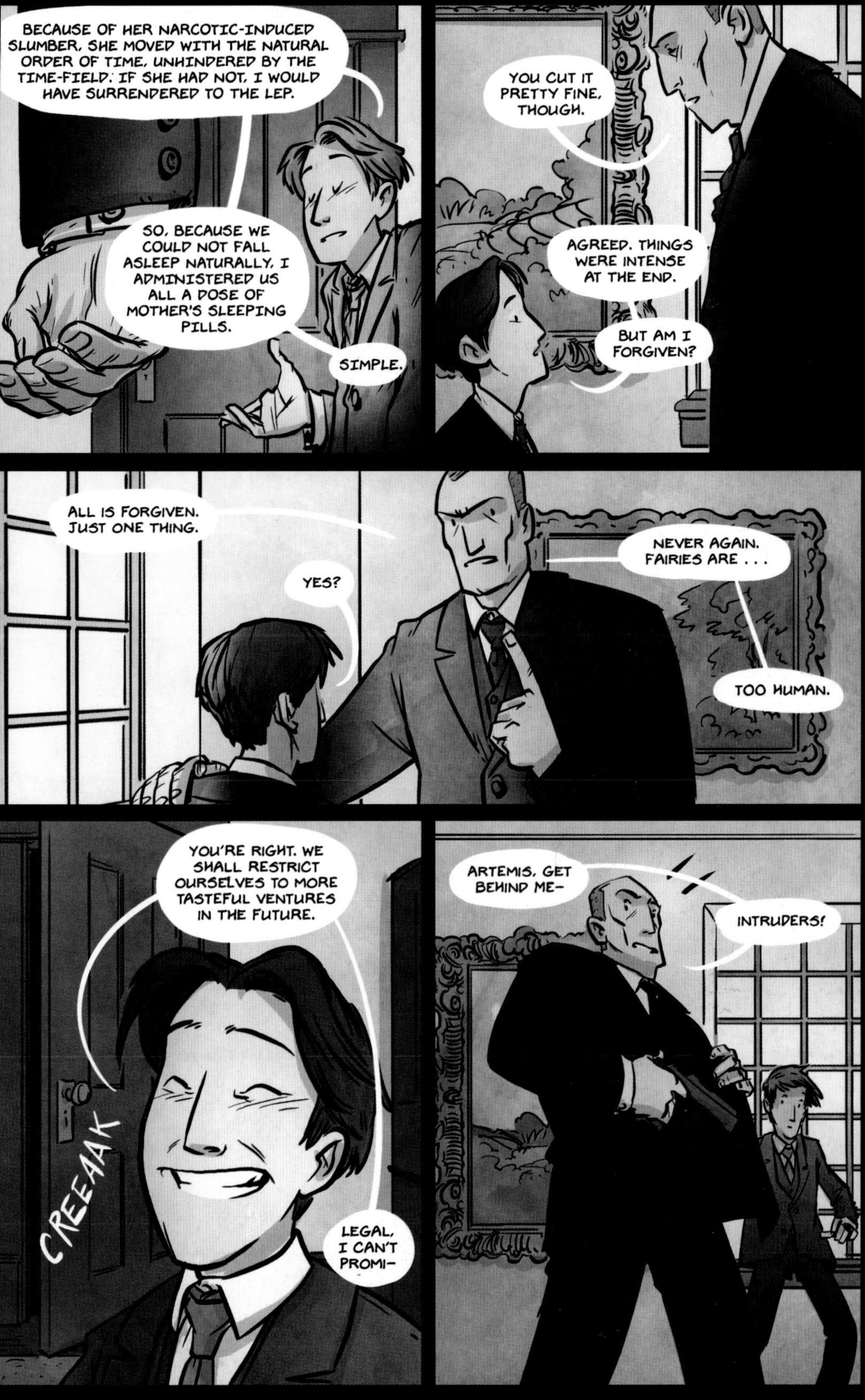
BECAUSE OF HER NARCOTIC-INDUCED SLUMBER, SHE MOVED WITH THE NATURAL ORDER OF TIME, UNHINDERED BY THE TIME-FIELD. IF SHE HAD NOT, I WOULD HAVE SURRENDERED TO THE LEP.
SO, BECAUSE WE COULD NOT FALL ASLEEP NATURALLY, I ADMINISTERED US ALL A DOSE OF MOTHER'S SLEEPING PILLS.
SIMPLE.
YOU CUT IT PRETTY FINE, THOUGH.
AGREED. THINGS WERE INTENSE AT THE END.
BUT AM I FORGIVEN?
ALL IS FORGIVEN. JUST ONE THING.
YES?
NEVER AGAIN. FAIRIES ARE . . .
TOO HUMAN.
YOU'RE RIGHT. WE SHALL RESTRICT OURSELVES TO MORE TASTEFUL VENTURES IN THE FUTURE.
LEGAL, I CAN'T PROMI-
CREEAAK
ARTEMIS, GET BEHIND ME-
INTRUDERS!

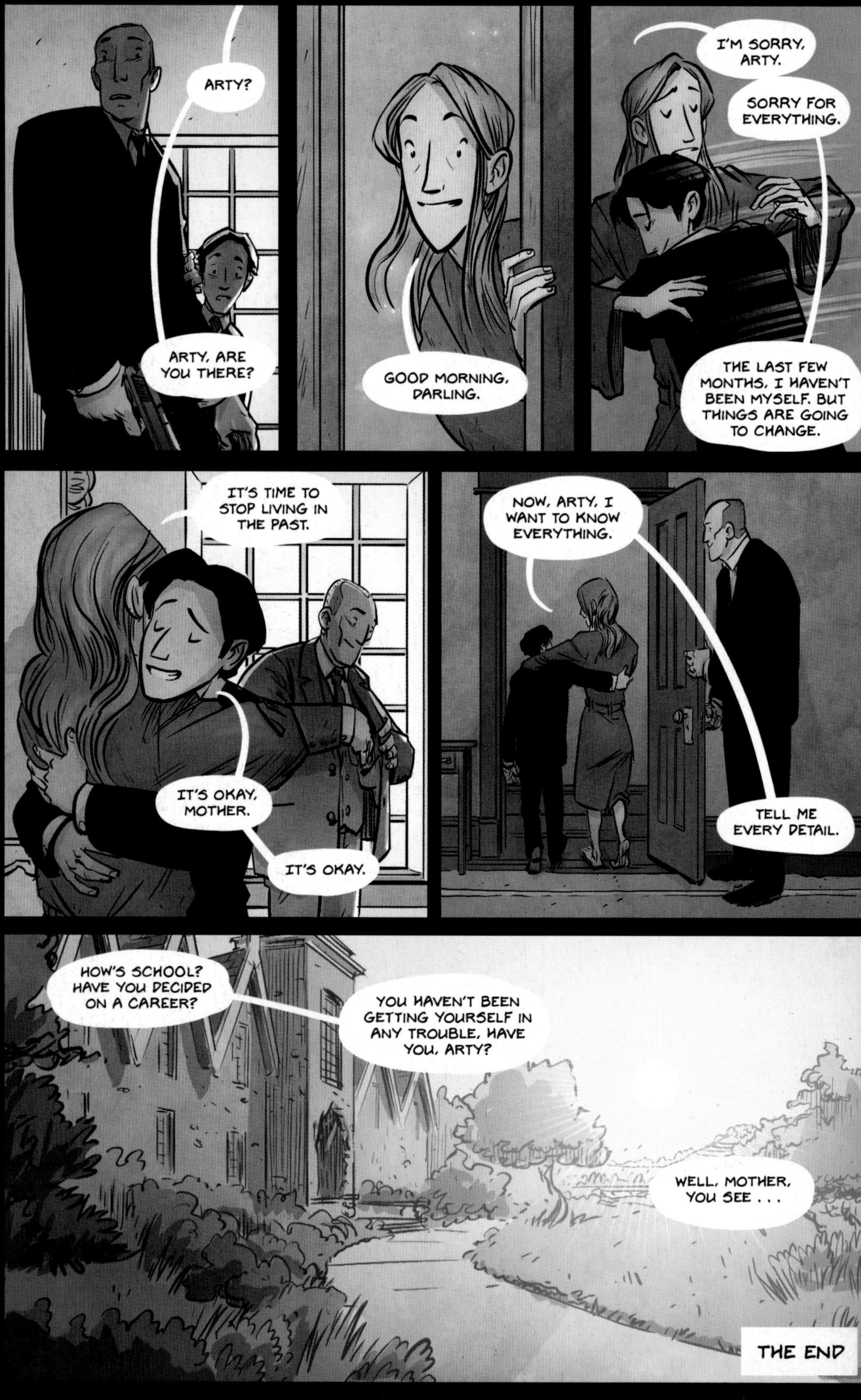
ARTY?
ARTY, ARE YOU THERE?
GOOD MORNING, DARLING.
I'M SORRY, ARTY.
SORRY FOR EVERYTHING.
THE LAST FEW MONTHS, I HAVEN'T BEEN MYSELF. BUT THINGS ARE GOING TO CHANGE.
IT'S TIME TO STOP LIVING IN THE PAST.
IT'S OKAY, MOTHER.
IT'S OKAY.
NOW, ARTY, I WANT TO KNOW EVERYTHING.
TELL ME EVERY DETAIL.
HOW'S SCHOOL? HAVE YOU DECIDED ON A CAREER?
YOU HAVEN'T BEEN GETTING YOURSELF IN ANY TROUBLE, HAVE YOU, ARTY?
WELL, MOTHER, YOU SEE . . .
THE END

Adapted from the novel *Artemis Fowl*

First Hardcover Edition, June 2019

First Paperback Edition, June 2019

10 9 8 7 6 5 4 3 2 1

FAC-038091-19130

Printed in the United States of America

This book is set in Colleen Doran/Fontspring; DIN Next LT Pro, ITC Novarese Pro, Neutraface Condensed/Monotype

Designed by Stephen Gilpin and Tyler Nevins

Library of Congress Cataloging-in-Publication Data

Names: Moreci, Michael, adapter. • Gilpin, Stephen, artist. • Adaptation of expression: Colfer, Eoin. Artemis Fowl.
Title: Eoin Colfer's Artemis Fowl : the graphic novel / adapted by Michael Moreci ; art by Stephen Gilpin.
Other titles: Artemis Fowl, the graphic novel
Description: First edition. • Los Angeles ; New York : Disney • Hyperion, 2019. • Summary: When a twelve-year-old evil genius tries to restore his family fortune by capturing a fairy and demanding a ransom in gold, the fairies fight back with magic, technology, and a particularly nasty troll.
Identifiers: LCCN 2018028370• ISBN 9781368043144 (hardcover) ISBN 9781368043700 (pbk.) • Subjects: LCSH: Graphic novels. • CYAC: Graphic novels. • Fairies—Fiction. • Kidnapping—Fiction. • Magic—Fiction. • Mothers and sons—Fiction. • England—Fiction. • Classification: LCC PZ7.7.M658 Eoi 2019 • DDC 741.5/942—dc23
LC record available at https://lccn.loc.gov/2018028370

Visit www.DisneyBooks.com

SUSTAINABLE FORESTRY INITIATIVE
Certified Sourcing
www.sfiprogram.org
SFI-00993
Logo Applies to Text Stock Only